# THE CASTRO CONSPIRACY

By

BRUCE T. CLARK

Bruce T Clark

This book is a work of fiction. Places, events, and situations in this story are purely fictional. Any resemblance to actual persons, living or dead, is coincidental.



ISBN: 1-4107-1182-X (e-book)
ISBN: 1-4107-1181-1 (Paperback)

This book is printed on acid free paper.

1stBooks - rev. 03/18/03

# *ACKNOWLEDGMENTS*

In little more than a thousand days, from January 1961, until November 1963, the world was rocked by an unusual number of political cataclysms. Just three months after his festive inauguration, John F. Kennedy's administration was all but destroyed in the aftermath of the Bay of Pigs Invasion. For the next year and a half, Jack and his youthful helpers played catch-up politics.

During those eighteen months the CIA was not idle. Since an armed invasion had failed to unseat Castro, they designed and implemented a different strategy. In league with the Mafia, the CIA made at least ten attempts on Castro's life—all of which failed.

Then, in October 1962, the Cuban Missile Crisis afforded the Kennedy brothers an opportunity to demonstrate their considerable skill and ability. Under Jack and Bobby's firm leadership, a situation that well might have become an even greater fiasco than the Invasion, became one of America's finest hours.

On November 22, 1963, President John F. Kennedy was assassinated. **BUT WHO KILLED HIM, AND WHY?**

For the next thirty years a flood of material hit the bookshelves that shed various degrees of light on many Kennedy-connected events. Participants like Bob Kennedy wrote about a few of them. Others were described by fringe players in the dramas. Some were penned by a handful of artful researchers. Vicarious speculators and "want to be insiders" produced many more explanations/exploitations.

On September 16, 1992, much of the speculation ended when 312 classified documents dealing with the Bay of Pigs and the Cuban Missile Crisis were finally declassified and published by the CIA. At one point, each of them was a secret, or top-secret, communication, letter, memo or report. Printed in a single volume and distributed by the Historical Review Program, this bevy of documents revealed an incredible tale of mystery and ingenuity, as well as a great deal of abject deceit and foolishness.

By the time I finished reading them, I was totally hooked on Kennedy's Thousand Days, the Bay of Pigs fiasco, and the absolute intrigue of the times.

I began studying all of the data that had become available in books, articles, and analysis papers, written by people that had planned or participated in the various debacles. I avidly devoured every scrap of information.

Then, in 1997, as I was completing *The Custer Legacy*, the State Department released a massive eleven hundred page volume—*Foreign Relations of the United States and Cuba, 1961-1962.* It plugged many gaps that still remained in a number of the great cover-ups. A final piece of the puzzle was supplied by former Mafia boss, Bill Bonanno, in his 1999 expose, *Bound By Honor, A Mafioso's Story.* The arcane curtain was at last lifted away, and the solutions to many heretofore mysteries were suddenly exposed. I now possessed a wealth of knowledge about the Kennedys, the Castros, the Bay of Pigs Invasion, the

Cuban Missile Crisis, the attempts to eliminate Castro, and the Kennedy assassination. I even uncovered an unsubstantiated but plausible story of an attractive Cuban agent who was recruited by the CIA, tried to assassinate Fidel Castro, failed, and was herself eliminated.

Over the years, ever more answers came to light. Some were generated by research, some by adding one isolated fact together with another to produce a probability, and, of course, the magic of the greatest hypothetical possibility organizer or all—the computer. One fascinating computer generation is the almost certain probability that there were at least three shooters in Dallas, not one. The sum total of the facts, probabilities, and innuendoes became *The Castro Conspiracy.*

As a series of favored people, whose opinions I trust, read *Conspiracy,* their most common query was, "Where did you find all of this information?" I have written this acknowledgment to satisfy their curiosity, as well as that of many readers who also might wonder.

Finally, bear in mind that *The Castro Conspiracy* is an historical novel, it is **not** a history book. Nonetheless it is 80% historically accurate.

A great many people have made that accuracy possible by the words they wrote, the interviews they gave, or the service and advice they so freely offered. I cannot possibly list them all, but I want to acknowledge my principal information sources.

Dean Acheson
Manual Artime
George W. Ball

Tracy Barnes
Richard Bissel
Bill Bonanno
Chester Bowles
McGeorge Bundy
Fidel Castro
Allen W. Dulles
John Foster Dulles
Dwight D. Eisenhower
J. William Fulbright
Roswell L. Gilpatrick
Andrei A. Gromyko
Jack Hawkins
Roger Hilsman, Jr.
J. Edgar Hoover
Haynes Johnson
Lyndon B. Johnson
John F. Kennedy
Robert F. Kennedy
Nikita S. Khrushchev
Lyman B. Kirkpatrick
Edward G. Lansdale
Lyman Lemnitzer
Robert A. Lovett
Arthur C. Lundahl
John J. McCloy
Robert S. McNamara
Richard M. Nixon
Erneido Oliva
Walt W. Rostow
Dean Rusk
Jose San Roman
Arthur M. Schlesinger, Jr.

Enrique Ruiz-Williams
Theodore Sorensen
Adlai Stevenson
Walter Sweeney
Maxwell Taylor
Llewellyn Thompson
William Tidwell
Peter Wyden
Valentin Zorin

They are the information donors who provided the infusions to my intellectual bloodbank.

My heartfelt thanks go out to the terrific people who worked backstage on the *Conspiracy.*

Readers: Hal Brock, P.J. Galligan, Mary Jo Gibson, Kay Graves, Carla Sayre, & Buddy "The Barber" Smallwood.

Production guys: Tom Nelson & Ray Newcomb

Editors: Iryna Woloshyn & Devin Pesta

&

Dr. Patrick Keats: Editor-in-chief, actor, teacher, director, dialogist, and friend extraordinaire. It has been said that a historical novel is divided into three parts. The story is its body, the author is its brain, and the editor is its heart. As I finish a second novel with Patrick, I totally agree—at least with part three.

Bruce T. Clark
Front Royal, VA
August 2, 2002

*NOTE: Nine years of research have gone into The Castro Conspiracy. It is more than 80% historically accurate.*

*There are over ninety historical characters, and approximately thirty fictional ones. The novel's chief protagonist, Ramrod Reynolds, is a composite of several real people.*

*To aid readers, I have added a character reference guide.*

*On April 17, 1961, a fight against impossible odds began at Cuba's Bay of Pigs. In a frantic effort to reclaim their beloved homeland, 1453 Cuban exiles came ashore in the middle of the Zapata Swamps, then spent the next fifty hours in a furious melee. Though destiny did not grant them victory, when the stinging smoke of sour defeat cleared, one more chapter had been added to history's illustrious list of heroes who refused to trade their honor for mere existence.*

*This story is dedicated to each of them.*

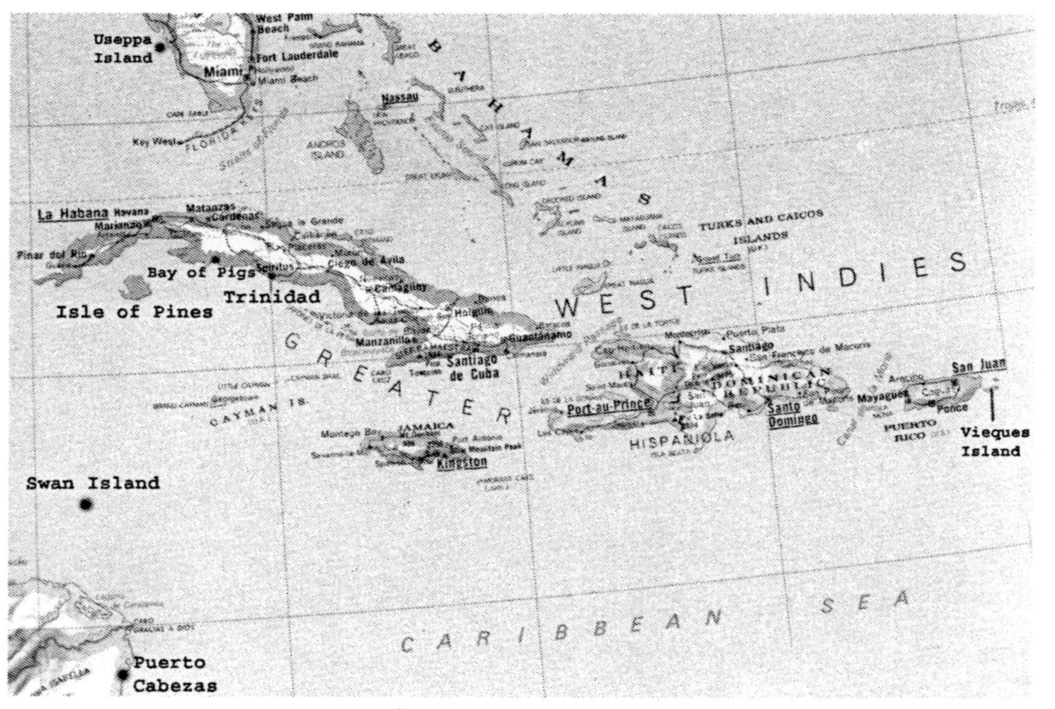

Useppa Island
West Palm Beach
Fort Lauderdale
Miami
Miami Beach
Key West
FLORIDA KEYS
Nassau
ANDROS ISLAND
B A H A M A S
TURKS AND CAICOS ISLANDS
W E S T   I N D I E S
La Habana Havana
Mariano
Matanzas
Cárdenas
Pinar del Río
Bay of Pigs
Ciego de Avila
Camagüey
Trinidad
Isle of Pines
Holguín
Manzanillo
Guantánamo
Santiago de Cuba
G R E A T E R
CAYMAN IS.
JAMAICA
Montego Bay
Kingston
HAITI
Port-au-Prince
Santiago
Puerto Plata
DOMINICAN REPUBLIC
Santo Domingo
HISPANIOLA
Mayagüez
Ponce
San Juan
PUERTO RICO
Vieques Island
Swan Island
C A R I B B E A N   S E A
Puerto Cabezas

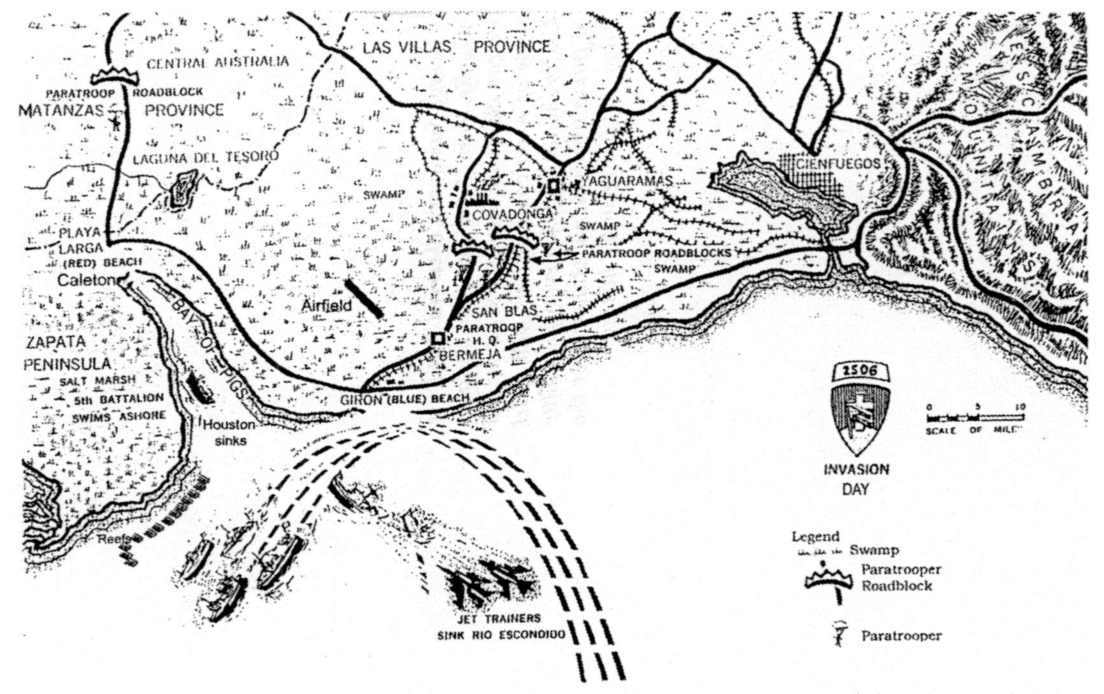
LAS VILLAS PROVINCE
CENTRAL AUSTRALIA
PARATROOP ROADBLOCK
MATANZAS PROVINCE
LAGUNA DEL TESORO
SWAMP
PLAYA LARGA
(RED) BEACH
Caleton
Airfield
ZAPATA PENINSULA
SALT MARSH
5th BATTALION SWIMS ASHORE
BAY OF PIGS
Houston sinks
Reefs
GIRON (BLUE) BEACH
BERMEJA
PARATROOP H. Q.
SAN BLAS
COVADONGA
YAGUARAMAS
SWAMP
PARATROOP ROADBLOCKS
SWAMP
CIENFUEGOS
ESCAMBRAY MOUNTAINS
JET TRAINERS SINK RIO ESCONDIDO
2506
INVASION DAY
0 5 10
SCALE OF MILES
Legend
Swamp
Paratrooper Roadblock
Paratrooper

*George Santayana observed that if we actually learn from our past mistakes we can eliminate them—if so, a careful study of American relations with Fidel Castro should eradicate every possibility of future international blunders for the balance of our recorded history.*

# *PROLOGUE*

# *THE EXECUTION*

## *HAVANA, CUBA, JANUARY, 1960*

A smile played at the corners of the executioner's mouth as he turned to confront his tightly bound and blindfolded prisoner. A greater contrast between the two men could not have been possible. The executioner stood over six feet tall and possessed a burly physique. Each time he moved he held an exaggerated pose for a moment, in an effort to impress the crowd with his lithe grace and athletic ability.

He towered over his prisoner, whose body was so racked with pain that merely standing was a heroic act. The gaunt, emaciated victim was lashed to one of the dozen blood-encrusted stakes that had been erected several months earlier at the base of the Morro Castle's towering front wall. Their bullet-shattered condition bore mute testimony to the stakes' frequent and efficient use.

The executioner began intoning the death sentence in a crisp, staccato voice. His vengeful bearing and harsh tone could not have been crueler if he were dooming an unrepentant sinner to hell.

"Manuel Martinez, having been tried by a military tribunal and found guilty of treason against the state, you are about to die for your crimes. Like so many others, you thought high position and great wealth would protect you; but you were wrong! There can be no escape for enemies of the state."

The executioner made no effort to conceal a sneer as he continued.

"Perhaps your death will teach a valuable lesson to others who might be foolish enough to become our enemies. Then, at least, you will provide a small benefit to the state."

Beaming with devilish joy at the prospect of issuing his next command, the executioner directed his order to the young officer in charge of the firing squad; but every member of the crowd also heard him and recognized the satisfaction in his voice.

"Lieutenant, proceed with the execution!"

A single glance at the lieutenant's face revealed the bitter agony his duty was causing him. Observers standing near him clearly saw glistening beads of perspiration on his brow and shimmering reflections of tears in his eyes.

He blinked away the tears and forcefully clenched his teeth in resignation before he shouted the required order.

"READY! AIM! FIRE!"

Eight shots ripped through the air. A moment later their echoes crackled back from the ancient fortress wall. Manuel Martinez was slammed against the splintered wood and then flung forward again by the force of the heavy bullets. He stiffened in anguish for a single instant, thinking in his last moment of life that he had been cheated somehow—this was not the quick and painless death he had expected. But the terrible pain was brief. His last breath escaped, then his corpse slumped awkwardly and hung limply against the lashings that bound it.

The people in the crowd were stunned. They stood motionless and breathless, unwilling to accept the terrible violence they had witnessed. Only the birds roosting high upon the castle's parapets were spurred into action. Hundreds of them instantly quit the wall and launched themselves into the air, eager to be gone from the manmade thunder and chaos below.

Murmurs and soft sobs began rippling through the throng of onlookers. Then a single voice rose above the restless hum.

"The birds are luckier than we humans this day!"

A stooped, elderly priest moved out of the crowd and shuffled forward, brushing aside all the guards' half-hearted efforts to stop him. He hobbled to a place between the executioner and his victim; then spoke in a clear and courageous voice.

"The birds, unlike all of us earth-bound creatures, can fly away from this insanity and escape, while we must remain here as your prisoners. Every Cuban is now captive! Last year, when you and your masters came to power, you promised us freedom. You gave us slavery! You promised us justice. You gave us tyranny! You promised us life. You gave us death! Will your ruthless vengeance never end?"

The executioner's face darkened in stunned shock. He couldn't believe anyone would display this kind of courage on the heels of a spectacle that had been staged in order to teach these people the sheer folly of resistance. He fought to recover his poise, then shouted in a loud, ominous voice:

"Watch your words, old man! You are speaking treason! If we decide that you are an enemy of the state, you will not be able to hide in your Church's shadow! Your clerical collar will not save you! Your blood will cover the ground, like that of this poor fool who just died for his crimes. You think we won't execute a priest? You and every other slave of religion may soon learn how foolish such a notion is!"

To emphasize his words and newfound power, the executioner walked past the old priest, shoving him aside in the process. Slowly he made his way toward the lifeless figure crumpled against the stake; then, with elaborate unconcern, he unholstered his pistol and fired a needless coup de grace.

A final trickle of blood rolled slowly across the sand and stopped at the feet of the brave old priest.

# *PART ONE*
# *THE NEW PROBLEM*

# *FORT KNOX, KENTUCKY*

# *JANUARY 16, 1960*

Captain Rodney “Ramrod” Reynolds smiled as he glanced over his shoulder at a long column of weary, fatigue-clad soldiers who followed him, desperately trying to match his brisk pace. Ramrod was ten years older than most of his men, but in much better shape than all but a few of them. His six-foot frame carried a lean hundred and eighty pounds on a body nearly devoid of fat. He had become a role model for most of his basic training recruits, and he knew it.

The formation was halfway up the second of two four-mile-long hills that formed a saddle on this eight-mile stretch of roadway. The pair of hills, each of which pitched upward at a twelve-degree angle, had long ago been aptly named Misery and Agony.

His gaze swept upward toward the crest of Agony Hill, whose lofty summit, although still two miles away, was clearly visible against the bright blue, cloudless sky. Those two miles were the ultimate challenge for his lead-legged troops, since the crest of the hill still lay nearly two thousand feet above them.

He pulled out of the column and stood looking back along the formation. Suddenly, he raised his voice in a fierce yet friendly challenge.

“Who are we?”

"The Bravos!" came the instant reply from a mass of proud, straining throats.

Once again his challenge rang out.

"How good are we?"

"We're the best!"

Now Reynolds demanded to know,

"How far are we going?"

"All the way!"

He rejoined the tail end of the column, and fell in beside the Company's First Sergeant, Jose "Apache Joe" Blackhorse.

"What do you think, Sergeant?"

"They finally got warrior's pride, Captain."

"About time. It's B Company's tenth speed-march. They coasted down Misery Hill today, and they're making good time climbing Agony. We'll give them a five-minute breather at the summit and let them get their second wind coming down Agony Hill. By then they ought to be in shape to double time all the way back up Misery."

"They've come a long way since the first speed-march. I was pushing the tail end of the column along almost a mile behind you when you and the first half dozen finished. The training's toughened 'em up and built their confidence. Except for a few 'goldbricks' we've got a good outfit, Sir. And we're always goin' to have a few 'bricks.'"

"The way they're running today, we might even break the post speed-march record."

"You're right, Captain! Even the weaker ones are gutting it out. I told the three sob sisters if they cost us a chance to break the record, I'd personally kick their sorry butts bloody. If Dolan don't fall out, the other two won't quit. Dolan ain't weak; he's just a lazy good-fer-nothin'."

Just then, a few yards ahead of them, one of the men who had been running in the outer file suddenly stumbled and fell heavily to the ground. His limp body rolled over several times, and finally came to rest on the grassy shoulder of the road.

"Don't let 'em slack up, Sergeant. I'll check out the downed man. He's lucky to be off the blacktop. This stuff is hot enough to fry eggs."

When he reached the soldier's side, Reynolds bent down and carefully checked the man's legs, rib cage, and arms. The exam disclosed no broken bones or any other serious injury. Reynolds carefully turned the limp man over onto his back and gazed down into the beet-red face of Evan Dolan, Apache Joe's number one goldbrick.

He disgustedly removed the canteen from his web belt and splashed water on Dolan's face and throat. The "unconscious" man's eyes popped open at once.

"I think my leg is busted, Captain," Dolan moaned.

"There's nothing wrong with either of your legs, Dolan!"

"It feels like a couple of my ribs are busted, Sir."

"There's nothing wrong with your ribs either."

"My head hurts real bad! Maybe I fractured it."

"You seem to have dropped your rifle just as you fell. That was mighty convenient! You were able to break the fall with your hands and field pack. You're goldbricking! Now get up and rejoin the formation. When we reach the company area, clean your filthy weapon, then do ten laps at high port around the perimeter. When you finish chow, report to the First Sergeant in his office."

"I can't get up, Sir! I need a medic!"

Just then, from the corner of his eye, Reynolds saw a stealthy, wriggling movement in the tall grass a few feet from Dolan's head. In a lightning-like draw that Wyatt Earp might have envied, Reynolds jerked his .45 Colt service automatic from its holster and fired a well-aimed shot into the ground. The effects of the sudden thunderous explosion were as dramatic as they were predictable. The snake slithered off into the dense undergrowth, while his "intended victim," saved only by the quick reaction of his commanding officer, went bounding up the steep road with far more energy and enthusiasm than he had ever shown before.

Racing behind him, Reynolds was grinning when he rejoined the column.

"It's amazing how fast soldiers' priorities change once the first shot is fired," he told Apache Joe. "And it's incredible how much alike black snakes and rattlers look at first glance. Let's get the rest of these young people motivated and see how much time we can shave off that speed-march record."

The Bravos raced back to their company area and shaved nearly a full minute off the old speed-march record. It was a tired but jubilant bunch of recruits who marched off to chow.

A few minutes later, as he and his friend Captain Felipe Orizaba sat enjoying a cold beer at the Officers Club, their Battalion Commander, Major Hugh Martin, came in. He was obviously agitated.

"Ramrod, I need to see you in my office right after chow. Something's come up." He turned stiffly and left the O Club.

"Ten to one," Reynolds told Felipe Orizaba, whose nickname was Avispa (The Wasp), "Evan Dolan, Apache Joe's number one goldbrick, ran screaming to the chaplain, who in turn talked to Major Martin. Well, I handled Dolan properly. I'll simply tell the Major what happened and then let the chips fall where they may."

Ramrod reported to Headquarters at 1830, and was met by the battalion clerk, who immediately escorted him into Major Martin's office. Reynolds saluted and remained at attention until his red-faced, visibly upset commander spoke.

"Sit down, Captain. As you can plainly see, I'm mad as hell! I just received orders detaching you for some kind of special duty. Without one damned bit of warning, the spooks in Washington are pulling out my best company commander. Losing you at this time will make one hell of a dent in my performance forecast."

He leaned back in his chair, fighting to control his temper.

"Well, there's no point in crying over spilled milk. You're ordered to report to Washington, Building K, at 0800, the day after tomorrow, for an assignment of undefined mission and undefined duration. It must be pretty damned important. They also issued you a Class One air priority. I will only offer one bit of advice. Be straight with the CIA types. They probably already know everything about you. If they want to know anything else, tell 'em!"

Martin rose and offered his hand.

"You're a fine officer, Ramrod! I hope we have another chance to serve together. Good luck on your new mission."

Reynolds shook hands, saluted, and left headquarters. As he headed back to the BOQ, he speculated about the assignment and wondered why he had been chosen. In his own mind, there was nothing special about him. Nothing set him apart from dozens of other officers—but for once, he was wrong.

Rodney Reynolds was nine days away from his thirtieth birthday that evening. He had been born in the winter of 1930, the first full year of the Great Depression. It was a time when uneasiness and an almost visible despair enveloped the country.

Rod and his younger brother, Ray, had grown up in a middle class neighborhood on Cleveland's East Side. His dad had worked two jobs, and his mom earned a few extra dollars sewing and dressmaking for the wealthy ladies of Shaker Heights and other high-class suburbs, but times had still been tough on the family.

A few weeks before Rod's third birthday, Franklin Roosevelt had been swept into the presidency and had offered Americans a New Deal. But it was not until the outbreak of World War II that the country finally emerged from the Great Depression. The day after Japan attacked Pearl Harbor, America declared war on Japan. The remaining Axis partners declared war on America, and the United States soon became the world's foremost industrial giant. Bombers and fighters, tanks and jeeps, giant artillery pieces, and every conceivable type of weapon and war product poured out of her suddenly busy factories.

In the spring of 1942, both of their parents had found employment at Graphite Bronze, a mammoth manufacturing plant on the outskirts of Cleveland. That left twelve-year-old Rod and ten-year-old Ray on their own for much of the time. This freedom curbed their impulsiveness and taught them to be self-reliant. In addition to paper routes, the boys cut summer grass and shoveled winter snow. These responsibilities taught them to think carefully before they made either decisions or commitments. The good judgment they developed had served them well ever since.

For the next three and a half years, in addition to a strong work ethic, the brothers shared numerous interests—from all outdoor sports, to hotly contested Ping-Pong games, to a mutual love of knowledge. Like most youngsters who grew up during World War II, they were acutely aware of the world situation and the involvement of American troops in the conflict. Rod could still remember President Roosevelt declaring that, "America's next Bunker Hill may not be in Boston; therefore, America must become the world's arsenal of freedom."

On June 6, 1944, America and her Allies invaded "Fortress Europa." From those wave-swept, blood-drenched beaches of Normandy, a new word blazed across the airwaves and entered America's lexicon:

***D-DAY!***

How proud he and Ray had been of the brave men on Omaha and Utah Beaches who refused to quit.

How proud America had been.

How proud the world had been.

In the final month of Rod's freshman year of high school, Germany had surrendered. The boys listened to General "Ike" Eisenhower's famous speech to the English Parliament. Rod never forgot Ike's words.

"No one hates war more than a soldier, for it is the soldier who knows best the horrors of war. For that reason above all others, let the word go forth from this place that we will work for peace, and we will pray that war may end for all time. But let us assure every aggressor who stands ready to break our hard-won peace, that neither London nor Abilene [Ike's home town], sisters under the skin, will ever sell her birthright or her freedom, for mere existence."

Ike received a key to the city, a sword of valor, and became an honorary *Citizen of London.* The time-honored ceremony was concluded with a sumptuous meal of fish and chips.

From that day on, Rod was committed to the life of a soldier.

Three years later, his commitment and hard work were rewarded when Congressional Representative Frances P. Bolton nominated him to the United States Military Academy. In the summer of 1947, Cadet Rodney L. Reynolds reported to the Plain of West Point, high above the Hudson River, and joined the Class of 1951.

During Christmas break of his senior year, Rodney Reynolds, now a Cadet Battalion Commander, took the train home to Cleveland. On New Year's Eve he was invited to attend a gala party at the home of another cadet, whose family lived in the swank suburb of Gate's Mills. It was the kind of spectacular affair that can only be crafted by the ultra rich who have amassed posh party skills along with their immense fortunes.

Rod and three other West Pointers in attendance had received the lion's share of attention, at least from the bevy of young women who were the classmates of the family's eldest daughter.

About nine o'clock, tired of the loud music and idle chatter in the smoke-filled room, he had drifted out to the ballroom's balcony. After the glare of the bright lights on the dance floor, it took several seconds for his eyes to adjust to the soft glow of the moonlight.

When they did he saw a sight that made him wonder if the crisp winter evening had conjured up a mirage.

She stood near a low, snow-covered stone wall. She wore a bright, holiday-red gown and a high-collared, silver fox fur jacket that framed her face and drew his gaze to her soft, auburn hair.

"I've been looking for you," he said. "This is our dance."

She had moved willingly into his eager arms and they had danced together, oblivious to the fierce and frigid gusts of the north wind that stung their cheeks and made them shiver—nor did they notice the people who were celebrating a short distance away.

When the cold finally forced them inside, they found a quiet corner. He discovered that her name was Amanda Mitchell and that she was in her senior year at Western Reserve University. For nearly an hour they had talked and sipped drinks, but most of the time they had simply looked at each other.

As midnight approached, the party had invaded their private corner and they were drawn back into the mass of swirling guests, where they were quickly separated. Moments later as he looked around the huge ballroom, crowded with more than a hundred happy celebrants, Rod suddenly realized that he felt terribly alone.

At one minute to midnight, just as the countdown to the New Year had begun, he felt a gentle hand on his shoulder. He turned and saw an excited, blushing, beautiful face and heard Amanda's whispered words.

"Do you have room in your arms for a lonely girl?"

No answer was necessary. None would have done justice to the moment. All he could do, all he needed to do, was hug her tightly and smile.

From that moment on there was never any doubt that they were destined to be together. Rodney's roommate, Charles Manning, swore that Rod never stopped smiling after he met Amanda. They were wed in the West Point chapel, on the third Saturday of June, and left for California: first to honeymoon on the beautiful Carmel Peninsula and then on to their first duty station at Fort Ord.

Those first months together—and as a harsh fate would decree, the only time they would ever have—were everything either of them had ever dreamed they could be. Each evening he rushed home as soon as his duties permitted. Twilight became a magical time of peace, and love, and togetherness.

Then tragedy struck. One foggy, dreary morning in April, as Amanda drove along the ocean highway, a speeding pickup truck, driven by an intoxicated driver, ploughed into her small car. The driver of the truck emerged unscathed, but not so Amanda and her unborn child. They were both killed on impact.

Rod descended into a deep, grief-stricken, melancholy pit of loneliness—a hellish place where he suffered alone—unwilling and unable to reach out for help. He performed his duties in an almost mechanical fashion—a constant dark scowl in place on his grim face.

A month after Amanda's death he was transferred to the staff of General Mark Clark. Clark was the tall, hawkish officer who, as a confidant of General

Eisenhower, had orchestrated the North African landings during World War II. He had gone on to command the men of the Fifth Army in Italy, as they fought and sloughed their way along the length of that muddy, mountainous peninsula. General Clark and his staff arrived in Tokyo on May 6, 1952, and he became the Supreme Commander of all United Nations Forces in Korea.

En route to Tokyo, Rod met a Japanese-American woman on board his PAN AM flight to Hawaii. A native islander in her late thirties, Tomiko Ishii was an associate professor of political science at the University of Hawaii. She instantly felt a protective, maternal sympathy for the darkly handsome young American officer with the melancholy smile and sad brown eyes. Since Rod was not scheduled to fly on to Japan for several days, Tomiko offered to show him the great wonders and beauty of the Hawaiian Islands that only a native Hawaiian can really know well enough to share.

On their last day together the new friends toured the island of Maui, then enjoyed a luau and the hula dancers at one of Hawaii's most famous restaurants. As they sat watching the sunset across Lahaina's roadstead, Tomiko shared with Rod the tragic stories of her two younger brothers. One of them had been killed in 1944, in Italy, while fighting with the American 442 Combat Team. Ironically, her second brother had been killed in the Philippines the same month—while fighting with Japan's Sixth Imperial Army.

Through Tomiko's eyes the typically naive young American saw the traditional Samurai mentality that had pervaded Japan in the years preceding World War II. She helped him understand the disbelief and sour disillusionment that followed their humiliating defeat, and the hatred that was engendered in the hearts of many Japanese by the atomic fireballs that incinerated their ancient cities of Hiroshima and Nagasaki.

For the first time, Rodney Reynolds realized that when America dropped the atomic bombs on Japan, she had also obliterated her reputation for fair play and justice in the hearts and minds of people in the emerging nations.

"Because of the horrible bombs, America will no longer be the clear choice as the principal leader of the post-war world she would have been," Tomiko-chan told Ramrod.

Then she added a prophetic observation.

"Our country has given the Communists a political and psychological club they will use to batter the helpless and vulnerable people of Europe and Asia into submission. The Cold War in Berlin and other parts of Europe, as well as the hot war now raging in Korea, are only a start. Democracy and Communism are now engaged in the last war to control the *lands* of men and the first futuristic war to gain control over the *minds* of men. You and I may be old and gray, perhaps long dead, before that struggle finally ends."

It was a much wiser young man who left Hawaii and flew on to Japan the next morning. For the first time Rod clearly saw a variety of issues that would continue to puzzle a vast majority of his countrymen well into the foreseeable future. In the next decade Tomiko's wise words would echo in his ears on many occasions, in many parts of the world.

His staff duty was both challenging and blatantly eye-opening. Very quickly Rod saw that Tomiko had been correct. The Cold War had begun. For the first time in recorded history, battles *were* being waged to control men's minds as well as men's lands. In a large part of the post-war world, to the surprise of naive Americans, the Communist *Red Menace*, with its propaganda and brain washing techniques, was actually winning converts, gaining momentum, and labeling all Americans and Western Europeans as a *White Menace*.

In prosperous post-war America, where a jubilant population still basked in the afterglow of the recent victory, threats to world peace and order were far too odious to be contemplated. Therefore, most trusting and fun-loving Americans simply refused to believe what was happening in many other, far less fortunate quadrants of the fast-shrinking world. At the same time America's more astute citizens wondered why Communism, with such a hard-to-sell product, was enjoying such phenomenal success.

Rod realized that until he met Tomiko, he had also been puzzled by the knotty problem. During his first months in Japan, although he was still a committed patriot, he was forced to reluctantly acknowledge that the atomic blasts that obliterated Hiroshima and Nagasaki and snuffed out 120,000 Japanese had also obliterated the moral ascendancy that America had long enjoyed in the rest of the trusting world.

In the eyes of many, America had joined history's ruthless conquerors—vile tyrants who employed the foulest of means to achieve victory. Hiroshima and

Nagasaki signaled the demise of the moral character and integrity that had been growing in America for centuries. Those characteristic virtues were charred as crisp and black as the Japanese citizens the atomic weapons had immolated. America earned the scorn of humane and compassionate men the world over. Millions of Asians imagined themselves and their children in fiery atomic infernos of similar intensity.

The propaganda value America's loss of respect provided for Communism was incalculable. During the Cold War years, because of America's immoral slide, every Communist claim, promise, and plan would be examined in the bright light of a terrifying atomic sun. When either the Russians or Americans extended a hand of friendship, Asians were forced to reluctantly take it, while knowing full well about the *treatment* that had befallen the unwitting enemies of these two super powers in the past.

On the general staff Rod met a few officers who still harbored the belief that A-Bombs had shortened the war. But considering the damage that Japan had suffered and the gradual acceptance by the Japanese people of an eventual defeat, prior to the use of the bombs, most of the staff members agreed that the war would have ended within a few months in any case. Some American lives certainly had been saved, Rod reasoned, but many more lives had since been lost in efforts to reestablish America's honor in the ensuing years.

Tomiko's prediction was correct. Atomic attacks on the two Japanese cities that tarnished America's honor had given global Communism a psychological club. They were using that club to beat the Free World's inhabitants into submission.

During his days in the Far East, Rod witnessed first-hand the folly of Roosevelt and Churchill at the 1945 Yalta Conference, where they had given in to Joseph Stalin and provided a long-term free ride for the Russians and their Communist minions. The two acknowledged leaders of the Free World "bribed" Stalin with the Kurill Islands and the southern half of Sakhalin Island, as well as access to Port Arthur and Darien. Their actions acknowledged Russia's preeminent interests in Manchuria and gave Russia a physical and political foothold in the Pacific that the ice-bound northern nation had yearned for since the reign of Peter the Great.

The enormous concessions had been made because Joseph Stalin promised to join the Allies in defeating Japan and made a firm commitment to support the establishment of the United Nations. But Roosevelt and Churchill conveniently forgot that the territorial possessions so generously ceded to Stalin were the rightful property of America and Great Britain's Chinese ally, Generalissimo Chiang Kai-shek.

Of course, every one of Stalin's promises had been broken in the days after World War II. Now the new war that was raging in Korea could be traced back to American and British capitulation at Yalta.

During Rod's West Point years, Russia had made a sustained effort to challenge American leadership throughout the world. The timing was perfect. After every war in her history, America couldn't wait to "bring the boys back home." World War II was no different. Rod still remembered some of the statistics his Professors of Military Science and Tactics had recited.

A year after the war ended, America's 15,000,000-man army had been cut to 3,000,000. By the end of 1947, half of those men were gone. As 1948 drew to a close, only 670,000 ground troops remained, and 250,000 of them were stationed in Far Eastern units. None of them were prepared for war. They had been trained as occupation troops—a police force to keep peace in Japan, not to fight a war should one arise.

Suddenly political observers in the Department of State and military experts in the Pentagon awoke to the fact that the depleted American forces were now incapable of coping with the "Red Menace" that was advancing into every corner of the world.

In an effort to balance the scales, the Department of Defense asked Congress for an appropriation of $20 billion and the conscription of all young men of military age. They hoped this universal draft would not only prepare a standing military force to cope with any emergency but would also re-kindle the proud feelings of patriotism that had enveloped the nation during World War II. West Point professors thought the move might finally alert the average American to the Asian threat that seemed ready to flare up at any moment. Rod remembered lengthy discussions about the various contingencies that could evolve. But America had remained true to her time-honored pacifist principles and isolationist mindset. The "panicky Pentagon alarmists" had been properly satirized, and the head of the American ostrich had remained firmly imbedded in the sand.

Fortunately, President Harry S. Truman was a man of proven courage. He wasn't a smooth statesman or a brilliant thinker. He was a simple, down-to-earth, middle-class haberdasher, but Truman usually made sensible choices in reasonably short order. Equally important was the fact that he had the courage to see his choices through. During the early years of the Cold War, President Truman stood toe-to-toe with Joseph Stalin, and Harry never blinked. Unfortunately, the majority of the nation's citizens were far less informed and committed.

On June 25, 1950, while Rod and his classmates were prepping plebes on the Plain of West Point, ninety thousand North Korean troops, accompanied by hundreds of tanks, had stormed across the 38th parallel—the international boundary that separated North and South Korea.

General of the Armies Douglas MacArthur was charged with two separate missions: defeating the North Korean invaders and protecting the rest of the Far East, from northern Japan to the southern tip of the Philippines. He was expected to accomplish both objectives with a ground force of less than 85,000.

When MacArthur's troops, most of them trained as traffic cops for Japanese occupation service, tried to combat the hard core regulars of the People's Army of North Korea, it was simply no contest.

The naval situation had been equally grim. The mighty US Seventh Fleet, the once immense armada that had struck fear into its wartime enemies, now consisted of a mere 14 ships. The Far Eastern Fleet, commanded by Vice Admiral C. Turner Joy, could only muster 13 vessels. No wonder the Communists enjoyed overwhelming successes in the beginning.

Thank goodness General MacArthur had regained the initiative with his surprise landing at Inchon, Rod recalled. He had pulled America's fat out of the fire, temporarily.

Unfortunately, General MacArthur was relieved of his UN Korean Command, by President Truman, after MacArthur's protracted criticism of Truman's Korean policy. The very capable General Matthew Ridgway replaced MacArthur.

MacArthur's removal had been a bitter pill for many Americans to swallow, particularly by fellow West Pointers who were convinced that he could win the war in Korea quickly and easily if only Truman would allow him. Every soldier who lived with a credo of *Duty, Honor, Country* echoed the General's criticism of President Truman.

Then in early 1952, General Dwight Eisenhower, the UN Supreme Commander, decided to seek the Republican presidential nomination. He resigned his military post, and General Matthew Ridgway took over Eisenhower's UN Command. Mark Clark then replaced Matt Ridgway in Korea.

When General Clark and his staff arrived in Korea, he had tried to negotiate a peaceful end to the war and an immediate exchange of prisoners. Rod and other staffers had believed they were getting close to an acceptable settlement. But the *peace negotiations* ground to a halt because the belligerent Communist attitude defied logic. Their meetings became *talking wars.* Then in September, the *talking war* became a *shooting war*. Mark Clark ordered an escalation of US airstrikes and the establishment of a new battle line twenty miles north of the 38th parallel. Once again, US troops were in the middle of a hot war.

"The Peace Talks" continued. So did the fighting and killing. When the talks began to lag, the battles grew hotter. So it was not until July 27, 1953, that the guns finally fell silent.

During the final weeks of conflict, Rod was able to resign his staff position and gain command of an infantry platoon. He underwent his baptism of fire, earned a Purple Heart and a Silver Star, and received his first promotion.

The stressful times also began to heal his heartache and desperate emptiness. Slowly he emerged from his world of darkness and began once again to take pleasure in his duties, his accomplishments, and his friends.

The following spring, Rod left Korea and returned to Japan. At twilight, on what would have been their third anniversary, he stood alone on a rocky cliff overlooking the deep blue waters of the Pacific. He and Amanda had often stood hand in hand during their wonderful year together, looking out over the great expanse of ocean. Somehow, it didn't seem to matter that they had enjoyed the power and majesty of the world's mightiest ocean from a headland in California, while now he stood on a picturesque precipice on the Japanese Island of Honshu. The ocean was a link that bridged the distance, the years, and the loneliness. They had been married only three years before, but in many ways it seemed much longer. West Point was a world away! More than that, it was a lifetime away. That had been a time of love and tenderness. Now he existed in a violent world—the world of a professional warrior—a hard, often bleak and bitter world, where sudden death, by familiarity, lost most of its terrors. He had come here tonight to bid a last farewell to Amanda and the world they had shared.

Suddenly he realized there was no need for good-byes. Amanda's spirit was here beside him. It always would be. Twilight was still a special time of love and togetherness. As if by magic, his sadness fell away, and he was at peace with the world—a new world that could be good or bad, right or wrong, bright or dark. The choices were his. Fate had been unkind when it had taken Amanda and their unborn baby, but that could never be undone. There would always be time to remember, but now it was time to move on. A time to revere the dead but also a time to let them go and to live his life in the present.

The happy grin that had been missing for so long re-appeared. With new resolve and commitment, he turned from the restless ocean and boldly faced the future of a professional warrior, ready to welcome whatever adventures that future might hold.

## *WASHINGTON, D.C.*

## *JANUARY 17, 1960*

In an effort to gather as much information as possible before his morning meeting with the CIA, Reynolds invited Captain Quentin Moultrie, of the Charleston, South Carolina Moultries, to dinner.

Quentin was the quintessential southern gentleman. He had been Rodney's classmate at West Point and was currently assigned to the G-2 (Intelligence) Section of the Pentagon—a position that gave him access to a great deal of classified information. Rodney was walking a thin line between the topics that he was eager to explore and the sensitive subjects that his friend had sworn to protect.

"What can you tell me about the CIA people I'm going to meet tomorrow?" Rod queried.

"Not a whole lot about their operation, Rod. That's hush-hush. The two dilapidated buildings they use, Quarters Eye and Building K, are a joke. They both look like they're ready to collapse. But the guys in the section are all top-notch."

"How about Tracy Barnes? The man I report to."

"The guy is a living legend. People say the only man in Washington more intelligent than Tracy Barnes is his boss, Richard Bissell. Barnes graduated from Yale and went on to earn a degree at Harvard Law

School. He was practicing law with a top Wall Street firm when World War II broke out."

"How'd he get mixed up with the spooks?"

"He joined the OSS [Office of Strategic Services], and served under Allen Dulles in Europe. The week before D-Day he parachuted into occupied France and won two Croix de Guerre medals for heroism. He's been Bissell's buddy since their prep school days. Barnes seems content to work in the big man's shadow and smooth all the feathers Bissell ruffles."

"Tracy Barnes sounds like a good man to work for; but I'm not so sure about Mr. Bissell."

"*Dr.* Bissell! He has a Ph.D. from Yale and is regarded as the brightest man in the government by Capitol insiders. Right now he's Assistant Director of the CIA. He runs the Plans Division with an iron-fisted discipline. He's virtually unknown outside of DC, but when Richard Bissell speaks, everybody listens, including the last three Presidents. The first time I met him I was awed by his bearing and brilliance. Since then I've discovered that everyone he meets feels the same way. Let me share an interesting story with you.

"A while back, Bissell was given a very difficult assignment—gathering strategic information about the Russians and their allies by his boss, the CIA Director Allen Dulles. Rumor has it that Bissell went out and recruited Kelly Johnson, the top designer at Lockheed Aviation and E.H. Land, the guy that developed the Polaroid camera. The three of them have designed an aerial spy system they call the U-2 Program. No doubt they'll develop plans for more sophisticated spy missions and eventually provide more data about Soviet secrets than we've ever had. Mother Russia's mysterious interior will be open to a full inspection by our 'eye in the sky.'

"Bissell and his staff also hatched the scheme for the 1954 Guatemala Coup, when the CIA engineered the overthrow of the government in a single week. Bissell's good—very, very good!"

During the rest of the evening, although Rod was able to learn nothing more about the mysterious goings on at Quarters Eye and Building K, he was glad to have some background on the two top men. But two burning questions remained. Why had they picked him, and what did they have in mind?

At 0750 the next morning, Captain Rodney Reynolds drove a motorpool jeep into the parking area of Building K and got his first look at one of the buildings Quent had described as somewhat seedy. He decided that his friend's appraisal had been too generous. During World War II, a row of barracks-like, "temporary" structures had been built close to the Potomac River. Now, twenty years later, their shabbiness stood out in stark contrast to the splendid Lincoln Memorial, which they overlooked.

Rod walked briskly into the building, found Tracy Barnes' office without delay, and entered at exactly 0800. The door to the inner office was ajar, and he observed an individual sitting at a large desk, talking on the phone. When the conversation ended, the man rose and strode into the anteroom.

A tall, imposing man, he wore a charcoal gray Ivy League suit, white button-down French linen shirt, and a Windsor-knotted, dark gray and burgundy tie. His receding but neatly trimmed silver gray hair and chic horn rim eyeglasses complemented his overall look of competence. If Rod had been asked to describe him in one word, he would have chosen "elegant."

Holding out a steady hand, he said with a friendly grin, "Hi, Captain Reynolds, I'm Tracy Barnes. My secretary will arrive shortly. Her first act will be to brew a pot of fresh coffee. Until then, come into my lair, and we'll chat for a while."

Feeling very much at ease, Rod followed Barnes into his inner office.

"Sit down and relax. How was dinner at the Chart House last night? I love that restaurant. I hope you had the turtle soup. It's always absolutely delicious."

He smiled his warm, friendly grin once again in response to Rod's unmasked look of disbelief.

"There are many eyes and ears in Washington, Captain. You find them in the most unlikely places! The first lesson we all must learn is the importance of continuous security and the need to be alert. Say nothing unless you want the whole world to share it. Another lesson is to refrain from giving out unrequired data to anyone. Quentin Moultrie forgot that lesson last night. You had no need to know about the U-2 System. He only told you to show off. I trust you'll forget everything you heard."

Barnes regarded his abashed visitor for several seconds before he continued.

"Today's most important lesson is a simple one. If you *need* to know something about the CIA, Allen Dulles, Dick Bissell, myself, or, for that matter, anyone in the company, ask me. *No one else!* Is that clear?"

"Yes, Sir!" Reynolds stammered.

Once again, Tracy Barnes flashed his friendly grin, but he had made his point. The men who staffed Building K and Quarters Eye were not to be trifled with. Rod hoped Quent wouldn't wind up in hot water, but he wasn't about to ask.

"Captain Reynolds, since you graduated from the Point, you've achieved a fine record. We reviewed your accomplishments in depth before we requested you. Dick Bissell and I concur that you are precisely the person we need to fill a very special slot on our staff. I'm familiar with your record, but I'd like to know about the things between the lines. What have you learned along the way? What did you bring out of Korea, besides a Silver Star and a Purple Heart? They call you 'Ramrod', don't they?" When Reynolds nodded, Barnes continued. "Tell me about the real Ramrod Reynolds. Start with your marriage."

Ramrod was somewhat stunned by the frank and personal nature of the request. He paused for nearly a minute—collecting his thoughts—then he began.

"Amanda and I were married three weeks after I graduated. We had less than a year together before she and our unborn child died in a traffic accident. Amanda was a terrific lady. She was so thrilled about the baby that she glowed with happiness. A foolish man who drank far too much and then tried to drive snuffed out her life in a single instant. He walked away without a scratch and Amanda died. The awful irony of that made me bitter for a long time."

"Soon after Amanda's death, your staff duty in the Far East began, didn't it?"

"Yes, six weeks later. When I arrived in Japan, the tragedy of her death was still uppermost in my mind. It seems strange to me, even now, but somehow my own misery made me more conscious of the grief and desolation of others. It was as if I had a special perception that allowed me to sense the vulnerability and feelings of the people around me."

Tracy Barnes could see how difficult this was for Reynolds. Dark sadness had crept into his eyes, and a wistful expression seemed to be frozen in place.

Suddenly the sadness disappeared, and a fierce look appeared in the steely gray eyes. His back straightened, and it was patently obvious that Captain Reynolds had regained control of his emotions. "Now I know why they call this man Ramrod," thought Barnes.

"I perceived the enmity that many Japanese still felt toward Americans. Although most of them tried to suppress it outwardly, I could feel their hostility and frustration. I realized the traditional confidence, that almost cocky attitude that symbolized Japan in the years before the war, was gone. It had given way to disillusionment and disbelief. A look of vacant emptiness was visible in many people's eyes. Others displayed righteous hostility, produced by the atomic fireballs that incinerated Hiroshima and Nagasaki. In '52, hostility was still quite intense. Maybe it always will be."

"Those were terrible times for most of us!" Barnes agreed. "I believe they may have been more difficult for President Truman than for anyone else. Tell me about your staff duty. Was South Korea's president as tough as they say?"

"Yes, Sir! In April 1953, General Clark assigned me, along with four other officers, to assist with the scheduled talks between Communist North Koreans and the United Nations negotiators. Although he was excluded from the peace talks, the South Korean President, Syngman Rhee, was adamant that any peace treaty had to expel every North Korean and Chinese Communist soldier from every inch of South Korean territory. I still remember the day he told General Clark he would withdraw all South Korean troops from UN command unless every Communist soldier was withdrawn. Rhee was so furious with the General that he vowed to fight alone if we didn't incorporate his terms.

"General Clark tried to explain that we had no hope of gaining concessions in peaceful negotiations that we had been unable to win in two and a half years of bitter warfare. But Rhee remained adamant that there would be no peace as long as one enemy soldier remained. Rhee began an all-out propaganda campaign designed to undermine the truce talks."

"As I recall, his campaign didn't work very well."

"It didn't work the way he expected. The Chinese leaders in Peking, who were pulling the strings of the Korean puppet leaders in Pyongyang, retaliated by escalating attacks against Rhee's South Korean troops. Both sides sustained major casualties, but the repeated assaults failed to gain very much ground. Communist strategists decided that heavy causalities would convince Rhee that continued resistance was sheer folly."

"How severe were those losses?"

"During that last offensive, our intelligence people estimated 25,000 North Korean and Chinese troops died and 72,000 were wounded. But the Communists finally succeeded in driving their 'no quarter' point home, and the guns were silenced on July 27, 1953."

"And you were in the thick of that fighting."

"I welcomed the responsibility of wartime leadership and the dangers of combat. Leading my troops, keeping them and myself alive, was a full- time job that left no time to brood about Amanda's death. During the last days of battle I was wounded and hospitalized. The next month I was promoted to first lieutenant and awarded the Silver Star."

"The army has kept you hopping ever since."

"Since I returned from the Far East they sure have! First, Advanced Warfare and Tactics School at Fort Leavenworth—then two years as a training officer in the Combat Engineer School at Fort Leonard Wood. In 1958, I was promoted to captain and assigned to Fort Gulick to assist with the establishment of the Advanced Jungle Warfare Training Program."

"Fort Gulick is in the Panama Canal Zone?"

"Yes, Sir. It's a beautiful part of the world."

Tracy Barnes smiled wryly.

"I'm glad you enjoy the tropics. By the way, will Special Forces training work throughout the army?"

"It's hard to say. I was a member of the first group to graduate from Special Forces Program. That SF School has evolved into the Rangers. Last October, I was assigned to the Fort Knox Advanced Warfare School as senior company commander. The recruits they sent us responded well; although the average man isn't Ranger material, the tough training they receive certainly will help them to become better regular soldiers."

"You've had a fascinating career, so far, Ramrod! Hopefully, you won't get too bored working with us. Let's grab some fresh coffee. Then we'll head over to Quarters Eye—you're going to meet the boss."

## *QUARTERS EYE*

## *JANUARY 18, 1960*

As Barnes and Reynolds entered the conference room, Richard Bissell and several staff members were discussing a scheme designed to hasten Fidel Castro's demise.

"What we need," said Bissell, "is a plan that rivals the '54 Guatemala coup. Engineering a government overthrow in a single week was brilliant. A textbook operation that included less than a hundred and fifty exiles and a dozen old World War II fighter planes. Obviously, compared to the Guatemala operation, this one will be miniscule. I don't cite the Guatemala coup because of its size, or even its methods. I cite it because of its operational thoroughness. The whole thing went off without a single hitch. We achieved near-perfect execution. Since we know that it can be done—let's do it again! Our mission is simple. We must oust Castro! That's all there is to it. So let's put on our thinking caps and lay out the groundwork."

*The bare bones of the new operation that would become Operation Trinidad were formulated that morning. They decided to use the same staging area they had employed for the Guatemala Operation, the all-but-abandoned US Naval Air Station at Opa-Locka, Florida. The man who made that suggestion would play a key, although covert, part in the Cuban Operation but would achieve far greater national notoriety a dozen years later as a result of the Watergate break-in. His name was E. Howard Hunt.*

As the brainstorming session neared a conclusion, Richard Bissell made his position perfectly clear.

"We can't afford to let this operation get out of hand. Nobody wants to rid the Western Hemisphere of Castro any more than I do, but we must be content with a modest beginning. Let's start with three basic objectives. First, we'll train a few hundred guerrillas. Next, we'll infiltrate them, a few at a time, onto the island. Finally, we'll select targets for our saboteurs that will cause maximum disruption when they're destroyed. Okay? Let's all get to work on this. Two weeks from today, I want a plan that includes a projected timetable, probable targets of opportunity, and photographs of everything—a plan I can sell to Allen—which means a plan he can sell to the President. That's it! Let's get on it!"

The staff members rose and filed out, but Bissell motioned for Barnes and Reynolds to remain.

"Welcome aboard, Captain Reynolds. I'm sure Tracy told you we have a unique assignment for you. We need to blend your knowledge of neo-modern military tactics with our knowledge and skills about clandestine operations. In any covert operation there are bound to be foul-ups. The only thing we can do to minimize glitches is to use highly qualified people in our projects—and lay out an operational plan that is close to foolproof. You have certain prerequisite tactical experience that we feel is needed to guarantee success in our current objective.

"Nose around in our Castro files for a couple of weeks. Study everything he says and everything he does. Try to learn to think like Castro, so you'll be able to predict his tactical responses. If I were you I'd start with the newspaper stories on his visit to Washington last year. If you need help, just holler."

***CASTRO ORDERS EXECUTION OF TWENTY-EIGHT MORE "REBELS"***
***TOTAL NOW STANDS AT 521***

Rodney read *The Washington Post* banner headline. He was studying an April 17, 1959 edition of the giant daily newspaper. That headline greeted Castro last April when he arrived at National Airport for the start of his "unofficial," eleven-day visit.

On April 18, the *Post* printed a front-page story.

**Big, impatient crowds gathered at Washington National Airport yesterday really did not know what to expect from the man who has engendered so much controversy.**

**What they got was a friendly, bearded, vigorous young man (32 years old) wearing battle fatigues and a very charming smile—a revolutionary who looked like a revolutionary, and obviously takes a great deal of pride in being a revolutionary. His boyish charisma seemed to captivate them.**

**Hundreds of well wishers shouted: *Viva Castro! & Long Live Fidel!***

**He mingled with the crowd, oblivious to any possible danger. He shook hands, kissed babies, and signed autographs. Then Castro held a two-hour press conference and assured his listeners that he "favored a free press because a free press is the biggest enemy of a dictatorship." All in all the Cuban dictator's visit began on a very successful note.**

CIA archives contained hundreds of newspaper stories, radio transcripts, and television tapes, as well as the various testimonies Castro had delivered to government leaders. The Senate Foreign Relations Committee was the recipient of one such oration, when Castro assured the senators that there would be no expropriation of US property in Cuba.

Rodney found a transcript of Castro's appearance on *Meet The Press*, in which he declared that he stood for "Cubanism" not "Communism."

Rod even found file photographs of Castro laying wreaths at the tombs of Washington and Lincoln.

In one interview Castro held Thomas Jefferson up for praise as "a man who understood revolutions and what revolutionaries should do."

Each time he spoke, Castro guaranteed Americans that he was their new friend, their "nuevo amigo."

It was obvious to Rod that Castro had told Americans exactly what he thought they wanted to hear. Radio transcripts, television film, and newspaper accounts seemed to indicate that American public opinion was evenly divided—many of Castro's eager listeners had believed him; many others had not.

Rod wondered what US leaders had really thought about the Cuban dictator's declarations of friendship and cooperation. What was concealed behind those headlines and the blatantly obvious observations? Rodney wished he could have been a fly on the wall or a bug in Castro's pocket for those fascinating eleven days in Washington during April 1959.

# *WASHINGTON, D.C.*

## *APRIL 19, 1959*

Dick Nixon sat in the den of his official residence with his old friend and substantial benefactor, C.B. "Bebe" Rebozo, who had jetted into Washington earlier that Sunday morning from his home at Key Biscayne. They were both sipping chilled Southern Comfort from tall glasses as they watched *Meet The Press*—but the refreshing icy liquor was having very little effect on Nixon's temperature or indignation. His curses blistered the wallpaper. Obscenities filled the air.

"How in the hell can anybody be stupid enough to believe that swarthy Cuban *******?" he stormed. "Nobody with his mind in gear can pay any attention to that greasy *******!"

He stopped his tirade as the camera swung away from Castro and returned to the show's moderator, a well-known news anchorman. The suave newsman posed a question to the Cuban dictator that invited a response designed to enhance Castro's position. Nixon exploded once again.

"Did you hear that *******, Bebe? Did you hear that simpleton's half-baked softball question? Every one of those Commie-loving ******* is exactly the same! They're all stupid *******! I'm meeting with

Castro at five o'clock, and he'd better not try to pull any of his ******* on me."

Aboard a sleek sailboat that was currently running before a fresh northern breeze on Chesapeake Bay, Dick Bissell was evaluating Castro for Tracy Barnes.

"Castro is an absolute wizard. He's one of the best manipulators in the whole world. If the CIA had a hundred agents like him, most of our troubles would be over. If you didn't know he's a classic villain, you'd have to believe this good guy image he projects. I don't like him, but we better never sell him short!"

Many knowledgeable Americans were just as sure as Dick Bissell that the Cuban dictator was only *playing* the good guy role. President Eisenhower, having no desire to meet with Fidel, spent the days of the Castro visit playing golf at Augusta National.

Cross-examination and overall evaluation of the smiling revolutionary's underlying purposes would normally have been the task of Eisenhower's most trusted advisor, the Secretary of State, John Foster Dulles. But Dulles was terminally ill. He announced his resignation a few days before Castro's arrival.

Since Dulles was unavailable, the confrontational meeting destined to become a classic was scheduled between Castro and Vice-President Richard Nixon in Nixon's office on Sunday afternoon, April 19th.

# *WASHINGTON, D.C.*

# *APRIL 19, 1959*

The jubilant Fidel Castro strolled into Nixon's office that afternoon, buoyed by the tremendous confidence his brilliant performance on *Meet The Press* had engendered.

Of this first face-to-face meeting, Nixon later said:

"His compelling, intense voice and sparkling black eyes are quite striking. Fidel Castro is intelligent, quite shrewd and, at times, an eloquent man who radiates vitality. At first, he gave the appearance of sincerity. But my favorable first impression was quickly tarnished, and I reverted to my preconceived opinion of him when I asked him tough questions."

"Premier Castro, you promised to conduct free elections, but so far there have been no elections. Why not?"

"Cuban people don't want free elections, Mr. Vice-President, because free elections very often produce bad governments."

"In an obvious effort to eliminate any and all opposition, you have executed more than five hundred Cuban citizens who disagreed with your policies. Why don't you give your opponents a fair trial?"

"The Cuban people don't want them to be tried. They want them executed as quickly as possible."

"That's a 'puppet-like' answer. One that I've heard often before from other Communist puppets."

"Since I'm not a Communist puppet, it's not a Communist puppet answer," Castro responded hotly. "It's a Cuban answer. I will do anything to protect my country!"

"You are currently accepting Communist aid. They are giving you a wide variety of materials. Commies never help anyone unless they attach political strings to their assistance. You already have Communists in your regime who will work from the inside to establish a Marxist-Leninist government right under your nose. Aren't you afraid of the vile consequences that a friendly relationship with those Communists might bring about?"

"I'm not afraid of the Communists or anyone else. I can handle them all! My most frightening enemies are not the Communists. Cuba is the same as every other emerging nation. Our enemies are illiteracy, poverty, and a lack of opportunity and jobs. Nothing can be changed until Cuba's industrial and agrarian bases are completely overhauled."

Castro quickly dismissed Nixon as a "lightweight."

He tried to explain to Nixon, but according to Castro, "Nixon listened, but he didn't learn."

The next three hours were spent with Castro trying to explain his willingness to accept Soviet cultural and economic advisors who would help the poor and unemployed of Cuba.

Nixon tried to convince Castro about the dangers of Communism: the subtle abilities of Red leaders to combine their assistance with political ideology. The advisors they sent would eventually infiltrate and seize control of the government.

The meeting ended in a standoff, but their face-to-face confrontation produced many far-reaching results.

Fidel Castro made an uncharacteristic, critical error in judgment by underestimating his opponent. An error he would sorely regret.

For his part, Richard Nixon discerned a dogmatic, indefinable quality, which, for good or for evil, made other men follow Castro. He recognized the Cuban dictator for what he was—a dangerous, unpredictable opponent. A rival to be reckoned with.

The next day Nixon wrote a twelve-page memo to President Eisenhower, Secretary of State Designate Christian Herter, and CIA Director Allen Dulles.

"Castro is either terribly naive about Communism, or he is already under Communist discipline."

But Nixon knew that if there was one thing Castro was not, it was naive! From then on, Nixon became the strongest and most persistent advocate for setting up a supporting and covert military operation designed to unseat his dangerous Sunday visitor.

Brigadier General Rowland "Rowdy" Stanton and his wife, Harriet, watched Castro's debut on *Meet The Press* while they enjoyed a steak tartare brunch on the patio of their home in Bethesda, Maryland.

When the network broke for an ad, Stanton, a baseball enthusiast in general, and a Washington Senators fan in particular, remarked to his wife,

"You know, Harri, Castro was a pretty fair ball player at one time! I heard he even had a tryout with the Senators. It's hard for me to believe that a guy who loves baseball that much can be all bad. We should learn a lot more about him at Dolly Iverson's cocktail party this evening. You can bet your boots he'll be there."

# *WASHINGTON AFTER DARK*

# *APRIL 19, 1959*

Dolly Iverson's estate, Ivy Hall, was a dazzling spectacle that evening, as Brigadier General and Mrs. Roland Stanton drove slowly around the huge, cobblestoned, horseshoe driveway that led visitors toward the mansion's main entrance.

Bordering the drive were a plethora of tiny, twinkling lights—warning lights that separated the replaceable cobblestones from the exotic plants that patiently awaited spring's arrival in their carefully marked and well-protected beds.

Rowdy Stanton brought his sturdy old Ford sedan to a temporary halt at the end of a long line. The humble vehicle seemed out of place in the column of elegant limousines, Cadillacs, Lincolns, and foreign sports cars that were inching their way toward the brilliantly lit white portico. As each car arrived, its occupants were greeted by one of the Ivy Hall servants, all of whom were clad in rich gold and maroon livery. The guests were ushered along an inviting maroon and gold carpet which extended up the front steps. The Iversons were proud patrons of the University of Southern California. Many years ago they had adopted Southern Cal's maroon and gold colors as a sign of allegiance.

As they approached the portico, Rowdy Stanton pointed to the Rolls Royce Silver Shadow that was parked in a place of honor near the edge of the walk.

## SENATOR

The Georgia license plate proudly proclaimed the Silver Shadow's ownership to the world.

"I see Old Fuss & Feathers is here tonight, Harri."

"You shouldn't call Georgia's Senior Senator 'Old Fuss & Feathers,' Rowdy, even though he can be rather stuffy at times. Who do you suppose Dolly has invited tonight besides the esteemed Senator Burgess, since Castro is scheduled to be the starring attraction?"

"Let's see. You and I are the obligatory General Officer and spouse this type of function demands. I would guess a few Congressmen, a Cabinet member, a Supreme Court Justice, and a high-ranking White House Staffer."

"We've attended so many of Dolly's parties over the years that figuring out the guest list in advance has become almost too easy for you. What about news people?"

"One high profile syndicated columnist, a pair of Capitol Hill news hawks, and three or four television personalities. No doubt one of them will be an anchor man," Rowdy added as an afterthought.

"Dolly also needs to invite people from the UN, doesn't she?"

"Oh, sure! To create an international flavor. My guess would be the Russians, to put Castro at ease; the British to offset the Russians; the French to add moral support; and a Middle Eastern diplomat. Their polished approach to neutralist appeasement is fun to watch. That's all I have time to speculate about," Rowdy Stanton concluded smugly, as they finally reached the portico.

Harri smiled sweetly at a liveried footman as he assisted her from the family sedan, then thought to herself, I bet Rowdy hits the guest list right on the nose.

They ascended the long flight of stairs and entered a mammoth front hall. The towering ceiling rose to a height of three stories. Wide, magnificent balconies provided access to the rooms on the second and third floors. They were greeted by their hostess, who was wearing an elegant dark green satin evening gown, which was capable of turning every other woman in the mansion bright green with envy. Dolly delicately touched her cheek to Harri's.

"You look marvelous this evening, Harri. That shade of light blue is a perfect color for you."

Dolly turned slightly, then flashed a brilliant smile at General Stanton.

"And it complements this handsome devil's dress blue uniform."

She looked over Stanton's shoulder at several arriving guests, smiled, and said,

"You two are old pros at this! Why don't you go into the ballroom and mingle, while I greet my other guests?"

They entered a huge ballroom that resembled the great Viking halls of the past. Each time Harri came into the ballroom she instinctively looked around for statues of Odin and Thor, or at least a window that overlooked a Norwegian fiord. They began circling the huge room, moving from one group to the next, pausing just long enough for a greeting and a few words of small talk. Of course, they made several exceptions. They spent several minutes with the British and French Ambassadors to the UN—the austere Lord Percy and Lady Pamela Brighton, and the delightful Claude and Simone de Vauclose.

Both ambassadors were eager for any information Rowdy Stanton could provide about the Pentagon's official intelligence position on the Castro visit. An expert at this international pastime of cat and mouse, Stanton talked a great deal but said very little while making both foreign dignitaries feel comfortable and privileged to be such integral members of a General Officer's in-group.

The Middle Eastern diplomat whose presence Rowdy had predicted proved to be the Lebanese Embassy's second-in-command, Rafik al Hariri. He did not hesitate long before coming to the point.

"Premier Castro seems to be making more friends than enemies in your country, General Stanton, do you not agree? Yet many of your newspapers are quite critical of his policies and methods. Therefore, my question must be, is Premier Castro a friend, or is he a foe, of your great country?"

"Mr. Deputy Ambassador, being the experienced, wise, and well-respected diplomat that you are, what do you believe to be the best strategy for America?"

"My government believes that everyone should be friends with everyone else. That is my government's official position."

"I wish Castro felt the same way! Unfortunately, he does not. He seems to regard the total annihilation of every opponent as his only logical course of action. What is your position on violence?"

"Of course, General, we abhor violence. However, my government has not established an opinion on the methods that Premier Castro is using. But rest assured that we are waiting and watching very carefully! That is our official position, I think."

Rafik al Hariri smoothly excused himself and turned to join another circle of conversationalists.

"Rafik al Hariri is even better at saying nothing than you are," Harri whispered to her husband.

A short time later Fidel Castro arrived, and for the rest of the evening he exerted his considerable charm in an effort to win friends and justify his cause. He assured everyone that he stood for Cubanism, not Communism. Cuba was destined to be a democracy, not a dictatorship. But Castro also reminded his listeners that omelets could not be made without breaking a few eggs.

Intercontinental Broadcasting Company's Evening News anchorman, Brendan York, was chatting with the Stantons when Senator Andrew Jackson Burgess joined them. Burgess, Georgia's Senior Senator, was Chairman of the Senate Armed Services Committee.

"Mrs. Stanton, may I say that you are looking especially lovely this evening. General Stanton, you are a very lucky man. By the way, I appreciated the candor you displayed during your testimony before my committee last week." He glared directly at the newsman. "It's too bad television networks don't exhibit that same type of candor, Mr. York!"

"Perhaps no one outside the US Senate is ready for absolute candor, Senator," replied Brendan York, his Irish temper peeking through his cool facade. "As you have often observed, there is such a thing as a need to know."

Suddenly, the already electric atmosphere was intensified. Fidel Castro and a small entourage that included the fiery Russian Ambassador Mikhail Potopovich joined their circle.

"Aha, Premier Castro, now we have found this gathering's key meeting," the Russian triumphantly crowed, "where the chairman of the Senate Armed Services Committee conspires with the Pentagon to destroy your country's chance for freedom. Then the American television networks will report that Cuba could only be saved by raining missiles down on your innocent and unsuspecting countrymen."

"Mr. Ambassador, your propaganda gets irksome! You know America's principal concern has always been the welfare of her neighbors. We've never had the slightest interest in imperial conquest!" Senator Burgess corrected him.

"A very pretty speech, Senator, but we Russians know better! We are not the fools that you suppose us to be. You placate us with morality today, but you will kill us with missiles tomorrow," he bellowed, loud enough for everyone in the great hall to hear.

"The Cuban people know who their real friends are! They also recognize their real enemies. You capitalists are confident of victory because Cuba lies only ninety miles from your shores. If our Cuban friends refuse to knuckle under, their defenseless cities will become easy targets for your arsenal of deadly missiles. But you, Senator Burgess, and every other American should understand that we Russians are loyal to our friends. We stand ready to help the Cuban people ward off your aggression."

His voice thundered into every corner of the ballroom as he issued his final warning:

"Remember, Senator, that if Cuba is only ninety miles from America's shores and American missiles, America is only ninety miles from Cuba's shores. And we have missiles, too!"

Having fired his last salvo, the Russian spun on his heel and walked away, leaving everyone within earshot absolutely dumbfounded. Meanwhile, his ominous threat hung in the air like a cloud of gun smoke.

# *THE WHITE HOUSE*
# *FEBRUARY 7, 1960*

Allen Dulles and Richard Bissell were President Eisenhower's first visitors of the morning. It was a routine monthly briefing when various CIA projects were discussed. Dulles decided that one of the day's topics would be Cuba.

"Mr. President," he began, "we need to consider the idea of infiltrating guerrilla saboteurs into Cuba. Men we'll train to cause as much damage and stir up as much disruption as possible. I brought along some photographs of possible targets where our saboteurs could begin."

Eisenhower had supreme confidence in the CIA Director and an understandable appreciation of Dulles' talent—abilities he had come to appreciate during the Guatemala Coup. He studied the photos and listened patiently before he replied.

"Allen, I realize the need to upset Castro's apple cart. I'm also sympathetic to the idea of trying to oust him completely. But this series of hit-and-miss forays won't even cause significant inconvenience, much less inflict any real permanent damage."

The President paused before he continued.

"If you want to institute a major effort, put your people to work on a real program that I can look at. Castro's been sitting on that island for over a year now, thumbing his nose at us. If we're going to do anything, let's do something substantial."

These words were like an engraved invitation to Dick Bissell. Less than a week later, he had drafted a top-secret policy paper entitled, *"Program for Covert Action Against the Castro Regime."* The next step was to present the plan to the 5412 Committee.

"The 5412 Committee," Tracy Barnes explained to Rodney Reynolds, "is composed of four high-level individuals, empowered by National Security Council Directive 5412/2, to make top-level decisions about covert operations. The Committee members are: the Deputy Undersecretary of State; the Deputy Secretary of Defense; the Director of the Central Intelligence Agency; and the Special Assistant to the President for National Security Affairs. During Eisenhower's Administration, the 5412 has become the most secret and powerful committee in government. I'm glad Allen Dulles is already sold on Dick's plan."

At the 5412 meeting, Reynolds saw Bissell in action for the first time. He was informed, precise, and absolutely brilliant.

"Gentlemen my operational plan has four principal goals.

1. Create a unified Cuban government in exile.
2. Establish a powerful propaganda offensive.
3. Establish a covert intelligence and action organization in Cuba that can respond to all manner of opposition.
4. Organize a paramilitary force outside of Cuba, and train it for all future guerrilla operations.

My plan accomplishes all of these tasks."

For the next hour, Bissell spun a web of intrigue, yet he did so in such a logical and simplified manner that he cast a magical spell over each of his listeners.

The 5412 Committee unanimously approved his plan.

The full National Security Council met twice in early March to discuss the Bissell Plan.

On March 10th, they talked about various Cuban exiles that might be recruited to fill the many posts and assignments that loomed ahead. Several members suggested joint actions with the OAS (Organization of American States) now or later.

The word "assassination" was carefully avoided, but the idea of making Fidel and Raul Castro, along with Che Guevara, simply disappear was a veiled desire of many NSC members.

On March 14th, the NSC met once again. At this meeting Admiral Arleigh Burke, the Chief of Naval Operations, was adamant in his opinion.

"To make this plan work, we need to recruit influential Cuban exiles that anti-Castro elements will trust and follow. Removal of the Castros should be a package deal, because many of the men around them are just as bad or even worse than they are."

Once again, the word "assassination" was avoided, but Bissell and Dulles knew they weren't the only ones thinking about it.

On March 17, 1960, Eisenhower approved Bissell's Plan. The effort to overthrow Castro was officially underway.

# *SWAN ISLAND*

# *MAY 24, 1960*

Bissell and his advisors decided that the time was ripe to set up a radio transmitter and bombard Cuba with anti-Castro information and carefully selected propaganda.

The individuals selected to design and install the system were the ones who did the same job so masterfully during the Guatemala coup. In order to reach as many Cubans as possible, the radio experts decided that they needed a fifty-kilowatt medium-wave transmitter.

That request was a difficult one to fill since the K-50s were extremely expensive and in short supply. Also, they were large enough to fill several boxcars when they were shipped. Since the operation was still essentially covert, a transmitter could not be requisitioned through normal channels. It had to be "borrowed" from an unwitting source. A perfect solution was found when a transmitter owned by the US Army, due to be turned over to the "Voice of America," was "discovered" on a railroad train in Germany by one of Ramrod's former subordinates. The entire system was quickly commandeered and prepared for immediate transshipment.

Once the transmitter had been obtained, another question arose. Where should it be set up? The most obvious answer seemed to be the Florida Keys. But knowing the Department of State would not condone such an overt act of diplomatic meddling, Bissell soon discarded that idea. The last people he wanted to know about the transmitter were the ones at the State Department or, for that matter, at the White House.

Then an ideal location came to light—Great Swan Island. Great Swan was a tiny spot off the coast of Honduras, in the western Caribbean, composed of equal parts of sand and guano. The island was a mile and a half long, and a half mile wide—a remote sand spit that America and Honduras had both claimed for the past hundred years. It was currently occupied by two dozen people and thousands of lizards. It was to this isolated oasis with its few scraggly palm trees that the transmitter, a temporary work force of Navy Seabees, and a small contingent of CIA radio operators were sent.

The first Sunday they were on the island, an international incident was avoided by traditional American quick thinking. Shortly after daybreak, a dozen Honduran college students arrived from the mainland. They planted their country's flag, sang their national anthem, then proudly proclaimed that on behalf of Honduras, they were seizing control of Great Swan Island. Fearful that the boisterous young Hondurans might damage the irreplaceable radio transmitter, the radio operators sent a call for help to a US destroyer that was hovering nearby.

Fortunately, cooler heads prevailed. The students were invited to join their hosts in drinking a large stockpile of beer that had been shipped to Great Swan. Each side attempted to out-drink the other for the rest of the day. At nightfall, the college students, by now the good friends of their "American guests," departed, secure in the knowledge that the national honor of Honduras had been preserved.

A few days later the installation was completed, and Radio Swan began its broadcasts. Another piece of the puzzle was in place.

The same afternoon as the Swan Island incident, Richard Nixon was sitting on the terrace of his residence chatting with his close friend, Bebe Robozo. Bebe could not help chuckling to himself as he observed the Vice-President's idea of casual attire. A gaily-colored Hawaiian shirt hung outside a pair of starched and bleached sailcloth canvas pants. Okay, so far. But it was Nixon's legs and choice of footwear that titillated Bebe's funny bone. He was wearing long, black, silk dress socks, supported by calf-hugging garters, and a pair of highly shined black and white wingtip shoes. His legs, in contrast to the black socks, were so chalky white and pale, Bebe decided Nixon's legs had seen no sun since he left the South Pacific at the end of his navy career.

"Bebe, I've been the Vice-President for the last seven and a half years. I've done my share and paid my dues. I deserve to be the Republican nominee in the 1960 Presidential Election, don't I?"

"There's no doubt about it. Nelson Rockefeller seems to be your only competition."

"That's true, but to be successful, I need to do two things. I need Eisenhower to actively campaign on my behalf. He was only elected to the presidency because of his record in World War II, but after almost eight years in the Oval Office, the old ******* is even more popular now than he was then—and not only with other Republicans! Most Americans genuinely like him. But getting his help may be tough. We aren't very friendly, you know. For some reason the old ******* hates my guts, and I can't figure out why! What have I ever done to him, Bebe? Hell, I even took up golf to please him! Can you imagine? Me, Richard Milhous Nixon, chasing a stupid ******* little ******* white ball over hill and dale!"

The affluent Floridian shook his head in apparent puzzlement but remained silent. Bebe knew, only too well, that being liked played an enormous role in Dick Nixon's comfort level. His major assets were his great intelligence and his astounding memory. His most serious flaw was an incredibly thin skin.

"My second problem is a lot easier to solve than the first. I need to speak out on a popular topic—an issue the average man on the street can identify with. The clearly obvious choice is overthrowing Castro. I'm going to request daily updates so I can stay on top of developments. Castro's a great issue, Bebe. No one I know likes that underhanded, swarthy *******."

From then on, the CIA delivered daily updates to Nixon on the Cuban situation. From these reports he plotted his course of action. He soon came to regard the unseating of Castro as a major political triumph for every single anti-Communist in the Western Hemisphere.

He pushed the CIA, on a daily basis, to move swiftly ahead with their plans, while urging the President, less frequently but just as vehemently, to authorize the necessary funding for the Cuban Project.

He frequently shared his views and ambitions with Bissell.

"If Castro can be overthrown before November's elections, we Republicans will get the lion's share of the credit for a worthy accomplishment. Republican candidates for every national and local office will be rewarded by votes from the admiring electorate. We'll be swept into office! And since I'll occupy the top spot on the ticket, it's imperative, to me, that Castro's overthrow be accomplished without delay."

Despite gentle but nearly constant prodding from Nixon and Bissell, President Eisenhower did not seem to regard the Cuban coup with any real sense of urgency.

At the August 18th Cabinet meeting, Eisenhower finally approved a $13 million budget for the Cuban operation but added a warning.

"I'll permit limited use of Department of Defense personnel and equipment in supporting roles only; no American military personnel are to be employed in any type of combat status."

Nixon was pleased, but apprehensive.

"One big question remains," he remarked to his executive assistant for national security affairs, retired Marine General Robert Cushing, Jr. "Can the CIA boys pull this off before the elections?"

Nixon called Bissell regularly to prod him into immediate action.

"We have our funding, so now I can afford to stall Nixon," Bissell told Tracy Barnes. "Realistically, it's too late to expect action before the elections. But I foresee another problem. Dick Nixon will give the go-ahead if he becomes President—but what if the

Democrats win? What do you suppose Kennedy will do if he becomes the next American president?"

Barnes left, and Bissell sat for a long time, staring out of his office window at a star-filled summer sky and wondered once again. What would Kennedy do?

# *WASHINGTON, D.C.*
# *SUMMER OF 1960*

Ramrod had known Tracy Barnes and Dick Bissell for six months and agreed with most people who knew them both. Bissell might be the only man in Washington smarter than Barnes.

Tracy was a quiet, unassuming man. He never talked about graduating from Yale, or earning a degree from Harvard Law School, or practicing law with a prestigious Wall Street firm. Only once, after a great deal of encouragement from Rod, did he share a few World War II adventures that he had had in Europe. He did talk about serving under Allen Dulles in the OSS but never mentioned parachuting into occupied France on the eve of D-Day or the missions that earned his Croix de Guerre. Rod knew Barnes and Bissell had been friendly since prep school. After all those years, Barnes was still content to operate in Bissell's shadow and smooth the feathers his often-abrasive boss constantly ruffled.

During the late evening hours of July 20, Avispa Orizaba and Ramrod were meeting with Tracy Barnes when Barnes received a cablegram from a CIA operative in Havana. The message was short and to the point.

"One of our Cuban agents will be contacting Raul Castro within the next few days. What kind of information should he try to obtain?"

In the early hours of July 21, Barnes sent a reply to Havana.

"Possible removal of Cuba's three top leaders is getting serious consideration here at HQ. Is your agent sufficiently motivated to risk arranging an 'accident'? This is your authorization to offer $10,000 for successful completion."

Reynolds knew Barnes would not have sent that message without approval from higher authority; yet within hours of the first encrypted radio message, a second message was sent to Havana.

"Do not pursue the matter under consideration. Drop it!"

Tracy Barnes also signed this message.

Rod was unable to discover why the initial plan had been quickly and completely scrapped, but the die was cast.

A comedy of errors and foolishness now began. The CIA tried to sabotage Castro's charisma-filled speeches by bribing one of his writers.

But that didn't work!

Next, they tried to find a way to fill a broadcast studio with a chemical similar to LSD that would induce disorientation during one of his speeches.

No way could be found!

An attempt to give Fidel a box of cigars injected with stupor-inducing drugs was the next idea. Before that plan got off the ground, it was decided to coat the cigars with botulism toxin in hopes that the disease would prove fatal as soon as the first cigar touched Castro's lips.

The cigars were prepared but never delivered!

The most insane and comical scheme was the one designed to coat Castro's shoes with thallium salts when he left them outside his hotel room overnight to be shined. The CIA hoped the strong depilatory would make his hair and beard fall out.

Finally, a halt was called to the farcical fantasies. It was time to get serious. Time was running out. Ramrod could see Bissell's mounting impatience. They decided to establish new training facilities and operational headquarters. For security reasons they selected far-off but friendly Guatemala to house the base. Training in a remote area would begin as soon as living quarters for the recruits, and a meager but serviceable airstrip, could be constructed. That would solve the most pressing logistical problems.

Meanwhile, they would continue working on two important strategies: a realistic plan to assassinate Fidel and continued attempts to enlist the aid of the foremost Cuban exiles now living in Miami.

Howard Hunt and Gerry Droller were dispatched to ferret out and round up every influential Cuban who might be beneficial in establishing a valid Cuban government in exile.

By mid-August Bissell was no longer impatient—he was furious! He raged at Barnes and Reynolds.

"What else can go wrong this month? Droller and Hunt are having almost no success ferreting out the important exiles we need to recruit in Miami. The Tech Services people are stymied in their attempts to poison

Castro or to make his hair and beard fall out. Torrential downpours in Guatemala have slowed construction on the barracks and airstrip to a muddy crawl, and the November Presidential Election is now being called a dead heat."

He rose from his deck and paced about the room. He did not speak again until he regained his composure.

"Dick Nixon is pushing me for a quick completion of the project, and worst of all, if Jack Kennedy wins, we may not even *have* a project."

Early next morning Barnes and Reynolds entered Bissell's office with a man at their heels. He was Colonel Sheffield Edwards, Director of the CIA's Office of Security. He laid out a plan for Bissell's consideration.

"When Castro overthrew Batista," Edwards began, "he confiscated all of the plush hotels and gambling casinos the American underworld had owned. Castro cost the mob billions of dollars then. He continues to cost them a ton of money every month their hotels and casinos are closed. The Mafia has even more and better reasons to assassinate Castro than we do."

Edwards observed that he had Bissell's undivided attention, so he continued.

"Since the Mafia lost the most, they should be the most eager to retaliate. Let's find someone to go to them, make a deal, and let the Mafia solve the Castro problem for us."

"That's a great idea," Bissell agreed, rubbing his hands in anticipation. "Cull our files and find a likely candidate. Keep me up to speed, Shef."

"I've got a former Chicago hood in mind, Boss. I'll get right on it."

A few days later, a go-between named Johnny Rosselli, an old time "fixer" for Scarface Al Capone's mob, was recruited to begin negotiations with the Mafia.

Shef Edwards and Ramrod Reynolds met Rosselli at the Yankee Clipper Hotel in Fort Lauderdale.

"You can tell your people that when Castro is overthrown, they'll get much more cooperation from the next government," Reynolds assured him.

Edwards then picked up a large briefcase and laid it dramatically on the table. When he released the clasps and opened it, Rosselli saw more than a dozen packets of currency—each of them was bound by a $10,000 wrapper.

"You're gonna have some start-up expenses connected with this deal, Johnny. Here's 150 grand to get you going."

"I'll do it. But you guys gotta understand; I'm not doin' it just for the money. It's my patriotic duty. Believe it or not, I'm a right guy!"

*Rosselli's right guy image was somewhat tarnished in 1968 when he was convicted of bilking six famous show business personalities, including Harpo Marx and Phil Silvers, out of more than $400,000, by cheating them in card games.*

Rosselli soon recruited a pair of Mafia bigwigs—Momo Salvatore "Sam" Giancana, Capo de Capo of Chicago; and Santos Trafficante, the former Mafia chief of Havana, who currently resided in Miami.

Rosselli gained access to Sam Giancana through their mutual friend—a high-priced call girl named Judith Exner Campbell, who was also rumored to be one of Jack Kennedy's "good friends."

Shortly after the "contract" was made on Castro, Giancana flew to Miami to meet Santos Trafficante. The assassination operation was ready to be set into motion. When he reached Miami, upset by many persistent rumors, Giancana spent his first day on the telephone talking to his current paramour, Phyllis McGuire, lead singer of the popular McGuire Sisters who were then appearing at the Sands Hotel in Las Vegas.

"Phyllis, I hear that bum Rowan is hanging around you again. You tell Mr. Smart Ass Rowan, the Rowan and Martin comedy team is going to be short one dead comic unless he keeps all his funny stuff on the stage. Tell the bum to go out and find a nice broad who ain't spoken for. And tell him I got people watching him."

Next day Sam Giancana called his CIA contact.

"I want you bums to know I'm dropping this assassination business and flying to Vegas unless you bug Dan Rowan's crummy house. That bum's trying to muscle in on Phyllis."

"We can't afford to get involved in your personal problem with Dan Rowan, Sam!" the CIA agent told him.

"Okay! Then deal me out of the Cuban party!"

"Sam, I'll tell you what I'll do. I've got a buddy who's a private eye in Vegas. I'll pay him, out of my own pocket, to rig a bug in Rowan's house. That's the best I can do."

"I don't care how you do it. Just get it done, or I'm out!"

A week later the detective reported that a bug was in place and operational. The very next day, the bug was discovered by Rowan's cleaning lady who turned it over to local authorities.

Las Vegas Sheriff's Deputies removed the bug and arrested the private detective. He was immediately bailed out of jail. His rescuer was none other than Johnny Rosselli.

Sam Giancana heard about the fiasco and thought it was hilarious. The episode had served his purpose. There was no doubt in Dan Rowan's mind as to who instigated the covert bug operation. Such knowledge, Sam hoped, would keep him far away from Phyllis McGuire. Giancana also concluded that if this was a sample of the organizational capability of the people plotting the assassination, then Fidel Castro was in absolutely no danger.

Shortly after this series of fiascoes ended, a far more serious one occurred. Giancana told Judith Campbell, or perhaps Phyllis McGuire, about the assassination attempt. On October 18th, Richard Bissell received a very disturbing memo from FBI Director J. Edgar Hoover, explaining that the CIA plot to assassinate Castro, utilizing Mafia killers, was now common knowledge, and advising him to cancel the arrangement with "Sam" Giancana and his friends. Bissell had no choice. The whole plan was quickly scrapped, and another gaffe was added to the growing list.

But other parts of the plan were finally beginning to jell. Bissell couldn't help smiling as he briefed Allen Dulles at their September 16th meeting.

"Things are falling into place. This past month we've been able to hire fifty qualified pilots from among the Cuban exiles living in South Florida. The Retalhuleu, Guatemala airfield has been finished, and a contingent of B-26's, C-46's, and C-54's has been ferried in. Day and night practices on takeoffs and landings have begun. Our air cadre is instructing pilots in dropping supplies and in close air support of ground troops. Guatemala Air Force insignias have been painted on the B-26 fighter/bombers. They are pretty badly worn, but the cargo planes are almost new. They're also unmarked."

"Do the pilots know where the planes came from?"

"They do now. They found bundles of letters, postmarked 'Formosa,' on board the planes. Most of them suspect that the Chinese Nationalist Air Force might have been the previous operators."

Dulles scowled darkly.

"As you know, Boss, the leading exiles have been gathered together to form a *de facto* Cuban government in exile. We're calling it the Frente. Unfortunately, their many points of view don't allow harmonious or pleasant relations. Members of the Frente still aren't making much of an effort to get along with us; but most of them are at least starting to get along with each other. Reynolds and Orizaba are having more success in their Miami recruiting efforts than Howard Hunt and his people. They've already recruited enough volunteers to staff and man three small battalions."

"That's encouraging! They've done very well!"

"That's not all! They've also brought in Pepe San Roman. He's a Cuba Military Academy graduate who was at the Fort Benning Special Warfare School with Reynolds and Orizaba. They hold him in very high regard. I only met him once, but I concur. I expect San Roman to eventually become the overall commander of the Cuban forces. As I say, things are starting to look pretty good."

"Keep me up to speed," Dulles ordered, a short time later, as Bissell prepared to leave.

"I will, Allen. Have a good weekend. Get some rest."

"I intend to keep him up to speed on most things," Bissell told Tracy Barnes an hour later, as they prepared to leave for a day of sailing on Bissell's boat. "The biggest problem we're now facing are all the different factions developing among the Frente. Some of the people are campaigning for positions in a post-victory government that doesn't exist—one that may never exist. Every faction seems to have a different idea of how to win the big victory that, to them, seems inevitable. We need to keep a lid on this, Tracy."

"That might be easier said than done."

"Pepe San Roman might be the answer to our problem. Obviously, he's the man to take charge and carry out orders."

"His experience in Army Training Command is a plus. Despite the tough training his volunteers have received in Guatemala, there have been very few injuries, and I believe only one fatality."

"Yes! Last week a soldier named Carlos Santana Rodriguez fell to his death from a 2,000-foot cliff.

Since his serial number was 2506, the unit has been renamed the 2506 Brigade in his honor. That new designation should improve troop morale, and higher morale should produce excellent results—our main concern must be results.

"I'm sure there'll be more casualties and some discontent, but those things are part of the price of success," he reminded Barnes, as they parked near the dock and headed for a pleasant day on the water.

Of course, the anticipated price of success, when analyzed by seasoned strategists in air-conditioned offices or on stimulating Chesapeake Bay outings, is far different than the actual price being paid by 2506 trainees in steaming jungle camps. No *dolce vita* here. Mountainsides with treacherous, slippery slopes and lightening-quick, deadly vipers were the order of the day—perilous places where a single false step or a momentary loss of vigilance could mean instant death. If he had been making his evaluation from the dark interior shadows of a jungle hut rather than from the holystoned deck of a sleek, sunlit sailboat, Richard Bissell might have foreseen the gargantuan problems that lay ahead. If he had, he might have quit the Chesapeake Bay and sailed straight south to Guatemala.

As the November elections approached, it became clear that a commando force could be recruited from the Cuban exiles already residing in Miami barrios; but pilots with combat experience could not be found so easily. They would have to be recruited elsewhere. The CIA, in order to keep the operation as covert as possible, could not afford to use pilots who were already on active duty. Therefore, they were forced to draw them from Air National Guard Squadrons in order to reach their quota. Prospective new recruits were assembled in small groups of less than a dozen. All of them were told the same story.

"A group of wealthy Americans with business interests in Central America are interested in hiring you to assist with a coup against one of the banana republics. For now that's all you need to know. If you're interested sign one of these sheets before you leave."

The story worked quite well until Cuban radio stations began broadcasting daily warnings about a forthcoming invasion. But by then, the CIA had rounded up a sufficient number of pilots committed enough, desperate enough, or just plain crazy enough, to man the strike force's aircraft.

Late in October President Eisenhower decided that Jack Kennedy should be briefed on current White House policies. Within hours, Democratic political strategists, now aware of a covert operation, decided Kennedy must assert himself in the area of foreign policy. The time was ripe for him to curtail his verbal bombasts against the Soviet Premier, Nikita Khrushchev, and concentrate on Fidel Castro, the leading Communist in the Western Hemisphere. International struggles between totalitarianism and freedom would become personalized confrontations of Communism vs Americanism, hopefully between Castro and Kennedy!

Since many political pundits were portraying him as an "international lightweight," and "a rich man's son, who might be soft on Communism," Kennedy completely agreed with his advisors' assessment.

The next morning national headlines proclaimed:

***KENNEDY REQUESTS AID TO HELP CUBAN REBELS DEFEAT CASTRO***

The afternoon headlines added:

***KENNEDY URGES SUPPORT OF CUBAN EXILES AND FREEDOM FIGHTERS***

Nixon was furious. He and Jack Kennedy had been friendly since they were elected to Congress in 1946.

"I've always thought of Kennedy as a man I could trust," Nixon told to his staff. "That ******* not only compromised national security, he stabbed me—a friend who trusted him—in the back! That dirty low-down *******!"

Now that Castro knew the invasion was imminent, CIA recruiting and training in Guatemala intensified.

As Election Day drew near, Nixon and Kennedy debated the issues on television three different times. For the radio audience, Nixon was the clear winner. For TV viewers, Kennedy won by a landslide.

Unfortunately for Nixon, the viewers outnumbered the listeners. John F. Kennedy won history's closest presidential election. Out of every 10,000 voters, 5,003 voted for Kennedy — 4,997 favored Nixon.

Two days after his inauguration, Jack Kennedy convened a meeting with the Joint Chiefs. Unlike President Eisenhower, Supreme Commander of Allied Forces during World War II who seldom required any military assessment other than his own, Kennedy felt compelled to consider advice from a great many quarters. His lack of experience, as well as his desire to see each facet of every issue, would prove to be his ultimate undoing. These traits, coupled with a rampant desire to spawn a mistake-free administration, caused him to err on the side of caution. Perhaps Kennedy forgot the ancient adage that admonishes, "the only people who never make mistakes are people who are too indecisive to make decisions."

The wisdom in that adage was proven correct when Kennedy's lack of decisiveness and reluctance to act became principal contributing factors in the Bay of Pigs tragedy.

# *PART TWO*
# *THE NEW PRESIDENT*

# *WASHINGTON, D.C.*
# *FEBRUARY 1, 1961*

Jack Kennedy peered up at the dark night sky and watched jagged streaks of lightning dancing among the rain-laden clouds. The bright twinkling lights of the metropolis that so often cheered and distracted him when he was troubled were barely discernible. All the familiar landmarks from which he seemed to draw his power were intermittently hidden by patchy winter fog, or veiled by opaque sheets of pelting rain that hammered in vain against impenetrable panes of bulletproof glass that protected him from the crazies who lurked beyond his window, in the sometimes deadly, but always precarious world.

As his reverie ended and he prepared to refocus on the overwhelming problems that confronted him, he concluded for the thousandth time that the poets had been wrong. It wasn't ancient Bagdad that concealed the great mysteries of the ages from view or Merry Olde England that accorded the greatest adventures. Far more intriguing mysteries and enigmas happened every day—right here in Washington—than any ever dreamt of by Omar Khayyam, and more daunting challenges than any ever undertaken by the Knights of the Round Table. Jack Kennedy smiled as he turned away from the glass, secure in the knowledge that he was living in the golden days of the real Camelot. King

Arthur had only been a pretender to the throne. Arthur had Excalibur, but Jack had the Oval Office.

"Bob," he said to his brother, the United States Attorney General, "this Cuban business has to look like an independent operation. Whatever we do to assist the rebels must be done in an absolutely covert fashion. If any of this can ever be traced back to my administration, Cuba's government will be solidified and Russia will start screaming about American imperialism again."

"Jack, at this very moment, an American cadre is helping to train the Cuban Brigade in Guatemala. American pilots, hired by the CIA, are flying around in American fighter planes, planes that are scheduled to provide air support for the exiles. My contacts in Miami are telling me that every Cuban refugee in South Florida is talking about the invasion force that's going to throw Castro out and take over the island. How can we pretend that we're not involved in an operation that everyone seems to know about?"

"Think of it as a replay of FDR's Lend-Lease Plan. I have made it perfectly clear that I will not stand by and allow a Communist state to exist ninety miles off America's shores. The issue here is not one of assistance, but one of any direct involvement. We will look like heroes to the world if we are seen helping exiles to recover their birthright, but we will be called imperialists if we take a direct part in the overthrow of a foreign country."

"It's like eating ham and eggs for breakfast," his brother chuckled. "A chicken is marginally involved, but the pig is completely committed."

"That's a good analogy, but I will add this. After blustering about protecting this hemisphere during the election, we must act in a positive manner or we'll appear to *be* chicken. On the other hand, if we employ intemperate means, we'll be branded as capitalistic pigs, eager to feed at the trough of third world misfortune."

He paced up and down for a few seconds. Then his jaw set in firm resolve as he continued.

"Last March Eisenhower approved a plan designed to train a few hundred guerrillas and infiltrate them into Cuba. Their mission was simply to make a few hit-and-run raids—insurgent action designed to annoy and disrupt Fidel Castro. Nothing about an invasion was even mentioned! Suddenly we're on the brink of an extensive project labeled *Operation Trinidad.* This is no modest plan of infiltration and harassment. It's a brand new mini D-Day—a major military project. Naval and air elements, joined by guerrilla units from the mountains and an invasion force from the sea will make an amphibious landing and attempt a coup d'etat in mere days rather than the months that were originally projected."

The President's face was crimson with rage and frustration.

"I can think of a hundred reasons not to go through with this, and another hundred that compel us to try *something*. The Joint Chiefs of Staff can't even agree whether or not the operation is feasible. The entire scenario is an enigma!"

"Jack, let's order Colonel Hawkins up here from Guatemala for a conference. I think we can count on him to level with us, and he's in a better position than anyone to evaluate the state of the Brigade's readiness. Second, we should send someone we trust down to Base Trax to evaluate it from the outside. Finally, we need to know if the division among the members of the Cuban Frente in Miami can be closed and determine if any consensus remains in their thinking. Reynolds and Orizaba are the most logical ones to evaluate that situation."

"I agree. And I think it would be wise to move the proposed invasion site farther toward the west. Trinidad seems to be too exposed to counterattacks from every side. These tactical maps of Cuba reveal many better sites all along the southern coast. I'll check on that possibility with Colonel Hawkins. And I'll make one thing crystal clear to him and the others. There can be no direct involvement of Americans in the landing, or even with the Cuban guerrillas. If such an involvement were discovered it might rally some misguided men to Castro's cause. My administration might be discredited or even crippled.

"Friends and foes alike, around the world, will be watching very carefully to see how I handle these problems and fulfill my promises. America's long-term reputation is on the line. We cannot afford to falter! I'm willing to sacrifice lives, up to a point, but I will never sacrifice prestige! All right, Bob, get Hawkins up here as soon as possible."

# *MIAMI, FLORIDA*
# *FEBRUARY 3, 1961*

Many people could not understand the Kennedys' animosity toward Fidel Castro, because they idolized the Cuban dictator. Dolores del Negro certainly did. She had since the first time she heard him speak. She smiled, remembering the glorious 1959 Ano Nuevo, when she had learned that Batista, that cochino, had fled from Havana, clearing the way for Fidel, Cuba's beloved El Caballo, to take the reins of power and lead his tortured homeland toward a bright and promising future.

She could still picture herself in a motor caravan as it came down from the Sierra Maestra Mountains on the first day of that New Year. For seven days they had driven triumphantly along the Central Highway of Cuba, for six hundred miles, toward Havana and destiny. Jubilant crowds, alerted by the presence of a menacing red/black helicopter that flew protectively over the long procession, lined each mile of the road.

Most of them wore red and black clothes, and waved red and black flags that symbolized the July 26th Movement. Parents told their children that this was a proud day in Cuban history. They were gazing upon a thirty-one-year-old miracle worker—a man who had begun three years earlier with twelve helpers—a man who had overthrown a tyrannical government. Fidel was a great man! Fidel was a legend! Fidel was their savior! Fidel was their future!

On January 8, when the big procession arrived in Havana, a hundred thousand happy revelers cheered along the Malecon Seaway and stood upon the high ramparts of a flag-festooned Morro Castle. A fleet of warships in the harbor fired welcoming salutes as they drove along on the journey to Camp Columbia. When they arrived, Fidel strode directly toward a podium equipped with a bank of microphones and began to speak—as he did, a man in the audience released three white doves of peace. One of the birds flew directly to Fidel and perched upon his shoulder. Not even the most hardened skeptic in the crowd could question the obvious significance of this wondrous miracle.

Ever the showman, the new Cuban Dictator waited until the last gasp of awe had dissipated, and then proclaimed:

"There are no enemies left in Cuba!"

For a single heartbeat there was absolute silence; then, as if by a prearranged signal, a thunderous roar burst from a hundred thousand trusting throats and exploded across the square.

It was still difficult for Dolores to believe that this glorious time in her life had begun only four years before. So much had happened to her since then. It seemed like only a few months since she and her sister, Tranquilena, had hitchhiked from Havana, all the way to the Oriente Province, where they became eager freedom fighters in the service of El Caballo.

Unlike her gentler sister, Dolores had relished the hardships and primitive conditions that were part of the initial training and subsequent guerrilla actions for which the intensive training had prepared them. Tranquilena believed that tenderness and feminine softness were the classic attributes of a lady—but Dolores knew the hardcore truth. A guerrilla fighter could never afford to be soft. She learned that lesson well! Softness meant weakness, and weakness meant death! When indoctrination and basic training ended, Tranquilena had become a cook, but Dolores had gone on to become an integral part of a hard-hitting paramilitary attack force.

Then one day, Captain Felipe "Avispa" Orizaba joined Fidel's burgeoning rebel force. The first time Tranquilena met the handsome young officer, who reminded many people of the movie star Tyrone Power, she fell hopelessly in love. Avispa, the Wasp, stung her poor sister. Marriage was inevitable for Tranquilena and Felipe. They were wed a few weeks later. Now my stupid sister is big as a house with her second child, thought Dolores disdainfully.

A dark frown spread across her beautiful face at the idea of her whipcord-hard body, in which she took great pride, being disfigured by an unwanted pregnancy.

Along with her three sisters and seven brothers, Dolores had grown up in one of the poorest barrios of Havana. She had often gone for days at a time with an empty belly, and always had been forced to wear tattered clothes. By the time Dolores was in her middle teens, she had learned to use her sharp wits and good looks to get what she wanted. A dazzling smile and flattering words quickly bent most men to her will. On her sixteenth birthday, her sugary words, and tempting promises, which she had no intention of fulfilling, had gotten her a party dress and a delicious meal at a fine restaurant. Let the fools of the world pray for deliverance and see what they got in return. She was smarter than all of them.

Since then, Dolores had been a trader. Sometimes she traded favors, but mostly she traded men—always dangling a man, like a puppet on a string, until she could improve her financial or social position by trading upward. Most men she met found her attractive. She often saw excitement shining in their eyes. Her pathetic, drab sister called her an Enchantress; but the worldly-wise and hardened Dolores knew, only too well, that she could dominate most members of the opposite sex. Most men were not only brute animals; they were fools, as well. Her friend, Ernesto "Che" Guevara, was right! The world was a vast collection of idiots who desperately needed keepers. Wise people, like Che and his friends, were the best hope for all those fools. Just as clearly, Communism was the only sensible way to help them.

It was Che who had suggested that she go with her sister when Felipe Orizaba deserted from the Cuban army and fled to the refuge of Miami. It had been obvious to Cuban leaders that the rumors about an invasion were true. America was no longer the stalwart protector of the tiny banana republics in the Western Hemisphere. The Americans would attempt to overthrow the lawful government of Cuba just as they had done several years earlier in Guatemala.

The Russians thought American intervention was imminent. Dolores remembered that the week after America cancelled Cuba's sugar quota, the Soviet

Ambassador, Anastas Mikoyan, arrived in Havana, and Raul Castro flew off to Moscow.

A short time later the U-2 missions had ended in absolute disaster, as had the Paris Peace Conference.

In July, the heat of a tropical summer had been intensified when Castro seized $700,000,000 worth of US property. The next day, Soviet Premier Nikita Khrushchev had threatened the United States with missiles if they tried to intervene in Cuban affairs. He also offered to help the Cubans oust American military forces from their Guantanamo Naval Base and announced his disdain for the Monroe Doctrine. Finally, Che Guevara added even more fuel to the raging political fire by announcing that Cuba was firmly on the road to Marxism.

American response was predictable. President Eisenhower countered Khrushchev and Guevara by announcing that the Monroe Doctrine was alive and well and that America had no intention of allowing a Communist state to exist anywhere in the Western Hemisphere.

The die was then cast, thought Dolores. As word spread throughout the length and breath of Cuba, all the cowards had run to seek refuge under the thumb of Big Brother America.

Dolores had come to Miami with the Orizabas—but not for refuge. She was on an assignment. Since Che was certain Felipe would join the anti-Castro forces, Dolores had been sent to spy on the invasion contingent, to report as much about their current plans as she could and, if possible, to infiltrate the rebel organization.

Tonight, a perfect solution to her problems was about to fall into her lap. Felipe was bringing home an American friend for dinner. An army officer who was apparently a key figure in training the rebels and in the invasion planning. His name was Rodney Reynolds. According to Felipe, he had lost his wife in a terrible traffic accident a few years ago. Felipe hoped she would be able to cheer up his friend and make him relax.

A wry, wily smile that had become her trademark crept slowly across Dolores's face. When a man was lonely and sad, he could be counted on to be indiscreet about a lot of things. Rodney Reynolds didn't know it yet, but she was going to strum on his heartstrings as if they were a flamenco guitar. She would make him ecstatic with joy. She was simply too good at what she did to contemplate any thought of failure. Reynolds would be her next conquest! By next week he would be eating out of her hand like a foundling puppy, eager to tell her whatever she wanted to know. Her sister Tranquilena was wrong. She wasn't an Enchantress; she was La Arana Negra, the Black Widow Spider.

Ramrod and Avispa were as frustrated with the members of the Cuban Frente as with anyone they had ever known. It seemed as if each member favored a different plan of action.

"It's worse than dealing with Syngman Rhee," Ramrod told his friend. "Rhee was a hard-headed man, but at least he knew what he wanted. There's been so much confusion and upheaval in Cuba in the recent past that most of the Frente members have, at one time or another, been enemies—many of them still are.

They don't seem to realize that Castro is the real enemy—not each other. Every day we're confronted by foolish men who believe a subtle infiltration of subversive agents can overthrow Castro's government. All of our efforts to explain the futility of such a plan have been stonewalled."

"I don't know how else to explain it to them," Avispa said. "They must know that the increased awareness in Cuba makes supplying guerrilla forces with airdrops nearly impossible. They don't seem to realize that Cuba's new allies, within the Soviet bloc, are supplying them with vast shipments of armaments and ammunition. Our agents in Havana estimate that nearly thirty thousand tons of military supplies have been delivered, so far. Castro's control over his expanded militia and civilians is far more effective and tighter than we ever anticipated. For some reason we can't make the Frente see that a military force, ten times bigger than anything ever assembled by any of Castro's predecessors, makes for real problems. That combination of factors dooms even the most persistent guerrilla activity to ultimate failure. But, regardless of what we say, they don't believe us."

"Knowing what we know now, 'Vispa, I think this new plan is crazy. What in the world would possess the CIA to change the plan in November, four lousy days before the Presidential Election? The ideas of infiltration and guerrilla warfare have been virtually abandoned. The total number of infiltrators is reduced to sixty. We're looking at a full-scale World War II type landing now. I guess the size of the invasion will be Jack Kennedy's decision. I just hope they don't hang the 2506 out to dry. If the President really lets

Jack Hawkins take charge, most major problems might be behind us. Let's hope so!"

A week after the election, Colonel Hawkins was named overall commander of the Cuban operation. He immediately summoned Ramrod and Avispa to Washington for a briefing. The following day, together with Hawkins and several other staffers, they left for Guatemala to inspect Base Trax, where they were appalled by the overcrowded living conditions and the lack of a great many essential items, including knives, forks, hot water, and worst of all, weapons.

Construction of modern barracks began the next morning, along with a fully equipped kitchen and a brand new electric plant. Planeloads of fresh bedding were flown in. Serviceable weapons for every man appeared as if by magic. Suddenly, supplies galore were available. In a single week, Base Trax was propelled out of the Stone Age and into the Space Age.

When the inspectors reached Base Trax there were 430 men in camp. Sixty of those best qualified for advanced guerrilla training were detached and sent to Fort Gulick, in the Canal Zone, the Army's Special Jungle Warfare Operations Center.

Hawkins appointed Pepe San Roman as Brigade Commander, then the remaining recruits were assigned to the four battalions. Pepe promoted Alejandro del Valle to command the First—the Paramilitary Battalion. Hugo Sueiro took over the Second Battalion—Infantry. The Third Battalion, Armor, went to Erneido Oliva. Roberto San Roman, Pepe's brother, took the Fourth—the Heavy Weapons Battalion.

To fill the Table of Organization & Equipment Colonel Hawkins needed at least 450 additional volunteers.

Ramrod and Avispa were assigned to recruit them—they thought it would be a cakewalk; but they didn't anticipate the obstacles the Frente was about to place in their path.

# FORT LAUDERDALE
# FEBRUARY 4, 1961

It was after 1 A.M, and Rodney Reynolds was still sitting in the Coral Reef Lounge of the Castaways Hotel, sipping Johnny Walker Red Label Scotch on the rocks, and thinking about his daylong date with Dolores del Negro.

He had met Felipe and Tranquilena Orizaba, and her sister Dolores, at 8 A.M. for breakfast at the Yankee Clipper in Fort Lauderdale. As they enjoyed sumptuous Eggs Benedict, Rod studied Dolores. Felipe had tried to prepare him for someone special but had not done justice to the overpowering Dolores del Negro.

For openers she was ravishing. Her dark eyes, soft mouth, and delicate nose were set in an oval face almost too perfect to be real. Her long, soft auburn hair framed and accentuated her loveliness. She was wearing a short, white terrycloth robe over her bathing suit when they met, but it did not conceal her slim, tanned, and beautifully shaped legs.

During breakfast Dolores made him feel as if he were the most fascinating person she had ever met. Strangely enough, his feeling wasn't engendered by her words, but rather by her smile, skin fragrance, and unique, captivating charm. She made him feel as if they belonged together. It was a strange euphoria that he had never experienced and couldn't begin to explain. Rod almost felt privileged to be sitting next to her, but at the same time, he found the magnetism she projected to be almost eerie.

When breakfast ended, he and Felipe left the girls and went to change into swimming suits.

"Well," asked Felipe, with a sly smile, "did I tell you?"

"You didn't tell me half enough, amigo! She's absolutely incredible. What a glorious girl!"

"Be careful! For some reason, the better I know her, the more sinister Dolores seems to become."

"You're imagining things, old buddy!"

"I hope so! After all, she is my sister-in-law. All the same, be careful, and play it safe for as long as you can."

The friends returned to the dining room, rejoined the sisters, then they all walked across the highway to the beach.

When Dolores dropped her terrycloth robe on the sand, Rod gazed in wide-eyed astonishment at her white-clad angelic form. His first thought was a Churchillian paraphrase—that Dolores might well have been God's finest hour. For the first time he began to fathom Felipe's warning. Rodney shuddered in spite of the unseasonably warm mid-winter morning. The seductive Dolores del Negro might very well wind up causing more trouble and heartaches than he could begin to imagine, much less try to handle.

The four of them spent the rest of the day enjoying the nearly deserted beach, then returned to the modest apartment building where the Orizabas and Dolores lived. Tranquilena and Felipe's large suite was on the ground floor, while Dolores' smaller apartment was on the fourth floor.

Rod assumed that he would shower and change for dinner in the Orizabas' apartment, but as he began following them down the hall, Dolores paused with one foot perched on the lowest step and said in a husky voice, accompanied by a Mona Lisa smile,

"You're welcome to come up and shower in my place instead of using Felipe and Lena's." She added teasingly, "If you want to."

"I'm worn out, Dolores. I don't think I can climb three more flights of stairs until I recuperate," he told her, following in the wake of the Orizabas.

"I'll bet I could help you to recuperate, Captain America," she cooed, beginning the long climb up to the fourth floor.

They all went dancing at the Fountainbleu, and for the first time in his life Rod saw looks of open envy on the faces of the men and unmasked jealousy in the eyes of women, as he and Dolores glided around the dance floor. But it was easy to understand the reactions of the other dancers. In her black strapless evening gown and golden tiara, Dolores looked like a reincarnation of Queen Marie Antoinette, dancing with Louis XVI at the Palace of Versailles.

At midnight they left the Fountainbleu and adjourned to the Castaways for a nightcap. An hour later, the Orizabas made their excuses and Felipe went to get the car.

"Are you coming home with us?" Tranquilena asked her sister.

"Give me a moment with Rod before you leave, Lena."

Tranquilena headed for the ladies room and Dolores smiled at Rod.

"You've had a devastating effect on me, Captain America. I've never felt this way about any man, especially after such a short time. I know you feel drawn to me, too. Please don't think that I'm a brazen hussy for saying this, but I'm falling in love with you."

"Dolores, you're a very beautiful woman. I pity blind men who will never see you! We've had a wonderful day enjoying each other's company, and having tons of fun; but we've just met. Forgive my directness. I don't mean this as a rebuff, but it's a time for caution, not rashness. I hope you understand."

"I do understand. You're much wiser than I am. I appreciate your counsel as well as your wisdom."

When Tranquilena returned, Rod escorted the sisters to the Castaways' entrance where Avispa was waiting with his car. He helped Tranquilena into the front seat, then swung around to face Dolores.

"It's been a wonderful day, Senorita. Once again let me say that I like you very much. I'll call you tomorrow. Now I'm going back to the bar and enjoy a nightcap as I think about our terrific day."

Dolores moved into his arms and kissed him—it was a friendly kiss that reflected new willing patience. She whirled and walking halfway to the car, then turned back and said, "You're quite a guy, Ramrod Reynolds."

Moments later she was gone—the car's taillights blending with hundreds of others on Ocean Drive. All that remained was a hint of her exotic perfume.

Rodney returned to the Coral Reef Lounge and sat at the bar, mentally replaying the day, and knowing in his heart that he had met 'quite a girl.'

A few miles away, Dolores sat smiling in the dark interior of the Orizabas' automobile, convinced that she had sunk her harpoon with as much professional skill as one of Ahab's whalers. It was just a matter of time, she told herself, before the upright but naive Captain America would be playing the game by her rules. And then he would tell her everything she wanted to know.

The following afternoon Ramrod and Avispa were sitting in a barrio tavern, drinking Carta Blanca beer with a few Cuban refugees. The bar had become one of the best unofficial recruiting stations. The pending invasion had become so popular in the Cuban barrio that lately Ramrod and Avispa were only recruiting men with previous military experience.

The tavern owner, Pepe Fulano, laid a copy of a Spanish language newspaper now being printed in Miami on the bar, and pointed to the headline.

**SEVENTEEN HUNDRED CUBAN REFUGEES ARRIVING WEEKLY IN MIAMI**

"According to this article," Pepe told the group, "there are 700 anti-Castro groups right here in Miami. Here's a picture of a hundred men, lined up and waiting to volunteer for the invasion force. The other night, a bunch of us went up to Opa-Locka and watched the 'blackout' planes taking off for Cuban invasion headquarters.

"Everyone on the whole island over the age of six knows the invasion is coming. If either of you guys gives us a date for the invasion, Castro will probably know about it before most of the people right here in this barrio! Some secret operation you've got here!"

"The Germans knew the Allies were coming on D-Day," Rod reminded him, "but that invasion worked for a lot of reasons. No one knew the exact landing site, or time! The invaders were well trained, had an excellent tactical plan, and were totally committed to liberty. Scores of partisans, eager to be free, rose up and helped the invaders who were risking their lives to liberate France. The same elements hold true for the Cuban Invasion. We have a great many reasons to expect success!"

An elderly, aristocratic gentleman, rumored to be a member of the Cuban Frente, spoke up. He was very difficult to understand because of his thick accent.

"Your expectations puzzle me, Senores! Castro has 40,000 men in his army, and 200,000 in his militia. If rumors about the size of your invasion force are correct, you'll be outnumbered a hundred to one. Yet you sit here and tell us that you will win. Will you also tell us how such a miracle can possibly occur?"

"We believe there is much unrest and dissension on the island," Avispa told him. "We expect mass defections from the militia, as well as some from the regular army units. We also believe the people will rise up and help us overthrow a tyrant who intends to lead them into the iron jaws of Communism. Cuba's people will not permit Castro to succeed. They know they must help themselves if they hope to be free. All the invaders need is a toehold in the sand."

The old man sighed sadly before he replied.

"I am an old man. Perhaps I no longer see things as clearly as I did. But our countrymen have seen the folly of resistance for the past year. Most people who tried to resist are dead. Firing squads are kept busy shooting Castro's political enemies. No, my young friends, you are wrong. Where you hope to find courage, you will find fear. Where you hope to find victory, you will find defeat. Instead of toeholds, you will find graves. I wish it were not so, but I fear that it is! Castro will repel your invasion attempt and become an even bigger hero to those who still believe in him. Then he will become an even more powerful enemy to those who oppose him or who fear him. Either way, you will play directly into his hands."

The patrons of the tavern were almost evenly split. Some of them believed everything the old man said; others believed none of it. Before they left the tavern, Ramrod and Avispa succeeded in recruiting three more experienced soldiers, then set up drinks for the house.

Ramrod slid behind the wheel of their car, then sat quietly, obviously deep in thought. Finally he looked up and turned to face Avispa.

"'Vispa, if only half of what the old man said is true, the Brigade is going to catch hell on those damned beaches. My God, Castro's people will have a turkey shoot."

"When you asked me to get involved in this thing, I jumped at the chance for two reasons. First, I want to set my country free. Second, because I trust your judgment. You convinced me that the CIA could bring this thing off. After everything we've seen and heard both here and at Base Trax, do you still feel that way?

Do the Quarters Eye people really know what they're doing, and are Bissell and Barnes still as confident as they once were?"

"The only honest answer I can give you at this point is, I don't know. I know it's not the answer you want. Hell, 'Vispa, it's not the answer I want either; but it's the only one I have. I can only add that I'm still hopeful. We're scheduled to leave for Guatemala tomorrow; maybe things will look better down at Base Trax."

# *WASHINGTON, D.C.*

# *FEBRUARY 5, 1961*

During the Eisenhower Era many insiders regarded Allen Dulles only as Secretary of State John Foster Dulles's kid brother. In addition to his high cabinet post, Foster Dulles was also President Eisenhower's right-hand man. Now Foster Dulles and Eisenhower were both gone. John F. Kennedy occupied the Oval Office. With the ascendance of a new Commander-in-Chief, many CIA agents were openly speculating about Allen's future. Would he be able to emerge from his brother's long shadow, or would he simply disappear from the national limelight?

That question seemed to be answered when Jack Kennedy reappointed Dulles as CIA Director and J. Edgar Hoover as FBI Director. The reappointments, which were among Kennedy's first presidential acts, were deft ploys designed to place a presidential seal of approval on both directors, and also to establish a sense of permanence and well being within their respective agencies.

J. Edgar Hoover had been Director of the FBI for thirty-seven years, and he was firmly rooted in his Justice Department post. The cagey old super sleuth also was rumored to have personal files on many of Washington's rich and famous—massive files that contained tediously gathered information that would be extremely embarrassing if it were ever released to the press.

Government workers, and everyone in prominent positions, were zealous in their efforts to obtain, and to maintain, J. Edgar's good will. Joseph P. Kennedy, formerly ambassador to England, as well as his son John, the new president, and several other Kennedy family members were said to have starring roles in a number of Hoover's most salacious files.

"Junior," J. Edgar Hoover often told his long-time friend and assistant, Clyde Tolson, "we have nothing to fear from any of those Kennedys."

Allen Dulles, on the other hand, was very wary. Obviously, he could never match Hoover's clout. So he decided that his interests would best be served by solidifying his relationship with the new President, as well as with Kennedy's circle of close advisors.

Shortly after the Kennedy Inauguration, twelve of the CIA's top guns met twelve of their White House counterparts. They were all Allen Dulles' guests for dinner at the Alibi Club. The Alibi was so exclusive that few Washingtonians were aware of its existence. The occasion was an informal icebreaker.

Dulles' plan worked like an absolute charm!

From then on, at least on the surface, the White House and CIA worked on an intimate basis. First names were the rule. Telephone calls were promptly returned, and inquiries were quickly answered. When a CIA agent was assigned to prepare a briefing memo for President Kennedy, he could be confident that the President would actually read it.

Stuffy information-gathering committees that had flourished during Eisenhower's Administration now disappeared completely. The intelligence business was fun again. It was a great time to be a spook!

The dramatic changes created a great opportunity for one CIA man in particular. Believing that Allen Dulles might want to retire before much longer, Richard Bissell saw this as a perfect time to sell himself to the only man who really mattered: the President of the United States.

Less than a month after dinner at the Alibi Club, Kennedy confided to McGeorge Bundy, the Special Presidential Assistant for National Security Affairs:

"By, golly, I don't care what it is; but if I need a piece of information, or an idea fast, the CIA is the place I go. The State Department takes several days just to give me a simple yes or no."

"The CIA guys love your new regime," Bundy assured him. "When you ask them for something, they come in at three or four in the morning to get it ready, because they know the data they produce will get to you without wandering through lots of hands."

Richard Bissell's future brightened considerably a few days later when the recently appointed Under Secretary of State, Chester Bowles, asked President Kennedy to appoint Bissell as his Deputy.

"It's a very crucial position, Mr. President. I need Bissell to make sure this job gets done properly," Bowles told the new President.

"Well, you can't have him!" Kennedy responded. "Richard Bissell is one of the smartest men in government, even if he is a Yale man. On July 1st, he's going to replace Allen Dulles as the Director of the CIA."

The scene was set. Whenever Bissell needed the President's ear, not only was Kennedy available, he also listened carefully to everything Bissell told him. He was particularly interested in Bissell's pet Cuban project.

But the President was also eager to know what the leaders in the principal Caribbean countries were thinking. Until he did, no decision about Cuba was possible.

Kennedy decided to send Arthur Schlesinger, Jr., one of his "special advisors," to pay America's official respects to the heads of six Latin American nations.

Arthur Schlesinger, Jr. had been called "Little Arthur" for many years in deference to his famous historian father, because of his diminutive stature, and because of the gentle appearance he projected from behind a huge pair of dark, owlish glasses. However, in Arthur's case, appearances were quite deceiving, because Arthur Jr. was a mental giant. A political historian of great note in his own right, he won his first Pulitzer Prize before his thirtieth birthday.

"Your actual, covert mission," Kennedy confided to him, "is to sound out the Latinos and see how they would respond if a group of Cuban exiles unseated Castro. The CIA is currently working on such a plan. You can get an update on the whole thing from Dick Bissell. You know him, don't you, Arthur?"

"Yes, Mr. President. We worked together on the Marshall Plan, back in the forties."

When Schlesinger visited Bissell, he learned very little about the Cuban Plan, because Bissell decided not to compromise security, and Schlesinger was too embarrassed to press him for information.

Schlesinger originally had met Castro at Harvard University during Castro's first American visit. He found the Cuban Dictator both witty and congenial.

Because of this first impression, Arthur Jr. felt that people might think of Castro as a young man who defied the odds—who gathered a few reliable friends together and overthrew a government composed of a bunch of evil old men. On the eve of his departure for Argentina, Schlesinger sent Kennedy a memo of warning. "An overly dramatic foreign policy may fix a malevolent image of your administration in the minds of millions."

Obviously he was still completely unaware of the pending action against Cuba.

Arthur Schlesinger, Jr. was not the only person Bissell was keeping in the dark. He followed a similar pattern with many others, including the American Ambassador to the UN, Adlai Stevenson. Stevenson would remain ignorant of the plans for Cuba until the day on which the invasion occurred. Ironically, it began on the morning the United Nations was scheduled to hear the grievances Cuba had filed against the United States.

Stevenson later said, "The coincidence occasioned the most embarrassing moment in my entire career of public service."

A cone of silence also descended on the State Department. West Point graduate Roger Hilsman, who had distinguished himself during World War II while serving with Merrill's Marauders in the China-Burma-

India Theater of Operations, had dinner with his friend, Allen Dulles. He concluded, from Dulles' remarks, that the 2506 Brigade might soon see action.

Hilsman was the State Department Director of Intelligence and Research—the one man who should have been completely appraised of the entire Cuban situation. He went at once to his boss, the new Secretary of State, Dean Rusk.

"Mr. Secretary, from everything I've learned and can surmise, I've concluded that an invasion of Cuba is imminent. World War II taught us that invading a hostile shore is a very perilous undertaking. For this handful of invaders to have any chance of success, two things have to happen as soon as they land. First, a very large number of Cuban soldiers and militiamen must defect and come over to the invaders. And second, the Cuban populace must rise up in revolt.

"My information coming out of Cuba suggests that neither of those necessities is going to happen. If you give me your approval, I'll run a quick feasibility analysis. We'll have every answer we need within a week, Mr. Secretary."

"I'm sorry, Roger! I can't do it," Rusk replied. "This whole thing is being too tightly held."

"I guess that means the CIA is running the show, and no one is being permitted to interfere, or second guess them!"

"You're right about the interference," Rusk replied grimly. "But I suspect there'll be a lot of second guessing, particularly if the operation fails."

Different opinions now came from every quarter:

Better to wait since Castro might be losing strength!
Better to wait since he might be gaining strength!
Better move now, since he might be losing strength.
Better wait a while, since he might be gaining strength.
Time is definitely on our side!
Time is definitely working against us!

Late in February, the Pentagon took a hand. Three general officers with diverse combat experience were sent, incognito, to inspect every element of the invasion force which, since their training was over, was now poised and waiting in Guatemala. Two of the officers were impressed by the commitment of the exiles and also by their state of training. But the third man, an Air Force officer, concluded that if even one Cuban aircraft, armed with 50-caliber machine guns, should survive pre-invasion airstrikes, that one plane would be able to sink or destroy the Brigade's entire invasion force.

On February 27, the inspectors submitted reports. Despite their collective pessimism, the Joint Chiefs concluded that Operation Trinidad (the city nearest the invasion site) would probably succeed. However, ultimate success would hinge on the initial assault and the ability to precipitate an uprising among anti-Castro elements throughout the length and breadth of the island. Of greatest concern were the fragile vessels that would transport the invaders and support them from the sea.

The Joint Chiefs decided a complete reevaluation of the entire logistics plan was warranted before the invasion plans were finalized.

# *THE WHITE HOUSE*
# *MARCH 11, 1961*

President Kennedy agreed with the Joint Chiefs; but in addition to their input, he wanted to gather as much intelligence data and pertinent information as he could from as many quarters as possible.

The morning after Schlesinger, Jr. returned from his Caribbean tour, he was ordered to report to the White House. When he arrived, he was taken to the President's largest conference room. As he entered, he was amazed to see the Secretaries of State and Defense, three Joint Chiefs, and several Presidential Special Assistants.

Allen Dulles was speaking. He had the attention of everyone at the long conference table.

"If we decide against this invasion, we'll have a huge disposal problem. We'll have to bring the exile force back to Florida because we cannot demobilize them in Guatemala. If we do, they'll wander about Central America and tell anyone who'll listen about their training and the projected invasion. And we can expect to have one hell of a lot of trouble when we ask them to give up their firearms."

"Even if we successfully disarm and disperse them, their stories will sweep across Latin America like wildfire, and then around the entire world," spat out the President. His clipped Boston accent sounded harsh in the stillness of the large conference room. "The rest of the world will say we turned tail and the Republicans will laugh at us. That's a combination we can't afford. It would not only cost us votes in the next election, it could also precipitate attempts to establish Communist governments elsewhere in our hemisphere. We have no alternative; we must let the exiles go to the destination of their choice, and that destination seems to be Cuba. So we need to do two things: convince the exiles they need to establish a representative and liberal front, then re-evaluate the operation and develop a more workable scenario."

For the next hour, various suggestions and ideas flew wildly about the room. Finally Richard Bissell offered a plan. *Proposed Operations Against Cuba.* He recommended amphibious and airborne assaults near the coastal city of Trinidad. His new plan still had invasion forces coming ashore at Trinidad, the location proposed in his original plan, but now all of the air support was scheduled during the invasion. No "softening up strikes" prior to the landing were contemplated. He emphasized the importance of establishing a beachhead, as well as the need to seize other accessible, adjacent areas. Finally, his key strategic goal was to quickly establish a provisional government as soon as a beachhead was completely secured.

After a great deal of discussion, Bissell's plan was rejected for several reasons. Kennedy called it "overly spectacular." Some others opposed the landing area because the Trinidad airstrip could not handle the operation's B-26s. Brigade planes had to operate from adjacent sites to continue the facade of an unsupported, independent raid, as well as to fly future punitive sorties against Cuban military and air bases. Most of the participants agreed that the plans for invading Trinidad should be discarded, and a better location should be selected.

President Kennedy summed up the meeting.

"It seems the more we diminish our political risks, the more we increase our military risks, and vice versa. We need a plan that brings the two risks into a more equal balance. Mac, summarize these ideas we've come up with in a memorandum."

McGeorge Bundy went to his office and prepared National Security Action Memorandum #31, which proclaimed:

*The President expects to authorize US support for an appropriate number of patriotic Cubans to return to their homeland. He believes that the best possible plan, from the point of view of combined military, political, and psychological considerations has not yet been presented, and new proposals are to be concerted promptly. ACTION: Central Intelligence Agency with appropriate consultation.*

McGeorge Bundy had been Castro's host when he visited Harvard during his American visit. He impressed Bundy as a well-organized individual—a man with a plan. On this windy March day, Bundy couldn't help wondering what Castro was planning.

# HAVANA, CUBA
# MARCH 11, 1961

As harsh winter winds slashed across the Potomac, bringing with them fresh assaults of driving snow, coupled with stinging sleet—as thousands of pink-cheeked Washington pedestrians struggled toward destinations with dogged determination and resolve, far to the south it was an idyllic day in Cuba. The wind was also on the march here, but no one seemed to mind. In this Caribbean paradise, it was a warm wind that swept across a deep blue, white-capped sea before singing through the swaying palms, and gently caressing the unhurried beachcombers.

In downtown Havana, Fidel Castro was conferring with a group of his most astute military and political advisors. Sixteen men were seated in an elaborate duplicate of the Pentagon War Room that Fidel had seen and admired during his last visit to Washington.

The room was the nerve center of Cuban military headquarters. The walls were covered with dozens of tactical maps of the Caribbean. Strategic overviews of America's southeastern cities and states were on display, as well as aerial topographic photographs of the most likely invasion sites along the northern and southern seacoasts of Cuba.

Overhead viewgraphs and motion picture cameras, equipped with slow motion capabilities, had been installed—hopefully they would be used to review film from the wing cameras of Cuban fighter planes as they shot down invading aircraft. Banks of phones and radios provided direct communication to every Cuban military installation and outpost. The entire area was a wartime commander's dream come true.

The sixteen men who sat around the circular oak conference table were a study in contrast. Half of them were seasoned soldiers who had helped Castro to overthrow Batista and had served with him ever since. The others were honors graduates from some of the world's most prestigious universities. It was simple to tell them apart. The hardened warriors were all wearing cheap fatigue uniforms and beards; the scholars sported expensive Ivy League suits and were well groomed and clean-shaven.

The meeting had been called to assess the risks that Kennedy's New Frontier Administration posed to Cuba.

"Do any of you believe that Kennedy's belligerent attitude toward us may soften?" Castro asked them.

"Kennedy can't afford to change," replied a rather insignificant-looking young man, who had graduated at the top of his class at Harvard Law School. "He committed himself quite strongly in his presidential campaign. I'm convinced that his position will get tougher, not softer."

"I agree with Dr. Ramirez," said an elderly scholar who, for many years, had taught political science at a well-respected West Coast college. "One phrase in his Inauguration Address spelled out his intentions quite clearly. He said, 'the torch has been passed to a new generation.' Because he is in his early forties, many

Americans are skeptical about his youth and lack of experience; therefore, he must talk tough and act tough. And Kennedy's speechwriters have an uncanny ability to take a phrase that appeals to a listener's emotions and make it sound like pure logic. Kennedy himself has become a much better orator. His improved delivery permits writers to compose speeches for him that have far greater impact. It makes him a very powerful speaker."

"I concur with my distinguished colleague," Dr. Ramirez responded. "Kennedy's favorite subjects of impact are the Cold War and Cuba. He must send an invasion force. And he must send it soon."

"Latinos in Miami are all talking about invasion," injected Raul Castro. "Kennedy would look like a promise breaker if he didn't send some kind of token force against us. I know they're coming. My agent, La Arana Negra, reports that the training of exiles, going on in Guatemala, is almost over. Very soon, I expect her to discover the invasion site, as well as the date."

"I hope you're right, Hermano!" Fidel replied. "Our island has more than two thousand miles of coastline. I won't even try to guess how many of the miles are barren. Countless coves, bays, cays, and remote beaches make Cuba an invader's paradise."

"What about our fifty pilots who are being trained on Russian MIG fighters in Czechoslovakia?" asked a young man who sported a Phi Beta Kappa key.

"They won't be combat-ready for at least six more months," Fidel told him, "and Kennedy won't wait that long. But there is something we can do right now. Several thousand Russian and Czech artillery pieces and anti-aircraft guns have arrived, and many more are en route. We need to train thousands more of our people to operate those heavy weapons."

"Russian weapons experts conduct classes every day—all over the island," Raul reminded his brother.

"I know that, Raul, but it's taking too much time. How many of our soldiers are in those classes?"

"I would estimate there are over a thousand."

"All right. This is what we will do. Every evening, when they get home from school, every man in those classes will teach twenty other men what he learned that day. Very soon we'll have twenty-one thousand guncrew leaders, instead of one thousand. Let the rebels deal with that kind of firepower."

"Comandante, the invaders may not invade Cuba. They may strike elsewhere," suggested a squat, dark, ponderous man, who looked like a villain in an old silent movie. "They might content themselves with seizing and occupying the Isle of Pines."

"You're right, Augustino. That thought has been in my mind as well. A determined force that set up a puppet government on the Isle of Pines would be almost impossible to dislodge. Particularly so, since a great many counterrevolutionaries are confined on the island—all of whom would be willing conscripts. Our naval and air forces are much too small to win a protracted battle. German Field Marshall Rommel once said: 'We must stop them at the water's edge, on the beach, before they are able to land.' We must follow the same plan. Send a strong force to garrison the Isle of Pines immediately, Raul, and place Major Pedro Augustino in command."

"Comandante, it's time we took extra precautions to insure your safety," said Felix Duque, an older man who wore a major's uniform, the highest rank in the Cuban army. "American agents might make another attempt on your life. We must be ready."

"Felix, my faithful friend, we are no longer hiding in the Sierra Maestra Mountains, fighting Batistas and dodging bullets. All leaders, particularly in Latin America, must expect a few assassination attempts. When I am out in the open, I feel like a dove at our shooting club, but what else can I do? Living under a cloud of assassination becomes a habit. I believe our security is such that no one can kill me unless he is willing to die with me—and there is no way to guard against fanatics or crazies. I appreciate your concern, Felix. Now tell me how our agrarian reform project is going at Cienfuegos."

"We are a little bit behind schedule, Comandante; but a hundred and eighty concrete bungalows and bathhouses have been built. We are building motels and recreation centers on the east side of the bay— and we have now installed powerful floodlights on twelve-foot-high poles, so the construction can go on both day and night."

"Tomorrow, we'll drive over to Giron. I want to see the progress with my own eyes."

The meeting covered several additional matters, and finally adjourned in the late afternoon.

The next day the Castro brothers and Felix Duque drove to Fidel's pet project in his black Lincoln Continental. When he arrived, Fidel demonstrated his displeasure at the minimal progress that had been achieved. He stalked around the entire project, firing questions at foremen and workers alike.

"Why haven't more of these motels been finished? Why haven't many more bungalows and bathhouses been built?" he demanded to know.

"Delivery of the materials is often delayed, and we have a critical shortage of technicians," he was told.

Three hours later, Castro walked down to the shore of the bay with Felix Duque and told him,

"I want you to drop everything else you're doing and make this project your top priority. Many will argue that this is not strictly agrarian reform. I agree, but I want it done anyway. I like this place. I always have. I used to come here to fish when I was a boy. I'm counting on you to get things moving, Felix. I want the Bay of Pigs to become Cuba's showplace."

Felix Duque could only nod in acquiescence. He was well aware of Fidel's special feeling for this swampy wilderness that covered most of Cuba's largest peninsula (1,172 square miles), but he was even more aware that he would need a miracle if he was going to fulfill Fidel's impossible dream of a Cuban showplace.

# *GIRON, CUBA*

# *MARCH 12, 1961*

The Castros drove off a short time later, and Felix Duque retired to his small but comfortable office. He opened a frosty bottle of Carta Blanca beer, then sprawled out on his large, well-padded couch and reminisced as he relaxed.

Fidel was very good at making dreams come true. *La revolucion* was itself a dream. When Fidel and his first twelve recruits had forted up in the Sierra Maestras in December 1956, the revolution had not even reached the dream stage. It was still an absolute fantasy. Then, tens of thousands of Batista's soldiers began hunting them. They were constantly on the run. Never sleeping under a dry roof. Never staying in the same place for more than a day at a time. Supplies of all kinds ran perilously short. Men wore tattered clothing and ate whatever they could forage. Fidel ordered them to grow beards so they could more easily identify each other. Felix smiled. He still suspected the beards were only grown to hide Fidel's double chin. Finally, ammunition supplies grew so short that Fidel himself began issuing bullets to each of his followers.

But slowly, their fantasy had become an obtainable dream as the force, calling themselves the *Barbados, the bearded ones,* had grown. In mid-February 1957, Castro granted an interview to Herbert Matthews, a

*New York Times* reporter. The entire interview had to be conducted in hoarse whispers, since the Barbados were completely surrounded by Batista's troops. To Matthews, Castro was a reincarnation of Washington, Jefferson, Madison, O'Higgins, and Simon Bolivar all rolled into one—and he depicted Fidel that way in *The Times.*

After two additional years of successful guerrilla warfare, the Barbados emerged from the Sierra Maestras and marched into history. How proud we were, Felix remembered, as we received cheers from thousands of our grateful countrymen. Americans could not begin to understand how we felt. I suppose it's impossible to understand tyranny unless one has lived with it. I bet Americans who lived during the revolution with England would have understood.

His beer and rest completed, Felix wandered out to confer with his foremen and discuss new strategies that would speed up the project's completion. When his meetings ended, he stood for a long time, staring across the murky black waters.

Over the centuries, since Columbus had discovered this place, few humans had found it friendly, much less habitable. La Bahia de Cochinos was thirteen miles long. Its average width was four miles. Bahia inhabitants were few—only two small groups of fishermen who lived in huts. One village was at the far end of the bay, at Playa Larga (Long Beach). An even smaller settlement lay near the bay's entrance, at Playa Giron. It had been named Giron in honor of the captain of a French ship who had lost a sea battle, and then his head, to a victorious Spanish ship's captain. Over the years, very few men had been brave enough or desperate enough to tackle the Bahia, with its ravenous mosquitoes, abundant and poisonous guao plants—or its impenetrable marabu bushes with their inch-long, flesh-tearing thorns.

Felix remembered reading about the first attempt to drain the vast swamps. A group of New Yorkers formed a company called the Zapata Land Company, and hired the best-qualified engineer they could find—a man named Cosculuella. A few weeks after they began, Cosculuella and his men returned, and reported that the 500,000-acre swamps were absolutely impenetrable.

"The swamps are a place where fog, death, and alligators are absolute masters!" Cosculuella told them as he departed.

Felix Duque turned away from the terrible swamps that bordered the Bay of Pigs and headed back toward the refuge of his office, grateful that such a place of safety existed in this stark and inhospitable landscape.

Little did Felix dream that in little over a month, refugees from a failed invasion at the Bay of Pigs would be slogging through the swamps, desperately seeking a refuge that simply did not exist.

## *CHICAGO, MIAMI & HAVANA MARCH, 1961*

Bissell was convinced that a sufficient length of time had passed since J. Edgar Hoover's discovery of his deal with Giancana and Rosselli. He decided to assassinate Castro with a "gangland-style hit"—an execution just like the ones in Chicago during the days of Prohibition. So he offered Johnny and Sam a second chance to orchestrate the assassination.

Rosselli telephoned Giancana with the good news.

"Sam, the Castro hit is on again. They just want a triggerman to come out blastin'. Real blood and guts. There's fifty grand in it for the shooter."

"You're as crazy as they are, J.R.," Giancana told him. "The security around that Cuban ******* is tighter than the fairways at Oakmont. A shooter is out of the question. The button man would get killed even if he hit Castro. Tell the Washington spooks I'm gonna take him out nice and clean. I got a guy in Havana who used to take kickbacks when we were runnin' the casinoes. He owes me a big favor, and he hangs around a place where Castro likes to eat. For fifty big ones, he'll slip something into Castro's food or one of his drinks. Bingo! It's all over! No mess! Call 'em up and tell 'em to send us something, J.R."

"Okay, Sam!"

Bissell referred the problem to the CIA technical section. He needed a pill that would kill Castro with no trace of foul play. The first toxin they concocted failed to dissolve in liquid, but the second batch was nearly perfect. It quickly infected the victim with a deadly strain of botulism. The lethal tablets were sent to Rosselli, who forwarded them to Giancana's pigeon.

A week later, the assassination conspirators were thrilled by Cuban newspaper and radio reports. Fidel had been stricken by an unknown ailment, and was confined to a hospital in Havana. Johnny called Sam.

"Our guy musta got him, Sam! He musta got him!"

"Yeah! A couple more days, then bingo! No more Castro!"

The excitement was short lived. Castro recovered.

The pills were returned a week later with a note.

"He don't eat here no more!"

A Castro "hit" proved so difficult that the CIA set up a special section whose responsibility was "the general ability to disable foreign leaders, including their assassinations as a last resort." This section was designated—E*xecutive Action/Cryptonym/**RIFLE.***

The Castro assassination was dubbed *AMLASH;* but with the date of the Cuban Invasion looming so close, all further efforts to assassinate Castro, before the Bay of Pigs, were temporarily scrubbed.

*Giancana and Rosselli did not fare as well as Castro. In June 1975, after several years in prison and only five days after Johnny Rosselli testified before Senator Frank Church's Senate Intelligence Committee, Sam Giancana had seven .22 bullets pumped into his head by an unknown assassin.*

*Fourteen months later, Rosselli's decomposing body was found floating in the Atlantic Ocean, off the shore of Miami Beach. His final resting-place was a fifty-five-gallon oil drum.*

*Did Fidel Castro orchestrate these murders? Very few people will ever know for sure.*

# *LATE MARCH, 1961*

The scheduled invasion was only a matter of days away, but suddenly everything seemed to go wrong. A Cuban Frente spokesman, Tony Varona, called a press conference and said:

"We now have sufficient forces to overthrow Fidel Castro. Our troops have just completed training at camps in the Western Hemisphere."

The former Cuban premier, Jose Miro Cardonna, now the president of the New Cuban Revolutionary Council, told the press:

"We will transform our present group into a provisional government as soon as we establish a military foothold in Cuba."

"There go all of our hopes for surprise," Bissell complained to Barnes.

The next evening, Robert Amory, the CIA Deputy Director of Intelligence, appeared at a local costume party wearing starched army fatigues, a forage cap, and a Fidel beard. Everyone at the party howled with laughter—Allen Dulles was not amused!

Information about the invasion that heretofore had been zealously protected was beginning to leak into many new quarters. Wherever and whenever the data surfaced, it was greeted with expressions of disbelief or dismay.

Undersecretary of State Chester Bowles laughed off the invasion rumors until he substituted for his boss, Dean Rusk, at a security briefing. He listened in horror as Dick Bissell, his longtime sailing buddy, covered the impending invasion in great detail. When he thought about the possible repercussions, Bowles was stupefied.

"America's irrational support of Batista created the opportunity for Castro," he told his assistant. "The thought of attempting to topple his regime by force is mind boggling. We may wind up making Castro a modern martyr and giving him a stranglehold on Cuba for the next forty years."

Violent opposition to the invasion continued to rise in nearly every quarter, but it never reached the Oval Office. Whenever his brother brought the growing unrest and incredulity to his attention, the impatient chief executive responded:

"Bob, my only opposition is coming from egghead liberals and the people without guts."

Robert Kennedy said no more.

When Secretary of State Dean Rusk returned from the SEATO Conference in Bangkok, Thailand, Bowles was waiting with a memo he had prepared.

"Mr. Secretary," Bowles began, "the White House has scheduled a meeting for April 4th. The purpose is to make a decision about this Cuban situation. I have gathered as much information about the project as possible. I have also spoken with every person I can find who will talk. Although there are very few of them, they all have one thing in common. They share the universal belief that this invasion cannot succeed without direct support from US military forces. Such support would violate the Bogota Act that governs the

Organization of American States. I realize that a great deal of money, and a great deal of time, have been invested by a great many people; but Mr. Secretary, we must not persist simply because of that. This is not an avalanche! It can be stopped! It must be stopped! I respectfully request that you go to President Kennedy, give him my memo and, as forcefully as possible, try to convince him that this fiasco can only spell tragedy for the Cuban exiles and long range embarrassment for the United States. You are the Secretary of State! If the President will listen to anyone, Sir, he will listen to you."

"I'll make my decision after I study your memo," Rusk concluded.

Rusk waited until the April 4th meeting before he made a decision about Bowles' request or the memo.

Prior to that, another man who had Kennedy's ear made a strong case against the impending invasion. During a phone chat with the President, Arkansas Senator William Fulbright mentioned that he was going to Del Ray Beach for the weekend.

"Jackie and I are going to Florida, too, Bill. Why don't you and Betty fly down with us on Air Force One?"

"That's very thoughtful of you, Mr. President. We'd both be delighted."

Jack Kennedy greatly admired the Senator from Arkansas, who had been an Oxford scholar, and had served as the president of the University of Arkansas before coming to Capitol Hill. He was the Senate's most brilliant member and one of the few eggheads Kennedy really liked. As reigning chairman of the powerful Senate Foreign Relations Committee, Bill Fulbright had taken the youthful Junior Senator from Massachusetts under his wing and made certain that Jack Kennedy was placed on several of the most important committees, including his own CFR.

Kennedy would have nominated him as Secretary of State if Fulbright had not unadvisedly signed an anti-desegregation declaration called *The Southern Manifesto*. Kennedy often called Ted Sorensen his intellectual bloodbank, but Bill Fulbright was the man to whom Kennedy turned when he needed a transfusion.

For several days before boarding Air Force One, Fulbright and his staff gurus prepared a 4,000-word position paper, forcefully presenting his plausible objections to invasion.

The Fulbright Memo contained three principal concerns.

***1. The invasion of Cuba is an ill-conceived idea that has become an open secret.***

***2. Statements by the weak Cuban Frente have already blown away all hope of surprise or success.***

***3. An invasion will defy the Bogota Act, disregard several long-standing treaties, and break a great number of US laws, including Title 50, Appendix, Section 2021; and Title 18, US Code, Sections 958-962—laws prohibiting an enlistment or recruitment for foreign military service in the United States, the preparation of any foreign military expedition, or the outfitting of foreign naval vessels for service against friendly powers.***

On March 30th, as soon as Air Force One lifted off the runway, Fulbright and Kennedy retired to the rear of the plane where the small presidential private office was located. They sat in comfortable chairs and accepted beverages from a cabin steward before Fulbright handed his position paper to the President.

"Before you read this, Mr. President, I want to say that any covert effort to assist with an invasion of Cuba is tantamount to hypocrisy and cynicism of the first order. It is exactly the kind of conduct for which America and her free world allies denounce Russia. If we persist in this course, our actions will not go unnoticed by our allies or by history."

Kennedy read the material at his usual breakneck speed. When he finished, he capsulized the situation but did not express any of the doubts that Fulbright had hoped to hear.

"Bill, several questions need to be answered. First, can the exiles succeed without direct intervention by US forces? Next, what will the repercussions be if we *do* take a hand? Finally, if the invasion bogs down can we in good conscience abandon a group of committed freedom fighters that are counting on us for aid? In other words, we have a very difficult set of problems here."

"Yes, but our decision must be tempered by the knowledge that Castro's regime is a thorn in our flesh—not a dagger in our hearts. As Chairman of Foreign Relations, I advocate a policy of isolation and patient tolerance for the time being."

"Tolerance is one of the biggest questions. How much more injustice can the Cuban people tolerate?

And how much longer can we tolerate a Communist state less than a hundred miles from our shores? We need to address those issues, and many similar ones, at our April 4th meeting, Senator Fulbright."

# *AIRCRAFT CARRIER ESSEX NORFOLK NAVAL BASE MARCH 31, 1961*

Rear Admiral John Clark was seated in the office of his superior, Admiral "Denny" Dennison. He had just been briefed on the tiny fleet of five ships that would be sent to invade Cuba. A navy captain from the Pentagon had conducted the briefing.

Out of uniform John Clark looked like a bank clerk or librarian, but his looks were quite deceiving. He was currently on a tour of duty as *Commander of Hunter-Killer Force Atlantic*. His force consisted of one aircraft carrier, six supporting destroyers, and a complete complement of jets. They were at sea for two weeks out of every four, conducting searches for Soviet submarines. Their missions required dogged, unending persistence. Every two weeks an identical fleet sailed from Norfolk to relieve them. Year after year the intense surveillance continued. The purpose was to provide a first line of defense against nuclear strikes. The duty demanded steel nerves; Clark had them. They were one reason he held his command.

"Johnny, I'm sending you back to sea with *Essex*, and five screening destroyers. I've ordered VA-34 Squadron, who are flying AD-4-2 *Skyhawks* out of Cecil Field, Jacksonville, to report aboard *Essex*. The squadron's called the 'Blue Blasters' and they're very good. They just returned from a tour aboard *Saratoga* in the Med. Hopefully, the *Skyhawks* will only serve as a safety measure. All of Castro's aircraft should be eliminated before any landings.

"Eduardo Garcia, a Cuban national, will command all of the civilian ships in the invasion group. Your taskforce will secure all approaches to a rendezvous point, well outside the Bay of Pigs, then send a pair of destroyers in to that rendezvous point, where they'll meet Garcia's ships. The two destroyers will then escort his ships and the invasion force toward the beach. None of your ships are to actually enter the Bay. I don't want *Essex* or any of the other destroyers anywhere near the Bay.

"Before you leave Norfolk, all of your destroyers' numbers will be painted out, and I want a different course assigned to each ship's captain. Order them to stay out of visual range of each other. Your force must appear to be a group of isolated ships carrying out a series of independent missions."

A wry smile crept across Dennison's deeply lined face.

"Make sure the invaders get to the beach, Johnny. Eliminate any and all interference, but do it without letting anybody see you."

"In other words, we're going down there armed to the teeth, in order to do nothing?"

"I'm afraid that's about the size of it. I'm sorry to stick you with this incredible fiasco."

"Admiral, this crazy stunt might just work because of its sheer brazenness and stupidity."

"I hope so, Johnny! I surely do hope so. Here's a package of info the spooks sent in from Washington. It makes hilarious reading," said Dennison, handing over a thick folder. "Here's your operations order," he concluded, passing over a thinner one.

John Clark left and returned to his quarters, where he spent an hour reading the CIA briefing and top-secret orders. Denny was right. They were hilarious.

The first two pages of an eight-page order outlined the vital importance of maintaining absolute secrecy, lest any hint of the impending invasion might leak out. The order continued in such confident terms that it might have been describing a stroll in the park.

"When the first shot is fired," it said, "most Cuban civilians will welcome the invaders—so will most militiamen. Many of Cuba's crack troops will defect and promptly lay down their weapons. Political prisoners from the Isle of Pines can be expected to join the invaders on their triumphant march across the island. Total victory is all but assured!"

Then, in a virtual reversal, the order went on to establish the tightest security measures Clark had ever seen. False reports were to be filed with the Atlantic Fleet Movements Reporting Center. No unnecessary record was to be filed, and all records needed during the operation were to be destroyed as soon as the mission ended. He was forbidden to tell anyone, except vital personnel, about any phase of the mission. Well, Clark decided, as he closed the file and locked it away in his safe, a few people needed to know now. For one thing, *Essex* wasn't equipped to handle the *Skyhawks.* Several things had to be changed before the faster jets could operate. *Essex's* captain, "Pete" Searcy, must be told at once, but the destroyer captains could be kept out of the loop until a few days before they sailed. For now, everybody needed to think they were simply going out on another anti-submarine warfare patrol.

# *FLORIDA & NICARAGUA*

# *MARCH 31, 1961*

Eduardo Garcia and the captains of five merchant ships that would transport the 2506 Brigade to their invasion sites were sitting in a stuffy conference room, listening to a cocky, self-important CIA agent, whose ill-fitting hairpiece kept sliding off to one side of his head. He introduced himself as Joe Doe.

"*Blagar* will be the command vessel," Doe told them in a voice filled with condescension. "*Blagar* will also carry a thousand troops, together with their weapons and equipment. *Barbara J.* will transport half as many troops and their equipment. *Houston* and *Rio Escondido* will carry fewer men since they'll be transporting most of the munitions and fuel.

"Captain Tirado," Doe said, addressing the *Rio Escondido's* short, dark, normally merry captain, "your ship will also carry two teams of frogmen and their catamarans. I'm sure most of you have already guessed your flotilla will be transporting the Cuban invasion force.

"Your objectives are twofold: first, get the troops ashore; then, lay offshore until you're ordered to unload your cargoes by a beachmaster, or by the guerrillas who've already infiltrated into the attack zone. You will not be given the exact location or date until you are underway. I presume that some of your crewmembers may not wish to participate in the operation. If that is the case, anyone opting out will be interned in Nicaragua until the operation is over. The location of the Nicaraguan staging area will not be revealed until you are at sea. Any questions?"

It was the usually jovial Captain "Gus" Tirado who said:

"My cargo manifest includes tons of ammunition and other munition stores, 54,000 gallons of aviation gasoline are stowed in the hold, and two hundred 55-gallon drums are lashed on the decks. When my ship was hired, I was led to believe that my cargo was destined for the government of Nicaragua. Suddenly we learned that we are all bound for a combat zone. I have become captain of a munition ship. If a single bomb or stray incendiary shell hits *Rio Escondido* we'll all go up like an A-bomb."

"Captain Tirado, your ship need never go within shooting or shouting distance of the beach. By the time the invasion is launched, the Cuban airforce will no longer exist. There is no cause for concern. Of course, if you object, internment in Nicaragua is an option."

"No! I'll go! I've always enjoyed fireworks and skyrockets, Mr. Doe. I just don't want to become one of them myself."

That evening the ships sailed for Nicaragua. They arrived a few days later in Puerto Cabezas. Once in port, their supplies were replenished and .50 caliber machine guns were mounted on the decks of all the ships. The fresh supplies of whiskey and chocolate were most welcome; but the combat veterans in the crews were skeptical about the guns' performance, since they had not been attached to the decks with welded plates. If those heavy weapons had to be used, the old timers predicted, the vibration alone might well sink the old ships.

Captains of four American destroyers were now preparing to get underway, still believing they were going to conduct a normal ASW (Anti-Submarine Warfare) mission. The ships were *Eaton*, known as 5 &10, because of her fleet number, 510; *Murray,* which along with *Eaton* would be assigned to lead the invasion force to the beach; *Cony;* and *Waller*.

Two hours before they sailed, Commander Gilven Slonim summoned the destroyer skippers to *Waller* for a briefing.

"The Squadron Commodore has directed me to tell you that when we sail this morning we won't be heading to Point Pete, because we won't be conducting ASW drills for the next two weeks. It's fair to assume that we'll be gone a little longer than usual. Nevertheless, you are forbidden to communicate with your wives or anyone else before we sail. You're authorized to inform only one officer aboard your ship—I presume your executive officer. *Essex* and *Conway* are already on station. I have all of your orders here. You will open them, and follow them to the letter, as soon as you sail. Commodore Crutchfield will be the senior officer. He will be in overall command of all naval forces. That's it for now. Godspeed, gentlemen. I'll see you all at the rendezvous."

# *WASHINGTON, D.C.*

# *APRIL 1, 1961*

It was April Fool's Day that Saturday morning, as Bissell, Barnes, Reynolds, Orizaba, E. Howard Hunt, and three other CIA staffers sat in Bissell's office. Ramrod noticed that Bissell's large desk was now adorned with a beautiful scale model of the new high-altitude reconnaissance aircraft dubbed the U-2.

He grinned when he noticed tiny letters carefully painted on the plane's fuselage. RBAF. Obviously they stood for *Richard Bissell's Air Force.*

"I got you in here this morning to make sure we don't wind up looking like a bunch of April Fools," Bissell announced, as the meeting began. "President Kennedy called me at home last night and asked a lot of questions. I got the impression that he has some reservations about the Cuban plan. He's concerned that the Cuban business may gum up his talks with the Soviets about Laos. If so, he believes the war in Southeast Asia may escalate. He also seems dubious about airstrikes taking out the Cuban air force. I reminded him that Cuba has only sixteen operational aircraft. We'll destroy them before they can take off. But somebody's got Kennedy's ear."

"It's Arthur Schlesinger," Howard Hunt told him. "For the past few days, he's been hustling harder than a New Orleans hooker during Mardi Gras. I bet he's trying to convince the President that the Cuban citizens won't help the Brigade."

"I think you're right, Howard. Kennedy pressed me on that point last night. I assured him that 2,000 to 3,000 Cubans now belong to active resistance groups and another 20,000 are auxiliary members. Ramrod, you and Avispa are on top of that situation. What's your estimate of Brigade support? Can we count on some help when we establish a foothold?"

"We expect to get at least token support from about 25% of the people. We lost a large number of our former partisans after the airdrop fiascos."

"Nobody can blame them for getting panicky over that mess," a scowling Bissell agreed.

*Several airdrops to guerrilla and partisan forces hiding in the hills had gone haywire. On one occasion, two thousand .45 caliber automatic pistols were dropped with a million rounds of .38 caliber ammunition, making the automatics useless for anything other than overpriced clubs. On another night, the campfires of a Cuban force in hot pursuit of local guerrillas were mistaken for signal fires surrounding a drop zone—fires that had been lighted by the same group of rebels the Cuban soldiers were chasing. Castro's troops were both astonished and grateful when two planeloads of supplies, including nearly a ton of food—far more appetizing than their usual drab rations—came floating down out of the night sky.*

"We do have some good news," Bissell told them. "Here's an intelligence report filed three days ago by one of our agents in Cuba. I'll share it with you.

*Opposition to Castro's regime is becoming more open and unguarded. Grumbling about government policies has become commonplace. Working classes are now violently against Castro. The secret police are currently detaining members of lower classes on a regular basis. A continued shortage of food and other necessities is causing growing dissatisfaction. Resistance and sabotage are increasing throughout Cuba, despite increased punishment and attempts at suppression. Yesterday, anti-Castro rebels set off twelve bombs in Havana alone.*

"If we take this report at face value, it would seem the 25% you expect to aid the Brigade may be an army in themselves. Okay. For now, the President has pushed D-Day back from April 5 to April 10. He hasn't yet given his final approval, but at least he hasn't cancelled us out. Let's head down to the war room and see what the U-2 photos and Arthur Lundahl's analysis tell us about this new invasion site."

*Art Lundahl was a professor of Geology at the University of Chicago when World War II began. He was assigned to a brand new field of endeavor—the art and science of aerial photographic analysis, or photogrammetry. Since the field was brand new, Lundahl had to learn as he went along. An extremely ingenious and persistent fellow, he discovered and developed most of the techniques that would become standard for everyone who followed in his wake. Lundahl was responsible for analyzing scores of prospective invasion sites, and determining the feasibility of success. In 1953, Richard Bissell persuaded him to join the CIA. When Lundahl came aboard, the photographic analysis section had a total of five members. When he retired twenty years later, the number had swelled to two thousand. He was fond of saying that he turned a sneaky cloak and dagger business into an enterprise of scientific technology. Upon his retirement America awarded him a National Security Medal, and Queen Elizabeth II knighted him.*

*Despite his distinguished record, Bissell kept Lundahl in the dark about the Cuban invasion until the last minute. When he finally found out he said: "It looks like the company is going to conduct a Pearl Harbor of its own."*

A Cuban Operations War Room had been set up on the ground floor of Quarters Eye. It resembled something that Ian Fleming might have created for 007 and his associates. The windows were painted black. Every wall was covered with huge maps and tactical overlays. Entry to the war room was gained by entering a numbered code in the door panel. Few people had enough of Bissell's confidence to acquire that access code.

As the staff entered the war room, Colonel Jack Hawkins, the military commander of the Cuban Operation, met them. He walked directly to a giant wall map of Cuba, and pointed to the eastern end of the island before he spoke.

"Well, gentlemen, we aren't going to land here, at Trinidad, after all." He pointed to another location, a hundred miles west of the original site. "Now, we're going to land here, at La Bahia de Cochinos. The Bay of Pigs."

"How can we expect the Cuban populace to rally to a place called the Bay of Pigs?" one agent asked.

"That's one hell of a long way from our original objective! How are the guerrillas, who are hiding in the mountains near Trinidad, going to get to the Bay of Pigs?" queried a second man.

"That landing site is right next to the biggest and most treacherous swamp in the entire Caribbean," objected a third. "If Castro's troops drive the Brigade off the beach, and into those swamps, the invasion will be over before it starts."

"The airstrip looks pretty rough," Arthur Lundahl observed, indicating one of his greatly enlarged aerial photographs. "I'll bet half our planes cartwheel on it when they try to land."

"It's the site we've been given, and it's the site we have to work with," Bissell told them. "So, let's quit complaining and get on with it."

"When did the lunatics who picked this location get out of the asylum?" a thoroughly disgruntled agent asked.

"Don't call the President and his top advisors lunatics," Richard Bissell advised him.

President Kennedy phoned Senator William Fulbright after breakfast on Monday and invited the Senator and his wife, Betty, to return to Washington aboard Air Force One. During the flight Kennedy was friendly and chatty but made no reference to the lengthy memo Fulbright had given him a few days earlier. The plane landed at Andrews Air Force Base about 4:30 P.M. As they were getting ready to disembark, almost as an afterthought, the President said:

"Today's meeting is scheduled for the State Department rather than the White House. I have a few details to clean up before the meeting starts; but if you want to ride along with me, Jackie can drop Betty off on her way home."

So the First Lady took Betty Fulbright in her limousine and the Senator went with the President.

When they arrived at the State Department, the President waited patiently while three gentlemen representing Governor Archie Gubburd, of South Dakota, awarded him a golden shovel; then they attended a swearing-in ceremony of Ambassador to Spain designate, Anthony Drexel Biddle. Finally, Secretary of State Dean Rusk, fresh from his meeting with the British Prime Minister, Harold Macmillan, joined them. Macmillan had come to Washington to consult with Rusk and Kennedy about the cease-fire currently being negotiated in Laos.

When the trio arrived at the Secretary of State's conference area, many of the scheduled participants had been waiting for a reasonably long time. They had been instructed to come separately, to safeguard security; also, Kennedy arrived later than anticipated.

As soon as Fulbright entered, he got two distinct impressions. First, there was a lot of uneasiness and apprehension among the dozen men jammed into the room. Secondly, this meeting was interrupting really important events of the day.

Richard Bissell began the meeting by getting the President up to speed on the latest developments. The complexity and size of the invasion that Bissell detailed appalled Fulbright.

When Bissell finished, the uneasy men who sat at the round table posed many thoughtful questions.

"What about the Cuban Air Force?"

"Is the Brigade ready for the invasion?"

"How strong is their commitment?"

"How is their morale?"

"What is the mood of the Cuban people?"

"Can the Brigade count on Cuban assistance?"

"If we should decide to abort the invasion, how will the members of the Brigade be disbanded?"

Fulbright expressed the same doubts that had been outlined in his memo. Kennedy listened carefully as he conducted his critique. Fulbright had known Kennedy well, both as a friend and colleague, for many years. He sensed that his objections concerned the President as well.

Dean Rusk listened to Fulbright's impassioned plea but was not swayed. When the President asked for Rusk's input, he said:

"Mr. President, when an irregular military action succeeds, it immediately becomes self-legitimizing. That's exactly the way Fidel Castro himself came to power. And the price of each failed coup is the same. Our founding fathers braved England's wrath when they rebelled against the Crown and Parliament. If they had lost, they all would have been hanged as traitors. Our answer to the Cuban issue is the same as the answer to the question that has been asked since the first man was enslaved. Can any price we are required to pay for liberty ever be too high?"

Rusk said no more. He didn't need to. He had won the day. No one could continue to protest in the face of such eloquence.

A few tactical and strategical problems surfaced, but they were all quickly resolved. They decided to go ahead with the invasion, but to delay it for one additional week.

Exit *Operation Trinidad.* Enter *Operation Pluto.*

"All right, gentlemen. For better or for worse, the invasion will kick off April 17th." Kennedy smiled. "That's an ironic date. On the night of April 17, 1775, Paul Revere waited for a signal to be hung in the Old North Church of Boston. One if by land. Two if by sea. Then he rode through the countryside, shouting, 'The British Are Coming.' I only hope that there is no such church in Havana where two lanterns can be hung. The very last thing we need is a Cuban Paul Revere, riding about the countryside, shouting, 'the Yankees are coming.'"

# *WASHINGTON, D.C.*

# *APRIL 5, 1961*

Edward R. Murrow telephoned the CIA at 8 A.M. and asked for a meeting with Allen Dulles. Murrow was a famous, well-respected news correspondent, whose nightly radio broadcasts from bomb-ravaged London during World War II kept most Americans apprised of the conduct of events from Europe.

In the late 1940's and early '50's, his television shows, *See It Now* and *CBS Reports*, made him a familiar face to every American. His clean-cut, straightforward image of integrity became as much a symbol of America around the globe as Uncle Sam.

For all these reasons and because Ed Murrow had been his friend since the war and was the current Director of the United States Information Agency, Dulles agreed to see him at once.

"Allen, we've learned, from a highly-reputable source, that an invasion of Cuba is imminent. Do you care to comment?"

"Ed, I'm in no position to comment one way or the other," Dulles told him. "I'd like to help you. I really would! But I simply can't. I'm very sorry."

Murrow left Dulles' office minutes later, realizing that a refusal to answer was just as good as an affirmative reply. If the allegation had been false, Dulles would have been vehement in his denial.

Murrow returned to his USIA office and a short time later received a call from McGeorge Bundy, inviting him and his chief assistant, Donald Wilson, to lunch at the White House. Over a pleasant meal, Bundy gave them a thumbnail sketch of the plan.

"Mac," Murrow exploded, "this is the craziest story I've ever heard! Wanton aggression against a small nation is counter to everything America stands for! And using Cuban exiles as your 'front group' is deplorable. Nobody in his right mind will fall for such ridiculous chicanery. These 'naive innocents' aren't Cuban invaders; they're American dupes. America's real role can't stay hidden for very long. As sure as I'm sitting here, history will record this operation as nothing less than a sneak attack."

Murrow paused for a moment before adding in a calmer, but chilling tone of voice.

"I fear that future American generations will be merciless in their criticism of this folly you are now poised to perpetrate!"

"Sir," Bundy replied, "there is a great deal of merit in what you say. I don't disagree with your position. But the operation has gone too far! It simply cannot be stopped. I have only been authorized to share this information because everyone at the White House has infinite respect for you. It is highly confidential, and, of course, none of this can be divulged. Lem Jones will release information to the wire services as soon as it becomes available. Neither of you may be familiar with the agent who is assigned to security for this operation. His name is E. Howard Hunt. He will be responsible for the information coming out of Quarters

Eye. Gentlemen, I want to thank you both for your cooperation."

Bundy reported to the President that Murrow and his people were sworn to silence; but the President was becoming increasingly disturbed by the mood of uneasiness that he felt pervading the Capitol. One of his major problems concerned the power brokers. Perhaps it was time to host another big White House party. A gala affair designed to create a gigantic and impenetrable smokescreen. Something that would placate the power set and give the news media something new.

*At every important White House social function for the past hundred years, representative members of the Executive, Legislative, and Judicial Branches have been among the invited guests. So, too, have been selected players from the Diplomatic Corps and a handful of the nation's most deserving military leaders.*

*Less apparent, but far more important, are the always present, stealthy string-pullers. Those international high rollers, power brokers, industrial magnets, and opinion makers who really choose America's leaders, as well as those of every other industrialized country. The world's most important people. They are practiced and adept at creating a voter-pleasing, highly desirable public image for their selectees. They are the star-makers that gleefully finance and succor proteges who will be the leaders of tomorrow. The enormous investments are wise indeed, for when their future political stars, so carefully chosen, finally occupy center stage, the clever benefactors will reap far greater rewards than any they sowed. Their harvest will yield a single crop.* ***POWER!***

*Records of incurred favors and debts are catalogued and stored away, as carefully as any other promissory note, by these shadowy men. Pseudo Galahads—idolized, charming, invulnerable, clad in a thin veneer of altruism that is far more efficient than the armor worn by the knights of olde. They stand ready to slay any dragon that threatens the way of life that they have ordained for the masses. They are major stockholders in world finance and economy. Like every other stockholder, they must be informed, consulted, and allowed to vote on any contemplated action which might upset the equilibrium over which they preside.*

In the hectic week that preceded the invasion, John F. Kennedy heard from a great many powerwielders. Perhaps the biggest and most visible of them all was the President's own father, Joseph P. Kennedy, the former American Ambassador to England.

# WASHINGTON, D.C.
# INVASION WEEK

On Friday, April 14, 1961, invasion force aircraft began bombing strategic targets in Cuba. Pressure on President Kennedy, already tremendous, escalated to a fever pitch. On the afternoon of the 15th, together with his wife, Jacqueline, and their children, Kennedy boarded a helicopter for the short flight to Glen Ora, the family's weekend retreat near Middleburg, Virginia. Once there, an aura of casual observation was established at the new presidential command post.

Saturday, April 15, was a very busy day in New York City. By 10:30 A.M., members of the Fair Play for Cuba Committee were marching up and down in front of the United Nations, shouting, "Cuba si, Yankee no!"

Most passersby ignored the seedy young man that shouted the loudest. His name was Lee Harvey Oswald, and he would become Fair Play's most notorious player.

When President Frederick P. Boland, of Ireland, gaveled the UN General Assembly meeting to order, Cuban Foreign Minister Dr. Raul Roa demanded to be recognized for a point of order. When Roa was acknowledged, he said:

"I wish to inform this Assembly, which is the supreme forum for the expression of international conscience, that this morning, at 6:30, United States aircraft—"

"Mr. Ambassador," interrupted Boland, "you are out of order. Your point is not one of order, it is one of substance."

"Thank you, Mr. President," responded Roa, "but it seems to me that this great Assembly should be more interested in a breach of the international peace than a breach of procedure."

"I agree, Mr. President," shouted Valentine Zorin of the Soviet Union. "This unwarranted aggression against Cuba must be discussed immediately."

After several sharp exchanges of angry words and accusations, Boland ruled that the UN's Political Committee, which he ordered to meet immediately after lunch, would discuss the Cuban situation in an emergency session. The ruling pleased both factions. It gave the Cubans and their allies time to add to the list of allegations, and it provided the US delegation with an opportunity to frame a suitable denial of Ambassador Roa's charges.

The man on the hot seat was the US Ambassador, Adlai Stevenson. He had been kept in the dark by the White House, the State Department, and the CIA. Now Stevenson and his staff had to uncover more information in the next few hours than they had been able to ferret out in the past several months.

Stevenson aide Harlan Cleveland made the first inquiry. It went to the State Department's Bureau of Latin American Affairs.

"We don't know anything about Cuba over here," he was told, "but we'll check with the CIA and get back to you."

A few minutes later, Cleveland received a return call from a low-level intelligence officer.

"Mr. Cleveland, please assure the Ambassador that the bombing was carried out by defectors from the Cuban Air Force."

Cleveland sent his deputy, Joseph Sisco, who was waiting in Washington, to the State Department to consult Dean Rusk's top-level aides. If a statement of denial was to be issued, it had to be rooted in fact!

Once a statement was drafted, it had to be reviewed by Richard Pedersen, a legation legal officer, before it was delivered to Stevenson.

Sisco phoned Pedersen's secretary at the UN from Rusk's office and dictated a statement. As she typed the transcript Pedersen listened on an extension.

The four-point statement began by reiterating President Kennedy's promise of April 12.

*Under no circumstances, I repeat, under no circumstances, will the United States send military forces into Cuba!*

*The United States will do everything it possibly can to make sure that no Americans participate in any actions against Cuba.*

*The United States will consider defecting pilots' requests for political asylum.*

*Cuban pilots have begun landing in Florida. They are flying aircraft that are, to the best of our knowledge, Castro's planes.*

Moments after the statement was completed, a wire service photo was received. It showed a Cuban plane parked on a runway at Miami. Clearly visible were the

Cuban star, and the letters F.A.R. (Fuerza Aerea Revolucionaria).

The photograph was the ultimate proof Stevenson needed to refute Roa's allegations.

"Mr. Stevenson," advised Pedersen, "you must authenticate the photo. We must know the picture and the statement can stand up against the challenges that are sure to come."

Stevenson called the State Department and spoke with the Assistant Secretary for Public Affairs.

"Can I use this statement and the photograph? Are they clean?"

"Mr. Rusk and I are both convinced that they are."

Minutes later, Stevenson read the statement and displayed the photo to the committee, as well as to a huge television audience.

Here was plausible deniability at its best. Majestic rhetoric at its finest. Unfortunately, the totally honest, well-meaning individual who delivered the magnificent denial had been hoodwinked by his own government. Adlai Stevenson firmly believed in America's top Foreign Service officer, Secretary of State Dean Rusk. Did Rusk lie? Definitely not! Rusk had also been hoodwinked by Richard Bissell's cone of silence. It had worked to absolute perfection.

Now only a matter of hours remained before the invasion would begin, and many Brigade members were beginning to have serious doubts about their probability of success. When they saw the five old, dilapidated vessels that would transport them, their concern escalated. Conditions aboard *Rio Escondido* were so overcrowded that more than a hundred men had to sleep topside, wherever they could find a few inches of space between the drums of aviation fuel that were lashed to the decks.

Spirits fell even lower when they learned that the Brigade's forward observer, who had been infiltrated into Havana two weeks earlier, had been caught and executed by Cuban troops. A short time later it was reported that Castro had a force of 66,000 men ready to meet them. Brigade morale hit a new low when they learned that "softening-up bombing missions" had been cancelled and that ten of the Brigade's sixteen A-26 aircraft had been grounded. Only six of the old planes would now provide air support during the landings.

Then a blizzard of rumors began to circulate. The other ten A-26's wouldn't be needed. The American aircraft carrier *Essex,* loaded with supersonic fighter planes, would be standing by offshore. Her fighters would orbit the landing sites and form a protective umbrella over the invasion force.

"God help anyone that Castro sends against us," they reassured each other.

Sometime later, when they spied two American destroyers on the horizon, a rumor spread that a taskforce, consisting of a dozen warships, would escort them ashore and quickly destroy the members of any guncrew foolish enough to open fire on them.

Perhaps the most incredible fabrication of all was one that proclaimed the existence of a dozen other brigades, just like the 2506, that had been trained at various locations. Supposedly, these brigades were now steaming toward a dozen different objectives around the perimeter of the Cuban coast.

How else could any rational invader explain their 1453-man force, attacking an army that numbered more than 66,000?

Attempting to offset the overwhelming feeling of dread and to raise morale, each battalion commander delivered a remarkably similar assurance to his own troops.

"There *will* be pre-landing bombing runs!"

"There *will* be continuous air cover for the entire duration of the assault!"

"A majority of our countrymen are eager to help us overthrow Castro and his henchmen."

Aboard each of the wallowing, rusty ships, men cheered.

At the Guatemala airstrip, no one was cheering. The latest U-2 high-altitude photographs spelled out another extremely critical situation. Only five Cuban aircraft had been destroyed in initial bombing raids. Although several others showed various degrees of damage, most had escaped unscathed. In some of the photographs, a number of planes, Sea Furies and T-33 jets, could be seen parked next to the runways. The missiles slung under their wings were clearly visible. The pilots' morale also began to plummet.

The CIA Air Ops Commander in Guatemala sent a desperate message to his boss, Colonel Beerli, at Quarters Eye:

"I request immediate approval for additional airstrikes against the Cuban air field closest to our objective. Six of my planes can do the job at sunset,

Sunday, if they come out of the sun at low levels. Please advise."

A one-word response came quickly: "Negative."

The refusal made a huge impact on Stan Beerli. He and his air operations staff spent Saturday evening and the early morning hours of Sunday perusing new U-2 photos that Art Lundahl and his staff interpreted for them. By dawn, representatives of the collective intelligence sections had chosen targets of greatest opportunity and maximum impact.

Before noon, pilots in Guatemala and Nicaragua had their new assignments and were committing topographic features of each objective to memory.

Meanwhile, ground crews were servicing Brigade planes for the last time and loading bombs and ammunition aboard.

That Sunday President Kennedy spent some quiet hours with his family at Glen Ora. He and Jacqueline attended the late morning Mass at St. John's Catholic Church in Middleburg. When they returned, they joined their weekend guests, the Stephen Smiths, and hit golf balls for an hour before lunch. The gloomy and obviously disturbed President confided to his brother-in-law (Smith) that he was "worried as hell about the whole damned Cuban business."

At Quarters Eye, Bissell was beginning to fret. He was powerless to make another move without the President's express permission. He'd asked Kennedy to call before noon in order to accommodate the sailing schedule of the tiny fleet of merchant ships waiting expectantly in the harbor of Puerto Cabezas. But knowing the way of presidents and most other high-ranking men, Bissell had built in a fudge factor of four hours.

One o'clock slipped by, then one-thirty, as Bissell sat staring out of his office window and wondered if the pessimistic naysayers had finally convinced the inexperienced President that a Cuban coup was nothing more than a forlorn dream.

At 1:47 his desk telephone shattered the oppressive stillness. He had been waiting expectantly; but the sudden sound seemed as deafening as a claxon horn announcing a jailbreak. He lifted the receiver to his ear, hoping for confirmation but expecting rejection.

Jack Kennedy's clipped Bostonian inflection was unmistakable. The President uttered the two words Bissell longed to hear.

"Go ahead."

The elated Bissell returned the phone to its cradle and reflected that the worst might finally be behind them. Seldom in the annals of recorded history has anyone been so terribly wrong!

Bissell's euphoric feelings were short-lived. A few minutes after he received presidential authorization, Charles P. Cabell, the CIA's extremely unpopular Deputy Director, entered Bissell's office and planted himself in a chair. A retired general, Cabell had held his post since 1953, principally because of his long friendship with Allen Dulles.

*Several months earlier, Cabell had discovered that some of the supply planes that were flying weapons and ammunition to the guerrilla fighters, who were hiding in the Cuban mountains, were only half full. Cabell ordered the crews to fill all of the empty spaces with heavy bags of rice and beans. Since neither heavy cargo slings nor cargo parachutes were available, when they reached the rendezvous, crewmembers simply dragged the sacks to the door of the plane and heaved them down into the darkness below.*

*Suddenly, huge bulging burlap bags began raining down on the unsuspecting and unprepared guerrilla fighters. Although a few of the sacks came perilously close to killing some of the troops before they could dive for cover, fortunately none did. Since that night, retired General Charles P. Cabell had been known as* ***Old Rice and Beans.***

"Allen's gone for the weekend, so I'm in charge until he gets back," Cabell told Bissell, referring to Allen Dulles. "I thought I'd better stop by and let you bring me up to speed."

Before the unhappy Bissell could reply, the CIA's Airforce Commander for Cuban Operations, Stan Beerli, entered and stood expectantly near Bissell's desk. Moments later he was joined by Barnes, Hunt, and several other top-level aides.

"How did the initial airstrikes go, Stan?" Cabell asked.

"Not quite as well as I hoped they would," Beerli responded.

"What, exactly, does that mean?"

"We were able to inflict some minor damage, but Castro's air force is still pretty much intact."

Cabell glowered at Bissell.

"Do Kennedy and Rusk know about this? Do you still have solid approval for this mission?"

"Of course I do!" Bissell assured him.

"Well, I don't like it! I'm going to call Dean Rusk."

"Damn it, General. I talked to President Kennedy a few minutes ago. He gave me his personal go-ahead," Bissell assured him.

"Just the same, I want to talk to Rusk. Don't do anything until I get back."

He spun on his heel and walked out of Bissell's office.

"That tears it, boys!" Bissell told his staff. "If Old Rice and Beans calls Dean Rusk, Rusk will call an emergency meeting with a dozen of his advisors who, in turn, will have to hold even more meetings with their advisors. We could be looking at a major delay."

"A further delay might spell disaster to the entire operation," Barnes interjected. "Since Allen's out of town, Charlie Cabell just wants to flex his muscles and prove he's still the same old take charge guy. He's going to rip the whole invasion apart just to pad his own ego. He sees a perfect opportunity to step out of oblivion and grab a moment in the limelight!"

Ten minutes later, Cabell returned.

"I talked to Mac Bundy. The President just issued a new directive. There will be no airstrikes until the Brigade secures the Giron airstrip. Every subsequent attack must originate from there."

"Without those preliminary airstrikes," thundered Beerli, "the whole invasion is doomed to failure."

"I'm going to call Bundy," Bissell says. "Without air cover, the poor ******* will never get anywhere near the Giron airstrip!"

"It's too late to catch up with him. He's en route to National Airport. President Kennedy ordered him to hotfoot it up to New York to pacify Stevenson. The two of us are scheduled to meet Rusk and his people at the State Department at seven, Dick. I agree with you about the air cover; but we need concurrence from Rusk and the President."

Cabell and Bissell headed for the door. Barnes followed in their wake.

A half-hour earlier, Secretary of State Dean Rusk had phoned the naval member of the Joint Chiefs.

"Admiral, I'm beginning to believe the odds of a successful Cuban invasion are only about 70%. Do you agree?"

"No, Sir!" came the instant reply. "I think the chances of success are less than 30%."

"Thank you for your candor, Admiral."

His next call went to Fort Myer, to the residence of the Chairman of the Joint Chiefs.

"General, I just spoke with one of the other Joint Chiefs, reference the Cuban invasion. He thinks the probability of success is only about 30%. What is your opinion?"

"I think that evaluation is far too optimistic, Mr. Secretary. This thing may turn into a complete rout."

Rusk's final call went to Glen Ora.

"Mr. President, the cover story Adlai Stevenson gave the UN today, about air attacks being staged by Castro's planes, flown by Cuban defectors, has been exposed. The cat is out of the bag. In my opinion, if we allow another strike to be flown from Nicaragua, we can expect the international mood to reach a very dangerous level."

"I agree, Dean. Unless there are sudden 'overriding considerations,' all future strikes must be launched from airfields in Cuba. We can't afford to jeopardize our talks with the Soviets about the de-escalation in Southeast Asia. Khrushchev loves to bluster, and it doesn't take much to get him started. I sent Mac Bundy to the UN to help Adlai keep the lid on there, but you need to keep it on here as well. Call me if there is any change."

At precisely 7 o'clock, Dean Rusk admitted Cabell and Bissell to his private office but asked Tracy Barnes to wait outside.

"I spoke with the President," Rusk told his visitors. "I recommended that the Monday morning strikes be cancelled, and President Kennedy agreed."

"Mr. Secretary, we need those dawn airstrikes to protect the ships while they're unloading, as well as to provide air cover for the landing forces," Bissell protested.

"According to the Operational Plan, unloading is scheduled to be completed under cover of darkness. It must be finished before dawn. As soon as Giron's air strip is secured, the airstrikes can begin."

"As you know, Sir, one of the basic elements in the success of any military operation is the morale of the troops. Without the air cover, the entire operation will be endangered, and we will seriously deflate Brigade enthusiasm and determination," predicted Cabell.

"We're committed to the landings, Mr. Secretary," added Bissell. "Everything is already in motion. It's too late to call the landing off. Can't we at least give those poor ******* a fighting chance?"

"All right," Rusk agreed reluctantly. "I'll call the President again."

Rusk called Glen Ora, explaining that Cabell and Bissell were in his office and that both felt the entire operation would be seriously jeopardized unless the air strikes proceeded as originally planned.

"I agree! The air strikes are important," Kennedy replied; "but are they an overriding consideration?"

"Considering the risks we'd run in the Southeast Asia talks, as well as at the UN, I still say no, Mr. President. I think the airstrikes must be cancelled as a matter of national security."

"Very well," Kennedy acknowledged. "We'll stand pat. Does General Cabell wish to speak with me?"

"Do you wish to speak to the President, General?"

"No! I don't suppose it will help very much in the face of your recommendation, especially since he's already rejected the plan twice."

When Rusk relayed this message, Kennedy asked to speak with Bissell. The conversation was short.

"How many planes are scheduled to provide air cover during the actual invasion?"

"We're going to use sixteen A-26's, Mr. President."

"That's far too many, Dick. I've told you over and over, I want this thing kept to a bare minimum. Cut the sixteen down to six. Is that perfectly clear?"

"Quite clear, Sir!"

"Okay! Put Dean back on."

Rusk listened for less than a minute, said good-bye to the President, and rose from his chair. The action indicated that a final decision had been made.

"Gentlemen, the President and I would like to help you. We want to see this overthrow succeed. But the invaders are going to have to do it without airstrikes that can be alleged to have come from outside Cuba. Such allegations might provoke a political disaster. If the invasion fails, we may have a very unpleasant incident—but if it succeeds, principally because of American intervention, we may blunder into World War III."

Bissell was certain that any attempt to prolong this meeting was useless. His frustration was beyond all description. Why, he wondered, couldn't everyone else visualize what he saw so clearly? This was the moment of climax. All of the planning, scheming, training, blustering, and most of all, the waiting, was finally over. It was D-Day! It was time to fly, to sail, and to invade. Perhaps, for some, it was time to die. But it certainly wasn't a time to pull back! It was a time to charge forward. The words, waiting, delays, and excuses finally had to end. With or without air cover, it was time to go for all, or for nothing.

At Quarters Eye, Beerli and all the others were in a state of disbelief. They were emotionally drained. In Puerto Cabezas the planes carrying the paratroopers had lifted off; so had the far slower PBY sea-rescue planes. Radio reports from Cuba told of thick clouds and a dark, moonless night.

It was well past nine o'clock when Beerli and the others finally heard from Bissell. There would be no air sorties on D-Day other than reconnaissance over the invasion beaches. The disheartened Beerli sent a top priority message to his squadron commander in Puerto Cabezas:

"CANCEL…CANCEL…CANCEL… All D-Day sorties except recons."

The squadron commander immediately radioed a reply to Beerli.

"My A-26's cannot hope to eliminate Cuban planes over the beach. We must destroy them while they are on the ground. Respectfully submit your previous order be amended."

The terse reply from Washington came quickly.

**NEGATIVE YOUR REQUEST! NO STRIKES ARE AUTHORIZED FOR FORTY-EIGHT HOURS!**

The sentiment of the pilots was predictable.

"Don't they have the guts to kill us themselves? Why make Castro do it for them?" asked one.

"We spent a hell of a long time getting ready, and now they're tearing the whole damned thing apart, one small piece at a time," added another.

"Pity those poor ******* on the beaches without any air cover," from a third.

When Bissell, Barnes, and Cabell returned to Quarters Eye, Cabell was assailed by a half dozen staff members who called him every name they could think of that meant: inefficient, timid, and gutless.

"The success of this damned invasion hinges on the premise that none of Castro's planes will get off the ground," Howard Hunt screamed at Cabell.

"The best planes Castro has are his T-33 trainers. Intelligence sources told us he only has two or three of those jets, and none of them may be airworthy. We're not sure that any of the planes are armed. I can't believe those old T-birds are going to be much of a factor," Cabell assured him.

"Well, I hope you're right. Because you're betting the lives of more than a thousand men on your opinion," Beerli sighed.

"I feel confident in taking that chance," Cabell told him.

"Sure you do!" Hunt stormed. "Because it won't be your ass that gets shot off on some lousy Cuban beach. If Allen were here, he'd go back and raise more hell with Rusk than he could handle. It's just too damned bad you don't have the guts to do that."

For the next hour, voices grew louder, insults grew stronger, and the frustrated pounding on Cabell's desk grew more vigorous. Several men lost control and wept openly—some howled—many faces turned purple with rage. They tried every conceivable tactic to place Cabell on a guilt trip, but nothing worked!

**Invasion was on! Air sorties were off!**

At 0200 the Chairman of the Joint Chiefs of Staff, General Lyman Lemnitzer, was awakened in his quarters at Fort Myer, by an insistent buzzing of his doorbell. On his front porch Generals Wheeler and Gray stood waiting.

"They scrubbed the airstrikes," Gray announced.

"That's unbelievable," Lemnitzer replied. "Pulling the rug out from under those people is reprehensible. Worse than that, it's downright criminal. Let's check with the situation room for confirmation."

The call to the Joint Chiefs' War Room confirmed the worst. The air cover was definitely cancelled.

"The CIA guys want to get some kind of air cover from *Essex*—at least until the beachheads are secured," General Wheeler explained to Lemnitzer.

"Call Admiral Dennison in Norfolk, tell him to prepare an order for an aircap umbrella from *Essex*." As Gray started for the telephone, Lemnitzer added: "That crazy cancellation must have come from the top. Tell Denny to clear with the State Department before he issues any orders."

In the wee small hours of the morning, badgering by all of his staff members finally paid off. Whether motivated by a guilt trip or the slowly accumulated knowledge that without air cover the invaders were doomed, we shall never know. But regardless of the cause, at 4 A.M. Cabell arrived at the Sheraton Park apartment of Dean Rusk.

Cabell had always liked and respected Dean Rusk. Most people did. It was hard as hell not to like him. As he rode up in the elevator, Cabell put his rapid-recall memory to work and clicked off everything he knew about the Secretary of State.

Rusk had been born in 1909 on a small, red-clay scratch farm in Cherokee County, Georgia. He had worked his way through Davidson College, then earned a Rhodes Scholarship to Oxford University.

Rusk's years in Europe coincided with Hitler's rise to power. Careful study and analysis of Nazi tactics instilled in Rusk a rabid distrust of totalitarianism.

Cabell remembered that Rusk had been called to military duty in December 1940, a full year before Pearl Harbor. He had taken command of Company A, Thirtieth Infantry Battalion, in the Army's Third Division. However, the Department of the Army quickly recognized Rusk's talent and ability and, in October 1941, he was reassigned to the Intelligence section of the General Staff in Washington, then commanded by General George C. Marshall.

When the war ended Rusk continued working for Marshall and his chief aide, Dean Acheson, in the post-war State Department. During the ensuing five years, Rusk played an instrumental role in several of State's "Hot Projects"—establishment of the United Nations, the Marshall Plan, the birth of Israel, and the onset of the Korean War.

In 1950 he became President of the Rockefeller Foundation. Rusk was still there in 1960 when Jack Kennedy asked him to anchor the State Department. Rusk was no lightweight; he had served a very long, complicated apprenticeship. Although he listened to every opinion, he was extremely difficult to sway.

Rusk answered Cabell's first light tap on the door, then ushered him through a spacious living room and down a long hall to a cozy, book-jammed den.

Cabell sank gratefully into the wide, black leather chair that stood in front of Rusk's carved oak desk. Then he came right to the point.

"Mr. Secretary, at least give us some air support from *Essex* during the unloading and withdrawal of the supply ships. All the planes that were originally scheduled for the aircap are still in Nicaragua. That means they're at least five hours away from where they're needed. They're so old they might not stand much of a chance against the Cuban fighter planes anyway. A few jets from *Essex* would at least give the Brigade a fighting chance to succeed."

Rusk rose and walked toward a tiny bar that stood in the corner. He poured a generous quantity of dark amber liquid into a tall glass and handed it to Cabell before he resumed his seat behind the desk.

"General Cabell, take a big swig of that sour mash and try to relax. Please understand I'm as concerned as you are. But also understand that we are sitting on several powder kegs that are ready to explode at any moment. The President and I are watching a number of critical issues very carefully—arms control, the nuclear test ban, the escalation of the Southeast Asia scenario, and of course, there's Berlin. Juggling blowtorches might be easier than this. Nonetheless, I will phone the President and convey your concern."

He called Glen Ora and spoke with the President. To Rusk's credit, he presented Cabell's request in the most favorable light and then listened intently.

Cabell saw him nod several times, then listen again for what seemed an eternity, before he finally said:

"I'll issue those orders at once. Good night, Mr. President."

Cabell waited expectantly. It sounded as though the President might have relented.

"The President is adamant in his refusal," Rusk told Cabell. "First of all, he made a nationwide declaration that American forces would not take part in an invasion. He feels compelled to hold firm on that. Secondly, Russia and China are threatening some type of retaliatory action—if not in Cuba, then perhaps in Vietnam, in Laos, or in Berlin. We can't afford to stick our necks out any farther than we have already. President Kennedy has ordered *Essex* to stand out to sea. She is to remain thirty miles off Cuba's coast until further notice. Please understand that this is not a decision that either the President or I want to make; the hard ones seldom are. But our decision must be predicated on national security."

As a crestfallen General Cabell left the apartment of the Secretary of State, his mind was filled with the images of rusty, antiquated ships as they plowed through dark, alien seas, and moved ever closer to the danger of a hostile shore—toward a foreboding strip of mud and sand where those aboard might encounter sudden and bloody death—where a dream might end for more than a thousand brave men who longed for liberty and justice in the land they loved.

Cabell walked quickly across the richly appointed lobby, stopped beneath the brightly-lighted portico, and squinted up at a night sky that was now scant moments away from the new dawn. He stood and wished that he could be aboard every one of those lumbering vessels in the far off, deadly Caribbean for a few moments. If I could just be there long enough to talk to each one of those brave, expectant freedom fighters, he thought—just long enough to say: my friend, you're not alone. Our hopes, our dreams and, most of all, our prayers are with you. We desperately want you to win!

Suddenly, he felt violated, naked, and dishonored in the glare of the bright lights from this building where he had suffered his most humiliating defeat. To General Charles Cabell, America was no longer the land of the free and the home of the brave. It had become a sinister place where political expediency and caution had replaced legitimacy, honesty, and traditional morality.

He pulled his hat far down over his eyes and walked quickly into the darkness, seeking anonymity and solace in the blue-black velvet of the night.

# *PART THREE*
# *THE INVASION*

# *THE BAY OF PIGS*
# *APRIL 17, 1961*

Minutes after midnight on Invasion Day, a fresh wave of Radio Swan propaganda began. Across the length and breadth of Cuba, wherever short wave radio was available, strange messages were heard.

"Beware of the spiny purple fish."

"Many dogs growl when they hunt."

"The tall palm tree sways gently."

"Juan has a long mustache."

Of course, all the messages were bogus. Their sole purpose was to convince the network of Fidelistas that the huge Cuban underground was being readied for immediate action. Unfortunately for the invaders, no action was possible since no underground existed.

Far into the night, as deep darkness covered the vast Caribbean, Radio Swan broadcast messages that were reminiscent of the hundreds sent on D-Day at Normandy.

"Gain control of the highway intersections and the railroad stations. Execute anyone who refuses to surrender or follow orders. It is vital to stop all Fidelist aircraft from leaving the ground! Sabotage them. Break cables and parts, or puncture the gas tanks. Rise up, Cuban patriots! Rise up, and win back your homeland!"

On D-Day, June 6, 1944, similar instructions had worked to perfection. Allied troops hitting the five Normandy beaches found collaborators at every turn. But on this D-Day, April 17, 1961, no one seemed to be listening. Efforts of the Radio Swan staffers were all but futile.

On this D-Day, the invaders were on their own!

A midnight briefing at the Opa-Locka Naval Air Station informed the Frente leaders that the air cover the Brigade had been promised was being withdrawn because of "political considerations."

Questions from the exiled Cuban leaders, many with sons or other relatives in the 2506 Brigade, now came thick and fast.

"What 'political considerations' are more important than keeping the promises that convinced us to go along with this attack?"

"Why are our men landing in the Zapata swamps?"

"What will be done to protect them, now that you have stolen their air cover?"

"How can they *succeed* without air support?"

"How can they *survive* without air support?"

"If the Brigade members need to escape, they were told to go into the mountains; but now the mountains are more than a hundred kilometers away. How can they escape? They will die in those dreadful swamps!"

The CIA agents did not have official answers to any of the questions posed by the angry members of the Frente. They could only assure the Cuban leaders that they shared the same concerns, and that answers to their questions would soon be coming from Washington.

The meeting soon erupted into angry and chaotic shouting matches. Curses and threats filled the air. In an effort to allay the fears of the Frente members, and to quell the near-riot, an elderly, dignified CIA agent repeatedly pleaded for attention until they finally, grudgingly listened. Then his authoritative, calm voice filled the angry Cubans with new hopes.

"My friends, what I am going to say is my own personal and unofficial analysis of our predicament. Since the dawn of our republic, America has always come to the aid of the underdog. And quite honestly, at this moment, the Brigade is the biggest underdog since David picked up his slingshot and went off to fight Goliath," he added with an infectious grin that brought smiles to many worried faces. "I am certain that President Kennedy and his advisors feel they cannot openly assist the Brigade in gaining a foothold in your homeland. It must appear that the Brigade succeeded on its own —without American assistance. Enemies around the world may doubt that such a thing could happen, but without tangible proof, it doesn't matter what they think!" He paused, giving his words a chance to register before he continued.

"When a beachhead is secured, and a new provisional government is established, the provisional leaders can then declare that they, and not Castro and his hoodlums, constitute the legal government of Cuba. That will be the time to call upon America to recognize their claim and come to their defense. Radio Free Cuba will fill the airwaves, and Americans will rally to your cause and your call. If American armed forces are employed *then*, the US will be seen as a defender of freedom and justice, not as an imperialist warmonger.

The United States will not allow your sons to die on the bloody sand of a forgotten beach. Believe in us, as we believe in you."

For the moment the impasse was forgotten, as spontaneous applause filled the room.

In New York City, McGeorge Bundy called Adlai Stevenson and invited him to an early breakfast. It was then that Stevenson finally learned about the invasion.

"I've been required to do many things in the service of my country," the UN Ambassador told the presidential messenger, "but this is the first time I've ever been asked to impersonate a fool."

At the stroke of midnight, the captains of all the American destroyers were helicoptered aboard *Essex*. When the last one arrived, Admiral Clark uncovered a large area map of the Caribbean. On the map were several zigzag tracks, marked with tape, that led from their present position toward the Cuban coast.

"Gentlemen, our mission is to escort certain 'unidentified, insurgent craft' to the coast. Each of you will be responsible for the navigation of one of those vessels. You are to stay out of visual contact with the 'unidentified ships' at all times. To effect course corrections, bounce the beams from your largest searchlights off the clouds and send Morse code messages. Each of you will receive a silhouette of the 'unidentified ship' that is your assignment. Remember that it is not, I say again, this is not, an official mission. It is not a mission at all! So stay loose and look casual. Any questions?"

Each of the destroyer skippers looked blankly at each other, and at the Admiral, but said nothing.

"Good! Get back to your ships, and remember that your executive officers are the only ones who are to be informed about any of this."

An hour later, American destroyers became the shepherds of shadowy phantom ships that officially did not exist.

It was now time, while the flotilla was still beyond sight and sound of the land, to check their meager weapons.

Aboard *Atlantico*, the second officer decided to test fire the machine gun that had been mounted on the afterdeck. Shortly after the firing began, the poorly mounted gun broke loose and began spraying bullets in all directions. Before he could stop, one man had been killed, and two others were seriously injured.

On the CIA ship, *Barbara J.*, Andy Pruna and his squad of frogmen tried to fire the M-3 submachine guns they'd been given. It was a good thing they did because the weapons were useless. They discarded the M-3's and replaced them with Browning Automatic Rifles *(BARs).* The team objective was Red Beach, at Playa Larga, which was situated at the northern end of the Bay of Pigs. The BAR's would prove to be a good choice, because they would need all the firepower they could muster before the day ended.

American destroyers, together with the shadowy ships that were now their responsibility, began stringing out in a long column, being careful to maintain a gap of a thousand yards between ships. Of course, crewmembers were not permitted to actually see anything beyond the limits of their own ships.

The CIA ship *Blagar* was anchored two thousand yards off Blue Beach at Playa Giron. Most of the Brigade's personnel, as well as a majority of the expedition's leaders, were aboard. Nearby, *Houston*, escorted by *Barbara J.*, was preparing to head west toward an anchorage at the mouth of the Bay of Pigs that led to Playa Larga. She carried the seasoned Second Battalion and the fledgling, scarcely trained Fifth Battalion. It was here that, for the very first time, Brigade Commander Pepe San Roman, aboard *Blagar*, questioned CIA intelligence reports, as he saw a beach at Playa Giron that was supposed to be dark and deserted, ablaze with hundreds of bright white lights. He shook his head in disgust and smiled grimly.

San Roman turned away from the shore and saw Reynolds and Orizaba meeting with an elite contingent of frogmen at the rail of the ship. The men all wore black rubber suits, swim masks, and flippers, and were weighed down with weapons, ammo bandoliers, and signaling lights. This small amphibian force would be the first to land on Blue Beach at Playa Giron.

Blue Beach was located at the eastern side of the Bay of Pigs entrance, at the very edge of the Zapata Swamps. Until recently it had been a place time forgot. Now Playa Giron was the site of dozens of cottages, constructed on orders from Fidel Castro, in the hope that Playa Giron would someday become the Cuban Riviera. Blue Beach also guarded a road that ran southward from San Blas and Covadonga. A road that might bring troops to repel the invaders.

Ramrod Reynolds and Avispa Orizaba finished meeting with the frogmen a short time before they were scheduled to deploy. Moments later, the assault team received a final blessing from a Brigade priest. As they rose to their feet and turned around, they were surprised to see Ramrod and Avispa coming toward them. Both "advisors" carried BARs and wore bandoliers across their chests.

"Where do you two think you're going?" asked the frogman team leader, Jose Alonso.

"I'm going in with your group, and Avispa's going in with Andy Pruna and his squad from *Barbara J.*"

"No way, Rod! Look, we're grateful for everything you've done; but this is where it ends. You're supposed to run this show from a command post, here, on the radio. That's your job. Hitting Blue Beach is our job!"

"I don't plan to stay long, Jose. I'm coming right back. But I can do a better job here, after I go in with you and see what's going on, instead of getting second-hand feedback. When the rest of you transfer to the raft and go in to scout the beach, I'll stay aboard the catamaran and bring it back."

This assault team's job was to act as pathfinders. They would leave *Blagar*, which was anchored two thousand yards offshore, in a very fast eighteen-foot catamaran, powered by a pair of 70-horsepower outboard motors. Behind them they would tow a low profile rubber raft, with an 18-horse motor. As soon as they sighted the beach, they would transfer to the raft, move inshore, indicating any submerged obstacle in the landing craft approach lanes as they went, mark the optimum landing sites with red and white lights, and neutralize anyone who might be lurking on the shore that could raise an alarm.

U-2 photographs pictured a promontory jutting out from the beach. Near the seaward end of this rocky jutland stood a small building that housed a grocery store, or *bodega*. Since it would shield them all from the view of anyone ashore, the bodega became the team's first objective. Fortunately, they were landing in pre-dawn darkness. The construction workers who were employed at the nearby seaside resort probably would still be asleep.

The first leg of the short trip went well; but when they saw the beach they were unpleasantly shocked. The Cubans had recently installed brilliant, vapor lights on tall towers. The whole area was now as bright as day. Under one of the light standards, a small group of men stood talking; since none of them happened to be looking seaward, they didn't notice the catamaran or its astonished passengers bobbing on the waves.

Ramrod analyzed the situation and reached three obvious conclusions.

The intelligence reports they had were useless.

The primary landing site had to be abandoned, and another one had to be selected.

No one else aboard the catamaran had combat experience. Therefore, he would have to reconnoiter the forward area himself before he recommended an alternative site to the Brigade's commanders.

While the assault team paddled just hard enough to keep the small vessel from drifting closer to shore,

Ramrod studied the beach through a pair of night binoculars.

To the right of the original landing site was a relatively dark area. Ramrod examined that section of the beach and detected no movement of any kind. It seemed to be pitch black and deserted. His night glasses revealed a service road leading away from the construction site that followed the curve of the shore before it disappeared in the distance. Directly behind the road he spotted a large patch of thick woods; obviously that was the area to scout out as the first alternative landing zone. According to the latest intelligence reports, there were fewer than a hundred troops stationed at the Bay of Pigs. He smiled grimly in the darkness and wondered if that estimate had been formulated by the same sources that failed to notice the light towers and had predicted a bunch of sleepy inhabitants.

"All right," he told the team in a hoarse whisper, "this is what we're going to do. One man will stay here and hold the catamaran against the waves. The rest of us are going in to check on alternative landing sites. Jose, you handle the motor. Head for the middle of that dark section of beach just to the right of the arc lights. We must find out what's in the woods behind that shore road. Bring along a half dozen of those red signal lights."

Ramrod and the assault team members transferred to the small rubber raft and Jose Alonso started the outboard motor, which had been muffled. About a hundred yards from shore, one of their red and white signal lights began blinking. The seawater that had accumulated in the bottom of the raft had shorted it out. Jose Alonso quickly threw his poncho over the defective device, and another man tore all of the wires out to make sure that it could not betray their presence again.

Suddenly the outboard motor hit an underwater obstruction and stopped. They had run hard aground on one of the reefs that guarded the Bay of Pigs. The CIA photographic analysis section had mistaken these reefs for harmless seaweed.

The frogmen jumped from the raft into the knee-deep water that covered the reef and began hauling or pushing the stubborn raft shoreward. Meanwhile, Reynolds lay prone in the bow, his BAR pointed toward the beach.

About fifty yards from shore, above the noise of the waves, he heard the sounds of an approaching jeep. Reynolds quickly ordered the frogmen to lie down behind the raft, hoping the jeep's occupants would fail to see them in the deep darkness of the moonless night.

They later discovered that the jeep was driven by guards who, seeing the blinking red light, assumed that it came from a fishing trawler and hurried down the beach to warn the fishermen about the dangerous reefs.

Unfortunately for the guards, when they reached the spot directly in front of the bobbing rubber raft, with its crouching occupants, they turned on a searchlight that was mounted on the front of the jeep. Instantly, the assault team was bathed in bright light.

Ramrod had no choice! He opened fire. He drained a whole twenty-shot magazine before two other BARs and the four submachine guns joined him. Since every third round was a tracer bullet, they could all watch as fire from their automatic weapons poured into the jeep and killed the occupants. The guards were the first casualties at the Bay of Pigs Invasion.

Ramrod leaped out of the raft and, with members of his spread-out assault team, began wading toward the beach. At that precise moment, every light in the construction area and on the light standards went out. Ramrod called *Blagar* on his walkie-talkie.

"We had to knock out a patrol jeep. We're now en route to place signal lights and mark the landing site. Out!"

As they passed the jeep, he paused long enough to examine the two Cuban soldiers who lay in silent, grotesque positions. Once again, Ramrod agreed with Sherman. "War is hell!"

The team sprinted down the beach toward the promontory, raking the bodega with sustained fire from their automatic weapons as they ran.

When Jose Alonso, the first frogman to reach the building, burst through the door, he found two more guards lying on the floor. They were both dead.

"Our element of surprise has disappeared, but that really doesn't matter," Ramrod told the assault team. "We'll simply readjust our plans to conform with the new conditions. Jose, take half the team and check out that patch of woods along the road. Then set up a couple of outposts that can sweep the whole area with rapid fire."

Ramrod's walkie-talkie suddenly crackled to life:

"There's a truck heading for your position," said a bodiless voice from *Blagar*.

"Okay," Ramrod responded, "move the ship into position to lend supporting fire, just in case we need help. Meanwhile, get the rest of the troops moving. We need them in here on the double."

"They're loading aboard landing craft right now. They'll be shoving off in a couple of minutes."

Just as the message ended, a large truck rolled to a stop a short distance away, and two or three dozen men got out—a few carried flashlights. All of them carried weapons. Ramrod and his men hunkered down behind the bodega and began firing into the massed troops. Moments later, gunners aboard *Blagar* opened fire with machine guns and recoilless rifles. The surprised militiamen quickly melted back into the woods.

When the firing stopped, the radio crackled again.

"We're on our way. We're almost at the beach."

Ramrod suddenly realized that he had not warned the other boats about the reefs. He grabbed a radio, but it was too late. The first fragile vessel hit the rocky reef at full speed, flipped high into the air, then quickly disappeared beneath the waves. The ruined boat's occupants struggled back to the surface and waded the rest of the way ashore. Although they were badly shaken, none of them appeared to be seriously injured.

Ramrod decided that since there seemed to be a lull in the action, it might be an ideal time to send the catamaran out for Pepe San Roman and the battalion commanders.

San Roman came ashore a short time later with a second contingent of troops and directed them to positions near Playa Giron, where they opened fire on the brightly colored beach resort in which Fidel Castro took so much pride. Since there was no answering fire, or any type of opposition, San Roman assumed the resort was deserted and issued a cease fire order.

Ramrod joined Pepe and his staff as they walked along the promontory toward the bodega, where they discovered an old Chevrolet in the shadows at the back of the building. One of the Miami recruits who was adept at hot wiring cars performed his magic; then San Roman and his staff climbed into the ramshackle vehicle and set off to capture the airstrip. In the Chevy's wake, a group of soldiers followed along at a dogtrot.

"Pepe, I'm going back to the ship. I'll take Third Battalion to Green Beach," Ramrod shouted after the ancient car. San Roman turned and waved to indicate that he had heard.

As Ramrod raced back toward the catamaran his radio came to life.

"An important message just in from Quarters Eye. They want you back aboard *Blagar* ASAP."

The message was a warning from Bissell.

"The Cubans still have several operational aircraft. You might be hit at dawn! Get your troops and supplies unloaded before first light, then take all the ships out to sea."

"Bissell must know something we don't," Ramrod confided to the leaders of the Third Battalion. "The pre-dawn airstrikes were designed to knock out all of the planes. Bissell probably feels that if a few of their planes are still undamaged, they might slip in and hurt us. Let's get everything ashore and send the ships back to sea. It never hurts to be overly cautious," he concluded, still completely unaware that airstrikes imperative for the mission to succeed had been cancelled.

He reached Pepe San Roman on his walkie-talkie.

"Pepe, I'm under orders to send all the troops and equipment in pronto. They want the ships as far from the beach as possible by dawn. But we can't land the tanks and heavy equipment before high tide. Today, high tide is at 0700. Anytime before that, the heavy stuff will simply hang up on the reefs."

"I recall them mentioning high tide in one of the briefings. What do you think we ought to do?"

"It's your call, Pepe; but I don't see any alternative. We have to wait until we're sure the heavy stuff can clear the reefs."

"I concur," Pepe San Roman told him. "If we try to get the tanks and other heavy equipment in before high tide we'll probably lose everything. If we wait until 0700, we might lose everything anyway, but at least, that way, we'll have a fighting chance."

"Okay, Pepe. I'll come ashore and do whatever I can. Buena suerte! I hope to see you all very soon."

The orders from Quarters Eye were disregarded—and at 0700 the tanks and the other heavy equipment came ashore without a hitch—it was one of the few things that went right during the entire invasion.

As Ramrod left *Blagar* and headed toward the beach, he saw *Houston* moving toward Red Beach at Playa Larga. Aboard *Houston*, Second Battalion was assured there was no need to worry about opposition while they established a beachhead.

"Castro has no communication capabilities within twenty miles of your landing zone!" a CIA advisor told them.

Lt. Hugo Suiero, of Second Battalion, had been an officer in Castro's army until a few weeks before. Now he asked.

"When were the microwave radio units removed?"

"I don't understand your question," replied the CIA man.

"There were operational microwave radios at Playa Larga and Playa Giron last year. Have they been knocked out?"

"They must have been," the CIA man countered, "because there are no transmitting capabilities within twenty miles of either of our invasion beaches."

Suiero and his friends breathed a collective sigh of relief. They had absolute faith in the United States. If this man said the radio stations were gone, they must be gone.

Thirty minutes later, Suiero was in the bow of the first boat from *Houston* to come ashore. Since they had been warned about the reefs, they carefully avoided them and got to a point a mere fifty yards from Blue Beach before the stillness was broken by a thunderous staccato of machine gun fire from the woods beyond the beach. Suiero ripped a full magazine of shots through his BAR, and the enemy machine gun fire died.

Cautiously, they moved toward the beach and left the boat when the water became shallow enough to wade. Crouching low, they dashed forward, dove onto the wet sand at the water's edge, and assumed prone positions.

While the men in the squad covered them, Suiero and two others cautiously advanced toward a low building Suiero recognized as the former microwave radio site. Wary of possible enemy opposition, the three riddled the small building with concentrated rifle fire before they advanced and took possession of the structure. Inside they found an impressive array of microwave radio equipment. Although their hail of lead had ruined everything, the transmitters were still warm. Once again, the CIA's forecast had been wrong. Dead wrong!

## CASTRO HAD BEEN WARNED!

Rafael Moreira was nearing the end of his twelve-hour night shift as the invaders came ashore. When the attack began he had been driving a slow-moving tractor, and hauling a large tank that contained two thousand gallons of water destined for the Playa Giron Recreational Center's swimming pool. As he drove along a shore that would soon be known as Blue Beach, Rafael reflected that no one in Giron even had an indoor bathroom, few even had running water, yet here he was hauling water to fill a public pool. Life was certainly full of strange events.

As he neared the Recreational Center, he suddenly saw a bright light coming toward him from the sea. A moment later he was engulfed in a cloud of tracer bullets. Somehow they all miraculously missed him and went screaming across the sand toward the buildings along the Playa Giron.

For several seconds Rafael was too frightened to leave his high perch. Then suddenly he sprang into action. He switched off the tractor lights and began running, as low to the ground as possible. He wanted to reach the nearby military post—the one with the microwave radio station. He was very proud that he would be the one to warn the local authorities that the invasion was underway; but he found even more satisfaction in the fact that he had remembered to turn off the lights of the tractor. No one would ever be able to say that Rafael Moreira had provided a beacon for the invaders. He tried to crouch even lower. More bullets seemed to be screaming over him, and each one seemed to be coming closer.

He bent lower and ran faster than he ever had before.

Rafael was one of the least confused individuals at the Bay of Pigs that morning. Several hundred yards offshore, a pair of American sailors were dangling in bosun's chairs off the fantail of the destroyer, *Cony*, whose fleet number was 508. They had been ordered to paint over the "8" in an effort to disguise the ship.

Aboard the aircraft carrier *Essex*, fighter pilots of the Blue Blaster Squadron became uneasy when they were ordered to leave all of their identification and dogtags in the ready room just in case they took off at any time during the day.

"Hell with that crap," stormed their usually icy Executive Officer, Jim Forgy. "If we get shot down without our ID, we can be shot on the spot as mercenaries—or worse, pirates."

"The orders came from the top," his Commanding Officer, Commander Mike Griffin, told him.

"Skipper," Forgy replied, "I'm a naval officer. I'm going to fly as a naval officer—wearing tags and carrying my wallet and ID. Anybody who doesn't do the same thing is nuts!"

The orders were clear, but so was the attitude of the Blue Blasters.

Aboard *Atlantico*, the ship's doctor could not stop shaking. The rusty ship was so overcrowded with men and equipment that he had been forced to sleep underneath a rickety lifeboat. Gasoline fumes polluted the air. It was so dangerous that the men had been forbidden to heat their rations or to smoke. All around him crazy daredevils puffed on cigarettes while they waited for orders. "I don't have to go ashore to die," Dr. Sordo decided. "I'll be killed before I can get off this old tub."

Captain Tirado of *Rio Escondido* was in his cabin, sorting out the hundreds of navigational charts he had been given by the CIA before sailing for Cuba. The only one that seemed to be missing was the one detailing an area around the Bay of Pigs.

Tirado was glad to leave the cabin and go topside, because the stench from the fuel drums was making breathing nearly impossible. For the hundredth time he decided that if a single incendiary shell hit *Rio Escondido,* she would explode like a huge Roman Candle.

Aboard *Houston*, which was now anchored a short distance from the mouth of the Bay of Pigs, things were going poorly. The ship carried nine flimsy, plastic, unstable boats that were scheduled to transport the invaders up the entire length of the Bay, to Red Beach *(Playa Larga),* a journey which, in the miniature landing boats, would take twenty minutes. Avispa Orizaba and *Houston's* Captain, Luis Morse, had to move away from the rusty winches as the first of the plastic boats was lowered over the side because the loud screeching from the corroded pulleys was simply too painful to endure.

"If Castro didn't know about the invasion before, he sure does now," Avispa shouted. "The noise has to carry at least as far as Havana. Maybe we could dispense with the winches and simply drop the boats over the side."

"That won't work," Morse told him. "Those damned boats would disintegrate when they hit the water."

It soon became apparent that the light boats lacked stability. Seven of the nine quickly capsized and sank, long before they even reached the mouth of the Bay. The two remaining boats would have to accomplish a mission that nine had originally been scheduled to carry out.

"It's a real fiasco, Luis!" Avispa said. "I'm going ashore for a look see. It doesn't seem possible for anything else to go bad, but I have a hunch something will. I'll call you on the radio as soon as I've sized things up at Red Beach."

A short distance away, the construction workers and their families were awakened by a series of loud bangs that sounded like shots. They were temporarily housed in tiny, one-room straw huts that lay clustered behind spacious resort cottages being built along the shore at Blue Beach *(Giron).*

Among the couples whose slumber was interrupted were the Mejiases, Narciso and Alejandrina.

"Those loud noises sounded just like shots," Alejandrina exclaimed to her sleepy-eyed husband.

"They probably are shots," he agreed. "Crazy touristas from Oriente Province come over here, get drunk, then celebrate getting drunk by shooting off their pistolas. Go back to sleep and don't worry about them. They're all harmless enough."

Reassured by Narciso's blase attitude, Alejandrina checked on her seven-year-old son, Gregorio, who was still sleeping soundly a few feet away. Satisfied that her son was safe, she crawled back under the thin covers and carefully pulled the bug-proof netting tightly around the perimeter of the bed, in a futile attempt to ward off the hordes of bloodthirsty Zapata Swamp mosquitoes whose ferocity was legendary throughout the entire Caribbean.

Moments later a bullet shattered one of the long poles that supported the straw walls of the hut. More bullets hit their fogon, the tiny charcoal burner that served as a combination stove and furnace. A third salvo ripped through the thin headboard of their bed, less than six inches from the terrified woman's eyes.

The Mejiases scrambled out of the bed that had suddenly become a popular target. Alejandrina grabbed Gregorio and pulled him down next to her, huddled and shivering beneath the old straw mattress, protecting her son with her own body. Then they heard a man's frightened voice:

"Ships are shooting at the buildings on the beach."

"So much for your crazy, pistol-shooting Orientales," giggled Alejandrina, now nearly insane with fear. "They'll have to find a new place to celebrate getting drunk."

"Fidel said those Saturday air raids were made by American planes. The ships that are shooting at us must be American ships. Soon Cuba will be invaded by thousands of American soldiers," reasoned Narciso.

The shooting stopped as suddenly as it had begun. One minute the air was filled with whistling lead and the thunder of gunfire; a single heartbeat later, expectant silence. Narciso crawled from beneath the mattress and helped Alejandrina to her feet.

"I'm going to run to the Recreation Center and see what the sergeant-in-charge wants us to do. I'll be right back." Narciso dashed out the door.

As Alejandrina began to restore their meager possessions to some semblance of order, she noticed a large puddle of water on the earthen floor near the back wall, under a small iron tub that she used for her family wash. She moved quickly toward the tub, almost afraid to look inside. When she did, her worst suspicions were confirmed. A dozen bullets had ripped into the tub and its contents. One by one she slowly withdrew articles of sodden clothing and examined them. They had all been shredded!

To vent her frustration and exasperation, as well as her fear, Alejandrinio did what any other woman might have done in similar circumstances. She wept.

She was still holding the mass of sopping rags and sobbing when Narciso returned a few minutes later.

"Sergeant Mendoza has no extra weapons for civilians to use. He says we must leave Giron and hide in the swamps."

"Let's go quickly before all of us are killed!" Alejandrina cried, taking Gregorio by the hand, and heading for the door.

Some fifty yards from the small dwelling that was about to be evacuated by the Mejias family, in the backroom of Enrico Blanco's combination general store and tavern, Felix Rivera—bartender, cook, and handyman—had been jolted awake by a crash of gunfire.

Like his friend, Narciso Mejias, Felix suspected that either the local militia or Orientales on a spree were the source of the loud explosions, until he heard a loud voice that he didn't recognize, proclaiming:

"Come on, *mi companeros*, we are on Cuban soil at last!"

Fidel is right, he decided. An American-sponsored invasion has begun. He heard the same loud voice shout:

"Lie down on the floor of your huts and you won't be hurt."

Felix decided to stay in bed. Over the years he had seen a lot of American war movies and had yet to see one person get hurt while he lay safely in his own bed.

He heard the strange voice commanding:

"Everybody in the huts, come out! Right now!"

Reluctantly, Felix rose, donned his soiled cook's uniform with its greasy, tall white hat, then ambled slowly toward the *cantina door*. When he emerged, a dozen soldiers in dark green uniforms surrounded him.

"Have no fear, amigo," one of the green-clad men called to him. "We have come from America to save you from Castro's terror."

Felix recognized the speaker's accent as native Cuban and saw that the majority of the men were Cuban. As he glanced around the circle his gaze stopped when he reached Ramrod Reynolds. Maybe this man was American, maybe not, but he was no Cuban.

Three soldiers ushered Felix back into the *cantina* and set an impressive radio transmitter up on the bar. When a blare of static burst from the speaker, a radio operator began speaking into the microphone, calling for re-enforcements. He called over and over again, but no one answered him.

The operator paused, then said to Felix:

"Why don't you join us? Fight with us, amigo! You could be a big help. Since you live here, you must know a lot about the area."

"I don't know anything about guns or fighting. I've never even fired a gun. I'm frightened of guns. And I would be no help to you as a guide. I just moved here, from Oriente, last week," lied Felix, who had lived nearby for many years.

The radio operator shrugged his shoulders and turned back to his microphone. His relentless drone for help began again.

The shaky Felix Rivera collapsed at one of the cantina's rickety tables and breathed a sigh of relief. No way would he shoot off a gun or get involved in this fighting. If you shot at someone, he always shot back at you. A man could get hurt, even killed. Not me, decided Felix! I've seen too many men die in the American movies to be fooled. He wished he could go back to bed. He always felt safer there.

Several miles away, at the uppermost tip of the Bay of Pigs, in the area known to the Brigade as Red Beach, a lone sentry, named Victor Cabellero, stood guard. Six of his companions were sleeping fitfully aboard a small, insect-infested motor launch that was moored a short distance away. Victor did not have a uniform, but he was wearing a bright red armband, and carrying an old rifle. He wondered if his rusty weapon would really shoot. Well, it didn't really matter. Nothing ever happened here anyway. The .50 caliber machine gun stashed aboard the motor launch also seemed ridiculous to Victor. For that matter, standing guard seemed stupid to him and to every one of his amigos.

Suddenly, he was jolted out of his complacency by several loud popping noises. Moments later, a large ship appeared around a sharp curve in the bay, and tracer bullets from heavy weapons began screaming overhead. Victor screamed at his friends on the boat in an effort to wake them, then quickly realized that they were already raising the small anchor and preparing to make a run for it. Unfortunately, it was low tide, and the water was too shallow to allow an escape.

The lieutenant in charge of the guard detail ordered his men to abandon the launch and remove the machine gun.

The heavy weapon was soon transferred to the beach, along with a big supply of jute sacks and several shovels. The men began filling sacks with haste borne of desperation, then they were placed in a semicircular sandbag wall facing toward the water. Although a two-foot-high wall offered very little real protection for the gun or its operators, it did make them all feel a little more secure.

The lieutenant scurried back to the launch and switched on the radio. If he could only alert headquarters, they might send help; but all he heard was static.

Then a loud voice came out of the massive loudspeaker on the deck of the ship that confronted them.

"We've come to liberate you from Communist oppression. Fidel Castro is our prisoner. If you do not surrender, we will take your position by force. You have one minute to decide."

In response, the lieutenant ordered Victor to open fire with the machine gun. The guns on the ship returned fire, and bullets began thudding into the sand around them. Two of the men were wounded; one was hit in the foot, the other in the head. Victor carried the man with the injured foot a short distance back to the tiny fishing village of Caleton where they all lived. He deposited the man in his hut, then raced on to his own dwelling, where his wife and three young children lay on the earthen floor, crying. Every object in the hut seemed to be riddled with bullets.

"Florentina, take the children and run away from the shore. Go into the village and hide behind one of the stone walls. You'll be safe. Run fast, children! Stay as low as you can!"

"Come with us, Victor," his wife pleaded.

"I can't. Americans are attacking us. A man is not a man unless he is willing to fight for his family and his country. Vaya con Dios, Florentina. Take care of our little ones!"

Victor hugged Florentina and his children, then started them on the short journey toward the first of the village's high stone walls. As soon as they reached that comparative safety, he turned away. Then, bent nearly double, he raced back toward the beach and his waiting machine gun.

Moments after he reached the beach, the automatic weapon fire from the invaders' ship (*Houston*) increased dramatically. Bullets screamed overhead, pinning him and the rest of the squad to the sand. Nearby, Caleton residents lay huddled and terrified upon the earthen floors of their huts.

Then the firing stopped abruptly. For the next few seconds the sudden silence seemed louder and more oppressive than the turmoil that had preceded it. From the loudspeaker on the deck of the ship, the powerful voice was heard once more.

"We've come to free you from Communism! Stop shooting at our ship. One portion of our force has already landed. They are marching down the shore toward you. As they enter your village, come out of your houses and surrender to them. You will not be harmed. We are here to help you, not to harm you! This is your final chance to surrender!"

As the last echo of the message died away, the sound of an approaching engine was heard, and moments later a man in a Cuban Army uniform, riding an ancient Indian motorcycle, roared into sight. He stopped near Victor and his squad, in a shower of sand, and shouted loudly enough to be heard by the villagers.

"Trucks are on their way to pick up everyone from Playa Larga and Giron. They'll carry you to safety. Airplanes and soldiers are coming to repel these imperialistic invaders. Fidel will not fail you in your hour of peril! Do not fail Fidel! Resist these bloodthirsty Americanos!"

In response, a chorus of shouts erupted from the village.

"Patria o muerte!" *Fatherland or death!* The revolutionary slogan.

The villagers had not long to wait. Five minutes after the motorcyclist disappeared, a pair of low-flying aircraft, bearing Cuban FAR insignia, came thundering in from the sea. They began diving and strafing a target of opportunity that lay hidden beyond the villagers' vision. However, when they heard a terrific explosion and saw a ball of fire leap into the sky a few hundred yards away, they knew that one of the planes had scored a killing hit on an invader vehicle.

A long flatbed truck rumbled into the village of Giron, and slid to a halt just long enough for the terrified inhabitants to clamber aboard.

As soon as the last villager had secured a perch, the driver smacked the truck into gear and headed northeast along a road that paralleled the railroad. But alas, the journey was destined to be tragically short.

Halfway to San Blas, the truck and its inhabitants were caught in a vicious, deadly crossfire, as rebel paratroopers and Cuban militia units shot it out with submachineguns from the railroad tracks and the far side of the road. The driver was the first to die—shot through the head. Unguided, the large truck careered off the roadway and headed directly toward a freight train that the rebels had forced to a halt. The vehicle slammed into a 40,000 gallon pressurized tank car that carried liquefied petroleum (volatile propane gas under extremely high pressure); as it did, its gas tank ignited. The truck's passengers were now caught in a no-man's-land, where the curtain of gunfire was so intense that bullets soon riddled almost every one of the villagers. Still, the firing from automatic weapons continued. Limp, lifeless bodies danced like bizarre puppets on the ends of invisible strings.

When the deadly crossfire paused for a moment, a large pile of unidentifiable bloody rags was all that remained to mark the place where moments earlier a crowd of desperate refugees had huddled.

Maria Carena, a very pretty, rosy-cheeked young newlywed, lay quietly in the midst of the carnage for several seconds after the firing ended before she sat up and began assessing the damage to her body. She was covered with blood from head to toe yet felt no pain. Frantically she searched her body for wounds, but was surprised to discover that by some quirk of fate—or more probably by a miracle—she had not even been scratched. All of the blood had come from the bodies of her friends and neighbors who lay in lifeless positions around her.

Gingerly, Maria reached out to touch her husband, who lay precariously balanced on the far edge of the truck. Her tender touch was enough to tilt the scales. Dumbfounded, she watched as his limp body rolled over the edge, then, with a quiet thump, fell to the blood-soaked road below.

Screaming in a tortured anguish, born of disbelief and terror, Maria crawled off the flatbed's slippery floor and crouched over her dead husband, pulling him; imploring him to move; pleading with him to rise and run with her from the terror and the horror and the death.

The firing began anew, and a soldier from Cuba's 339th Militia left a comparatively safe haven in the bushes along the road and rushed to Maria's side.

"If we don't get off this road, we'll be killed," he shouted into her ear. "Come with me! I'll help you!"

His arm protectively encircled her waist, as he propelled Maria off the roadway toward safety. She managed to crawl through a roadside drainage ditch and stumble into a copse of low bushes. When she looked back to thank her benefactor, she discovered that the Good Samaritan had been far less fortunate than she. He lay half in and half out of the ditch—his body neatly stitched by .30 caliber machine gun bullets from his waist to the base of his skull. The agonized Maria turned away from his broken body and saw several other survivors in various stages of distress. Some lay writhing on the bloody ground, moaning or screaming. Others, too helpless to move, lay praying for deliverance from the terrible violence that had invaded their once peaceful world and caused it to suddenly go mad.

The 40,000-gallon tanker car suddenly exploded with all the fiery force of an erupting volcano. Maria was hurled violently to the ground. A millisecond later, piercing heat from the thousand-degree inferno reached the bushes along the road, gobbling oxygen, and suffocating everyone in its path. The grotesque bodies of the dead, the inhuman screams of anguish, and a sickeningly sweet odor emanating from small piles of charred and burning flesh would have made any living person believe they were gazing upon a horrible scene from Dante's *Inferno.*

Mercifully, Maria and her friends could no longer see or hear the fury. They were dead long before the blast furnace heat from burning liquefied petroleum reduced their bodies to smoldering, unidentifiable heaps.

Back at Red Beach, Victor Cabellero and the rest of his squad were thrilled when a Cuban Sea Fury zoomed directly overhead and flew toward the huge ship that confronted them. They watched as a rocket was released from the aircraft and hurtled down toward the ship. The missile struck amidships, near the waterline, and tore a huge hole through the ship's side. Victor waited eagerly for an accompanying explosion; but there was none. Apparently, the rocket had been a dud.

Nonetheless, the big ship had suffered serious damage. The firing stopped completely. Victor and his friends jumped up and shouted for joy when seawater began rushing in through the gaping hole in the rusty hull and the object of their hatred began listing to port. Victor and his jubilant friends then saw bright flames spouting from a cargo hold. The spreading fire was soon followed by a thick column of black, oily smoke, which quickly engulfed a squad of men who stood on deck, directing a thin stream of water at the searing flames from the nozzle of a tattered hose.

The Sea Fury circled, then began another strafing run on the old ship that now lay dead in the water, wallowing helplessly on the suddenly unfriendly sea. The plane thundered directly toward the cluster of laboring men, machine guns spitting fire as it came, bringing mayhem or death to everyone in its path.

The plane zoomed over and past the blood-covered deck, its mission accomplished. The fire hose no longer worked—it had been riddled by dozens of bullets. But that did not really matter since there was no one left to hold it. All of the men lay upon the deck—the fortunate ones were dead! Others lay moaning in agony, or staring in mute terror, as unchecked flames continued a relentless march toward the bloody and battered crewmen who were unable to crawl away.

On *Houston's* bridge, Captain Luis Morse received an urgent message from the engine room.

"Captain, there's so much water coming in through this hole the pumps can't stay ahead of it! The engines are in danger of flooding out!"

"Give me all the power you can before they die," Captain Morse ordered. "We'll beach the ship, or try to get close enough for the Fifth Battalion to wade ashore"

But alas, *Houston's* stern was sinking so quickly that the ship was halted when she bottomed out more than seven hundred yards from the beach. With 130 green, barely trained troops aboard, Morse ordered the ship's two lifeboats to be lowered. Everything went smoothly with the first; but as the second was being lowered over the side, davits that held the lowering cables pulled out of the rotten wood. The heavy boat plummeted downward, killing several of the men who had jumped overboard earlier. Their comrades stood beside the rail of the sinking ship, looking helplessly down at the bodies of their friends as they bobbed up and down upon the oily sea. They knew they also must jump overboard, but many of them were too paralyzed by fear to move.

"Get off the ship! Slide down the lowering cables and make your way ashore!" Captain Morse shouted. "You must get moving before another air attack."

At that moment one of the frogman teams arrived in a rubber boat. Their language was not as gentle as that of Captain Morse.

"Let's go, you miserable bunch of cowards! This is your damned war, not ours! So you'd better start fighting it!"

On the opposite shore from Victor and his friends, the Deputy Commander of the Brigade, Erneido Oliva, quietly remarked to the Brigade Surgeon, Dr. Rene de la Mar, whose bullet-broken arm dangled at his side:

"Rene, if one miserable Sea Fury can do this much damage in so short a time, the whole expedition is doomed to failure."

The doctor grunted in pain and nodded.

"When *Houston* sinks, my entire field hospital, and most of our medical supplies, go with her!"

Moments later *Houston* lost her battle for existence and slipped beneath the muddy waters of the bay, taking with her vast quantities of equipment and munitions that had never been unloaded—materials that would be sorely needed in the days ahead.

When the survivors of the ill-fated Fifth Battalion finally reached shore, Oliva gathered them together and summed up the tactical situation.

"We must get off this lousy beach and move inland! I'll be damned if a handful of locals with one old machine gun are going to keep me pinned down. In five minutes we're going to move out, around the perimeter of the shore, and rout those people. I could care less if they run away or if we have to kill them; but they have to go, one way or the other. The Second Battalion will lead, and the Fifth will follow. Any questions? Okay! Get ready to move out."

The battalions moved out and made their way northward along the Zapata Peninsula on the western shore of the Bahia. As soon as the Second Battalion sighted the machine gun emplacement of Victor and his squad, they laid down a ragged, but murderous, barrage of rifle fire. It was so heavy that the machine gunners were forced to quit their position and flee back to the village. En route, three more of them were killed.

Oliva dispatched two men to skirt the village and watch for any sign of approaching Cuban troops or vehicles. He radioed Pepe San Roman, who was directing operations at Blue Beach and requested more troops, tanks (if possible), but most of all, air cover to support his isolated position. San Roman assured his deputy that help would be arriving soon. For now, all the Second and Fifth Battalions could do was sit tight, wait, and worry.

A short time later, on the northern edge of Caleton, they saw a flash of light, followed by an explosion. Minutes later, one of the scouts that Oliva had dispatched came racing back toward them and dropped down next to the commander.

"A transport, carrying about fifty soldiers, came down the road. As it passed the place where Jose and I were hiding we tossed a pair of white-phosphorus grenades into the back and blew it up; but several of the soldiers escaped."

"You and Jose did well, Miguel; but the soldiers will carry the word back to the nearest unit with a radio. We can expect a bigger force to hit us the next time. Pepe's reinforcements better get here before Castro's people. I'll send a squad from Second Battalion back with you. String them out along both sides of the road. Send Jose out to the northern point of the line with a landline telephone. Hightail it back here as soon as he reports the first sign of trouble."

Less than an hour later Miguel scurried back from his outpost with alarming information.

"Fifty or sixty trucks are moving slowly toward us. Each of them is carrying between ten and twenty soldiers. We can't stop a column that big without reinforcements!"

"Well, we can sure as hell try, Miguel. We're here to take back our homeland. To do that we have to win some battles. So this war might as well begin—right here, right now!"

He had barely finished the pronouncement when a pair of miracles suddenly happened. First, he heard a rumbling sound that came steadily closer until a tank Pepe San Roman had promised appeared. Then his radio crackled and a decidedly American voice, with a strong southern accent, announced that two of the Brigade's B-26's were inbound, prepared to provide air cover.

"B-26 leader, there's a large column of troops just north of Caleton. Try to stop them from getting to us. Hit them with everything you've got."

"No problem, Amigo. Consider it done!"

Moments later, the optimistic B-26 leader and his wingman thundered overhead and continued for a short distance toward the north before they attacked the Cuban column with bombs and rockets.

The battalions' expectant wait was quite short. Only a few seconds after the planes attacked, multiple explosions and sudden fires sent flames high into the air and demonstrated their effectiveness. An area north of Caleton was ringed by a burnt orange glow as ever more fuel tanks ignited and popped.

The B-26 leader radioed to Oliva.

"The trucks are kaput! So are most of the troops. The few that are left are high-tailing it back up the road. They're not a problem anymore, Amigo."

"Many thanks," Oliva responded. "You've pulled us out of a tight spot."

"Glad we could help. We'll stay in the area as long as we can."

The B-26 victory celebration and helpfulness were destined to be tragically brief. Two Cuban T-33 jets and a lone Sea Fury suddenly appeared and dived on the pair of nearly helpless old B-26s. The fight, if such a one-sided affair can be called a fight, was over almost before it began. The B-26s were shot down in full view of Oliva and his suddenly sad and silent troops.

The Cuban aircraft departed, but they were soon replaced by a band of vultures. It was now their turn to circle and dive, to swoop and fly, as nature's cycle continued to spin until a precarious balance of order was restored.

Things were no better for the men at Blue Beach. A mile off shore *Rio Escondido* lay wallowing in the choppy sea near the Bay of Pigs' eastern approaches.

Captain Tirado's orders were to hold his ship in place until Blue Beach had been secured; then he could move inshore and offload the communications van and the two hundred barrels of highly volatile aviation gasoline that were lashed to the main deck.

Tirado was livid with rage. The dangerous cargo had been scheduled for transfer to the beach under cover of darkness. Yet here he sat in a rusty old hulk that would probably sink if it were struck by a half empty bottle of tequila.

"Hell," he raged under his breath, "we might as well have a big red bullseye painted on the deck to provide a nice clear target."

The next moment a Cuban Sea Fury came winging in from his port quarter and fired a series of eight air-to-ground rockets. One rocket hit the main deck and ignited some of the aviation fuel. The pilot hadn't needed the bullseye, Tirado decided; he had done pretty well without one.

Tirado raced into the radio shack.

"*Rio Escondido* to any American support unit. Come in."

Ramrod Reynolds answered from *Blagar*. Tirado thought his voice sounded unusually strained.

*Minutes earlier, as Reynolds was firing at an incoming Sea Fury, his .50-caliber machine gun had broken loose from its mount, and toppled Reynolds over onto his back before he could stop firing. Had the guncrew been less alert, he would have been severely burned by the red-hot barrel, as he lay pinned to the deck.*

"This is *Blagar*, Tirado."

"This old bucket is ready to go up like a rocket. I'm giving an order to abandon ship," Tirado replied.

"Do it now, Amigo! I'll send as many small boats as I can to help you."

Captain Tirado and his crew quickly jumped into the sea and began bobbing up and down, supported by bright orange vests. Ten minutes later, three small boats appeared. They hauled the crewmen and their captain aboard, then sped away from *Rio Escondido.*

The ship was now ablaze; shooting flames soared a hundred feet and more into the bright morning sky. Ramrod's boats had arrived in the nick of time. They were less than a quarter of a mile away when three quick explosions, so closely spaced that they sounded like one, tore the old ship apart. The ensuing fireball and mushroom cloud rose high enough to be seen for dozens of miles around.

"My God," said one of the sailors aboard *Blagar*, "the Cubans must have dropped an atom bomb!"

"Not quite," Reynolds assured him. "That was the end of *Rio Escondido*. Unfortunately it was also the end of our communication network. All we have left are these little hand-held radios which don't seem to work very well when they get wet."

Reynolds didn't then realize that most of the radios still wouldn't work after they dried out. The invasion was still in its earliest stages, but communications were on their last legs. If a soldier were wounded, he now had no way of letting anyone know he needed help—and even if he found a way, all of the medical supplies had been destroyed. Fidel and his troops had certainly won round one!

At noon, Ramrod began receiving radio messages, routed to *Blagar* from Washington, warning him that loyal Castro forces were closing in on his position.

"Get out of there, at once!" headquarters advised. "Take the ships to sea. Save what you can and go, before they close in."

"Close in hell," Ramrod shouted, letting fly with another volley of automatic weapon fire at the circling Cuban fighter planes. "Those explosions you hear aren't being caused by a July Fourth celebration.

"San Roman and his men will run out of ammo by the end of the day. They won't be able to defend themselves unless we offload the reserve ammo that's still aboard *Atlantico* and *Caribe*. We can't just turn tail and desert them!"

"Captain Reynolds," boomed an ominous voice from the radio, "you are ordered to take every vessel that is still afloat, and retreat beyond the twelve-mile limit—get the ships into international waters. If you stay where you are, everything will be sunk. You can't do much to help San Roman from the bottom of the ocean. Out there, the Navy can provide cover and security. Offload the ships and transfer their cargoes to the LCUs. Send them back tonight under cover of darkness. Now, get the hell out of there!"

"Okay," Ramrod hollered back, relinquishing his weapon to an eager crewmember. He switched the radio to the combat channel and told Pepe they were pulling out. He wished he could share the new agenda with his friend, but could not because the Cubans were almost certainly monitoring the open channels.

"Don't leave us high and dry," Pepe admonished.

"We won't, Amigo, I promise!"

He radioed Commodore Crutchfield aboard *Eaton.*

"Heads up! We're coming out."

It was a slow, lumbering retreat, with the clumsy LCUs leading and the ammunition ships, *Caribe* and *Atlantico*, tucked safely in behind them. Since they had the greatest firepower, *Barbara J.* and *Blagar* brought up the rear.

They were able to travel nearly five miles before the first attack came. A Cuban A-26 appeared about a mile and a half away, flying near the surface of the sea; it headed directly toward *Blagar.*

As the Cuban plane closed to within a half mile, Ramrod began firing tracer bullets at it. They began striking the plane at about two thousand yards.

"All ships! Open fire!" he shouted into his radio!

It sounded like thunder as every automatic weapon in the fleet opened up. The plane began wobbling as hundreds of rounds smashed into it, and the Cuban pilot began losing control. The plane kept coming. A thin stream of gasoline vapor trailed behind it.

For a moment Ramrod thought the pilot intended to crash into *Blagar;* but less than a hundred yards from the side of the ship, the plane suddenly erupted into a bright red fireball, as its gas tanks and unfired rockets ignited. The remains of the plane pancaked onto the sea and cartwheeled toward *Blagar*. A small part of one blazing wing actually landed on the deck of the ship and had to be extinguished by the crew.

As they neared the twelve-mile limit they were attacked again. They were unsuccessful in their attempts to destroy the Cuban plane, but did succeed in driving the attacker away after he fired a pair of ill-aimed rockets that did no damage.

*Blagar's* Captain Swen Ryberg was visibly shaken. As two ships appeared on the horizon, he rushed up to Ramrod.

"Those must be our cover ships. Let's radio a request to lay to under their lee. If they don't protect us, the Cubans will sink us for sure!"

The ships were identified as *Eaton and Murray*.

"Commodore Crutchfield," Ryberg radioed, "we're now outside the twelve-mile limit. We request your protection."

Ramrod and Ryberg were stunned by Crutchfield's reply.

"My heart is with you; but I have orders not to engage."

"Do you think those damned cowards in Washington will allow him to pick up survivors when we sink?" Ryberg asked Ramrod.

"We've done pretty well by ourselves so far, we'll just have to keep going; but we have another, even bigger problem. *Caribe* and *Atlantico* took off during that last air raid, and now they're nowhere to be seen."

"Let's check them on radar," Ryberg suggested.

Radar quickly revealed the whereabouts of the fleeing ships. It also verified the fact that they were getting farther away every second. The two ships carried all of the Brigade's ammunition. If they disappeared, every possibility for victory would disappear with them.

In the air, and miles inland from the beach, things were no better; but the aircrews and airborne troops were blissfully unaware of the rapidly deteriorating situation.

At dawn, the first of six C-46's that were scheduled to fly the Brigade's 177 paratroopers to drop zones several miles northeast of the invasion beaches spotted three large ships directly ahead of them, about seventy-five miles offshore.

"See if you can identify the ships," the pilot, Coco Ramos, yelled to his co-pilot over the thunder of the C-46's engines.

"It's an American carrier and a pair of destroyers. They're heading for the beach," responded Chico Mendez.

"Hooray!" Coco cheered. "With that kind of help we can't lose. Take over, Chico. I'm going back to share the good news with our passengers."

When he told the thirty paratroopers about the presence of the American squadron, there were shouts of joy. They could hardly wait to jump.

Twenty minutes later, they flew over the Brigade ships that were anchored near Blue Beach. During the final ten miles of the flight to the drop zone on San Blas Road, Coco descended to eight hundred feet. As they approached the road, Coco and Chico saw three armed soldiers in a Cuban jeep. The Cubans opened fire on the plane, and succeeded in hitting it several times. But good luck prevailed—only minor damage and no injuries. Coco decided to fly beyond the drop zone far enough to assure a safe landing for the paratroopers. A mile farther on, he pushed the green jump light, and the men dove out of the open door at two-second intervals. Two minutes later they were all on the ground and ready to repel any enemy attack, other than one of mammoth proportions.

As soon as the paratroopers were safely on the ground, the two pilots circled their C-46 back toward the beach. They had orders to fly over the airstrip at Giron to make sure it was still in usable condition. Just as they reached the airfield, a lone A-26 came diving out of a distant cloudbank toward them.

"Hey," Chico yelled, "that's one of our own fighters."

Suddenly, the wings of the approaching aircraft blossomed with dozens of bright orange, flashing dots of light.

"If he's our guy, he's either stupid or badly confused, because he's trying to shoot us down."

"I don't see how we can stop him, Coco. That A-26 is a hell of a lot more maneuverable than we are and a hundred miles an hour faster."

"Since we can't outmaneuver him or outrun him, we'll have to outsmart him."

Coco throttled the lumbering C-46 all the way back, applied full flaps, dropped the landing gear, and pointed the plane's nose straight up. The effects were startling and immediate! Deprived of speed and airworthiness, the old C-46 stalled and plummeted earthward while Coco fought to regain a measure of control. A bare fifty feet from disaster he was able to level off and streak toward the sea where the guns of the fleet could protect them from prowling Cuban fighters.

Then, a short distance above and behind them, the Cuban hunter found another of the C-46s. But this pilot did not have Coco's skill or good fortune. The attacker's bullets quickly found their mark, and the plane exploded. It looked like an enormous fireworks display as millions of tiny pieces went cartwheeling into space.

"Madre de Dios," Chico said sadly, "I thought we were goners, too. I feel pretty stupid, Coco! While you were saving our lives, all I could do was sit here like a dummy and wet my pants."

"If you think you're the only scared pilot aboard this kite, you're crazy. The puddle I'm sitting in isn't spilled coffee."

It was a long, wet, and uncomfortable flight back to their base at Puerto Cabezas; but their discomfort went unnoticed. They had been granted a wonderful blessing. They would live for at least one more day.

Other members of the Brigade's support force were not as lucky. At the beaches, as well as inland, the old A-26s were little more than slow-moving targets for the Cuban T-33 jets and Sea Furies. A few A-26s, and almost all of the far slower and more vulnerable C-46s, crashed onto the sand or into the swamp. Some managed to avoid the onslaught. They headed south, away from the devastating curtain of deadly gunfire. The sea seemed much safer than the land. A few of the pilots did find safety—but many others only found death.

"May Day! May Day! We're hit and losing fuel!" radioed one plane.

"We're losing altitude. We're going to ditch," called another

Radio calls for help filled the air, but no help would ever arrive. Frustrated *Essex* pilots, held in check by presidential orders, sat sadly in the carrier's ready room, listening to the radio as it blared a blow by blow account of terror and woe. The Brigade's fragile aircraft fell, one by one, into the sea and sank beneath the waves, never to be seen again. Aboard *Essex*, frustration and anger swelled to a fever pitch.

Since the Brigade flights were becoming suicide missions, many former hot shot fighter pilots began to lose enthusiasm. A sudden rash of malingering swept the command. When a few planes finally did take off, physical ailments, mechanical difficulties, and airworthiness problems caused most of the missions to be aborted close to their origination points.

In an effort to "put iron in the bellies" of the pilots, Dick Bissell finally authorized a pair of CIA pilots to lead a tiny squadron of six fighters on a search and destroy mission.

"Smith and Jones" led this force over Blue Beach and spotted a column of reinforced Cuban infantry heading for the invasion site. The fearless fliers fell upon their enemies with napalm, rockets, and fragmentation bombs. Ten minutes later they had inflicted two thousand casualties and knocked out half a dozen tanks. As they turned to run for home, Smith called Jones.

"A good strike, buddy. We really clobbered them!"

"Yeah," came a reply, "we were lucky! This whole damned operation is doomed unless we get some help from *Essex*, and I don't mean sometime next week! This is a hell of a way to fight a war. The fuel tanks leak! Guns won't shoot! And these worthless flying buckets can barely stay in the air! Somebody better do something before they have to clean up what's left of us with a sponge or a blotter!"

Meanwhile, aboard *Essex*, a curious two-part message was received. The Blue Blasters would now be permitted to assist the remaining Brigade planes; but the AD4 fighters would not be permitted to leave the deck until all the US identification and the squadron insignias had been painted over.

Since no spray paint was available, and there were very few paint brushes aboard, the mystified crew began splashing dull gray primer paint on every sleek, silver-gray fighter plane.

From every corner of the ship, crewmembers that were not otherwise occupied grabbed mops and began flailing away. Two hours later the once noble planes looked like a bunch of tawdry patchwork quilts; but they were now ready to help the Brigade's struggling fliers. However, there was a rub! The second half of the message limited the Blue Blasters to frightening off Cuban aircraft. There would be no gunfire or rockets! Such conduct might precipitate a serious international incident; therefore, it had to be avoided at all costs. But those costs were high—and they would be paid with human lives!

# *INVASION DAY IN THE CUBAN CAMP*

Fidel Castro was in a vile mood. At 0100 he had been awakened and informed about the invasion at Giron. His first act had been to phone one of the few men he almost trusted—Ramon Jose Fernandez, the man in charge of Cuba's military training program. Fernandez was only slightly surprised when he was awakened at 0115 by an orderly. Since the state of training was high on El Comandante's priority list, Castro often called him but not at this hour of the night.

Since there was no phone in Fernandez's Spartan quarters, he rushed down to his first floor office.

"This is Fernandez, Comandante," said the sleepy-voiced Fernandez.

"They're here!"

"Who's here, Comandante?"

"Who do you think? The rebels! They're landing at several locations around the perimeter of the Zapata swamp."

"That's one of the most isolated places on the island," Fernandez alertly replied.

"Isolation is good for them and bad for us. If they can gain a foothold, they will announce the formation of a provisional government. Since they landed in a remote area, where there are very few roads, it will be very difficult to ferret them out. Nonetheless, it has to be done and done quickly. Our planes will hit them at dawn and our ground forces as soon after that as possible. I want you to leave at once. Go down there and organize a counterattack. I'll call the Cadet School at Matanzas and tell them to mobilize. They're sixty-five miles from you, so they can be ready to go by the time you arrive. They'll be your initial strike force. Do whatever is necessary to prevent the rebels from establishing a beachhead. I'll get more army and militia units down there as soon as I can. Get in your car and go! I will remember the loyal people and their successes for a long time. I will also remember foolish people and their failures! Conduct yourself accordingly, Ramon!"

The phone clicked as the line went dead.

The thirty-seven-year-old Fernandez, trained as an artillery officer by the US Army, was ecstatic. Today would be a Day of Atonement. He hadn't been with Fidel and the others in the Sierra Maestras. Fernandez felt that his absence there was the only blemish on an otherwise perfect record.

He would have been there if the choice had been his. But during the time that Castro was building a revolutionary army in the mountains, he was serving a two-year sentence, as a political prisoner, on the Isle of Pines—convicted of treason for conspiring against the former Cuban dictator, Fulgencio Batista. The puerco! His absence was decidedly involuntary! Nonetheless, he yearned to erase that single black mark.

Fernandez alerted his staff and ten minutes later they left for Matanzas.

A little over an hour later they arrived at the Cadet School. The instructors and staff had used their time well. The cadets were ready, and a curious collection of large and small, new and old vehicles had been commandeered to transport the "troops."

Fidel called five minutes after they arrived.

"Ramon, why haven't you left yet?"

"We'll be ready soon. First I must reorganize and appoint unit commanders. Remember, por favor, that this is a training school, not a combat command."

The impatient, irate reply made Castro's position perfectly clear.

"You better turn it into a combat command pretty fast or you won't have a command of any kind! Now get moving!"

Castro's next phone call went to an airfield at San Antonio, twenty miles from Havana. Enrique Carreras, who had been the "ready pilot" since midnight, answered the phone in the control tower. The voice at the other end of the line was clear and unmistakable. When Fidel Castro called at 0400 it meant trouble!

"Who is this?" Castro's impatient voice demanded.

"This is Captain Carreras, Comandante."

"Oh! Good! I remember meeting you last week when I was there."

"What are your orders, Comandante?"

"Rebel invaders are landing at Playa Giron. But don't worry about them. Concentrate on their ships. Sink them before they can get away. If you can destroy them before they have time to unload, so much the better; but whatever you do, don't let the ships escape. When ships sink, the cargoes go with them. The end of their ships means the end of their supplies. Then we can annihilate the poor fools who think they can beat us."

"Have no fear, Comandante. We will win!"

"We must win, Carreras! Since you're my best pilot, you must show others the way. Now, go out and sink the ships!"

*Castro was right about Carreras. If not Cuba's best pilot, he was certainly the most experienced. Although he had never flown in combat, he was a veteran of the US Air Force; a graduate of the Air College, at Montgomery, Alabama; and the first Latino to fly at supersonic speed. But his Air Force experience at various air bases was not a pleasant memory. In fact, the opposite was true. He nurtured a healthy dislike for Americans in general and Air Force pilots in particular. They were hopeless egotists. All of them did their best to treat him and every other Cuban like idiots.*

Carreras sat at his desk and considered his options. Here, at San Antonio Airfield, a variety of aircraft were available. He considered T-33 jets. They were fast and maneuverable. But Castro was concerned about invasion ships, and jets were not best for sinking ships. Other pilots in the squadron could bask in the glory of flying T-33's and shooting down rebel planes. He and his wingman would fly Sea Furies. They were old and slow, but they could handle much bigger payloads of bombs.

He sent his messenger to wake the other pilots. Takeoffs would begin a half-hour before dawn and there was much to do before then.

The first faint glow of dawn had not yet begun to light the eastern skies when Carreras led a dash from the control center to the waiting planes. Scrambling into his Sea Fury, he taxied into position, facing into the wind. Moments later, Sea Fury 541 left the ground and reached for the sky. In his lurching cockpit, Carreras grinned as he watched a string of T-33s, Sea Furies, and A-26s leave the runway and follow in his wake. He turned away, his mind's eye picturing blazing fires aboard sinking ships, enemy aircraft plummeting into oblivion, and invaders perishing in the deadly swamps that surrounded the Bay of Pigs.

Many Cuban pilots did not share Carreras' dreams. As he took off in a T-33 jet, Rafael del Pino harbored no visions of enemy planes blowing up. Instead, he hunched forward in the cockpit, hoping and praying that his own plane would not blow up.

In the first place, he didn't hate Americans; in fact, he liked and admired many of them. He had attended boarding school in Knoxville, Tennessee, in 1954, and those folks had treated him as if he were a family member. He didn't really believe America was an aggressor; but orders were orders. They had to be obeyed. Besides, he didn't want to let Enrique Carreras down! 'Rique was his commander, his teacher, and his role model. But 'Rique had far more faith in these obsolete planes than he himself did. Most of the time the automatic starters on the British Sea Furies didn't work. Mechanics had to start the engines with pull-ropes, just as he did at home with his lawnmower. God help you if your motor died during a flight. You couldn't climb out and try restarting the damned thing with a stupid piece of rope. If you were lucky you might have enough time to pick a good place to crash! That was about it!

The T-33s weren't any better! Their burners were so worn out that the jet engines often overheated and flamed out. If that happened on takeoff, your plane crashed. Last month, 701, the T-33 he was flying, had crashed. Luckily he walked away. He had been assigned to 713; but 713 was quickly grounded because it lacked airworthiness. Mechanics had scavenged enough parts from 701 to repair 713. And, he had to admit, it had flown for ten days before it flamed out on takeoff and crashed.

For today's mission, against a probably superior force, he was flying 711. He squinted through the oily, bug-covered windshield and prayed that 711 wouldn't crash. In addition to praying, he rooted for the T-33's success by crossing his fingers. You could never say enough prayers or have enough luck when you were piloting one of these flying coffins. He laughed to relieve his tension and thought, "I can't cross my legs while I fly; I wonder if crossing my eyes might help."

Suddenly he tensed. Every thought about personal danger vanished. A short distance ahead and slightly below, Rafael spotted an enemy plane. He remembered Rique's oft-repeated advice, "Close in before you shoot!" He flew so close to the other plane that it filled his entire gunsight. Only then did he depress his firing button.

One moment the enemy plane was there, the next instant it was gone. Pieces of the exploding aircraft hit his T-33 before they fell into the bay. Suddenly an icy chill enveloped him. He had forgotten to jettison his rockets before he attacked. If a piece of the flying debris had struck one of his rockets his dead body would be floating in the sea with the pilot he had shot down.

Recovering his composure, he absorbed a fact that every warrior must know if he hopes to survive. War is not a game. War is a deadly, serious business!

Ramon Fernandez and the troops from the Cadet School of Matanzas had finally arrived at the Jovellanos military base, which was located several miles north of the swamps. As they pulled into the courtyard, the base commander beckoned Fernandez from the doorway of his headquarters and shouted:

"El Comandante is on the telephone! He wishes to speak with you!"

Fidel Castro's voice was crisp with agitation.

"Take your force down to the Central Australia Sugar Mill, pronto! I'll contact you there." The line went dead.

"Good news?" asked the local commander.

"Yes," Fernandez told him, "the rebels have stuck their necks in a noose. I'm on my way to tighten the rope and hang them all."

Enrique Carreras had timed his flight perfectly. He reached the Bay of Pigs just as dawn began to streak the eastern skies. Flying a mile above the sea, he was astonished by the myriad of activity he saw below.

Tiny shadows were darting in toward the shore. No bigger than water bugs at this altitude, Carreras recognized them as landing craft. As the daylight grew stronger, he saw a cluster of large ships lying offshore. One vessel that appeared to be a warship was steaming toward the upper end of the Bay. A smaller ship was following a few hundred yards behind. These people are serious, he thought in a moment of dismay. How can we defeat this force with a few rickety planes and a bunch of inexperienced pilots?

He turned back toward the two vessels in the Bay, suddenly aware that the ships were firing at him. He also realized that the two heavy bombs slung under his wings had reduced his airspeed to the point of making him a sitting duck. If he didn't drop both bombs pretty soon, the rebels would make him a dead duck!

He angled in toward the ship farthest up the Bay (*Houston*) and dropped both bombs. Because of a defective bombsight he failed to hit the ship; but he didn't miss by very much. He began a climbing turn as soon as he passed over *Houston,* then circled back around for a second run. When he was lined up on the vessel's stern he fired his eight rockets. As he swept over the ship he saw fuel oil gushing from her tanks.

Carreras looped around for a third run and strafed the ship with machinegun fire until his ammunition ran out. His fuel was now so perilously low that he was forced to fly directly to his base at San Antonio.

Behind him, the water around the ship was subtly changing from pale aqua to a shabby shade of rusty black as it was invaded by leaking oil tinged with blood.

Even at this stage of the invasion, Castro was not convinced that the landings at Giron and Playa Larga were the major assaults. He sat and stared at a large-scale map of Cuba and remembered Adolf Hitler's similar dilemma on June 6, 1944, as Allied landing forces stormed the beaches at Normandy.

Hitler had reasoned that the enemy would be foolish to invade Normandy. He was certain that the real assault would come at the Pas de Calais; but Hitler had been wrong. Castro was fairly confident that the rebel landings in an area as inhospitable as the Zapata Swamp were only feints to draw his troops away from the real objective; but, he pondered, where would it be?

There were a hundred better, easier places to come ashore. Many of them were quite near mountains where he, himself, had gained power and enlarged his army while he conducted hit and run raids.

An hour later his telephone rang. It was the manager of the sugar mill at Jaguey Grande.

"We estimate about 150 rebel paratroopers have landed at the northern edge of the swamp, Comandante."

Growing more confident that the Zapata Swamp really was the main invasion site, Castro replied,

"Fernandez and the Matanzas cadets are on their way there. I want them to attack those paratroopers and stop them before they secure a position. Have Fernandez call me as soon as he arrives. He must get the cadets into action at once!"

Shortly after 0800 Fernandez called.

"We're at the sugar mill, Comandante."

"Send out patrols! Find those paratroopers! These landings began seven hours ago, and all we've been able to do so far is inflict a couple of bee stings with our air force. We need to teach these rebels a lesson they'll not soon forget. Hurt them, Fernandez! Make them bleed."

Enrique Carreras was as eager for blood as El Comandante. He had just arrived at the Bay of Pigs for his second mission of the day. He flew directly toward the ship he had attacked earlier and saw the vessel lying dead in the water with her stern awash.

He turned back toward a second ship that had been trailing behind (*Rio Escondido).* As he neared it, a pair of enemy B-26s attacked him. His Sea Fury's engine whined as it was hit by at least one cannon shell. He began evasive tactics and seconds later was in a position to fire a short burst from his own guns into the trailing B-26. It spouted smoke and dove toward the sea. The other plane darted toward *Rio Escondido,* seeking the protection of the ship's guns.

Carreras circled around, headed back toward the ship, and fired all eight of his rockets in one gigantic burst. He could scarcely believe the instant transformation that he witnessed.

Captain Tirado of *Rio Escondido* had been correct with his forecast. When his old, frail ship was hit it "had exploded just like a skyrocket."

With his protesting engine emitting an ever-increasing set of ominous sounds, the elated Carreras headed back toward San Antonio—trailing a cloud of black smoke behind him.

Back in the village of Covadonga, dozens of villagers who were hastily fleeing from their homes were confronted by a small group of farmers that were bringing produce to market.

"What's going on here?" asked a farmer named Diego, who had been one of Fidel's earliest recruits.

"Banditos are coming after us," a village woman shouted back over her shoulder, as she stumbled along, herding her brood of small children. "Run for your lives! Banditos are coming down from the sky."

"That makes no sense!" Diego told his friends. "Banditos come in from the mountains, not out of the sky! Paratroopers come from the sky. Where else do they come from? From America!" he declared, providing his own answer. "If we have to stop the whole American army, we're going to need some help. Fan out. Collar every militiaman we can find!"

Ten minutes later the farmers returned to the plaza with a group of frightened, reluctant militia members. Three of them carried ancient weapons; but one man cradled a bazooka. An ideal anti-tank weapon. Diego grabbed the bazooka and headed toward the San Blas road, shouting for his hastily recruited force to form up and march behind him. If invaders were headed for Covadonga, they would have to come through San Blas.

Twenty minutes later, a mile and a half from Covadonga, as they neared a sharp curve in the road, they heard the sound of slow-moving vehicles coming toward them.

"Get down behind the low wall over there," directed Diego. "We'll ambush these invaders. You three, with the muskets, don't fire until I do. When you do fire, pour it into them! We can't let anybody escape. We can't let them warn anyone else. And most of all, we need to capture their weapons. We can't even win a little war with what we've got to fight with now."

Agonizing minutes passed before two large trucks loaded with men came into view and moved slowly toward the wall that shielded Diego and his helpers. The lead truck was only fifty yards away when Diego jumped on top of the wall and fired the bazooka. The rocket landed short, but bounced into the front of the vehicle, where it caused tremendous damage.

Diego and his men were badly outnumbered and out-gunned, but surprise was on their side. A ten-minute firefight ended when the invaders abandoned their trucks and fled up the road to safety, leaving behind an arsenal of submachine guns, rifles, and pistols, as well as cases of ammunition, and an assortment of concentrated food rations bearing American military markings. The truck floors, rolled-up parachutes, and the ground around the vehicles were all covered with blood. The ambush had been a brilliantly executed stroke of success.

"If the rebels can be beaten this easily," Diego assured his friends, "this war will be over before it even gets started."

"What if Americans come to help the rebels?" wondered one of the others.

"It would still be a short war, amigo; but none of us would be around at the end."

They unloaded the wrecked trucks and began walking back toward Covadonga. In the mind of every man was the same question. Where were the Americans? Would they try to help the rebels?

The American pilots aboard *Essex* were eager to help the Brigade. Four of the Blue Blaster Squadron's *Skyhawks* were orbiting over the Bay of Pigs at that very moment. However, there were many problems connected with their flight. The pilots had been ordered to avoid contact with Cuban planes. They had also been ordered not to attack ground targets. And they had been forbidden to fly below 20,000 feet. From a height of four miles, American pilots, flying formidable, unmarked, mop-painted, million-dollar planes, watched helplessly as the situation at the beaches deteriorated. The *Skyhawks* were simply invisible, wraith-like presences. They provided neither aid to their friends, nor a threat to their enemies.

Because of the presidential order, the four lethal war birds' only accomplishment was providing ringside seats for their pilots to witness one of America's most colossal disasters.

At 1000, Fernandez called Fidel from Central Australia.

"The Matanzas Cadet Battalion has arrived, Comandante. The 225th Militia is also here."

"Good! Start the Cadets toward the Bahia at once. Hold the Militia in reserve, for now."

"The Militiamen are willing enough, Comandante; but they have only a few old Czech rifles and very little ammunition."

"Duque is on his way to Covadonga with the 117th Militia, and enough weapons to supply everybody. If the 225th moves south, they'll have plenty of weapons. Get the Cadets going!"

Duque was jubilant when his column arrived in Covadonga at noon. The Russians had shipped large numbers of portable heavy weapons to Cuba, and he had brought many of them along—122-millimeter howitzers, 137-millimeter antiaircraft guns, and 185-millimeter cannons were strung out for a mile along the road. However, Duque's jubilation was brief. Very few of the guncrew members seemed to know anything about the shiny new weapons. They looked a lot more like high school kids getting ready for the first fiesta of the season than gunners.

He decided to leave half of his troops, and most of the guns, in Covadonga, and press on toward Giron with the remaining men and the mortars.

Barely a mile along the San Blas Road they were attacked by an aircraft that bore the Cuban insignia. Huddled in a protective ditch, Duque cursed the pilot's stupidity as well as the lack of a serviceable radio to either call off the attack or to warn the rest of his battalion back in Covadonga.

Fortunately, the errant pilot inflicted very little damage before he withdrew. Only one of the trucks was destroyed, but three of its occupants were killed.

After an hour delay, the column continued toward San Blas.

Minutes later, and a mile down the road, the lead truck was suddenly ambushed as it approached a newly-fortified rebel outpost. Duque halted the column and ordered two mortar squads forward to lob shells into the enemy position.

The battle raged throughout the balance of the afternoon. At one point, the mortarmen ran out of shells, and a jeep was sent to Covadonga for more.

After a delay of more than three hours, they finally expelled the rebels, and the column was able to move forward once again.

When they finally reached the outskirts of San Blas at dusk, they were attacked for a third time. It did not take Duque long to realize that this enemy position was much stronger than the two others had been. These rebels were well dug in, had tanks to re-inforce them, and were defending an extremely narrow roadway that was bordered on both sides by virtually impenetrable swamps.

Before he could pressure the rebels, he would need the rest of his troops and the equipment he had left behind at Covadonga. He could then move them into position under a cover of darkness while his badly battered men that had borne the brunt of the rebel attacks rested and licked their wounds. Things had to be better tomorrow, he decided. They sure as hell couldn't get much worse.

About the same time as the foolish Cuban pilot was attacking Duque's column, Ramon Fernandez and his taskforce reached their first objective. He telephoned Castro.

"We've taken Palpite, Comandante. There was no resistance."

"The rebels are collapsing, just as I suspected they would. We've all but won. We're sinking their ships, destroying their planes, and killing the fools on the beaches. It's almost over. Go down to Playa Larga right away. Shoot anyone who resists, and round up the rest of those fools. Duque will be phoning at any minute from Giron to report his success. Celebration time is getting close."

But Duque wasn't celebrating. He was thinking about the impending battle and wondering how many more men would die before he was able to storm his way past San Blas and fight the final battle along the shore of Giron or in the surrounding swamps. He hoped Castro would be patient.

By 2200, it was clear to Castro that if Playa Larga was to be taken any time soon, he needed to go down there and take command personally. He left Point One, his military headquarters in suburban Havana, and drove southeastward. Since he was familiar with the area, he was able to guide his driver along barely passable, seldom-traveled, mud-sodden roads that ran through the vast Zapata Swamps, until he reached a position less than a mile west of Playa Larga.

"I've ordered a squadron of tanks to meet us here," he told an aide who sat huddled in the back of the jeep beside a guard who crouched over a floor-mounted heavy machine gun

"As soon as the tanks arrive, we'll lead them along the back roads and hit Playa Larga from the rear. Then we can go on to Giron and finish off the rebels who are pinned down there."

The impatient Castro sprang out of the jeep and began pacing back and forth on the spongy road. His muddy boots made a loud sucking noise each time he extracted them from the clutching, sticky goo.

An hour passed, but the tanks had still not arrived. Fidel was furious. Lieutenant Reyes, his aide, called out to him.

"A radio message from Point One, Comandante. Colonel Vargas."

Castro rushed back to the jeep and seized the microphone.

"Go ahead, Vargas!"

"Comandante, another rebel landing force is reported at the Bahia Honda, off the north coast of Pinar del Rio Province. They can easily march into Havana from there, if that is their intent."

"Are you sure about this? Do you have confirmation?"

"Yes, Comandante. There is no doubt. The landing craft are approaching the beach as we speak. The last report says contact has been established between the rebels and our local militia."

"Very well. I'll leave Reyes here with a detailed map of the area. He can stay with the second jeep, and lead the tanks into Playa Larga when they arrive. I'll start back at once. I'll be at Point One by dawn. We have the rebels bottled up here, but if another rebel force has arrived from Miami we must repel it. Keep me informed. My radio may only work intermittently— I'll be going through dense portions of the swamp, but keep trying until you contact me if there is anything new!"

Castro drew a crude map of the area, as well as detailed eight-point instructions for Major Augusto Sanchez, the tank battalion commander, and handed them to Reyes.

"It looks like the main battle will take place near Havana after all, Reyes. It seems strange to me, since I was just about convinced that this local effort was the rebels' major thrust. It still might be! Convey to the commander of the tank battalion the urgency of striking at the rebels hard and fast. He is to capture Playa Larga, pronto. I will accept no delays and no excuses!"

Castro arrived at Point One a few minutes after sunrise and received some bad news. His tanks were bogged down in the swamps and could not attack the rebels. He was also informed that the landing force at Bahia Honda had only been a feint. There was no landing force. Not a single rebel had come ashore.

The personnel at Bahia Honda who issued the report could not be blamed for falling for the CIA's elaborate ruse.

Eight powerful, forty to fifty-foot long boats, each towing several smaller vessels, had sailed from the Florida Keys to a position a few miles off the Pinar del Rio coast. The boats had been loaded with electronic equipment, high-intensity lights, and a wide variety of sound and pyrotechnic devices.

The CIA personnel who manned the flotilla did a great job. Although no boat or man came within five miles of the beach, they convinced onlookers that the biggest invasion force in history was ready to pounce on them, sweep aside resistance, and drive overland to Havana. Recordings of battle sounds, played on loudspeakers, convinced the retreating guards that a furious fight was taking place at the water's edge, between groups of mythical invaders and non-existent defenders. At dawn, all the lights went out, the recordings were turned off, boats reversed course, and the phantom invasion force simply disappeared.

At 0600 Duque's force was still bottled up a quarter mile from San Blas. During the night his patience had dwindled while his resolve intensified. He knew the village of San Blas quite well. It consisted of twenty houses and a few assorted huts and sheds. He decided to level the town in order to drive the rebels out. He ordered his two cannons and some smaller mobile weapons forward and positioned them on the spongy ground along both sides of the narrow roadway. Then Duque issued a drastic order.

"Reduce San Blas to rubble!"

For the next two hours, the guns fired nonstop. The gunners were hip-deep in shell-casings, and the cannons had sunk into the soft ground when Duque finally gave the cease fire order.

At 0800, he ordered his troops to move in and occupy the village. His orders had been carried out to the letter. The village was a rubble. Almost nothing was left other than dust and splinters. One of the few exceptions was the booby trap that killed two of his men.

Ten minutes later, as Duque sat in his jeep writing a report about the destruction of San Blas, a courier arrived with a message from Ramon Fernandez.

"I've taken Playa Larga. I'm now reorganizing my troops. You are ordered to stay where you are. DO NOT, I repeat, DO NOT, attempt to capture San Blas!"

"Is there any reply?" the courier asked.

"Yes. Tell Fernandez that San Blas no longer exists; but we have captured the place where it used to be."

The messenger left, and Duque slumped in the seat of the jeep, convinced that he was a player in a maelstrom of chaos.

"If we're going to win this fight, the rebels will have to be crazier and even more disorganized than we are," he told his driver, "and I'm not sure that's possible."

At Playa Larga, Ramon Fernandez continued to receive messages from Fidel Castro.

*1000 Advance on Giron! Immediately!*

*1200 Stop wasting time! Finish off the rebels!*

*1600 You must take Giron by 6 P.M. Close the trap!*

But at 1800 Fernandez and his battalions were still more than twenty miles from Giron.

A string of five more couriers arrived. Each of them carried a message designed to goad Fernandez.

1. *The time is psychologically right to strike the rebels with a ferocious blow.*
2. *The rebels are completely surrounded.*
3. *Another force is approaching Giron from the east; hurry up or they'll be there before you are.*
4. *Now is the moment—while they are helpless!*
5. *Muerte al invasores (Death to the invaders).*

Fidel must be dreaming, Fernandez decided. If the rebels are helpless, who is killing my troops? Who is making us pay for every inch of this roadway? Someone should tell these poor devils that they're surrounded and helpless. They don't seem to understand how hopeless their situation is.

Despite Castro's demands and his own eagerness to strike a ferocious blow, Giron was still twenty miles away, and every mile of road was being defended by determined rebels. Those twenty miles would soon be coated with the blood of bloating corpses. Fernandez could reluctantly look forward to another long and deadly night in the God-forsaken swamp.

At midnight it occurred to Felix Duque that he and his men were in a place they should not be. If Fernandez's column of tanks came along the road and saw troops in San Blas, they were liable to assume a rebel force had captured the village, and open fire.

He jumped into his jeep with his driver, and a well-armed militiaman as a guard, then sped down the road in an effort to intercept the armored force. Minutes later, as they rounded a sharp bend, they spotted a lead tank. Duque's driver blinked his headlights to alert the tank crew, then approached at a snail's pace. Suddenly, they were all bathed in the bright glow of a searchlight and confronted by a group of men in camouflage uniforms. They had run directly into a rebel tank column.

"Who are you people, and what are you doing here?" demanded one of the rebel officers as soon as Duque and his militiamen were disarmed.

"My name is Duque. And I think I've made a big mistake."

"What are you doing here?" the rebel officer asked again.

"I'm an agricultural consultant. I'm on my way back to the village of Covadonga."

"If you're a civilian, why are you riding around in a Cuban Militia jeep?"

"As I was driving along, a bomb landed close to my car. I lost control and wound up in the ditch. I'm lucky to be alive! I'd just crawled back onto the roadway when these men came along in their jeep and offered me a ride."

The rebel officer glared at the driver.

"Is that what happened? Did you pick this man up after his car went off the road?"

The driver looked unsteadily at the questioner and mutely nodded his head affirmatively.

"I don't believe you or him." He turned to a huge, burly man who stood on the fringe of the small group. "Sanchez, take these three innocents into Giron! Turn them over to our people at G-2. Let's see if the Intelligence Section buys their crazy story."

Felix Duque and his men were herded into the back seat of a late model convertible and driven swiftly back to Giron. Outside a small building the car slid to a halt. They were hauled out and pushed toward the door, over which hung a small, crudely lettered cardboard sign.

**G-2 HEADQUARTERS**

The three were separated and questioned in different rooms. Pepe San Roman and Manuel Artime interrogated Duque an hour later; but he steadfastly stuck to his story about the car accident.

Minutes after the two rebel leaders left, Duque heard jets thunder overhead and walked out to the front of the building. On the street and on the beach there was absolute jubilation. One of his guards told Duque that the planes were bringing in the reinforcements and supplies they had been expecting.

The jets disappeared as quickly as they had appeared. Less than an hour later, doom and gloom descended on the rebels in Giron like a thick blanket. Then Cuban planes arrived and began strafing the vehicles on the beach and the boats in the water. Everyone ran for cover. Madre de Dios, thought a fearful Duque, I've got to get out of here before I'm killed by friendly fire.

Once again, he headed toward the front of the building. But now no guards were in sight. He moved stealthily around the corner of the building and eased into the thick swamp behind Giron. He spotted a Cuban militia vehicle a short time later, identified himself, and hitched a ride back to Covadonga. There, in the middle of town, he found his car. It was covered by a three-day accumulation of dust and grime, but was otherwise undamaged. He drove quickly back to headquarters and reported to Fidel, who slapped him heartily on the back and exclaimed, "My friend you are blessed with as many lives as a cat!"

The CIA kept asking Commodore Crutchfield for updates on the situation ashore; but information from the combat sites was scarce at best. At noon on Wednesday, he requested and received permission to venture inshore for a closer look.

Thirty minutes later he stood transfixed on *Eaton's* bridge as the destroyer moved slowly toward the mouth of the Bay. But Crutchfield's orders made it perfectly clear that his ship was not to remain in Cuban waters one moment longer than necessary. *Eaton* circled the sunken *Houston* and transmitted a message informing Washington of the doomed ship's state. As soon as the circuit of *Houston* had been completed, *Eaton* headed back toward the open sea.

At that very moment, Rafael del Pino arrived in his T-33 jet for yet another attack on the enemy force at Giron. He was dismayed to see a big modern warship that he quickly identified as an American destroyer. Under orders not to attack any American ships or planes unless he himself was attacked, del Pino dove instead toward a dozen tiny craft that were doggedly plodding toward the beach in the area between the American warship and the shore.

Directly toward the small, laboring vessels he dove, strafing them unmercifully as he came. That'll give them something to think about, he concluded, pulling out of the dive. Then out of the corner of his eye, he saw the American warship reverse course, and head quickly toward the mouth of the Bay. Del Pino cheered widely inside his cockpit.

Suddenly, his plane wasn't a wobbly, old, foul-smelling relic that reeked of oil fumes. It was a deadly, invincible fighting machine that had made an American destroyer run for cover.

The jubilant Rafael del Pino turned for home, convinced that the battle was won. Although most of the landing craft below him were still heading for shore, he didn't take this attempt at another landing very seriously. How could the rebels hope to win when they were saddled with this kind of feeble support from their so-called mighty ally, he wondered? Nonetheless, he dutifully reported the offshore activities.

When del Pino's message reached Point One, the Officer in Charge, Sergio del Valle, was reluctant to issue further orders until he spoke with El Comandante, who was in transit back to headquarters. Since he couldn't reach Castro by radio, del Valle paced about Point One and cursed the enforced delay.

An hour slipped past before Castro called from Jovellanos.

"Another landing is underway, Comandante. Landing craft are shuttling more men ashore," del Valle told him.

"Impossible!" Castro thundered. "You've lost perspective! The boats aren't bringing rebels toward the beach; they're evacuating them back to the ships. They're running away! We have to stop them before the whole rabble escapes. The battles at the beaches have been won. I want you to issue orders for the destruction of every one of those landing craft. The rebels are pinned down on the beach. Let's keep them there. Let's teach them a lesson they won't forget. I want this invasion attempt to be the only such effort anybody ever tries against us. Now sink those damned little boats!"

Ramon Fernandez was furious. Fidel had ordered him to capture Giron by six o'clock last night. Now, here he stood, twenty hours later, still two miles away from victory, unable to move because of the terrible terrain. Swamps and rocks! Rocks and swamps! Damn them both!

His strike force had been under heavy fire for most of the day. The rebels had inflicted heavy casualties on his original force of two thousand men. He called his unit commanders to a conference and told them:

"We must get off this miserable strip of beach or die! Those are our options. Since we can't retreat, we must go forward."

"Our men are hungry, thirsty, and nearly exhausted," one of his officers complained.

"Your dead men have no needs at all, Gonzales. Get the rest of them up, and get them moving; otherwise every single man who has died will have died in vain."

As he said this, Fernandez turned toward the sea and, to his surprise, saw a flotilla of small landing craft heading for the shore, being shepherded by a pair of destroyers (*Murray* and *Eaton*).

"Line up the howitzers, mortars, and self-propelled guns along the water's edge," Fernandez ordered.

"What are you going to do, Major?" Gonzales asked.

"I haven't decided yet!" Fernandez told him and the others.

It was a knotty problem, all right! There were nearly four dozen small boats scooting about; some were coming toward him, but others seemed to be going toward the war ships. His orders were clear:

**DO NOT ATTACK AMERICAN SHIPS!**

If the American Navy aided the rebels, the ships were expected to stay in international waters, well outside the twelve-mile limit. But these destroyers were close—only a couple of miles away—certainly no more than that. "My God," he thought, "I can't start a war with America." Blowing up a few rebels is one thing; a war with the big boys is something else.

Fernandez had received his training at Fort Sill, Oklahoma. He had even gone to the Mardi Gras, in New Orleans, one year. He liked America. He liked Americans. But here he stood watching two American destroyers, in hostile postures, bearing down on him, well inside Cuban waters. He could easily hit the advancing ships with his 85-millimeters—AND THEN WHAT? The Americans were liable to wipe out all of them if they got riled up. "No," he decided, "I can't fire on the destroyers, but there is nothing to stop me from firing at the rebels in their landing craft."

Three armored Soviet half-tracks with their self-propelled guns rolled into position and zeroed in on the invading ships.

"Shall I open fire on the destroyers, Major?" the half-track commander asked Fernandez.

"Hell no!" was the response. "Shoot at the landing craft. If one of your shells comes anywhere close to one of those American destroyers, I'll put a bullet in your head. We're here to stop a small-scale invasion, not to start a full-scale war!"

As his guns carefully opened fire, Fernandez sent a dispatch to headquarters via a motorcycle courier. He explained this stalemate outside Giron, amplified the new invasion threat, and requested instructions on this new situation. Finally, he requested additional reinforcements. He needed far more men and equipment if he was going to force his way into Giron while, at the same time, he was coping with the landing.

As the messenger roared away on his errand, Fernandez stood looking seaward, unable to believe that the Americans would fire on his force. If they did decide to get involved, they surely wouldn't attack without air cover, and so far there were no planes in sight.

Earlier that morning he had seen American jets streaking across the sky at such high altitudes they looked like small dots. Those jets posed no danger. He felt safe in assuming the two American ships constituted no threat to him either. But what would they do? For the present all he could do was wait, wonder, and confine his reprisals to the men in the landing craft. Fernandez reflected that sometimes war truly was hell, but mostly it was just boring and frustrating.

He heard a new rumbling sound and moments later twenty more 85-millimeter howitzers came rolling in to take their places in the line of guns that were still firing out at the small boats in the Bay. The officer-in-charge of the howitzers rushed up to Fernandez.

"I request permission to open fire on the American destroyers, Excellency!"

"Absolutely not! I'm getting tired of telling you eager youngsters that we're here to stop an invasion, not to start a war. I'm absolutely sure the Americans won't open fire on us. And I'm just as sure that very soon they'll turn tail and head back to open sea. As hard as it is to believe, these Americans are even more confused than we are."

Half an hour later, just as Fernandez had predicted, the American ships reversed course and disappeared from view.

He was also right about the confusion the Americans were experiencing. Fernandez would have been interested to know that the confusion was not limited to the men who were at the invasion site.

In Washington, the CIA was still insisting that a multitude of dissatisfied Cubans were sharing food and other supplies with guerrillas who comprised rapidly growing underground movements in the island's remote areas. These partisans who were supposedly hiding in the hills would link up with the invasion force as soon as it came ashore.

CIA bulletins to national news sources were sparse and incomplete. They were told that since Cuban exiles were in charge of the operation, the CIA had very little data. When updates became available, the press would be notified. For now, the fate of the men on the beaches was in limbo.

In the Oval Office, things were also in limbo. President Kennedy, his brother Robert, and a small group of their most trusted advisors huddled throughout the day.

"Things look bad, but they are not irretrievable," Kennedy told them. "The men at those beachheads must hold out until the ammunition and other vital materials can be replenished."

"Ships carrying ammunition and supplies are out beyond the twelve-mile limit."

"Yes, but they're scheduled to return at dusk. We must help the Brigade if we can! They're counting on us! I know there's very little we can afford to do because of our international political concerns; but I don't want to look like a bum."

"One problem is being several hours behind on information updates," Dick Bissell acknowledged. "Communications are so poor that even when we do get data, it's only fragmentary. We've been unable to contact Ramrod Reynolds or the other advisors. We just can't make intelligent decisions or suggestions when we're groping around in the dark."

By mid-evening, although current data was still sparse, it was evident that a disaster was shaping up at the beachheads. Bissell sent Dick Drain, one of his staff members, to pick up Allen Dulles at the Friendship Airport in Baltimore and to brief him on the deteriorating situation as they drove back to Washington.

"Well, how are things going?" Dulles asked.

"Not very well, I'm afraid, Sir!"

"Give it to me in a nutshell, Dick."

"They seem to be hanging on by their fingernails."

"Why? Our initial airstrikes should have blown the opposition off the beaches and given the Brigade plenty of elbow room."

"The airstrikes were cancelled, Sir."

"Why would anyone issue an order that insane?"

"I don't know, Sir. But the invasion is going to hell."

A heavy stillness pervaded the Dulles Cadillac—a silence as still and as somber as death.

Dick Drain was the first to break it.

"When your brother was the Secretary of State, we never had the problems we're now having with Dean Rusk. While I was his special assistant, I handled the liaison between the State Department and your CIA people. Your brother could be absolutely miserable at times, no offense intended, and he was often impossible to satisfy; but he was an extremely decisive man. He didn't care who received the credit, or who got stepped on, as long as the job got done.

"President Eisenhower grew impatient with him at times; but he discovered that John Foster Dulles was right far more often than he was wrong. I see huge differences between Eisenhower and Kennedy. Ike asked for advice from qualified people who weren't afraid to speak up. JFK solicits counsel from less qualified people who seem to be deathly afraid of offending him. Dean Rusk, for example, says things he thinks Kennedy wants to hear, as do many other advisors. Kennedy's Administration has just begun, so understandably he doesn't want to make mistakes; but he seems more interested in preventing a loss than in producing a win. It's like the final quarter of those football games the President is so fond of; but he needs to remember that no team can score unless they have the ball. If you don't try to score, the most you can hope to achieve is a tie. In all candor, Mr. Dulles, I think President Kennedy's goal is to lose as gracefully as possible. I hope I'm wrong; but that's the way I see it."

"I hope you're wrong too, Dick. At least we should learn more at the morning White House meeting."

At 7 A.M. on Tuesday morning, the Cabinet Room of the White House looked like the aftermath of a wake.

Around a huge table sat the President; Allen Dulles; General Charles Cabell; Major General Chester Clifton, the President's Military Aide; MacGeorge Bundy and his assistant, Walt Rostow; Tracy Barnes; and, of course, Richard Bissell.

At this early hour, information from the beaches was extremely limited; but updates that had arrived during the night were extremely disheartening.

***Brigade members are trapped! Cuban forces are tightening the encirclement around both beaches.***

***The Brigade will soon be completely surrounded.***

***Without immediate and substantial assistance from US military and naval forces, the invasion force is doomed.***

Kennedy's Administration—The New Frontier—, after an existence of ninety days, was about to suffer a catastrophic disaster of such magnitude that the youthful President might never recover.

Throughout the day the outlook grew gloomier. Faces grew sadder, and eyes grew redder as the atmosphere grew heavier and the situation became more intense.

John and Robert Kennedy sat in the conference room throughout the day, carefully analyzing reports from the invasion sites, harboring forlorn hopes that the situation might miraculously improve; but every report painted a darker, more sinister picture.

John F. Kennedy got his first taste of the pressure that comes with the Oval Office.

Ambassador Adlai Stevenson telephoned.

"What should I convey to the United Nations?"

Press Secretary Pierre Salinger wondered.

"What do I tell the press and television people?"

Richard Bissell consulted with the President on a number of occasions before he relayed new orders to Ramrod Reynolds at the Bay.

Admiral Arleigh Burke, acutely aware that Jack Kennedy had never commanded anything bigger than a PT boat, pushed for some sort of intervention.

If Kennedy would not allow Navy fighter planes to attack Castro's forces, would he at least allow them to frighten and suppress the Cubans with a display of force and support?

"A show of American force might discourage the Cubans," Admiral Burke advised the President, "just as it would surely encourage the invaders."

In response to Burke's pleas, Kennedy walked over to a nearby table that supported an elaborate scale model of the Bay of Pigs. The position of each ship and element of the invasion force was continually updated here as situations changed. Deliberately, the President picked up a model of one of the American destroyers closest to the Bay of Pigs, and moved it over the horizon, far away from the beach. Admiral Burke had his answer before Kennedy spoke.

"Admiral, it seems we may be forced to participate in the Brigade's evacuation; but even if that becomes a necessity, I insist on a minimum exposure of US ships. They must remain beyond the horizon in order to establish a framework of plausible deniability."

"Mr. President, *Essex* has some unmarked aircraft aboard. Will you authorize an air reconnaissance of the beaches? At least we can get a better handle on the current situation."

"Very well, Admiral. Two unmarked jets may fly in, make one photographic circuit, and then fly out. Is that clear?"

"Perfectly clear, Mr. President!"

At 1330 the order for a reconnaissance flight was issued.

*Two observation aircraft are cleared to overfly the beaches. These planes are to be unmarked and unidentifiable as American aircraft. They are cleared to defend themselves only if they are attacked! I say again, only if they are attacked!*

Reports from the reconnaissance flights confirmed the worst. The life expectancy of the Brigade could be measured in hours unless reinforcements arrived. Their ammunition and food were nearly gone.

At 1500, Admiral Burke issued *Essex* new orders.

*Ready a flight of unmarked jet fighters for possible combat missions. This does not signify any intention of US intervention. It is merely a preparatory step.*

At 2000 the Joint Chiefs suggested that orders be issued to a flight of unmarked C-130 transports from Kelly Air Force Base.

"C-130s can airlift supplies to those beachheads. At least eight unmarked fighters should accompany them to provide protective air cover," they added.

Conference Room gurus quickly rejected the Joint Chiefs' recommendation, reasoning that with the time and distance working against them, the planes could not arrive before dawn. They further decided that the only plausible course of action that remained was to evacuate as many of the Brigade survivors as possible and hope the others could evade capture by hiding in the swamps.

President Kennedy summed up with a carefully worded official position.

***"A defeat at the Bay of Pigs will be regarded as an incident! It will only become a disaster if we openly get involved! American prestige will suffer a bit, to be sure; but what is prestige after all? Is it merely the shadow of power, or is it the substance of power?***

***"We must forget the former, and continue to work diligently to achieve the latter. I may get kicked in the can for a while, but I will not allow criticism of any kind to deflect my administration from its avowed purposes."***

Although the White House meeting had become philosophical, the one that raged at Quarters Eye had not. Richard Bissell sat in his office, surrounded by his most trusted staff members.

This was the first time Tracy Barnes had ever seen Dick Bissell unshaven and unkempt.

"Despite discouraging news from the beachheads, the President has rejected American intervention," Bissell told them.

"We all know what the President has been saying," Barnes added, "but none of us really believed that he would let the invasion go down the drain rather than authorize whatever assistance might be required to achieve ultimate success. We have fifty times more firepower sitting offshore than we need. A few Navy jets could turn the whole thing around."

"Tell you what," Bissell interrupted. "President Kennedy is hosting a reception at the White House tonight. Let's try one more time to get him to release a couple of jets. I'll call Kenny O'Donnell and ask him to set up a meeting with the President when the reception ends."

The call to the President's Appointments Secretary bore fruit. A midnight meeting was arranged.

The contrast between the rebels pinned down and bleeding on hostile beaches, and the participants at the meeting, could not have been more pronounced. President Kennedy, Vice-President Lyndon Johnson, Secretary of State Rusk, and Secretary of Defense McNamara all wore white ties and tails. General Lemnitzer and Admiral Burke wore their dress uniforms—both were resplendent with medals.

Richard Bissell's opening salvo made his position crystal clear.

"Mr. President, the situation can still be saved if you will authorize the use of jets from *Essex*."

Admiral Burke seized the initiative.

"If you'll permit me, Mr. President, I could order one of our destroyers to enter the Bay and knock out the Cuban artillery pieces that are lined up along the shore."

"An American war ship can hardly be disguised, Admiral. That would be an open admission of conspiracy," countered Kennedy.

"If not a destroyer, will you approve a couple of jet fighters from *Essex*? I guarantee they'll blow every one of Castro's flying relics out of the sky before noon tomorrow."

"Absolutely not!" the President thundered. "I've told you, Admiral, as I've told Allen Dulles and Dick Bissell, over and over, I will not commit American forces to combat."

"Would you permit unmarked jets to fly over the beaches with orders not to fire? It would be a show of force—nothing more."

"Admiral Burke, what happens if some crazy Cuban pilot shoots at one of our jets? We all know the answer to that! Our pilot shoots back. In a single instant, we would reject the role of a helpful neighbor, acting under the provisions of the Monroe Doctrine, which we have upheld and enforced since 1823, and become international warmongers. Imperialist aggressors, imposing our ideology on a sovereign nation whose policies happen to conflict with our own.

"I am currently trying to keep a lid on this unfortunate incident, an incident involving a defeat, from turning into the profound disaster that a rebel victory would produce, if that victory were procured by the direct intervention of American forces. A simple disaster might very well become a best case scenario. Your proposed actions suggest a far more likely scenario—the precipitation of World War III. I will not risk such a calamity. *Therefore, we will not get involved!"*

Struggling mightily to keep his temper under control, but not succeeding completely, Admiral Burke angrily replied,

"You don't seem to understand, Mr. President, that *we are already involved!"*

"And you do not seem to understand, Admiral, that *I am the President of the United States!"*

The heated discussion continued until 3 A.M.; but the two sides only grew farther apart. Those who agreed with Burke continued to champion the idea of ultimate success, while Kennedy, McNamara, and Rusk believed the opportunity for any measure of success had passed. Now their only hope was to minimize the political damage.

Finally, Dean Rusk made a proposal.

"Let's order the invaders to break off the action and escape into the mountains. Once there, they can act as a guerrilla force. They'll be able to harass Castro's government from within."

"I agree," chirped Robert McNamara. "Let's have them go guerrilla."

"There are at least four problems with that idea," Bissell shot back, with obvious frustration. "First of all, the Brigade is incapable of 'going guerrilla.' Second—they can't reach the safety of the mountains because they're too far away. Third—they're stuck in the middle of the biggest damned swamp in the entire Caribbean. Fourth—if we don't get them out, we'll be signing their death warrants."

For the first time, it occurred to Tracy Barnes that most of the men at this meeting, including President Kennedy, had no conception of the tactical situation.

Kennedy was familiar with the global picture, and his PT boat experience had given him the ability to think like a small unit commander, but he simply could not digest the urgency and desperation that the invasion operation now involved. Areas that the 2506 Brigade still held were being diminished and depressed like the victim of a boa constrictor's compressing coils. He was still alive but would soon be crushed if no way could be found to lop off the head of the snake.

As the meeting adjourned, the President did make one major concession. Whenever Nicaragua-based A-26s attacked the Cuban forces that were threatening the Brigade, six of the *Essex* jets would be permitted to fly high altitude cover over them; however, the jets could not strike targets in the air or on the ground, and could only defend A-26s that were in peril.

Bissell saw this as a softening of Kennedy's position. Maybe there still was some room for hope. When he left the meeting he didn't feel quite as desperate; but, for the first time, he sensed that President Kennedy was growing increasingly desperate.

*Jack Kennedy, the man, wanted to help the rebels. He truly wanted them to win! But John F. Kennedy, the President, simply could not afford to do anything that would openly associate the United States with any action that might be construed as international aggression. The Soviet Bloc might know that America had helped the rebels; but they must never be allowed to obtain any proof.*

*Although many called this overall concept wiggle room, Kennedy thought of it as plausible deniability. Regardless of the label, the need to sacrifice lives—and to forsake a just cause—seemed to be the price Kennedy was prepared to pay in order to cast long shadows of doubt over the entire Cuban Operation. Such political shadows were designed to deny a propaganda issue to America's principal cold war antagonists and also to protect Kennedy's suddenly vulnerable administration from the Republican watchdogs in Congress. To juggle that many loose ends, the inexperienced American President needed to perfect a myriad of artful skills that were seldom seen outside of the center ring at a circus. As a budding disaster loomed, John Kennedy had an increasing number of reasons to grow ever more desperate with each passing hour.*

As light began appearing in the sky at Giron, Pepe San Roman was also getting more desperate. Where were the supply ships that were supposed to come in, unload, and escape into the night? Nearly all of the ammunition they had brought ashore was gone. If it wasn't replaced very soon, they would be unable to continue the fight. Where the hell were the damned ships? Pepe agonized as the green flash heralded the sun's arrival over the horizon.

He and his troops would not learn until much later that the ammunition ships were in full retreat with *Eaton* in pursuit. They would receive no ammunition and very little help. Hereafter, misery, courage, and perseverance would be the only things in abundance.

At Playa Larga, Erneido Oliva, the Brigade Second in Command, had received reinforcements from San Roman the previous night. A heavy weapons squad brought six more mortars, two additional bazookas, and all of the available ammunition. An hour later, a pair of tanks arrived to bolster the defensive position Oliva's men had constructed around the perimeter they had established. The troops and weapons were "dug in," and tank traps had been neatly constructed wherever Cuban tanks might attempt to assault their perimeter.

Ten minutes later, Cuban tanks and artillery pieces arrived and opened fire. 122-millimeter howitzers bombarded Oliva's force for the next four hours. The concussion from more than two thousand shells caused most of the men to go into shock, and the deafening noise destroyed their hearing, at least temporarily.

At midnight, the cannonading stopped, and the first of twenty Russian-made Stalin tanks began to arrive. Since the surrounding swamps were impassable, the Stalins' only alternative was to force their way over, or through, the tank traps.

Oliva and his tank crews were ready. They fired from twenty feet—point blank range. Shells from the two rebel tanks and a shot from one of the bazookas knocked out the first Stalin. Another was rammed so hard by a rebel tank that the Stalin's cannon split open, rendering it helpless. A squad of bazooka men moved into position and disabled a third Stalin; but they were caught in a volley of machine gun fire and killed.

Cuban infantry arrived to support the tanks. From then on the battle was both fast and furious. Thanks principally to Oliva's excellent defensive perimeter, there were far more casualties among the attackers than among the defenders. There was also a great deal of heroism.

One sixteen-year-old rebel soldier fired at a Cuban tank from ten feet away. When the concussion knocked him out, another enemy tank rolled over him before anyone could come to his aid.

As dawn approached, so did the end of the battle. Oliva and his men were out of water and food and nearly out of ammunition.

When a Stalin tank finally breached the tank traps and came directly toward Oliva's foxhole, the brave commander grabbed a bazooka and the last shell in sight, then dragged the bazooka up to the center of the road. Oliva's men stood in awe and watched the Stalin tank bearing down on him. Suddenly the tank stopped; then the crew climbed out and surrendered.

The tank commander told Oliva that the Brigade's 370 men had repelled a Cuban force of more than two thousand soldiers. When he took a muster, Oliva was surprised to discover that only twenty of his heroic band were dead.

It was not a Pyrrhic victory for Oliva and his men, but it was destined to be a short-lived one. Already snipers were infiltrating into favorable positions, and another full-scale attack could soon be expected. His men were exhausted, hungry, and thirsty. They could no longer hold Playa Larga without reinforcements and supplies. Since none were likely to arrive, it was time to pull back. The survivors climbed aboard five serviceable trucks and retreated to Giron. Shortly before 0900 they rejoined Pepe San Roman.

Now that Playa Larga had been abandoned, aside from Giron, the only pocket of resistance was in San Blas. Rebel paratroopers in that area had penetrated nearly to Covadonga before overwhelming numbers of Cuban soldiers repulsed them. Now paratroopers, aided by Brigade infantry units, were falling back, but inflicting heavy casualties among Cuban forces as they retreated. In Giron, a new strategy was being discussed.

"Let's consolidate our remaining forces and move east," Oliva suggested, "toward Cienfuegos and the Escambray Mountains. We can probably expect the heaviest counterattacks to come from the north and west. If major pressure comes from Havana, we'll be moving away and staying ahead of it. We might have to fight a few skirmishes, but that's better than staying here and having the Brigade forced into the swamps or into the sea and eventually killed. Every mile we travel toward the east is one mile closer to the mountains and safety."

"Erneido, there are a dozen reasons for rejecting that idea. We don't have enough ammunition to fight skirmishes. We're critically low on food and water, and we don't have a sufficient number of vehicles to transport the men. If we head east, it will be obvious that our first objective is Cienfuegos. Castro will have people waiting there for us, as well as along the roads we must use. We're no longer in a position to fight our way out of any trap. Finally, the Americans know exactly where we are as long as we stay here. I still don't believe they'll abandon us."

"Pepe, the Americans have already abandoned us!"

"I'll call Commodore Crutchfield again. I know he wants to help us. If he can't give us air cover, at least he might be able to send in enough ammunition to keep us going for a while longer!"

Aboard *Eaton*, Crutchfield was growing angrier by the minute—an anger born of frustration because he was unable to help San Roman and his men. He felt a personal responsibility to the Brigade; after all, his task force had brought them here and escorted them ashore. What in the hell were the top brass thinking about? If Navy help was going to be withheld from the Brigade, we should never have been sent down here. Navy pride was at stake, as far as Crutchfield was concerned. You simply didn't take a strike force to a hostile shore and then let them rot on the beach—especially when assistance was close and available.

A young naval officer, who was in charge of radio communications, rushed up to Crutchfield.

"Sir, a message just came in from the *Essex* pilots that are flying cap cover over the Brigade planes. They're shadowing some Cuban aircraft and request permission to shoot them down."

"No dice. Tell the pilots that unless we get direct orders to openly assist the Brigade, our hands are tied.

Tell them to fly close to the enemy planes and make threatening gestures. Maybe they'll vamoose!"

When he received a CB radio call from Pepe San Roman a short time later, Crutchfield could only say that he was aware of the critical situation ashore, and that he had relayed his concerns to higher authority.

Never before had he felt as angry or as helpless.

Aboard *Blagar,* Ramrod Reynolds was faced with a mutiny. Three of the survivors from *Rio Escondido* had seized weapons and forced the crew in *Blagar's* engine room to stop the ship. When Reynolds and a squad of six frogmen arrived, the mutineers were brandishing pistols and bemoaning the fact that they were going to die unless they escaped from the area. Of course, frightened, hysterical men were no match for Reynolds and his highly trained assistants. The three were quickly subdued and disarmed.

Ramrod couldn't blame the merchant sailors for being scared and angry. Cuban planes had destroyed their ship—planes they had been promised would be destroyed before they could leave the ground. Now the same planes were strafing the Brigade members who still clung to toeholds on the beach—toeholds that were crumbling at an incredible rate—because Cuban militia units that the CIA had been convinced would join the invasion force were closing in and doing everything in their power to kill the men that had come to save them. It was clear that every man in the Brigade was doomed unless ammunition and food were quickly replenished.

He radioed headquarters and requested permission to stop the fleeing supply ships before they escaped.

"HQ, this is Reynolds. If *Caribe* and *Atlantico* are not interdicted and turned around very soon, it will be too late."

"HQ to Reynolds. *Essex* is authorized to launch a search mission to locate the two vessels. Transfer to *Eaton* and go in pursuit. Try reasoning with the ship captains. If that fails, Commodore Crutchfield is authorized to use any available means. Do you have any questions?"

"No questions, HQ."

"Good hunting! HQ, out."

*Eaton* raced south at top speed. A short time later, the search planes located the fleeing freighters; but *Eaton* was running perilously short of fuel since her thirsty engines gobbled it quickly during high-speed pursuits. A radio call, requesting a rendezvous, went out to a nearby tanker, and a refueling operation was accomplished in mid-ocean without a hitch. Then the sleek destroyer charged on.

She overtook *Atlantico* about a hundred miles from the Bay of Pigs. Crutchfield and Reynolds convinced the captain to reverse course.

Hours later, more than two hundred miles from the Cuban coast, they sighted *Caribe*. They sent a dozen radio signals to the supply ship, to no avail. *Caribe* did not answer. Commodore Crutchfield was forced to order *Eaton* to bring *Caribe* to a halt by sailing across the errant ship's bows. Blinker light signals from *Eaton* demanded that the freighter heave to.

When *Caribe* complied, Reynolds and Crutchfield went aboard. Eduardo Garcia, the Garcia Ship Line's owner, was waiting for them when they arrived on deck. Garcia was contrite. The radios had gone out, and he had not heard *Eaton's* messages; but he was furious about being "double-crossed" by the CIA.

"They guaranteed all my ships would be safe from attack because Castro's planes would be destroyed. When they weren't destroyed, no one bothered to tell my crews or me that interesting fact. So my ships were blown up and my men were killed. Perhaps you and the others at the CIA don't understand the fact that I'm responsible for my men. Most of them have been with me for many years. The other fact you fail to comprehend is that when you change the rules of a game, you're obligated to tell the other players."

"Captain Garcia, you're right!" Reynolds admitted. "This whole thing has been a disaster from the start. We might not be able to save the operation, but we must try to help the poor guys who are still on that damned beach. I need your cargo of ammunition and food to give them a chance to help themselves. It's still dangerous, but I need your help. I'm asking you to turn around and come back with us."

With a great many misgivings, Garcia agreed.

At 0100 on Wednesday, Reynolds, San Roman, and Oliva met on the beach at Giron. Everything seemed to be improving. The three had begun to think they might succeed after all.

The arrival of supplies and ammunition made a big difference. The men dug in and temporally regained the ability to protect the perimeter. Loaded weapons and full bellies did a great deal to improve morale.

Rumors began circulating that wounded men would soon be airlifted to safety from a Giron airstrip and that a squadron of well-equipped fighter planes was inbound from Nicaragua.

"Things are looking bright again," Reynolds told Pepe, as he stepped into one of the remaining water bug boats. "Remember, in the morning, or any time things get too tough, we'll come in and take you off."

"Never! I refuse to disgrace the Brigade. We're here to fight and to win. Castro may beat us, but he will never make us quit. I will have no further talk of retreat or capitulation."

"All right, Pepe. I'll be back in the morning."

Back aboard ship, in the wee small hours of the night, Ramrod received a strange message from HQ.

"The navy is authorized to remove everyone from the beaches after sunset. Use all Brigade ships in this evacuation operation. For transport from beaches to ships, utilize Navy landing craft, manned by seamen wearing plain tee shirts."

Reynolds decided that he had better get some rest before the next crazy day began. As he dozed off, he thought about San Roman's commitment and about the paratroopers on the San Blas road.

Action along the San Blas road resumed at 0600, when a wobbly Brigade bomber strafed an area north of town where a unit of Cuban infantry was massing. On his next pass, the pilot dropped a pair of napalm bombs in the middle of the enemy formation.

The paratrooper commander, Alejandro del Valle, seized this chance to climb aboard a tank and lead a new attack on the enemy. His maneuver temporarily succeeded in pushing them back, but the victory was short-lived. They were now so low on ammunition that when Cuban soldiers began to move toward del Valle's troopers, and toward the men of the Third Battalion under Pepe San Roman's brother, Roberto, all they could do was slowly retreat, while inflicting as many casualties as possible on the enemy.

They fought, and they killed, and they died. It was a running, often crawling fight. Blood, sweat, tears, and pain bought each yard of ground for the fifteen long miles that separated them from their comrades on the beachhead at Giron. Roberto San Roman was wounded, but still they fought on, not knowing what they might find at the end of the agonizing journey. More and more of their friends fell with each passing mile, but still they fought on, and on, and on.

As del Valle and his men were inching their way toward the sea, Radio Havana made a startling announcement.

*"American participation in the aggression against Cuba was dramatically proved this morning when our antiaircraft batteries shot down an American plane, piloted by an American airman who was bombing our civilian population and our infantry forces in the area around the village of Central Australia. The pilot has been identified as Leo Francis Bell, of Boston, Massachusetts."*

**President Kennedy dismissed the Havana Radio claim as pure and simple propaganda. Because of the CIA's impregnable *Cone of Silence*, two years would elapse before he discovered that not one American pilot, but four, had died at the Bay of**

**Pigs. They had all been cleared for combat roles by Richard Bissell; however, State Department officials would continue to deny all American involvement for many years. The body identified as Leo Bell, but actually that of Leo Baker, remained in a Havana morgue and was not claimed by US authorities until the late 1970's.**

Aboard *Blagar* Ramrod Reynolds was handed a radio message.

"Four unmarked jets will fly over Blue Beach in forty minutes. San Roman should mark his perimeter with colored panels. Have him contact you when our jets are in sight."

Ramrod radioed Pepe with the good news.

"Jets are coming!"

"Thank God! When?"

"Very soon. Call me when you see them."

Forty minutes later, Pepe was back on the radio.

"They just flew over us, Rod."

"Are you sure it was them?"

"Must have been! No markings, but they wagged their wings at us."

"Where are they now?"

"They flew inland."

Several minutes passed before Pepe called again.

"We're being attacked by Cuban jets! Where in the hell are our jets?"

"I'll find out!"

Reynolds called *Essex*.

"The jets San Roman spotted were reconnaissance aircraft. We have a launch ready to go. Get the map coordinates of the targets he wants us to hit and call me back."

"Will this present launch hit the targets?"

"Negative! The first flight is for air cover and flak suppression, the next launch will strike the targets."

An hour went by, and then another, but no jets arrived. Reynolds called *Essex* over and over again but received no reply.

*Caribe* and *Atlantico* finally arrived at *Blagar's* position. Ramrod loaded as much ammunition as the LCUs could carry and prepared to head inshore. He radioed HQ to make them aware of his plan.

"Take the supplies in, and get back to sea before dawn."

"That's impossible. We're thirty miles offshore. The LCUs can't possibly run in, unload, and return by then. If we don't get our promised air cover, we're going to lose all of these ships anyway!"

"Stay where you are."

A short time later, *Eaton* and *Murray* steamed past them, headed for an inshore reconnaissance mission.

Unaware of the destroyers' mission, Ramrod and *Blagar* crewmen assumed it was to protect them. Of course, the LCUs couldn't keep up with the speedier ships, but they did plod gamely along in their wakes.

Ramrod radioed Pepe with the good news.

"We're on our way with ammo and supplies.

"You'd better hurry, or we'll all be dead when you get here."

On the road that connected Giron and Playa Larga, Erneido Oliva and his troops were fighting what they realized was a last ditch delaying action. Remnants of the Second and Fifth Battalions had thrown up temporary breastworks with logs and earth, and were holding off Ramon Fernandez's tank force with two of their own tanks, plus half a dozen bazookas, a few 81-millimeter mortars, and a small pile of white phosphorus shells.

The first Cuban tank was stopped by a blast from a bazooka; then an armored car suffered the same fate. Two more tanks were destroyed. Mortars were being fired so fast that their barrels were overheating.

The heat of the battle itself became too much for Fernandez and his men—grudgingly, they retreated.

Oliva decided to pull back and join San Roman at Giron. He tried calling Pepe, but received no answer. Blank static was his only reply.

Commodore Crutchfield stood on *Eaton's* deck as the destroyer sailed parallel to the coast of Giron with *Murray* in her wake. Between the two warships and the beach, which was still a mile away, several small boats bobbed up and down.

Suddenly, a column of tanks rumbled onto the beach and opened fire on *Eaton* and her consort. One shell landed fifty feet short—then a second round whizzed over the ship's bridge and landed about the same distance beyond.

"Commodore," said Captain Peter Perkins' voice over the bridge loudspeaker, "we've been bracketed. I request permission to open fire. Our main batteries are manned and ready."

"Negative, Captain. If the shells had come closer I would grant your request. As you know we are under orders not to engage unless we are threatened. A pair of stray shots from some hothead in a tank does not qualify as a threat. If they persist, or if a shell comes close, or if they bring up artillery, I'll countermand my order. Let's move seaward, away from the beach. I hate to leave those boats because they may contain people who are trying to escape, but that cannot be helped. We'd better get out of here before we are hit, because I'm angry enough to start a war of my own. Close on *Essex*."

Aboard *Essex*, Admiral Clark, Captain Searcy, and Captain Fickenscher were engaged in a blistering argument.

"Gentlemen," raged Captain Searcy, "we have all heard the relays from San Roman on the beach. Now a pair of our destroyers have been fired on. My God, Admiral, this damned operation is in its death throes; the rebels are hanging on by a thread. If we don't help them, the Brigade will be wiped out, and our national honor will be wiped out with them. Sir, I am highly distressed."

"Pete, I'm in your corner, you know that! You also know I've asked Washington, on several occasions, to change our rules of engagement. They've refused to do so. God knows, I don't want to dump hundreds of brave men on a hostile beach, then turn tail and run for cover when the going gets tough."

He turned to Fickenscher,

"Deacon, do you see any possible options?"

"Sir, as I see it, we have very few possibilities. We can try to soften up the enemy with airstrikes. We can move destroyers closer to the beach and cover an evacuation, or we can airlift the survivors off the beach with S-4 helicopters. I don't favor using the choppers, because they would be sitting ducks for the enemy."

"Unfortunately, if I implement any of those ideas, I may go down in history as the man who started World War III on his own initiative. We can't help the Brigade; but we are not permitted to *tell* them we can't help them. We can't go closer to shore; but we can't go farther out to sea without additional orders. We have to cool our heels until Washington changes policy. Unfortunately, if HQ doesn't turn us loose pretty soon, it won't matter to the men on the beach. They'll either be dead, or they'll be prisoners."

It was Ramrod Reynolds' sad duty to tell Pepe San Roman that the Brigade would receive no help.

"We'll hold out for as long as we can, Rod; but we can't do much more with what we have left."

An hour later, he received Pepe's last message.

"Enemy tanks are breaking through. We're going to destroy all of our communications equipment, and everything else of value, then head for the swamps. I hate to quit, but we have nothing left to resist with."

Delicate equipment was no match for rifle butts wielded by disillusioned men—within minutes a big pile of shiny rubble lay in the mud. Then Pepe San Roman and more than fifty others left the beach and quickly melted into the cover of the swamps.

Alejandro del Valle, and two dozen paratroopers, disdained the treacherous swamps and chose the sea. As artillery shells screamed overhead and machine gun bullets from Cuban jets pockmarked the sand, twenty-two men reached the water and swam out to a small sailboat barely big enough to accommodate them all. They managed to slip away to the open sea.

Two weeks later, an American merchant ship saw them and picked up twelve survivors. Alejandro del Valle wasn't among them. Their brave young leader had been buried at sea after dying of thirst.

Only minutes after the sailboat disappeared, Oliva and his meager force finally reached Giron, only to find the area totally deserted. He decided to execute his original idea—head eastward toward the safety of Cienfuegos. But he had led his weary troops less than a mile when they were discovered and attacked by Cuban planes. It was obvious to all of them that they were no longer soldiers. They were fugitives. With Oliva in the lead, they dived into the swamp and sought refuge. Their great dream of liberation no longer existed—neither did the 2506 Brigade.

Far into the night, Ramrod called Pepe San Roman on the radio; but no answer ever came. It was nearly dawn when he left the stifling cabin and went out on deck, hoping that the salty air and the rhythm of the sea would help to control his emotions. Never had he known such frustration and helplessness. For the first time he was tasting the bitter ashes of defeat—and for the first time he was ashamed of America.

# *WASHINGTON, D. C.*
# *APRIL 19, 1961*

Differing opinions abounded. In-the-know insiders who were privy to a maximum of knowledge could not agree on the next logical step. Robert Kennedy had attended very few of the planning sessions, but now he took over the White House Conference Room meetings. He found all of the presidential advisors to be sullen and silent.

"Whatever we do," Kennedy cautioned the group, "we must protect the President from unfair criticism. We must formulate responses and proper actions to meet this crisis or Moscow will think we're nothing but a bunch of paper tigers."

"Mr. Attorney General," responded Allen Dulles, "for the moment we *are* paper tigers. We're in the same shape as a prizefighter who just got knocked down. This is not the time to bounce back up and go after our opponent. We need to bob and weave, clinch and hang on until our heads clear. Then we can go get him. Have no fear. All of us, President Kennedy especially, will have plenty of chances to prove we're not paper tigers. Reliable information is still scarce. We need to know what's going on before we make a move. Since Castro can be expected to blister the Cuban airwaves, it also makes sense to wait until he sounds off. By then our heads will be clear. Then we can start counterpunching."

"That's good advice, Allen. Okay, we'll adjourn until morning. All of you get some rest. Meanwhile, keep mulling the situation over in your minds."

Allen Dulles returned to the CIA headquarters and began a string of meetings that lasted until 7:30 P.M. Then he went to Richard Nixon's office to brief his old friend on the current situation.

"The whole thing has gone up in smoke!" Dulles told the former Vice-President. "The invasion is an absolute and complete failure."

Nixon was stunned. He had just returned from his California home and knew nothing other than the information the news media was reporting.

"What went wrong? Why didn't we bail 'em out?"

"Everything went wrong. Most problems occurred because the President listened to political doves who tried to eliminate every risk by compromising."

"It has to be more than that! When I left town, the whole thing looked good. Somebody screwed it up."

"Well, in the first place, the operation should never have been moved from Trinidad to the Bay of Pigs. I say that for a multitude of reasons, not the least of which is that the rebels would have gotten support from the guerrilla bands hiding out in the Escambray Mountains. They also could have found sanctuary in the mountains if the invasion failed. The President's decisions to minimize the first airstrike and to cancel the second were two major contributions to defeat.

"Why the hell would the silly ******* do that?"

"The President told us he would rather look like a bum than an international imperialist."

"If he felt that way from the start, why did he give his approval to the operation? Does anyone know?"

"This afternoon I spoke with Maxwell Taylor. He summed up the fiasco better than anyone I've heard. He said, 'somebody should have looked Kennedy in the eye and told him his new plan was lousy. He should have been warned that the Invasion, at best, only had about a ten percent chance of success.'"

"Max Taylor's right! But nobody in the Kennedy administration has the guts to go toe to toe with him. They're all a bunch of weak sisters. McNamara and Rusk—all of them are too busy learning their new jobs to be worth a damn right now. If I had won, it would have been different. I understood the original plan! I helped develop Operation Trinidad, Allen."

"Max thinks Kennedy went ahead with it because he was in awe of Eisenhower. He reasoned that since Ike's the most successful military leader of his era—the man who orchestrated our victory in Europe—he must have been pretty confident of success when he approved the Cuban invasion. Obviously, Kennedy, a neophyte with very little experience, was reluctant to overrule a man with such a plethora of experience. If you think about it, Max's theory makes sense."

As Dulles finished speaking, the phone on the desk rang. Of course Dulles only heard Nixon's part of the conversation.

"Hello. Oh, hello, Jack. How are you?

There was a long pause as Nixon listened.

"I don't doubt it; you've had several brutal days."

Another long pause before Nixon ended the call.

"No, it's not an imposition. I'll see you at noon."

"That was Jack Kennedy, Allen. He invited me to the White House for lunch. He wants to know what I would do if I were in his shoes."

# *THE WHITE HOUSE*
# *APRIL 20, 1961*

Dick Nixon had known Jack Kennedy since they were freshman congressmen together in 1947. In all of those years he had never seen Kennedy so upset.

The President and his former rival sat in the Oval Office on comfortable couches flanking a fireplace. In a way the meeting reminded Nixon of the last few minutes before their first televised debate.

*They had been escorted to the stage an hour before airtime. When they were properly positioned, hot, bright lights had been skillfully adjusted to eliminate the majority of the shadows; then various camera angles were tried to find the most flattering ones for each of them. When all the video arrangements were completed, sound engineers had begun spinning an endless mass of dials, so the voice timbre of each candidate could be analyzed. Then the sound mixers reduced the variances and produced optimum audio balance. Since the television production engineers were professionals with a great deal of experience, they didn't need the hour that had been allocated. They completed their routines almost fifteen minutes before airtime.*

*During the unexpected down time, both candidates experienced last minute jitters while they tried to appear relaxed and confident in that final quarter hour before television cameras presented them to a national audience of nearly a hundred million.*

Kennedy smiled nervously, just as he had then; but his words made Nixon believe Kennedy intended to be quite candid with him.

"I met with the Cuban Council, from Miami, last night. I had another meeting with them this morning. Those meetings were two of the saddest experiences of my life. I lay awake last night for hours, almost wishing you had been elected to this damned office."

He stared at the fireplace and concentrated on the dull red flickering flames, as he struggled to regain his composure.

"The Cuban Council thinks it's my fault that all of this went wrong. I told them that I went ahead with the invasion because my advisors, men with great ability and experience, assured me it would succeed without intervention by US forces. I showed them a communication that Colonel Hawkins sent me from Nicaragua just before the Brigade left. My God, Dick, he made it sound as though the invasion force could lick their own weight in wildcats!"

Once again, he paused for several moments before he continued.

"Many of those people have lost family members. It's been a tragedy! No doubt about it! But I let them know I'm no stranger to tragedy. I lost a brother and a brother-in-law in the last war. I lost some of the crewmen who served aboard my PT boat. I told them that I'm not giving up on Cuba, but I also have other responsibilities to consider. Successful diplomacy, as you know, Dick, is like juggling hot plates with sticky fingers. You must focus on every component part, or you wind up with a pile of shattered dishes, and two handfuls of burned, broken fingers that you can't pry apart. Sometimes I wonder why any sane man would want this job."

Nixon found Kennedy's reference to the current crisis incredibly silly. Thanks to this man's inability to lead, more than a thousand men who had trusted America had been involved in a no-win battle. Now, the man most responsible was trying to justify his foolish behavior, soothe his conscience, and cover his sorry ass with a lot of rhetoric about shattered dishes and sticky fingers. He should be a hell of a lot more concerned about all the shattered lives he had caused! For a thousandth time, Nixon wondered how the American voters could have elected such a sorry ******* to be their President. He smiled smugly and waited for Kennedy to continue.

"One of the things that disturbs the Cubans the most is Fidel Castro calling all those brave invaders, 'mercenaries'! How dare he use that term? Those men are dedicated patriots, not mercenaries."

"How did the meetings with them wind up, Jack?"

"Last night they were livid; but they had calmed down quite a bit by this morning. Most of them are eager to go back and start the fracas all over again, if we'd give them the word. I asked you to come here today to get your opinion on a course of action."

He rose and beckoned to his visitor.

"Before you can do that, you need to be brought up to speed. Come over to the conference room and I'll brief you on everything I know. I've ordered lunch to be served. I hope you like tomato soup with sour cream, Dick. I don't feel much like eating today."

For the next an hour Nixon listened as Kennedy rattled off statistical data between gulps of tomato soup that had grown tepid. Although Nixon himself had an excellent memory, he was most impressed by Kennedy's analysis of the strategic overview and his ability to focus on vital details.

As Kennedy's story unfolded, Nixon saw a dozen flaws that virtually guaranteed failure. The operation was not remotely similar to the one Eisenhower had approved, or the plan he and Bissell had discussed on the eve of the election. Operation Trinidad had an excellent chance to succeed. He and Bissell agreed that no American troops would be needed to aid the invaders as long as Cuba's air force was neutralized. They had also concurred that the only way to insure neutralization was by unleashing naval airpower; but Kennedy had not allowed carrier plane participation. By making that critical decision he had turned the Brigade's old planes into a flock of sitting ducks, and had ended all hopes for victory.

"What would you do, now?" Kennedy asked him.

"I would make damned sure I was legally covered; then I would go after that bearded, ******* Cuban ******* with a full-scale airstrike."

"That means the end of plausible deniability!"

"It means armed intervention by American Armed Forces. With all the shenanigans Castro has pulled off, I think legal justification for reprisals would be very easy to establish."

"But if we attempt to disenfranchise Fidel Castro, Khrushchev may retaliate by moving against Berlin. I don't think we can afford to take that gamble at this time. As you know, we are currently in negotiations to deescalate Communist activity in Southeast Asia. I won't do anything to jeopardize those peace talks."

For the next hour, Nixon offered various reasons for acting, each of which was parried by Kennedy with reasons for *not* acting.

That night, Nixon called Bebe Rebozo in Florida.

"Hello, Bebe. Are you busy with anything?

"No! I'm relaxing next to a tropical fish pond and sipping Southern Comfort. What did you find out?"

"I found out Kennedy's a chicken *******! He has no guts! He's afraid of Khrushchev. Sure as hell, the more we let that Russian ******* get away with, the cockier he'll be. Those damned Bolsheviks only understand two things: hard resolve in negotiations, and if that fails, hard steel at the base of their spines. They'll go through us like a hot knife through butter if Kennedy soft-pedals them. Khrushchev has to be handled like any playground bully. If you let one of those ******* get away with something today, he'll try to get away with something more tomorrow. The next day, he'll have your lunch money in his pocket, and you'll be sitting there on your own dumb, panic-stricken ass, wondering what the hell happened. The sooner you kick the crap outta the big *******, the better. But you gotta have guts to fight, and Kennedy hasn't got them. I tried to tell him that we can either stand toe-to-toe with them now, or we can wait until later; but now or later, we're going to have to stand up and be counted. Kennedy doesn't believe me, Bebe; but one day, very soon, he will."

# *HAVANA, CUBA*

# *APRIL 20, 1961*

While Kennedy and Nixon were sitting in the Oval Office, Castro was lecturing on Cuban television. He related the story of the battle, emphasizing the valor of his friends and the stupidity of his enemies. He scoffed at the CIA for bombing useless aircraft at Campo Libertad and for underestimating the Cuban people's loyalty toward him.

"Imperialists think about geography and count up their cannons, tanks, and planes. But revolutionaries aren't concerned with those things, because we count on people. Imperialists have never discovered how important people are; but this week, we Cubans have taught them a great many new lessons."

Castro talked for four hours. He was alternately a prophet, an evangelist, a warrior, an orator, and a magician. He slipped from one role into another as easily as a highly paid Hollywood actor. By the end of his speech, Cuban citizens were well informed, deliriously happy, and outrageously proud.

In the Caribbean Sea, fifteen miles southeast of the Bay of Pigs, Ramrod Reynolds received a message from CIA headquarters authorizing rescue missions.

*US Navy ships and personnel will be permitted to extract the shipwreck survivors stranded on beaches along the west side of the Bay.*

Although he was fearful that Washington might rescind the order, Reynolds decided not to launch the rescue operation until the next morning.

Early the next morning, as soon as it was light enough to navigate, *Eaton*, with a big American flag unfurled, led the way into the Bay, past the sunken *Houston.* Almost at once the lookouts spotted four ragged survivors. The men hobbled out of the bushes and scrambled toward the beach, waving frantically. *Eaton* slowed long enough for Reynolds and Felipe Orizaba to lead two frogman teams ashore.

Eventually, they found twelve men. A few of them still wore shorts, but the rest were naked. All of them bore deep gashes caused by the long, razor-sharp, sun-hardened thorns that grew in clusters on bushes that abounded throughout the Zapata swamps. Each survivor was hungry, thirsty, and badly in need of medical attention.

At the next beach they found another group who had fared better than their compatriots. These five men still wore uniforms and carried weapons. Most surprising of all was the fact that they were neither hungry nor thirsty. *Houston's* Chief Engineer had taken charge of this group and provided an amazing amount of skill and leadership. The men had rested under shady trees during the heat of the day, marched only at night, and had found ample supplies of shellfish and crabs in the sand at the water's edge. They had quenched their thirst with rainwater they collected from the hundreds of hollow stumps along their forty-mile march route. Ramrod grinned when he heard the story. Unlike most of the other Brigade units, this group could have held out indefinitely.

Rescue missions continued for the rest of the day. A total of twenty-six survivors were picked up and brought aboard *Eaton,* where they showered, ate a hearty meal, received medical care, and gratefully donned fresh clothing. Although a pair of Cuban helicopters played a deadly game of cat and mouse with the survivors, strafing them on several occasions, they never threatened American ships or personnel.

The next morning, Captain Pete Searcy of *Essex* received a secret message that demanded personal involvement. He was ordered to destroy every order and log which had any connection with the invasion operation. Each deck, communications, combat, and navigation log, as well as every file and ledger, had to be destroyed. He was ordered to burn every shred of evidence personally. Searcy gathered it together, then summoned a Marine messenger. Together they carried the mass of papers and books to the lowest deck and threw them into the ship's big incinerator.

Searcy had been puzzled by the order's tone; but now the veteran warrior suddenly shuddered. Had he just conducted the first step in a widespread, sinister cover-up? If so, why? Who needed to be protected?

The next week, most of the Brigade's Cuban pilots and maintenance personnel were flown back to Opa-Locka, where they traded in their fatigues for white duck pants and tropical shirts. They were told that a switch was necessary so they would not look like a military group. Each man also received a legal-sized envelope. Inside they found three things: temporary parole papers, granting short term asylum in the US; from one to three hundred dollars in cash; and a note advising that no further compensation would ever be forthcoming.

On April 27th, an inquiry committee chaired by General Maxwell Taylor flew Ramrod and Avispa to Andrews AFB, outside Washington, for debriefing.

Having come directly from *Essex,* they looked like castaways. Sun-toughened skin was burned black—jagged scabs concealed the dozens of coral and thorn cuts that covered their faces, arms, and hands. They shivered constantly—a condition attributable to the lightweight, short-sleeved, tropical khaki uniforms they wore and bodies that had grown accustomed to the intense heat they had recently endured.

They were much too keyed up to sleep, so they sat up all night, sipping Jack Daniels, fighting the battle at the Bay of Pigs over and over again. By dawn, they had won each one of the replays, and the Black Jack was gone.

They were enjoying breakfast in the dining room of the Shoreham Hotel when Jack Hawkins arrived.

"I'm sure glad to see you two fellows alive. I was beginning to think you might not get out of there in one piece. By the way, are you still talking to me?"

"Hell yes, Colonel," Ramrod assured him. "This wasn't your fault; we know that, but somebody sure screwed up! We'd like to know who it was."

"The whole operation was taken out of my hands. After I lost control, the President gave all of us up!"

"So it's over for us; but what about those poor guys who are Castro's prisoners?" Avispa lamented.

"We'll hear from Castro pretty soon; but it isn't necessarily over for any of us. This kind of screw-up needs a lot of fall guys, and the big guys never take those falls. I'd advise you to stay loose and expect something very nasty to happen!"

# *HAVANA, CUBA*
# *APRIL 23, 1961*

Castro's prisoners were transported into the city in overcrowded buses and sealed trucks. As he entered Havana, Pepe San Roman was struck by the thought that being herded like cattle was very different from the arrival he had anticipated a few days earlier. But then, neither had he anticipated so many broken promises and treacherous acts.

At least Pepe San Roman was still alive when he reached Havana. Nine of his compatriots were dead. They died inside a crowded, closed, aluminum-sided truck. One hundred fourteen Brigade members were now dead. Another twelve hundred would become Cuban prisoners. The rest, approximately a hundred fifty, were never sent ashore or were able to escape.

For the first three weeks, the prisoners were held at Havana's Sports Palace. The thousand demoralized men were forced to sit in tiny hard chairs for more than twenty hours each day. Throughout those days and nights, at any hour, loudspeakers would blare a man's name and order him to report for questioning about his role in the invasion. He was encouraged to impugn the US government, admit his wrongdoing, and sign an incriminating confession. Each man was asked to write a letter to the UN Secretary General implicating US officials and condemning President Kennedy for his imperialism. Prisoners were assured that such acts would demonstrate a willingness to be rehabilitated and would weigh heavily when their punishment was decided. Cuban interrogators were amazed that only about 10% of the men cooperated, despite an overwhelming feeling that the American military and the CIA had abandoned the Brigade. Castro had predicted that plummeting morale would produce far greater results.

During the entire time they were forced to sit in the tiny chairs, the men were not permitted to bathe or shave. As many prisoners were still covered with filthy residue from the Zapata Swamp, the epidemic of dysentery that broke out was inevitable. Since there were only twelve toilets to accommodate more than a thousand men, the Havana Sports Palace became a living hell.

When this three-week "softening-up phase" had been completed, the prisoners were allowed to lie on vermin-riddled mattresses from 0300 until 0600.

Lying on the arena floor, under bright, hot lights, beset by fever and disease, a thousand men gradually decided that America had betrayed them.

They had been stupid to believe the CIA promises.

Cuban agents began screening men to find various types that were suitable for questioning on televised news shows. They selected prisoners that were weak enough to admit everything the Cubans demanded.

A second group was comprised of sons from rich and famous families, such as the Babuns, Varonas, and Cardonas. But the best coup of all was finding three men who had been condemned by the Batista regime as war criminals.

One of the men, Ramon Calvino, was a notorious criminal. He had tortured and raped a young woman and murdered two men. Calvino was not a Brigade member. He had been a crewmember of one of the sunken ships. After swimming to the beach, he had been captured in the swamps. But Calvino's presence provided Castro with a wonderful propaganda ploy. He used Calvino as a concrete example of the CIA's willingness to recruit vile mercenaries.

According to Castro, the Cuban invaders were the scum of the earth. Calvino's presence was another example in a mounting chain of evidence that these invaders were well-paid assassins, not dispossessed Cuban refugees.

In a span of four days, thirty-seven prisoners were paraded before television cameras. Although a few were contrite, the majority made strong cases against Castro. On the "contrite" end of the spectrum, Segundo de Las Heras expressed one point of view.

"I am very sorry for what has happened, and I ask the Cuban nation to accept my sorrow. I am ready to do anything I can to make up for what happened."

The opposing view came from Carlos Varona, who said to Castro:

"If you have so many supporters, why don't you hold free elections?"

And from Fabio Freyre:

"What I want for my country is the establishment of the 1940 Constitution, which gave us a free press and elections. Then the people can choose their own form of government."

Most prisoners refused to cooperate. Setting an admirable example of stoic behavior was Brigade Commander Pepe San Roman. Pepe didn't have a public interview—a private meeting with Castro was sufficient.

"How did you get involved in this business, San Roman?" the furious Castro demanded. "Why in the world did you come back here and attack your own country to aid our enemies—the damned imperialist Americans? You're a traitor! You've violated every law that matters. Every law of the world. Why have you done these things? You owe me an answer!"

"You'll get my name, rank, and Brigade number," spat out San Roman defiantly, "and nothing more!"

"If you don't cooperate, I'll have you shot!"

"Kill me, and get it over with; but don't play games with me. First the Americans, and now you! I'm sick of all your stupid games! I'd rather die than abide one more minute of your childishness."

"Obviously, you've been victimized by the CIA. Let's forget that you're the Brigade Commander and that I'm Fidel. Let's just talk, man to man. Okay?"

Castro spent an hour talking to San Roman, trying to justify everything he had done as dictator and ended the interview by promising to send in enough reading material to keep Pepe from being bored. The new tactic of compassion and understanding worked to some extent. San Roman began to feel that Castro was being more honest with him than any of the Americans had been.

At the end of their third week of captivity, the men were finally allowed to shower. They were divided into groups of ten, and one towel was issued to each group.

Then they were given fresh yellow T-shirts. Guards informed them that the yellow T-shirts were symbols of cowardice, because they were, after all, nothing but "yellow worms."

When the shower session ended, they were divided into groups, according to profession or social strata and questioned at length. After several hours, they were returned to their battalions and forced to sit in the same hard, tiny chairs, under the same bright, hot lights and maintain complete silence.

The tedious days and nights of captivity provided ample time for the Brigade members to ponder all of the foolishness that had led to their capture.

First of all, there had been no alternate plan. It had been all or nothing. The invasion attempt resulted in sixty-four hours of tough guerrilla warfare for which they had been inadequately trained. The Zapata Swamps were unsuitable for guerrilla tactics even if they had been trained.

Next, they had been assured that Castro's air and ground units would be neutralized and that had not happened. They were also guaranteed that the Cuban army and national militia would rise up in revolt and come to their aid—another forecast gone awry. The miscue had resulted in their being outnumbered forty-to-one.

Finally, the CIA guaranteed that if the invasion should fail, they would have air cover while they fought their way toward the Escambray Mountains. Now they all realized how empty that promise had been. The Escambrays were eighty miles away, and help from the US military never came. Each passing day, more and more prisoners decided they had been innocent lambs destined for a predictable slaughter.

These anti-American, pro-Castro feelings might have continued to escalate if Fidel had not made a major blunder.

Castro stood in the middle of the Sports Palace one night and gloated over the Brigade's misfortune and stupidity. He spewed forth his disdain until 0300.

Now, it was one thing to think about themselves as fools, but it was quite another to hear it from a man who was compounding their misery.

Once again, Fidel Castro became a bitter enemy! Once again, they realized that their homeland was in the grip of a maniac who must be stopped, regardless of the personal risk or cost to themselves.

After that night, although the Brigade leaders were threatened with death on many occasions, prisoners were treated better. His four-hour tirade seemed to have vented Fidel's fury. After a month of captivity, the men underwent a mass trial and were formally convicted and sentenced to prison.

Robert Kennedy, America's chief negotiator, asked Castro what he wanted in exchange for their release. Castro said he would let him know.

At the time, Kennedy could not begin to imagine that Castro would stall for more than a year and a half before he finally agreed to terms.

During those long months, in order to extract as large a ransom as possible, Castro eagerly gathered information from many sources—and to emphasize his strong bargaining position he issued a series of public and private ultimatums.

On October 15, 1962, Raul Castro delivered one of the ultimatums to Robert Kennedy, at the Kennedys' private compound in Hyannis Port, Massachusetts. Before that secret meeting, an immense amount of vital information would be gathered by dozens of Cuban agents working inside the United States and around the world.

One of Castro's agents was Dolores del Negro, La Arana Negra—the woman who had vowed to play Rodney Reynolds' heartstrings like the strings of a flamenco guitar.

Another agent, named Lee Harvey Oswald, would become much more famous. Oswald would become a key player in certain events that eventually would lead to a Cuban nightmare of forty years' duration and an assassination that would rock the world.

# *FORT LAUDERDALE*

# *JULY 4, 1962*

Dolores del Negro lay on the wide, luxurious strip of well-manicured grass that completely encircled the Olympic-size pool the owners of her apartment complex provided for their water-oriented tenants.

As she waited for Rodney to arrive, she oscillated between amusement and amazement. Her amusement stemmed from a string of middle-aged and elderly men who walked around the sidewalk that encircled the pool. They almost jogged up and down the other three sides, but when they turned the final corner and approached the spot where she lay, they slowed to the pace of a snail. Reluctantly, they strolled past her, all the while casting furtive, appreciative looks at her, adorned in a glistening white swimsuit that accentuated her deep tan. She enjoyed the covert antics of the bashful ones far more than those of the younger men and teenagers, who openly admired her. Dolores couldn't blame them; she worked out for two hours, three mornings each week, to stay in tip-top shape.

She looked past her parade of admirers and contemptuously glared at the dozen or more women who had sprawled out on deck chairs along the far side of the large pool.

Many Americans were disgusting. Right here at poolside, she could see more jiggling fat and flabby flesh in an hour than she would find in a whole day in her old Havana barrio. It was shameful the way Americans let their bodies go to hell.

She had discovered that most people tended to be lazy. They didn't take care of their bodies. Worse yet, they let their minds turn to jelly, as well. She had always been hungry for knowledge. In her early teens, she had begun walking long distances every week to salvage magazines and books from trash dumpsters in Havana's more affluent neighborhoods. She carted everything home in a big burlap bag. In a period of five years she amassed an amazing amount of knowledge on a wide variety of subjects.

When she came to Miami she had been surprised that many of the people she met couldn't speak proper English. That shortcoming was not confined merely to the Cuban refugees—many native-born Americans were even bigger offenders.

Dolores had become fluent in English, broadened her knowledge base, and increased her vocabulary by reading several library books each month. Whenever possible, she also attended free lectures on topics she found interesting.

The net result of her sustained effort was an ability to converse on a plethora of subjects and a new level of confidence that allowed her to move in any circle of erudite people.

Intelligent people made her think of Rod, and she felt a surge of anger. What in the hell was wrong with that man? She knew he was attracted to her. That was easy to see. For the past six weeks she had done her best to entice him into a romance; but she had run into a stone wall. At first she thought he might be victimized by weird religious scruples; but recently she had begun to understand that Rod was simply a very moral individual.

This morality presented two problems. First, she wasn't getting any useful information she could pass on to her Cuban control agent; and, perhaps of more importance, she was beginning to fall in love with Rodney.

Caring about another person as much as she cared about herself was an alien feeling for Dolores. With the exception of her family members, she had never felt this way before, and it made her a little uneasy.

Today would really prove to her where she stood. If Rod didn't react to her sleek new bathing suit, he never would. For one single fleeting moment she thought about marriage, then shuddered. Wake up, you fool, she told herself. Don't think such foolish thoughts! You have a life of your own to live, and it doesn't include an iron-willed Puritan, even if he does look terrific in his Special Forces uniform.

She thought once more about her family. They still lived in a small, crowded house in one of Havana's lower class barrios. Times were still very hard there. Occasionally, Dolores felt guilty about the luxurious life she was enjoying in America, while her parents and siblings struggled to survive in Cuba. But things would improve. They had to! Fidel would fix them!

Rodney and the others were terribly wrong about Fidel. He truly cared about the Cubans. He would do whatever was best for them. Fidel was Cuba's savior. She trusted him completely to make things right for her homeland and its millions of adoring citizens.

It was amazing that many people didn't trust Fidel. Of course, she rationalized, that was only because a great number of false charges had been trumped up against him. There had even been attempts on his life. She shuddered to think about such a calamity. She realized it was only jealous rage or ignorance that prompted such vicious acts. After all, great leaders were often targeted by assassins or misguided zealots.

Dolores was never fooled. She had recognized the greatness the first time she heard Fidel speak. Now she actually had become an agent, working to further Fidel's great plan. She was lucky to have the chance.

Her thoughts returned to Ramrod Reynolds as she wondered for the hundredth time how to prove that he was wrong about Fidel. How could the multitudes of unenlightened misjudge him? How could so many people hate him? Fidel was a good man. He would never hurt Cuba or a single Cuban. He was a man to be trusted. She had no doubt whatsoever about that!

# *PART FOUR*
# *THE MISSILES OF OCTOBER*

# *HYANNISPORT, MASS.*

# *OCTOBER 15, 1962*

The black and red helicopter swept in from the sea and hovered at the water's edge for a few moments, then moved two hundred yards inland and settled softly in front of a dimly lit beach house.

A pair of fatigue-clad toughs with dingy mustaches and beards that made them look like a couple of banditos from a Cisco Kid movie, emerged, leaped nimbly to the sand and peered suspiciously around. Carrying their light automatic weapons in the ready position, they moved slowly toward the cabana's entrance.

When they were still some distance away, Robert Kennedy emerged from the small building, walking between two men dressed in classical secret service business suits. Kennedy himself was dressed in a dark windbreaker.

One of the men addressed the newcomers in fluent Spanish.

"Tell Raul Castro that Robert Kennedy guarantees his safety. Everything is in readiness for their meeting. You two can come with him and keep the sidearms; but you'll have to leave the automatic weapons in the chopper."

The men turned around and sauntered toward the helicopter. One climbed back aboard while the other waited below. Apparently Kennedy's assurance was adequate because a moment later the man on the ground handed his automatic rifle to his companion who had reappeared in the helicopter's doorway.

An aluminum ladder was lowered, and Raul Castro descended. He moved directly toward Kennedy, held out his hand, and spoke in a calm voice.

"I'm glad we could meet in private, Mr. Kennedy. My brother is eager to end this foolishness. I'm sure your brother is too."

"My brother is the President of the United States. I trust you will remember that and refer to him with the proper respect."

"Your brother, the American President, did a very foolish thing when he attempted to muscle his way into Cuba. I hope you will remember that, Senor, and treat a situation, which you yourselves caused, with the gravity it deserves. Our meeting can be friendly or unfriendly, whichever you desire; but before I depart I intend to make several things very clear. So tell me, what is the tone of our talk to be?"

"Pleasant or unpleasant, it matters not to me; just remember that I represent the United States!"

"As I represent Cuba; but as you Americans are fond of saying, 'we have the hammer.' More than a thousand rebels are now confined in Cuban prisons. They are the men that your government lied to—a thousand men who will always curse their stupidity for believing that you and your brother were their friends—men whose freedom depends on your willingness to pay $100,000,000 for their release."

"We're here to negotiate fair and equitable terms. It is pointless to continue if you continue to take a hardline posture and employ inflammatory rhetoric!"

"I will not stray very far in these negotiations! And there is one condition that is not negotiable. The CIA has made several attempts on my brother's life. That must stop! If another assassination is attempted, we will be forced to respond in kind. I trust my warning is perfectly clear!"

Kennedy was stunned! A sudden look of rage and disbelief spread across his face, then slowly receded before he replied in a quiet voice.

"So there can be no possibility of misinterpretation, let me be certain that you have just threatened the President of the United States with death."

"Allow me to contradict you. I threatened no one. I just swore a blood oath! If another attempt is made to kill the Cuban President, the American President's life will be forfeited. On a more personal level, if we Castro brothers are left alone, you Kennedy brothers have absolutely nothing to fear. All of us can enjoy long and happy lives."

The rest of the meeting was short and unpleasant. Conversation was strained and stilted. When Castro left an hour later, his ominous threats of retaliation hung in the air like a dark line of storm clouds. But the next morning those threats against the American President were consigned to the back burner—for on the morning of October 16th, events occurred that would take the nation and the world to the brink of World War III.

# *WASHINGTON, D.C.*
# *OCTOBER 16, 1962*

Robert Kennedy's telephone rang at precisely 9 A.M. It was the President.

"Bob, we're facing some real trouble. New U-2 photos reveal a massive buildup of Russian ICBMs and atomic weapons in Cuba."

"How certain are the photo interpreters?"

"100%. The CIA will brief me at 11:45. I want you to attend that meeting."

The CIA briefing session was held in the Cabinet Room. Key members of the Kennedy Administration were present. A dozen high altitude photographs had been enlarged and were displayed on a big board.

A pair of senior CIA analysts, holding additional maps and charts, stood near the board. One of them pointed to an area in one of the photos.

"Gentlemen, if you look closely, you'll observe a missile base, designed to accommodate surface-to-surface ballistic missiles, being constructed at this site near San Cristobal."

President Kennedy, who was sitting closest to the photographs, voiced a concern that every civilian in the room shared.

"Your pointer seems to be resting on an area that could be a sports field or the construction site for a new house. They could be digging a basement just as well as working on a missile site, from the limited details I can see."

"I apologize for contradicting you so directly, Mr. President; but there can be no mistake. Over the past twenty years I've seen thousands of high-level photos of everything from Japanese cannons to covert Cold War buildups. There is absolutely no doubt, Sir. This is a Russian surface-to-surface missile base!"

The CIA interpreters left a short time later, and the meeting proceeded in earnest.

"Bob," requested the President, "remind us of the comments Soviet Ambassador Anatoly Dobrynin made in your recent meeting."

"He told me that the Russians were ready to sign an atmospheric test ban treaty, if we agreed to curtail some of our underground tests. I assured him that I would communicate his proposal to the President. I conveyed our deep concerns about the vast amount of military equipment they are sending to Cuba and mentioned the large naval base the Russians are constructing in Cuba—the base that our Intelligence people feel is being built to house submarines. They based the evaluation on CIA agents planted in Cuba, as well as a fairly large number of Cuban refugees who lived in the area of the shipyard; and, of course, from the U-2 flights.

"Ambassador Dobrynin assured me that our concerns were unfounded. They are building a fishing base for the Cubans—just to help them out. Khrushchev sent his personal assurance to President Kennedy that no offensive weapons would be sent to Cuba, and added that the Soviets would do nothing that might disrupt the relations between our two nations.

Dobrynin assured me that with our national elections coming up, Khrushchev would do nothing to embarrass the President whom he likes very much personally.

"Not wanting Dobrynin to suspect how much we really knew, I didn't push it. But I did point out that Khrushchev had a strange way of showing his regard for the President or of demonstrating the friendship he spoke about, by continuing to escalate military activities in the Caribbean. I told him that we would be monitoring their military buildup very carefully and that serious consequences would result if the Soviet Union placed missiles in Cuba. He offered me the strongest assurances that any such action was unthinkable. The same day I met with the President and Secretaries Rusk and McNamara. I conveyed the meeting's content and relayed my own skepticism. I suggested that it might be prudent to issue a strong statement making it quite clear that America will not tolerate a transfer of any offensive weapons to Cuba.

"On September 4, Nick Katzenbach and I drafted a communiqué for the President that offered a warning to the Soviets, pointing out the serious consequences that would ensue as a result of such a step.

"As you all recall, the next week the Russians made a public pronouncement that they had no need, or any intention, of transferring nuclear missiles to Cuba or any other foreign country. I also received a personal letter from Premier Khrushchev asking me to convey to the President, once again, the Premier's assurance that under no circumstances would surface-to-surface missiles be sent to Cuba."

"Thank you, Bob. It now appears that everything we were asked to believe was nothing but a pack of lies," Jack Kennedy reasoned. "At the very moment Khrushchev was giving us assurances, he was also authorizing missiles to be shipped to Cuba, and for the missile silo construction to begin. The Premier deceived us; but we also deceived ourselves. On four occasions this year, the United States Intelligence Board guaranteed that Russia would never make Cuba a strategic base of operations. They reached the conclusion because the Russians had never done that with their other satellite allies and because the intelligence people reasoned that Russia could not afford to risk certain retaliation by the United States that such a step would evoke, if it were discovered."

"It was just a couple of weeks ago when we heard rumblings that they might be up to something," interjected Robert Kennedy. "Our first inkling was the night Castro's personal pilot got drunk at the Havana Hilton and bragged about the nuclear missiles the Russians were shipping to Cuba. A CIA agent heard him on Saturday evening and nosed around Sunday afternoon. That was when we first suspected that the base at San Cristobal might be a surface-to-surface installation."

"We're no longer dealing with mere suspicions, nor second or third-hand suppositions," the President said grimly. "We now have cold, hard, photographic evidence. The missiles are there! We must act before they become operational. The question is not, should we respond; but rather, how must we respond?

"I'm designating this group EXCOMM (*Executive Committee of the National Security Council).* Your normal duties will continue but will be subordinate to this Missile Crisis. It is now Priority One. We'll meet again, at 5 P.M."

*The EXCOMM men who fought to save America, as we tottered on the brink of World War III, were:*

*President John F. Kennedy.*
*Vice-President Lyndon B. Johnson.*
*Attorney General Robert F. Kennedy.*
*Secretary of State Dean Rusk.*
*Secretary of Defense Robert McNamara.*
*Secretary of Treasury Douglas Dillon.*
*CIA Director John McCone.*
*Four Special Assistants to the President:*
*McGeorge Bundy, Theodore Sorensen,*
*George Ball, and Alexis Johnson.*
*Llewellyn Thompson / Russian Relations Expert.*
*Future Ambassador to the Soviet Union.*
*Roswell Gilpatric.*
*Paul Nitze.*
*The USIA's Don Wilson.*
*Presidential Special Assistant, Kenneth O'Donnell.*
*Joint Chief Chairman, General Maxwell Taylor.*
*Asst. Sec. State / Latin-America, Edward Mardin.*
*In absentia, Ambassador to the United Nations,*
*Adlai Stevenson.*

These were the nineteen men who held the future of the world in their hands for thirteen critical days in the fall of 1962—a time for courage, a time for prudence, a time for resolve, a time for gravity. A slice of time remembered as the *Missiles of October.*

As they walked back to the Oval Office Jack said:

"I want you to take charge of these EXCOMM meetings, Bob. We both know the mere presence of the President tends to intimidate people. Intelligent men who are normally clear, independent thinkers, suddenly feel impelled to say what they suppose the President expects to hear. We can't afford a stifled atmosphere. If I'm not in the room that problem will be eliminated. Encourage frank, open discussions; of course, let me know whenever I need to be present. There are a fair number of options open to us, but I can see a dozen reasons for eliminating almost every one of them.

"After the Bay of Pigs fiasco, airstrikes against a sovereign nation aren't appealing—and sending in ground forces invites retaliation, in some form, by the Soviets. At this point, I tend to favor a naval blockade. It's the most passive, yet active measure we can employ. It offers the lowest risk, the least involvement, and a chance for the fewest casualties, both theirs and ours. It's a limited form of pressure, but it can be increased if circumstances warrant. Most of all, it lets the Russians know that we really mean business.

"Push for a blockade at this afternoon's meeting. Thrash out the recommendations of the EXCOMM members and try to formulate the best plan of action—as well as the worst case scenarios."

Robert McNamara became the strongest proponent for a blockade that afternoon. He agreed with the Kennedy brothers that it would be a firm measure, but less than an overt confrontation—and it offered the opportunity to increase the pressure if necessary.

Two Joint Chiefs argued for limited airstrikes—"surgical strikes," against known missile bases only. The other Joint Chiefs were opposed to such a plan, pointing out that surgical strikes would not suffice. General Maxwell Taylor summed up the opposition position.

"Surgical airstrikes are tactically impractical. We will eventually have to destroy every single military installation in Cuba. And once we do that, the next step will become obvious—a full-scale invasion, an eyeball to eyeball confrontation with the Russians. It may come down to that, gentlemen; but first of all, let's try to solve our dilemma with diplomacy rather than brute force."

"The General is correct," Robert Kennedy agreed. "A blockade is, I think, the obvious starting point."

"A blockade does not force the removal of missiles that are already in place," Llewellyn Thompson, the White House expert on the Soviet Union, countered, "or deter the work that is currently underway on the launching sites. They may already have a sufficient number of missiles in place to carry out any plans they have in mind. In that respect, a naval blockade would merely lock the barn door after the theft of the horse!"

"My main objection to a blockade," observed Ted Sorensen, the man Jack Kennedy referred to as his intellectual bloodbank, "is direct confrontation with the Soviets. We'll be interdicting Russian ships on the high sea! In 1812 we declared war on England for doing that to us. If we can find a way, it would make more sense, and entail fewer risks by far, to pressure the Cubans rather than the Russians."

"Can you suggest a way?" asked Robert Kennedy.

"Begin by demanding the immediate removal of every Russian missile," Sorensen replied.

"If I were Khrushchev, and the United States made such a demand, I would, in turn, demand a removal of the thousands of missiles that currently surround the Soviet Union and her satellites. They would win by losing, while we lost by winning," countered Kennedy. "We seem to have as many possibilities as we have EXCOMM members. Let's think about this overnight and reconvene in the morning. New U-2 photos will be ready at 8 A.M. Meanwhile, we all need to pray for wisdom and salvation."

*So the first day of the Missiles of October ended. Nineteen intelligent, committed men went separate ways, knowing full well that each tick of the clock brought them ever-closer to a global war; knowing, too, that very few ticks remained before time ran out.*

The following morning, Wednesday, October 17th, the members of EXCOMM discovered that their worst fears had been well founded. New U-2 photos disclosed several heretofore undiscovered missile installations and as many as thirty-two missiles with a thousand mile-range capability. Highly skilled and experienced photographic analysts interpreted the images as they were projected on a large screen.

A few missiles, armed with atomic warheads, were already staged and aimed at various American cities. The chief evaluator summed up his analysis with a chilling statement.

"We estimate that if these missiles are fired, *we can expect eighty million Americans to die within twenty minutes."*

Minutes after the intelligence expert left, President Kennedy entered.

"Good morning. First of all, I would like to hear from the Joint Chiefs. In light of this new data, what are your recommendations?"

Air Force General Curtis LeMay replied first.

"Mr. President, we must hit them now, before they can launch their first strike. Yesterday, I favored a naval blockade, but it no longer seems prudent. We must take immediate and forceful action!"

"I regretfully concur, Mr. President," Max Taylor agreed. "Castro's finger is on the trigger. Strike now! Waiting invites disastrous consequences!"

"If we attack, what will the Soviet response be?" asked the skeptical President.

"There will be no response!" LeMay assured him.

President Kennedy shook his head and frowned.

"I disagree, General. They, more than we, cannot afford to let such an action go unanswered. After all their tough talk, they will not, they cannot, permit us to destroy the missiles, kill a bunch of Russians, and do nothing about it. Khrushchev would be ousted, and probably exiled to Siberia if he did not respond quickly and vehemently. If he did not choose to take action in Cuba, he might well do so in Berlin."

"Mr. President," LeMay rejoined, "if we don't act in a strong fashion, the Russians would figure that we are impotent and don't have the stomach for a fight. If that happens, they may very well move even more missiles into Cuba, and then make a new move on

Berlin as well. And that might only be the beginning. With all due respect, Mr. President, I feel that we must draw a line in the sand and then stand firm!"

Marine Corps Commandant General David Shoup added, "You're in a pickle barrel, Mr. President."

"And all of you are in it with me."

Everyone laughed, and the tension in the room was momentarily broken.

The members of EXCOMM took a short break. When they returned, Robert McNamara was the first to speak.

"Mr. President, let me make my position perfectly clear. I am not in favor of airstrikes! I still favor a naval blockade; but I think we should be prepared to go ahead with the strikes in case a blockade does not have the desired effect. My staff completed an in-depth feasibility study this morning. Here are their recommendations for attacks on every missile site and military installation. Also included are airfields, ports, and gun emplacements. Sir, if you issue orders for immediate mobilization, it will take several days to prepare; but if we begin at once, we can fly five hundred sorties on the 23rd. Next Tuesday."

A hushed silence filled the historical conference room that had been the scene of so many crises over the past century and a half. It was Robert Kennedy who ended the pervasive stillness.

"I strongly support a blockade—not because of an overwhelming confidence that a blockade will work, but because I cannot visualize America launching a surprise attack on unsuspecting people."

Kennedy shuddered before he continued.

"Five hundred sorties represent a torrent of bombs and terror. They also mean death or dismemberment for thousands of Cubans. Innocent citizens! I am ready to accept any other course of action, rather than brand the United States with a stigma that will live for as long as history endures."

Former Secretary of State Dean Acheson, a wise and prudent statesman, answered Robert Kennedy.

"I have no desire to see innocent Cubans die, sir; but I have less desire to see innocent Americans die! The principal duty of every president is to safeguard US citizens from foreign aggression. Attacking Cuba very well might provide a ready excuse for Russia to launch World War III. I readily admit that. But if the Cubans strike our East Coast cities with their nuclear missiles, we will be involved in World War III, like it or not; but eighty million Americans won't know anything about the war because they'll be dead."

"Mr. Acheson," Robert Kennedy replied, "you are advocating a surprise attack by a huge nation on a small nation. Despite all of the obvious military and political arguments that support airstrikes instead of a blockade, I must point out that American tradition and honor cries out against any such overt action."

"Mr. Kennedy, I once asked Harry Truman why he finally decided to drop the atomic bombs on Japan. He said he went ahead because he couldn't figure out what he would say to the mothers of the million American soldiers who would be killed when we invaded Japan. I ask you that same question now. What will you say to the families of eighty million dead Americans?"

"Mr. Acheson, regardless of the course we decide upon, we must safeguard our moral position here at home as well as in the rest of the world. Our struggle against Communism is ongoing. The ideological war will be lost the moment we sacrifice our ideals and morality."

"Self preservation is often a stronger motivation than idealism and tradition!" Acheson countered.

"Do you think many people actually believe that?" queried a still unconvinced Robert Kennedy.

"I think several million people do! For example, every citizen of Hiroshima and Nagasaki who saw his country in the aftermath of an atomic attack, and discovered what it meant to struggle for survival in cities that had been reduced to piles of radioactive rubble."

For the next several days heated debates continued for periods as long as eighteen hours, as Committee members sought a non-violent solution to a volatile situation. Unwilling to assume that a solution would ever be found, President Kennedy issued orders for implementation of the blockade strategy. Aircraft, crews, and weapons were readied in case airstrikes finally had to be flown. U-2 pilots took hundreds of high altitude photographs. Several times each day intelligence experts carefully analyzed the data and then briefed the EXCOMM members on up-to-the-minute details and developments.

Although the conferees' opinions remained divided, each proposal they submitted was rooted as strongly in moral principle as it was in tactical consideration. Should the airstrikes be conducted? If so, should the Cuban population be warned prior to the attacks?

Several members recommended that letters be sent to Castro and Khrushchev twenty-four hours before any scheduled bombardment, and that pamphlets and warning leaflets should be dropped over all potential targets to allow danger zone residents sufficient time to escape.

Many plans were promoted, then discarded, for tactical or moral reasons. The EXCOMM members' primary concern was the safety of the United States; but each of them was also confronted by standards of justice and integrity—ideals that have characterized America since her inception. Without respite, each man wrestled with his own conscience throughout the long, grueling hours of the day and the even longer, sleepless hours of the night. Impaled on a sharp double-edged sword of calamity, they carefully weighed options and probabilities.

Nearly all of the proposed solutions could rightly be characterized as 'soft.' Soft actions are often preferred because they are not only easier on the recipients; they are far easier on the devisers. But would any of the proposals actually work?

Some alternatives were hard and confrontational—aggressive responses that would only be utilized as a last resort. But in his heart of hearts, each of these wise and prudent men realized that the final strategy would have to come from a very short list of tough choices. They were debating more than a removal of ballistic missiles; they were facing a decision that could take the world to the brink of World War III—the brink of a cataclysm that might well turn a once bright green planet Earth into a scarred and charred atomic cinder.

In the midst of the EXCOMM turmoil the Soviet Foreign Minister, Andrei Gromyko, came to see the President. His visit had been scheduled before the missiles were discovered. The President considered canceling it.

"Should I confront him with the knowledge we already possess, or skirt the issue?" Kennedy asked his brother.

"I feel strongly that we should keep Gromyko in the dark for now, at least until we formulate and agree on a plan of action."

"I agree, Bob. I'll simply listen, and say nothing at all about the missiles."

President Kennedy received Andrei Gromyko in the Oval Office on Wednesday afternoon.

"Mr. President, I respectfully demand that you stop threatening our poor Cuban friends. Fidel Castro's principal goal is peaceful coexistence with America and the rest of the world's nations. In spite of the ramblings of fools, the Cubans are not interested in pressing their political philosophy on any other Latin American country. Cuba, like the Soviet Union, has one simple desire: to live in peace and harmony."

"The blasts of tough talk I hear from you Russian Communists, as well as the Cuban, Chinese, Korean, and Vietnamese Communists, make a bad case for your professed peaceful coexistence. You can't talk about peace one minute and then arm your satellites with new offensive weapons the next. Which posture are we supposed to believe, Foreign Minister?"

"You have been misinformed, Mr. President. We only aid our allies, as you do. We don't arm them!"

"Oh? Really?"

"Yes indeed. You see, we share a common enemy, Mr. President. That enemy is starvation. The Soviet Union gives her friends tools and farm implements, and sufficient knowledge to enable them to cultivate their fields and develop their lands. Our goal is to help the people of the world to feed themselves. It is our only purpose. All of this wild talk I hear about the Soviet Union's desire to dominate the Earth is foolishness." Gromyko smiled before he added, "It might make an exciting movie plot for your friends in Hollywood, but nothing more."

"Mr. Foreign Minister, do you deny that you are supplying weapons to your satellite countries?" demanded the President

"No, of course not, Mr. President. But they are all defensive weapons. As the great American, J. Edgar Hoover, says, 'you can't be too careful nowadays in such a dangerous world.' The last thing we would consider is furnishing offensive weapons to Cuba or anyone else. American newspapers would crucify us. There is an easy way to lessen the tensions between yourselves and the Cubans, Mr. President. Merely decrease some of the pressure that you are bringing against them."

Kennedy was startled by this presumptive and bald-faced twist of the truth.

"If you do supply offensive weapons to Castro, after Premier Khrushchev gave me his direct and personal guarantee that you would not, I would be extremely concerned, Mr. Foreign Minister."

The President opened a desk drawer and withdrew several typed sheets of paper.

"So that there is no mistake or misunderstanding, I'm going to repeat a statement I made on national television, on September 4th."

Kennedy read a carefully worded warning advising the Soviet Union of the serious consequences that would ensue if they ever placed offensive missiles, or any weapon with strike capability, on Cuban soil.

"I meant it then, and I mean it now. Don't push us too far, Mr. Foreign Minister. We've almost reached the end of our endurance."

Gromyko left a short time later, convinced for the first time that the young American president might be tougher than he and Khrushchev had imagined.

He hurried back to the Soviet Embassy and called the Kremlin on the scrambler telephone.

The EXCOMM members continued to wrangle until late Wednesday evening, and after a few hours of troubled sleep, began again on Thursday morning.

As the tedious day dragged on, there seemed to be more differing opinions than ever. Strong arguments were logically justified. Positions changed. Members reconsidered the options. Yesterday's militants often became today's wait-and-see pacifists. The militant hawks became doves for a few hours, then, without warning, flew back into the verbal fray with talons extended, eager for action. Uncertainty and flux were commonplace. With mankind's future hanging in the balance, each of the dedicated deliberators was faced with far greater pressure than he had ever known. At times, one of the men might seem to wriggle backwards, into a shell as uncomfortable as that of a hermit crab, before calling into play a surge of power, resolve, and fortitude that he never before had needed to employ.

A will to win pervaded every committee member. The will became so strong that it overcame despair, fatigue, and indecision; but nonetheless, the pressure on human frailties took its toll. Strain could be seen in the faces of every man—strain that was evidenced by their fits of impatience and angry outbursts.

As daylight hours ebbed, the shadows lengthened and tempers shortened. A variety of proposals were offered; but each of them seemed to contain inherent weaknesses, which were swiftly pointed out by other committee members, often with devastating effects that created deeply ingrained hard feelings.

At three o'clock President Kennedy phoned from Chicago, where he had just delivered an important speech to Midwest business leaders. He requested initial recommendations by six o'clock.

All of the sand in the hourglass was nearly gone!

The committee split into two groups and compiled preliminary recommendations. First, they outlined a plan listing all contingencies that might reasonably be expected; finally, they suggested various strategies that could be implemented to retaliate or respond to each contingency. Whenever a plan was completed, it was given to the other group for evaluation.

Every plan was examined and dissected. Strengths and weaknesses were analyzed and critiqued. Then these revised plans were returned to the formulators, who honed and improved their original ideas. The two sets of recommendations were finished minutes before the six o'clock deadline.

The group that favored a blockade offered:

1. *A legal justification for American action.*
2. *An agenda for a meeting with the Organization of American States.*
3. *An analysis of the UN's probable role.*
4. *Actual military procedure for interdicting ships.*
5. *Circumstances that might require military force.*

Those favoring military intervention detailed:

1. *The exact targets that would be attacked.*
2. *Arguments, justifying the strikes, to the UN.*
3. *Ways to gain support of the OAS members.*
4. *A communiqué to Khrushchev, discouraging any retaliation in Cuba, Berlin, or elsewhere.*

Robert Kennedy called the President, who decided to cut his Chicago trip short and return on Saturday morning. He told his brother to invite the EXCOMM members to the NSC meeting that was scheduled on Saturday afternoon at 2:30.

"We must decide on an immediate course of action Bob. Further delay is unacceptable! I plan to go on national television Monday evening and address the nation. We may all stay in session until five minutes before that broadcast; but by then, we must establish a workable plan and be prepared to stay the course. The Russians have to believe that we mean business! To convince Premier Khrushchev of that fact, I must have the support of a unified country."

The committee returned to their deliberations early on Friday morning. Throughout the day, they refined their plans. It was midnight by the time they finally felt ready to meet with the President and the NSC.

# *WASHINGTON, D.C.*

# *OCTOBER 20, 1962*

Jack Kennedy returned to the White House at 1:30 P.M., then went directly to the swimming pool.

While he swam, his brother sat in a lounge chair and briefed him on EXCOMM's current positions. Jack remained in the refreshing water for forty-five minutes. When he emerged, he dressed in casual clothes, and the brothers walked to the Oval Office.

By then, it was 2:30 P.M.

The session began promptly and continued until 5:15. Since it was a formal meeting of the National Security Council, every member who was unaware of the current situation had to be brought up to date.

Secretary of Defense Robert McNamara presented the plan for a blockade. Then one of the Joint Chiefs made a strong pitch for a military attack. He wound up his remarks by saying, "We should not hesitate to use our atomic weapons if the situation makes their use a necessity."

"How can we even contemplate the use of atomic weapons?" Robert Kennedy queried incredulously. "How can we justify such a decision?"

"We must make the Soviets believe that we *will* use our atomic weapons. If they think we're the least bit squeamish, they won't hesitate to use their entire armament again us."

"What if you're wrong, General? What if we use atomic weapons, and then the other side retaliates? We'll precipitate the world's first atomic war, won't we?"

"That won't happen! I give you my guarantee!"

"That's an interesting guarantee, General. If you're right, we'll all remember your brilliance. If you're wrong, it won't matter, because every one of us will be dead. There'll be no one left to say, 'I told you so.' We can't afford to lose, General; but neither can we afford a Pyrrhic victory!"

The President put a question to the Commander of Tactical Air Command, General Walter Sweeney—a question that was in the mind of every NSC member.

"If we commit our air forces to an all-out, major surprise attack, can we be certain of achieving total destruction of all the missile sites and every nuclear weapon in Cuba?"

"No, Sir! A surprise airstrike would eliminate the majority of their weapons; but I cannot guarantee more than about 75% success."

"Thank you! All right gentlemen, that resolves my final doubt. We cannot be sure that a naval blockade will remove all of the missiles. Since we are equally uncertain that an airstrike will accomplish anything more, I'm now ready to order a blockade. Airstrikes are certain to kill people! A blockade is not, unless it is met with resistance. A blockade is unquestionably a more moral and humane answer. I hope it will be judged as such by our friends and our foes alike."

"Mr. President," interjected Adlai Stevenson, who had left his duties at the United Nations in the hands of his deputy, and flown to Washington that morning to attend this critical meeting. "If you demand the removal of all of the Soviet weapons, I feel you must offer them something in exchange."

"What would you suggest?"

"Let Khrushchev know we're willing to remove our missiles from Italy and Turkey and abandon our Guantanamo Bay Naval Base."

"I am dubious about the strategic value of Jupiter missiles we currently have in Italy and Turkey; but this is the wrong time to consider their removal. And surrendering our Guantanamo Bay base is even more unthinkable. Mr. Ambassador, we must be cautious; but we cannot permit our adversaries to believe that our caution is occasioned by weakness. To curtail that idea, we must negotiate from the positions of firmness and determination, not compromise and appeasement."

Now that the decision had been made, it was time for implementation. Washington-based ambassadors from each of America's allies were informed of the crisis and the plan. They would be kept up to date with hourly bulletins.

Top White House strategists, led by Ted Sorensen, went to work on a position paper that would legally justify the proposed action of interdicting foreign ships in international waters.

On Sunday, an ever-increasing number of officials were called into their offices and made aware of the situation. Newsmen and television reporters began to sense that something was remiss and began tracking down each hint and innuendo. Although nothing had been substantiated when all the eleven o'clock news shows aired across America, most of the lead stories implied that a major crisis of unknown proportions was looming. Fearful that the morning newspapers might print speculative stories in their early editions, President Kennedy made more than a dozen phone calls to various power brokers of the press and used his influence to insure that nothing alarming would appear in any of the morning newspapers. In return, the cooperators were told he would make a major policy address on Monday evening.

The diplomatic corps worked diligently throughout that long night. By morning an impeccably legal and logical justification, under Organization of American States Charter, was completed.

The President contacted each of the OAS leaders and asked them to approve a plan to blockade Cuba. The grateful President received unanimous consent for quarantine. Suddenly the Russians and Cubans were not only opposing America; they were aligned against every free nation in the Western Hemisphere.

A transatlantic call to Britain's Prime Minister Harold Macmillan resulted in a pledge of his nation's unshakable backing.

French President Charles de Gaulle was often a very difficult man. Since de Gaulle admired Dean Acheson, the former Secretary of State, the President asked him to break the news to de Gaulle. Acheson explained the circumstances and offered to supply U-2 photographs of the missile sites before asking the French President for support. The offer proved to be unnecessary.

"You are doing exactly what I would do in your place," de Gaulle told Acheson. "I have no need for photographs! A great nation such as yours does not act without evidence."

The West German Chancellor, Konrad Adenauer, was just as encouraging as de Gaulle had been.

America's three major European allies would now add support to nations of the Western Hemisphere.

Canada's Prime Minister John Diefenbaker boldly approved the quarantine, but added,

"I only hope you can convince the rest of the world as easily as you've convinced me."

While the international coalition of nations grew, military preparations intensified. Missile crews were placed on full alert and more troops were moved into the southeastern states.

First Armored Division personnel, based in Texas, moved out, and began a trek around the Gulf Coast toward Florida. Five additional divisions were also placed on alert standby.

Strategic Air Command aircraft were dispatched to various places in the country and dispersed around civilian air fields, a move that increased capability and decreased vulnerability. The SAC B-52 bombers armed with atomic weapons stayed on twenty-four hour readiness. Half of the planes were always in the air—when one landed, its counterpart took off.

To reduce the risk of the Guantanamo Bay Naval Base being overrun, additional troops were flown in as reinforcements on Monday morning.

A few hours before the President's speech, Dean Rusk summoned Russian Ambassador Dobrynin and told him about its content. The newsmen who were on duty near Rusk's office later reported that when the

Ambassador left the building his shoulders were hunched and his chin sagged down on his chest. A few observers thought his attitude conveyed sadness; many others said he looked completely bewildered.

Monday afternoon was a busy time for President Kennedy. An official group was formally created by NSA Memorandum 196 to replace EXCOMM. The *Executive Committee For The Purpose Of Effective Conduct In Operations Of The Executive Branch In The Current Crisis* came into being. The President became the official chairman and directed members to meet with him every morning until further notice.

Next, he held his first full Cabinet meeting since the missiles had been discovered. The purpose of the meeting was to inform each Cabinet member about the crisis as well as the proposed action. As the Cabinet members filed out, a meeting for certain key members of Congress began.

Some Congressmen were extremely critical of the President's intentions, but a majority of those present favored air raids. A few felt that an invasion would be even more appropriate. A strong show of force, like air raids or an invasion—not a weak response, like a blockade—was the adamant, popular position of the day.

"Mr. President," drawled Georgia's Senior Senator Richard Russell, "I could not live with myself if I did not say, in the strongest possible terms, how vital it is that we act with greater resolve than that which you are now contemplating."

Senator Fulbright of Arkansas agreed with Russell.

"I strongly advocate some type of immediate military action! This is not the time for a weak step like a blockade!"

Most skeptical Congressmen remained silent, not because they agreed with the President, but because they thought it best for Americans to appear united during this moment of national crisis.

President Kennedy responded to every objection with great patience and obvious confidence.

"Please rest assured that I will not hesitate to take any step or employ any means in the defense of the United States; but I do not feel that an invasion, or even airstrikes, are warranted at this time. I want to avoid a devastating war! If possible, we must try to close this issue without bloodshed. For that reason, I am committed to the course I have outlined."

He paused for several seconds and gazed out at his listeners, evaluating the attitudes of these seasoned congressional leaders.

"The blockade is only a first step," he continued reluctantly. "Before the crisis ends, it may well be necessary to employ far more stringent military means; but I will order no such course of action unless it becomes our last resort!

"Meanwhile, in case there is no alternative, I have ordered a number of strategic units to full alert and moved others to stand-by. Rest assured, gentlemen, that the United States will not be caught napping."

The President let his words hang in the sudden stillness before he continued.

"The reaction of those who believe that a series of air raids are warranted is not unusual. It was my first reaction as well as that of nearly everyone on the

Executive Committee; but military aggression invites reprisals. I am not, nor are you, prepared to suffer a missile barrage on our eastern seaboard that could annihilate millions of Americans. Armed intervention is not an alternative until we have exhausted every other means.

"No champions are crowned after a shooting war! Wars only produce losers! Big losers or small losers, but losers nonetheless. I will not allow America to become a loser of any kind. We will prepare for a maximum confrontation; but we will try to settle this crisis with a minimum of force."

He stood up and uttered his final admonishment.

"I urge Nikita Khrushchev and Fidel Castro not to misinterpret my position. I am offering the simplest solution to an unacceptable situation. They should understand that the removal of every ballistic missile from Cuban soil is the only remedy the United States will accept. I am not offering a suggestion! I am issuing an ultimatum! And I warn them now, that if they reject my demand, they must be aware of the terrible risks they would be inviting. Justice and right are on our side, and I will act accordingly."

America's thirty-fifth president, John Fitzgerald Kennedy, addressed the nation at 7 P.M. His manner was dignified, calm, and confident. He detailed the current Cuban situation and enumerated the reasons that made him favor a blockade.

His speech strongly emphasized three points.

1. *A naval blockade might only be the first step.*
2. *Additional military action might be necessary.*

3. *If further action was required, every necessary preparation and precaution had been taken already.*

These steps would insure the success of any future action.

When his national audience was polled after the broadcast, the viewer consensus seemed to be that the situation was serious; but it was being handled well; and it was good to have the future of America in the hands of a leader as capable as Jack Kennedy.

The President himself felt no such elation. An hour before he went on the air he had been briefed by Defense Secretary McNamara. The invasion would require 250,000 troops. 90,000 Airborne troops and Marines would assault the beaches. 2,000 airstrikes would hit targets of opportunity. Pentagon planners estimated that 25,000 casualties could be expected before a complete victory was achieved.

President Kennedy was reluctant and somber as he approved these plans scant moments before he spoke to the nation in confident tones. During his speech, and in the difficult days ahead, confidence in his decision gave him a determination to persevere and gave a grateful American nation confidence in his presidential abilities.

The President stayed at his desk in the Oval Office until midnight. Before he retired he sent a special message to Nikita Khrushchev.

*"In our discussions and exchanges on Berlin and other international questions, the one thing that has most concerned me has been the possibility that your*

*government would not correctly understand the will and determination of the United States in any given situation. I cannot assume that you or any other sane man would, in this nuclear age, deliberately plunge the world into a war which is crystal clear that no country could win, and which could only result in catastrophic consequences to the whole world, including the aggressor."*

# *WASHINGTON, D.C.*
# *OCTOBER 23, 1962*

On the seventh day of the crisis, an Organization of American States meeting was convened for the sole purpose of voting on the naval blockade. In an organization that was famous for its lack of unity, the final vote was astonishing. The Latin American countries lined up behind the United States. 100% of the nations favored a blockade. No one was opposed.

An even greater surprise occurred when several member nations offered to supply men or war ships to supplement those already committed by the US.

The ten o'clock meeting of the 196 Executive Committee was filled with the first real elation since the preceding week when the Cuban missiles were discovered. An OAS endorsement had been one of their major sources of concern, and the 196 members were buoyed up by the outcome. A strong united front would confront the Russians and their allies.

The meeting began with a report from John McCloy, formerly a US High Commissioner to Germany, and Kennedy's top advisor for European affairs. McCloy had been recalled from Germany to assist Adlai Stevenson in presenting the US position at the UN.

McCloy, a Republican, had originally favored airstrikes followed by an invasion. When he was yoked with Stevenson, who held less aggressive views, a unique diplomatic tandem was formed, representing a rich vista of political ideology.

Capitol denizens idolized this strong bipartisanism because they were seldom able to bring it to fruition.

McCloy reported no substantial change in Soviet posture, either militarily or politically. No alerts had been called; however, admittance to the missile bases in Cuba was now limited to Russian personnel only and the missile sites were now being camouflaged. McCloy observed that the installations should have been camouflaged long ago. No one understood why the Russian strategists had waited so long to begin the process. McCloy concluded with an interesting question.

"Mr. President, what do you intend to do if the Russians shoot down one of our U-2 planes?"

Kennedy was prepared with an immediate answer.

"Our combat aircraft would retaliate at once! We will destroy one of their surface-to-air missile sites."

He turned toward Secretary McNamara.

"How quickly could we respond, Bob?"

"In less than two hours, Mr. President."

"We must be sure we don't start a shooting war by accident! I must have absolute verification of hostile action before I give the order to commit our armed forces. I want an immediate rescue of any downed pilot. I don't want another American flyer to fall into Castro's hands. Also, I'm extending current tours of duty for critical personnel, particularly in high-tension areas, such as Berlin, until this situation is resolved. Finally, I want the 101st Airborne placed on full alert. They must be ready to go to any trouble spot on an hour's notice. If Russian response to our demands makes retaliation or invasion inevitable, I want no time spent on preparations that can be done now. If we have to attack one of their installations, it is reasonable to expect them to attempt an attack on one of ours. Let's make sure that every military base within their strike capability distance is on alert, and let's be certain that all of our aircraft are well dispersed."

Maxwell Taylor, the 101st Airborne Commander during World War II and the man most responsible for forging the Division into the formidable fighting force it had become, slid a dozen U-2 photos across the table toward the President.

"As you can see, Mr. President, the Cuban planes are lined up, wing tip to wing tip. If we have to hit them, it'll be as easy as shooting fish in a barrel."

Kennedy examined the pictures, then remarked,

"You're right, General Taylor. All the more reason to make sure our planes aren't clustered. I don't want to supply any fish for Castro's barrels!

"Very well, gentlemen. This afternoon I'm going to communicate with each of our European allies. Let's plan to meet again at six o'clock, after the OAS announces their support."

For the next several hours the President spent his time on the phone, explaining the current situation and listening very carefully to the recommendations and ideas of the other world leaders. Throughout the day overflights of Cuba continued, and the Russian shortwave radio channels were closely monitored.

U-2 flights indicated that missile site construction was progressing at a feverish pace. Radio monitoring produced dozens of signals to Soviet ships inbound for

Cuba. Of course, there was no way to intercept or decipher the coded messages; however, not a single ship slowed or altered its course. On they came!

A terse reply to the Kennedy midnight message arrived from Khrushchev.

He declared that a blockade was a personal threat to him and the Soviet Union. He and his country would not acknowledge any type of blockade.

*"The actions of the United States with regard to Cuba are outright banditry or, if you like, the folly of degenerate imperialism. You are pushing mankind to the abyss of a world missile-nuclear war! Captains of Soviet vessels bound for Cuba will not obey the orders of your naval forces. If any effort is made we will then be forced for our part to take the measures which we deem necessary and adequate to protect our rights. We will do whatever is necessary."*

The 196 Committee reconvened at six o'clock.

The first order of business was the reading of Khrushchev's letter. After ten minutes of discussion the President read the strong reply he had drafted.

*"In early September I indicated very plainly that the US would regard any shipment of offensive weapons as presenting the gravest concern. At the time this Government received most explicit assurances from your Government and its representatives, both publicly and privately, that no offensive weapons were being shipped to Cuba. If you will review the statement*

*made by Tass in September, you will see how clearly this assurance was given.*

*"In reliance on these solemn assurances I urged restraint upon those in this country who were urging action in this matter at that time. Then I learned beyond doubt what you have not denied— namely, that all those assurances were false and that your military people have set out recently to establish missile bases in Cuba. I ask you to recognize clearly, Mr. Chairman, that it was not I who issued the first challenge in this case, and in the light of this record these activities in Cuba required the responses I have announced. I repeat my regret that these events have caused deterioration in our relations. I hope your Government will take the necessary action to permit a restoration of those relations."*

When the President finished reading, there were tense moments of expectant silence before he spoke again.

"I would like your recommendations, gentlemen."

The recommendations were twofold. The message to Khrushchev should be amplified a bit; and, they suggested that the President prepare a proclamation ordering the blockade to begin the next morning at 10 A.M.

A final paragraph was added to the communication for Premier Khrushchev. The President asked the Soviet leader *"to observe the quarantine which had been legally established by a unanimous vote of the OAS."* The message concluded, *"I have no desire to fire on any Soviet ship. I hope you will join my efforts to demonstrate prudence and to do nothing to make the current situation more difficult than it is."*

Then, in conjunction with the Joint Chiefs, the President and the 196 Committee decided on rules of engagement that would govern American ships if a foreign vessel refused to heave to.

To avoid a major international incident, one that could well provoke a war if any ship refused to stop, naval gunfire would be directed at the propellers and rudders. In that manner, it was hoped, a ship could be disabled without serious injuries or loss of life.

"What if, even then, the Soviet crew chooses to resist?" the President wondered aloud. "If we attempt to board uncooperative ships, we can reasonably expect a fire fight and any number of casualties."

"We don't have to storm aboard if the ships are dead in the water, unable to maneuver," speculated Robert McNamara.

"If you purposefully cripple a vessel on the high seas, you can't simply abandon her to the whimsy of nature," the former skipper of PT 109 interposed.

"We could tow any disabled vessels to a nearby port," McNamara suggested. "Like Charleston, or perhaps Jacksonville."

"Let me pose a worst case scenario," rejoined the President. "We cripple a resistant ship, then tow her to port. When the cargo is inspected, all we find is baby food, or something else just as harmless. Then what?"

"Only interdict ships that are visibly transporting military stores and equipment," offered McNamara.

"We must establish firm guidelines for the Navy. How do we decide which ships to stop and which to leave alone? Freighters can stow tons of military materials below decks. How can we know that if no evidence is visible? What criteria do we use?" Kennedy asked his advisors.

While everyone pondered this question, CIA Director John McCone entered the room and slipped into an empty chair.

"More bad news, Mr. President. Several Russian submarines are headed toward the Caribbean from three different locations."

"Tracking those subs must be a top priority, John! Bob, issue any necessary order that will protect all of our ships that might be exposed to any type of attack, particularly our aircraft carriers."

McCone and McNamara hurried from the room to set the wheels in motion.

"We must act in a prudent and resourceful way," the President concluded. "We cannot be stampeded into any foolish actions. God knows, during World War II, most nations stumbled into war before they were prepared—motivated by misunderstandings, idiosyncrasies, or just plain stupidity, while their real underlying reasons were security, pride, or simply saving face.

"We must not be forced into a war, gentlemen. Our mission is to keep the peace, not to precipitate violence. We must make every nation around the world, friends and foes alike, understand that we have done everything humanly possible to protect the peace. We must not miscalculate, misinterpret, or misjudge; and we must not force our adversaries into a destructive course of action, regardless of any future Soviet duplicity.

"Thank you all, very much, for all your hard work. We'll meet again tomorrow at ten."

As the others left the room, the President motioned to his brother to remain.

"You've always gotten along with Ambassador Dobrynin better than the rest of us, Bob. Call him tomorrow and set up an early appointment. On a personal basis you may be able to make him see our concerns. Make him aware of the great risks they're running with their adamant behavior and the uncomfortable posture they're forcing us to adopt."

Time dragged by slowly as a fretful, expectant America waited to see what Khrushchev would do—and, if Khrushchev did not forestall the crisis, what Jack Kennedy would do. For two tension-filled days Soviet ships steamed toward Cuba. While ashore, Soviet technicians worked at a feverish pace to complete launching sites for deadly IL-28 missiles.

Then, at 0724 on Friday morning, October 26, the first ship was stopped. At 0800 she was boarded.

She was *Marucla*, a Panama-owned, Lebanon-registered, American-built liberty ship. Chartered to the Soviet Union, she was bound for Cuba from the Baltic port of Riga.

*Marucla* had been spotted the previous evening, then shadowed during the long hours of darkness by a pair of US destroyers. *John Pierce* and *Joseph P. Kennedy Jr.* received credit for the discovery. *Kennedy* had been named for the President's eldest brother, a bomber pilot who died heroically during World War II.

President Kennedy selected *Marucla* personally for several reasons.

1. She was not a Soviet ship.
2. Therefore, it was not a personal affront to Khrushchev, and it did not require an immediate response.
3. It proved that the United States meant business.
4. It gave the Soviets additional time to formulate a response.

At 0900, *Marucla* was found to be carrying no contraband and was allowed to continue her voyage.

A new stage was set, and the waiting began again.

The Soviets remained adamant in their refusal to recognize a quarantine, and the preparation of Cuban missile bases went on as diligently as ever.

In response, President Kennedy ordered a gradual increase in pressure, one that stopped just short of a direct confrontation. The Cuban surveillance flights were increased from two a day to twelve. At night, photographs were taken with the aid of bright flares that lit up the island's countryside.

With each passing hour President Kennedy and his advisors became more certain that nuclear war with Russia was inevitable. If Khrushchev's position did not change or if his offensive weapons buildup continued, America's only possible response would have to be military force.

The morning meeting began with new reports from Robert McNamara and John McCone.

"If an invasion becomes necessary, our military forecasters predict very high casualties," McNamara told the group.

"It will be a long, difficult undertaking," cautioned McCone. "In Korea we found out how tough it is to drive even the greenest troops out of the hills. Cuba could very well become another Korea!"

"Long before we get to that point," interjected the President, "we're going to face bloody fights at the missile sites. We must acknowledge the possibility that a few of those missiles will be fired as soon as military operations begin. Invasion forces will suffer causalities; but missiles might also produce as many or more casualties among the civilians in cities along our Atlantic coast. For now all we can do is pray for peace, prepare for war, and wait for Chairman Khrushchev's answer."

At six o'clock the answer came.

*"We must not succumb to petty passions or transient things. We should realize that if indeed war should break out, then it would not be in our power to stop it, for such is the logic of war. I have participated in two wars and I know that war ends when it has rolled through cities and villages, sowing its seeds of death and destruction everywhere.*

*"The United States should not be concerned about the missiles in Cuba. They would never be used to attack America. They were there for defensive purposes only. You can be calm in the regard that we are of sound mind and understand that if we attack you, you will respond the same way. You will receive*

*the same if you hurl against us. I think you understand that. This indicates that we are sane people, that we can correctly understand and evaluate the situation. Consequently, how can we permit the incorrect action you ascribe to us? Only lunatics or suicides, who themselves want to perish and to destroy the whole world before they die, could do this.*

*"We want something quite different. We have no desire to destroy your country, despite our ideological differences. We want to compete peacefully, not militarily.*

*"I assure you, President Kennedy, that there is nothing to be gained by stopping our ships which are bound for Cuba. They are not carrying weapons. All necessary missiles and weapons are in Cuba already.* [**The first time Khrushchev admits that the missiles exist.**] *At our Vienna conference, you admitted that the Bay of Pigs was a mistake. I admired your frankness. We all make mistakes. I not only acknowledge the mistakes that we have made during the history of our state but sharply condemn them, as well.*

*"I sent defensive weapons to Cuba because the United States took an active part in trying to overthrow the current government, just as it took an active part in attempting to overthrow the government in my country after our revolution. My only objective was to help the Cubans to protect themselves. If I were to receive assurances from the President of the United States that you would sanction no further aggression against Cuba, and that the blockade would be lifted, then the question of the removal or destruction of missile sites in Cuba would become a completely different issue.*

*Armaments encourage disasters. When a nation accumulates them, this damages the economy; then if one puts them to use, they destroy the people on both sides. Consequently, only a mad man believes that armaments are the principal means in the life of a society. No, they are an enforced loss of human energy, and what is more, are for the destruction of man himself. If people do not show wisdom, then in the final analysis they will come to a clash, like blind moles, and then reciprocal extermination will begin. With all of those things in mind, here is my proposal.*

*"We will send no more weapons to Cuba. Those that are already there will be withdrawn or destroyed. You must reciprocate by withdrawing your blockade, and agree never to invade Cuba or interfere in any way with that sovereign nation. You must also stop treating Russian ships in a piratical manner.*

*"If you have not lost your self-control and sensibly conceive what this might lead to, you and we ought not to pull on the ends of the rope in which you have tied the knot of war, because the more the two of us pull, the tighter the knot will become. And a time may come when that knot will be tied so tight, that even he who tied it will not have the strength to untie it, and then it will be necessary to cut that knot, and what that would mean is not for me to explain to you, because you understand perfectly of what terrible forces our countries dispose. Consequently, if there is no intention to tighten that knot, and thereby doom the world to the catastrophe of thermonuclear war, let us not only relax the forces pulling on the ends of the rope, let us take measures to untie that knot. I am ready to do this."*

"What do you think, Bob?" the president asked his brother.

"In spite of all the verbose rhetoric, Khrushchev seems to be searching for some accommodation, some agreement. The very least it does is open the door for further discussions."

A telephone on the conference table rang. John McCone answered it. He listened for several seconds, then placed his hand over the mouthpiece.

"It's John Scali, from ABC News. The Soviet Embassy has given him a message for you."

"Put him on the speaker phone."

As soon as McCone complied, Kennedy said:

"Good evening, Mr. Scali. This is the President. What is the message?"

"Good evening, Mr. President. Ten minutes ago I was contacted by a Soviet Embassy official who asked me to convey information concerning the current missile crisis. They propose the removal of their missiles, under United Nations inspection and supervision. In return the United States will end its blockade and pledge never to invade Cuba. That was the end of the message, Mr. President."

"Thank you for your assistance, Mr. Scali, and good evening."

"It's interesting that they communicated through a newsman," observed Robert Kennedy.

"John Scali is an extremely honest and capable man," his brother reminded him. "This unorthodox means of communication gives the Soviets irrefutable documentation as to their offer. We should always remember to expect the unexpected from our Soviet friends. However, the tone of Khrushchev's note, in league with the Scali message, makes me guardedly optimistic. We'll meet in the morning as usual. That will give us all time to consider their apparent offer and to begin preparing a reply. I trust you will all rest well, gentlemen."

The President and the other Committee members certainly had a reason to be optimistic as they left the meeting and went their separate ways; but their optimism would be brief. Morning would bring new and startling information to light—information that would sharply diminish the Committee's boundless enthusiasm. And the bearer of those unwelcome tidings would be none other than J. Edgar Hoover.

It was only a few moments after daybreak when the telephone on President Kennedy's bedside table rang. The caller was FBI Director J. Edgar Hoover.

Kennedy detected an icy edge in Hoover's voice, but wasn't surprised by the other man's tone. J. Edgar Hoover disliked Joseph P. Kennedy, his sons, and every member of the Kennedy clan, nearly as much as they disliked him.

"I received information from my agents in New York City. Soviet personnel are apparently preparing to destroy all of their sensitive documents and materials."

"Are they absolutely certain of this, Mr. Hoover?"

"If I called you at this hour with unsubstantiated information that later turned out to be false, I would look like a fool. No FBI agent would ever dare to make me look like a fool."

The President grinned in spite of himself.

"My question was unguarded and unnecessary, Mr. Hoover. I apologize."

A grunt from Hoover confirmed the transparent validity of the presidential acknowledgement.

"Obviously, Mr. Kennedy, such action by Soviet personnel can only mean that they expect you to take direct action against the Cuban missile bases, or to continue interdicting Soviet ships. Destruction of the documents indicates that they would consider either of those moves tantamount to an act of war."

Hoover waited expectantly for a reply. When it came, it was not the one he had anticipated.

"Thank you for your call, Mr. Hoover. Please keep me informed of any situational change."

Kennedy broke the connection but did not hang up; instead, he dialed his brother's number and shared the Hoover information.

"The conduct of the Soviets, in New York, seems strange after the letter from Khrushchev, Jack. If we deciphered his statement correctly, he is anxious to find a peaceful solution. In essence, he handed us the solution to end the stalemate. Did we misinterpret him?"

"There is no mistaking his position, Bob. Perhaps the New York personnel are simply out of the loop."

"Perhaps we're out of the loop! Maybe the Soviet leadership in the Kremlin, particularly the Foreign Office, has overruled Khrushchev and decided to take a harder stance?"

"You might be right. If you are, we'll be getting a communiqué repudiating the Khrushchev letter and establishing a new set of ground rules. In any case, we should know a lot more before long. I'll see you at ten, Bob."

Kennedy rose, donned a pair of baggy black swim trunks, and quietly left the family living quarters. He always enjoyed a swim before breakfast, particularly when he was confronted with a knotty problem.

When he reached the pool, he eased into the water instead of diving. He had badly injured his back when PT-109 was torpedoed, and certain movements were still quite difficult, if not agonizing. He swam slowly up and down the pool, remembering his naval service in the South Pacific and recalling how serious that situation had seemed with his entire crew depending on him. Now an entire nation was depending on him. Well, he had not let the crew down then, and he would not let the country down now. His father had taught all of his children that a solution could always be found to any problem! All you had to do was determine your best course of action, then go ahead and follow it through.

Joseph Kennedy believed that follow-through was the principal difference between successful men and failures—and Jack believed that wholeheartedly.

At 10 A.M., just as the 196 Committee meeting began, a Navy chief entered the Cabinet Room.

"Pardon the interruption, Mr. President; but we just decoded this message from the Kremlin."

Kennedy took the clipboard, removed the decoded message, initialed the transcript receipt, and returned the clipboard.

"Thank you, Chief."

Kennedy scanned the message, then inserted it in a viewgraph projector that was positioned near him on the table. The letter was projected onto a huge screen behind the President's chair and was now seen as a 6 x 6-foot enlargement. Committee members read the communiqué with varying degrees of foreboding.

Gone was yesterday's conciliatory tone. In its place was a dictatorial ultimatum. The seasoned diplomats read the words, and they felt the sting of the Soviet Foreign Office. The message was concise and clear. There was no wiggle room, and no room for doubt.

1. *We will remove our missiles from Cuba.*
2. *You will remove yours from Turkey.*
3. *The Soviet Union will pledge not to invade or interfere with the internal affairs of Turkey.*
4. *The United States will pledge not to invade or interfere with the internal affairs of Cuba.*

"In itself, their demand is not unreasonable!" the President admitted. "I asked the State Department on several occasions, over the past eighteen months, to reconsider the removal of our Jupiter missiles, which are patently obsolete. Polaris submarines, stationed in the Mediterranean, can offer far greater protection to Turkey than those Jupiters ever did. The Soviets know that. Neither the United States, nor our NATO allies, would have suffered any net loss had we made such a move. We actually would have strengthened our position in Turkey. Now the Kremlin is using our Jupiter missiles as a bargaining chip to get the Soviet weapons out of Cuba, knowing we don't dare agree, because popular opinion would crucify us if we buckled under to a foreign threat. This isn't simply a propaganda ploy. Something more sinister is afoot!"

"The effort to finish the missile bases and launch capabilities has dramatically increased in the past twenty-four hours. If the Russians are ready to make a deal, why all of this furious activity?" Secretary Robert McNamara posed the question; but it was one that was uppermost in the mind of every man who sat around the table.

"Well, gentlemen," the President continued, "I don't mind telling you that I am furious about this entire scenario. I wanted those damned missiles out of Turkey eighteen months ago; but the people at State convinced me to wait, since their removal was a sore spot with the Turks.

"Last year, the State people again convinced me to wait, and we delayed once more. In May, I overruled the State Department and ordered the removal of the missiles despite Turkish objections. Now I discover that my direct order was not carried out. Because of that monumental foul-up, we are being held hostage by the Russians, with a bunch of our own obsolete missiles that I thought had been removed several months ago.

"In a way, I'm guilty for not bearing down and making sure my orders were carried out. I'm willing to accept partial responsibility; but in all probability, somebody's head will roll because of this.

"Since we cannot afford to remove those missiles under the shadow of a Soviet threat, our position has become extremely vulnerable, and the whole fiasco is our own damned fault. As a wise man once said, 'we have met the enemy, and they are us.'"

"You could send a letter directly to Khrushchev," suggested Robert Kennedy. "Since the tone of this message is so diametrically different, you could ask him to clarify his position."

"Meanwhile," McNamara countered, "construction on the missile bases continues, and the Cuban strike capability gets closer."

General Maxwell Taylor, Chairman of the Joint Chiefs of Staff, made the military position clear:

"The Joint Chiefs recommend an airstrike at dawn on Monday, followed closely by an invasion. With all due respect, Sir, we pointed out several days ago that a blockade was far too weak a response to the situation, and we predicted the probable outcome. Military intervention is the only thing the Soviets understand, Mr. President, and the only thing they truly respect!"

"I understand your position, General Taylor; but if we strike Cuba, and then invade, the door is clearly open for the Soviets to take reciprocal action against Turkey. We have the support of the NATO nations; but in this age of nuclear capabilities, any localized conflict might very quickly escalate into a full-scale atomic war. The very first nuclear weapon which is fired by the United States or the Soviet Union targets more than a missile base or even a country—it targets the future of mankind."

A phone next to the President rang. He answered at once. As he listened a look of sadness crept across his face. The call ended very quickly, and he shared the latest news.

"Major Rudolf Anderson, Jr., one of our U-2 pilots, has been hit by a Cuban SAM missile. His plane crashed. Major Anderson is dead."

"Mr. President," General Taylor said, "I grieve for my fallen comrade, but this tragedy only strengthens my position. The Cubans aren't just thinking about war, or even preparing for war. Cuba is already at war! American military action is no longer a threat to the future of mankind; it might be the only guarantee that mankind will have a future."

"I agree that this makes it an entirely new scenario, General. I won't risk any more U-2 pilots until we take out all of the Cuban SAM sites."

"Clearly, we must make as many major airstrikes as necessary to destroy those sites. Our fighters and bombers can be ready for full-scale attacks by dawn. Let's hit them then," Robert McNamara suggested.

President Kennedy asked each Committee member for an opinion. Not surprisingly, Major Anderson's untimely death seemed to solidify their resolve. Agreement on the dawn airstrikes, as a first step, was nearly unanimous.

"Obviously, until we have verification that Major Anderson's aircraft was destroyed by a Cuban SAM, we cannot proceed with a first step. But," cautioned the somber President, "we must think far beyond the first step. Imagine a space-age conflict as it escalates through a second step, then a third, and a fourth, and a fifth step—beyond that, it is pointless to speculate. Life would no longer exist. Earth would become a desolate planet where mankind's passage was only marked by the rubble of her once great civilizations: the only logical legacy for a world in which advances in technology became far more desirable than international stability and simple common sense.

"With those thoughts in mind, I want the warheads on each of our nuclear missiles to be defused. They are not to be reactivated without my direct order.

"We must update the NATO members about the current situation. If we attack Cuba, Soviet reprisals in Turkey are almost assured. In that case, NATO nations will face quickly-developing life and death decisions. They must be forewarned and forearmed.

"Once again, gentlemen, I reiterate, we are faced with a decision that will set off a huge chain reaction of events. It is our decision to make; but once it is made, there will be no turning back, and the future of the entire world will hang in the balance. I will only order airstrikes as a last resort; but we must be certain that we are in the last extremity before taking that action.

"Please remember the admonition Teddy Sorensen added to my inauguration address—'let us never negotiate out of fear, but never let us fear to negotiate.' We still have time to negotiate; our only question is the method."

"The Soviets' last letter leaves very little room for negotiation," General Taylor observed. "We have no right to the optimism the first conciliatory message produced. The latest communiqué can't be ignored."

"Why can't we ignore it?" Robert Kennedy asked, his face aglow with inspiration.

"I beg your pardon?" Taylor said.

"Why can't we ignore this second message, and proceed as though Khrushchev's first proposal were still on the table?"

"Bob," smiled a relieved President, "I think you've hit on the ideal answer! I'll simply reply to the first letter—the offer tendered through John Scali. Soviet missiles will be removed under UN supervision, and the United States, as well as every other Western Hemisphere nation, will pledge not to invade Cuba. I'm going to recess the Committee for an hour. Bob, I want you and Ted Sorensen to write a first draft of a letter to Khrushchev. When we reconvene the Committee we'll work on any and all refinements which seem advisable."

The Kennedy/Sorensen letter was delivered to the Committee an hour later. Then it was refined, agreed upon, typed, and signed by the President. It accepted the Khrushchev proposal.

***Dear Mr. Chairman:***

***I have read your letter of October 26th with great care and welcome the statement of your desire to seek a prompt solution to the problem. The first thing that needs to be done, however, is for work to cease on offensive missile bases in Cuba and for all weapons systems in Cuba capable of offensive use to be rendered inoperable, under effective United Nations arrangements.***

***Assuming that it is done promptly, I have given my representatives in New York instructions that will permit them to work out this weekend, in cooperation with the Acting Secretary General and your representative, arrangements for a permanent solution to the Cuban problem along the lines suggested in your letter of October 26th. As I read your letter, the key elements in your proposals—which seem generally acceptable as I understand***

***them are as follows: You would agree to remove these weapons systems from Cuba under appropriate UN observation and supervision; and undertake, with suitable safeguards, to halt further the introduction of such weapons systems into Cuba. We, on our part, would agree—upon establishment of adequate arrangements through the UN to ensure the carrying out and continuation of these commitments—(a) to remove promptly the quarantine measures now in effect, and (b) to give assurances against an invasion of Cuba. I am confident that other nations of the Western Hemisphere would be prepared to do likewise. If you give your representative similar instructions, there is no reason why we should not be able to complete these arrangements and announce them to the world within a couple of days. The effect of such a settlement on easing world tensions would enable us to work toward more general arrangements regarding other armaments, proposed in your second letter, which you made public. I would like to say again that the United States is very much interested in reducing tensions and halting the arms race; and if your letter signifies that you will discuss a détente affecting NATO and the Warsaw Pact, we are prepared to consider with our allies any useful proposals. But the first ingredient, let me emphasize, is the cessation of work on Cuban missile sites, and measures to render such weapons inoperable, under effective international guarantees. Continuation of this threat, or the prolonging of this discussion concerning Cuba by linking these problems to the broader questions of European and world security, would surely lead to intensification of the Cuban***

***crisis and a grave risk to the peace of the world. For that reason, I hope we can quickly agree along the lines outlined in this letter and your letter of October 26th.***

***John F. Kennedy***

"Bob, call Ambassador Dobrynin again. I think it might be wise to follow up on our letter with a personal visit to the Soviet Embassy. Let him know that we have considered the removal of our missiles from Turkey for some time now. But make him also understand that we cannot remove them until this situation is resolved and the echoes have died away. Promise him that as soon as it is practical, we will remove those missiles. Most of all, try to make him see that the sand in the hourglass is almost gone. I must have an answer from the Kremlin within the next twenty-four hours. Convey my deep concern and desire to resolve the problems that we face in Europe and Southeast Asia, as well as Cuba. We will work together to end the arms race, to end the need to stockpile nuclear weapons; but we will only talk about these things, the very heart of mankind's future, when the current crisis is behind us. Lay all of our cards on the table.

"Gentlemen, I suggest that you telephone your families and tell them that Washington may have to be evacuated within the next forty-eight hours. If they ask you where it will be safe, don't lie to them; tell them the truth. If the Soviets don't end their current threat, no place in America will be safe."

Robert Kennedy had a meeting with Ambassador Dobrynin and met a stone wall of resistance. When he returned to the Oval Office, his report was not optimistic. If anything, the Kremlin's position had hardened since Khrushchev's second letter arrived. Russia now seemed far more intent on provoking a nuclear war than in preventing one.

"Bob, we'll continue to hope for the best, but it's time to act in a realistic manner and prepare for the worst. I'm going to activate two dozen Air Force Reserve Squadrons. They'll be needed to transport the invasion troops. The Joint Chiefs agree that we can hit the beaches, in force, the day after tomorrow. If the Soviets do not reverse their adamant position in the next twenty-four hours, United States Armed Forces will invade Cuba on Tuesday morning. A day history may record as the start of World War III!"

"I told Dobrynin the United States is prepared for war, and that we are well aware of the consequences. I suggested that perhaps the Kremlin was unaware of our firm resolve. I concluded by emphasizing the fact that failing to accede to our demands not only could mean the beginning of a nuclear war, it might very well be the tragic end for all of mankind. I appealed to him, as a fellow human being, to call Moscow and try to save the planet from total destruction."

"On a scale of one to ten, what are the chances?"

"Six that they'll withdraw, and three that they won't?"

"That's only nine. What happens if they choose the tenth one?"

"We all get blown to hell!"

So the world tottered on the brink of annihilation as the Kremlin delayed and debated and the White House waited and prayed. Then on Sunday morning Robert Kennedy received a message from the Soviet Embassy. Ambassador Dobrynin would like to meet him again as soon as possible. Kennedy invited the Ambassador to see him in his office at eleven.

This meeting was destined to be very different from the troubling one of the day before.

"Chairman Khrushchev has decided to dismantle and withdraw all of the missiles from Cuba under adequate supervision and inspection. He is certain that everything will go smoothly. He sends his best wishes to the President, and for the first time he also sends his personal greetings to you. The Chairman is looking forward to meaningful negotiations on all of our international concerns," Dobrynin said, smiling warmly. Obligatory small talk ended a few minutes later, and the Ambassador took his leave.

A somewhat stunned Robert Kennedy raced back to the Oval Office with the news. Several members of the Committee arrived and joined the brothers.

Three of the men who were present that afternoon made very different observations about the end of the Cuban Missile Crisis.

"We went eyeball-to-eyeball, and the other fellow blinked!" summarized Dean Rusk.

"It was a very difficult time, but it's finally over," Robert McNamara said gratefully as he rose to leave.

"It's not over for some of the people who played vital roles and some others who made great personal sacrifices," the President reflected, as he sat at his desk and began a letter to the widow and children of Major Rudolf Anderson, Jr., the fallen U-2 pilot.

It was a difficult task to try to explain to this young family why a happy life in South Carolina suddenly had been left with such a large void.

He reflected on Winston Churchill's observations after the Battle of Britain. He had just lived through another of those perilous times in the course of history when so many owed so much to so few. Millions of Americans relaxing in their snug homes on this peaceful Sunday afternoon, or rooting for favorite football teams in cheering stadiums, would never realize how close they had come to extinction or fully understand the unique brand of courage that impelled Major Anderson and other brave heroes. Finally, no one would ever imagine how terribly alone Jack Kennedy had felt or how frightened he had been for his beloved country and her people.

He sighed in relief, breathed a thanksgiving prayer, and returned to his letter, feeling once more the great burden of responsibility. Americans would continue to enjoy their carefree days only for as long as the presidents they elected continued to hold the honor of the presidency inviolate. John F. Kennedy had many faults and had made mistakes—most of them were still closely guarded secrets; but his love for America was both deep and sincere. He hoped every president would place the nation's well-being ahead of his personal ambition; but in a fleeting moment of clairvoyance, he somehow knew that was not to be.

*So the Cuban Missile Crisis wound down. It ended peacefully because a young, inexperienced president performed brilliantly. He weighed each decision and examined the effect every proposed course of action would have on the Soviet Premier and his advisors.*

*He was careful not to disgrace Khrushchev, nor to embarrass or humiliate the Kremlin. He put himself in the Russians' shoes and asked, 'what would I do if I were in this fix?' If the answer indicated sharper, escalated responses because of security interests or national pride, the idea was discarded. A blockade, with three key elements, became the obvious answer.*

*The blockade was implemented by interdicting a neutral ship rather than by boarding a Soviet vessel. The blockade negated any need for airstrikes on the Cuban missile sites.* ***The blockade gave the Soviets a reason to pause before attacking; airstrikes would have given them a reason to attack before pausing.***

*He allowed no miscalculation, misunderstanding, or misinterpretation to exist. He exercised pressure, but eliminated humiliation! Kennedy himself said—"Action against powerful adversaries demands that careful logic be employed. If it is not, wars begin—wars that no one wants, wars that no one intends, wars that no one wins. In the final analysis, war's antagonists are seldom classified as winners or losers, only as big losers or little losers."*

*John F. Kennedy's patience, sound judgment, and statesmanship dispelled a crisis that might well have escalated into World War III. The Thirteen Days of October represent Kennedy's foremost achievement. They deserve an honored place in American history because they included many of our nation's finest hours.*

# *PART FIVE*
# *THE ASSASSINATION*

# *HAVANA, CUBA*

# *JUNE 7, 1963*

The peaceful stillness of the soft tropical night was suddenly broken as rifle butts slammed into the front door of a gaily colored, but otherwise shabby house in one of Havana's lower-class barrios.

When the first violent assault failed to gain either immediate entrance or instant acknowledgement, the ten-man, khaki-clad squad of secret police battered the flimsy door from its sagging hinges and burst inside, automatic weapons poised and ready.

"Manolo and Miguel del Negro," the officer-in-charge shouted, "you both have been identified as enemies of the state. I order you to surrender and come with us at once! If you or any member of your family attempt to resist, you, and they, will be shot. Come now! Be quick!"

The two young men were dragged from their home and transported to the ancient dungeons of the Morro Castle. They were taken to a subterranean area and thrust into a tiny, stone-lined cell that contained only two thin straw mattresses and a pair of rusty pots.

The sixteen and twenty-year-old brothers could not imagine why they had been arrested. What were they accused of? Who had accused them? They weren't the state's enemies. They weren't anyone's enemies!

Manolo, the elder of the two, tried to console and reassure his brother, as they lay huddled in the pitch-black dungeon.

"This is crazy! They've mistaken us for someone else. Don't worry. We'll see the prison officials in the morning and get it all straightened out."

"It's crazy, all right!" Miguel agreed. "But the guys who arrested us were deadly serious about shooting us if we resisted. It didn't sound like there was any doubt about us being the two they were looking for!"

"Look, if we have any trouble in the morning, Dolores can go see El Presidente. I'll bet she still has plenty of clout with Fidel. For now, let's try to relax and get some sleep. Everything is going to be fine."

They stretched out on the lumpy, vermin-ridden mattresses and made an effort to rest. Miguel tossed and turned restlessly for several minutes, then dozed off; but Manolo lay quietly staring into the darkness, trying to ignore the persistent insects and mosquitoes that crawled on his body and nipped at his flesh. He prayed that his brave words and predictions, meant to bolster Miguel's courage, would prove to be true; but in his heart he was afraid they might never leave this terrible place alive.

Manolo shivered, wondering what was in store for them. He tried to relax and ignore the depression that the damp cell and clammy, humid air were inducing; but several hours passed before his fatigue finally overcame his fear and he fell into a troubled sleep.

Forty-eight hours had passed and the brothers were getting desperate. They had been locked away in the oppressive isolation cell at 2 A.M. on Saturday. Now it was 6 A.M. on Monday. They had been fed six times. Each meal was the same. Coarse black bread and thin watery soup.

As the first light of the new day began creeping through their cell's single tiny window, positioned high enough in the slippery stone wall to prevent the prisoners from reaching it, they heard the heavy steel door at the end of the corridor creak open. Moments later they heard it slam against the bars of the first cell in the long row. It was breakfast time.

The day before, Manolo had complained about the food. The guard had responded by saying that if it were up to him the pair would get no food at all.

"Prisoners of the state should simply be starved to death. I don't know why we pamper traitors like you, even for a few days. Quick punishment is always best," sneered the brutish guard. "We save on bullets, as well as on food."

The brothers heard the guards unlock, then a few seconds later relock, the adjoining cell. They waited expectantly. Watery soup and stale bread might not be the most appealing food in the world, but after a twelve-hour fast their empty bellies would welcome it. But the guards did not pause. Manolo and Miguel listened as they shuffled down the corridor past their cell door, pushing a squeaky-wheeled food cart. The noise stopped at the adjoining cell on their left. For the next several minutes they were aware of bustling activity up and down the corridor. Then the clamor ended, and there was nothing but silence.

"Manny, what's going on? Why did they skip us?"

"I guess that loud-mouthed guard wanted to teach me a lesson after I complained yesterday. We'll just have to tough it out until the next mealtime. At least there's some water left in the pot. Don't think about food, Mig. We'll be okay until tonight."

An hour later, the cell door flew open. The brutish guard, along with a pair of confederates, entered and confronted them.

"As you've already noticed, you weren't required to eat 'the miserable slop that passes for food in this place.' I'll bet that made you feel very lucky this morning. Never fear, that lucky feeling will pass."

The other two men suddenly seized Miguel, threw him to the floor and handcuffed his wrists behind his back, and then repeated the process with Manolo.

"Why are you doing this?" Manolo demanded.

"You're going for a nice little walk on the beach," the chief guard chuckled. "But it won't take long; it's a very short walk."

They were hauled into the corridor and their ankles were shackled together with short chains; then those short chains were connected to a much longer chain, which already held five other prisoners.

The procession clanked its way slowly along the subterranean passage to a steep flight of stone steps. Handicapped as they were, it took several minutes for the prisoners to climb up to ground level.

When at last they emerged, they found themselves on a sandy patio that overlooked the Caribbean. But it was not the sea or sand that riveted their attention. It was the low stone wall and a long row of bullet-shattered stakes that held the horrified men's gaze.

Any hopes the seven prisoners had harbored about their fate vanished as a squad of armed men marched forward and took up positions ten yards in front of the stakes.

"My God, Manny, they're going to murder us!" the anguished Miguel shouted.

"It's some kind of bluff, Mig! We haven't done anything. Innocent people aren't shot. Even here!"

A guard began tying blindfolds across the eyes of the prisoners, and suddenly, it became horrifyingly clear to them that innocent men did get shot here.

It only took a few moments to finish blindfolding and securing the prisoners to stakes. Manolo tried to console his brother for the last time.

"Be strong, Mig. Don't say a word. Don't let these creeps get any satisfaction out of this. Just pray."

"Don't worry about me, Manny. I'll be strong! May God bless all of us!"

One of the prisoners, an upper-class attorney, shouted in protest.

"You can't just murder us! We have rights. You owe each of us a trial. A person has to be convicted of a capital crime before you can execute him."

"You seven are all enemies of the state. We owe you nothing! We have no time to waste on stinking trials for the likes of you," the chief guard growled.

Dismissing the attorney's plea, the chief guard turned his attention to the firing squad.

"Ready! Aim! Fire!"

Seven shots rang out as one, and seven lifeless bodies sagged against their restraints. Fresh blood crept across the soggy sand, heralding a new era in Cuba.

# *FORT LAUDERDALE*

# *JUNE 11, 1963*

The insistent ring of her front doorbell awakened Dolores del Negro. In that first moment, she thought something might be wrong with Tranquilena. Her sister was due to begin labor at any moment. But Dolores quickly discarded that idea. Tranquilena and her husband had gone through the rigors of childbirth before—they wouldn't need help—and even if they did they would telephone, not ring the bell. Her bedroom was nearly pitch black. The only speck of illumination was the soft glow from a tiny nightlight in the hallway next to the bathroom.

Reluctantly, she switched on a bedside lamp, and glared at her alarm clock. "Damn it," she blurted, "who the hell can be leaning on my doorbell at five in the morning?"

She picked up the expensive Japanese dressing gown Rod had given her from the littered floor where she had carelessly dropped it the night before, slipped it on, and padded toward the front door. Her bare feet, made hard by growing up in a family too poor to buy shoes for eleven children, made a sharply different sound when she left the soft surface of her bedroom's thick loop rug and slapped against the hallway's solid parquet floor.

She released the lock, but kept the heavy security chain in place. Through the narrow opening she saw two strange men in dark business suits.

"What do you want at this hour?" she demanded.

One of her visitors held up a folding wallet. In the dim light it looked like it contained a badge and an identification card.

"We're from the State Department, Miss del Negro."

"I can't see your ID. Hold it closer to me."

The agent moved the ID toward the opening and shined the beam from a flashlight on it.

"Okay, so you're from the State Department. What in the hell are you doing in my hallway at 5 A.M.?"

"We have information for you! Rest assured that if it weren't extremely important, we wouldn't be here at this hour. May we come in?"

Dolores' Cuban control agent had warned her that if and when the US government discovered she was a foreign agent, the Feds would show up and roust her on general principles. He had also mentioned that one of the federal agents' favorite tricks was to arrive between 4 and 5 A.M., while the "subject alien agent" was still asleep. Their arrival times were carefully calculated to catch the "subjects" off guard. In almost every case, uneasy feelings of intimidation and insecurity resulted. Of course, this allowed the spooks to quickly gain the upper hand. Dolores was not surprised by her visitors' early morning arrival.

She removed the safety chain, and then held the door open while the agents entered.

"All right, you're in. Now tell me what all of this is about."

"To begin with, I'm Charles Black. My companion is Randall Brown. I'm afraid we have some very bad news for you."

"Has something happened to Rod? Captain Reynolds?"

"No. Captain Reynolds knows nothing about our visit, or as yet, about our ultimate purpose. I wish there were a better way to tell you this," Black said sadly, "but unfortunately there is not. Your brothers, Manolo and Miguel, are both dead."

"What? When? How?"

"They were executed by a Cuban firing squad on Monday morning."

"A firing squad? You're crazy! Who are you people? What do you really want with me."

The older of the two men, Randall Brown, spoke for the first time.

"I can assure you that we are not crazy. We really are federal agents; and Manolo and Miguel really have been executed. But that's only half of the story. Apparently, several years ago, your father and two of your uncles made some very influential enemies while they were working for Batista."

"My father and my uncles drove Batista around and ran errands for him. All three of them were little more than peons. They had no reason or opportunity to make enemies—influential or otherwise."

"Part of what you say is true. They drove, and they ran errands, but every now and then they performed special jobs as well."

"What kind of jobs?"

"They were enforcers. They assaulted people who refused to do Batista's bidding. The three of them were part of a group known as the 'Bone Breakers.' They earned that name because they kept breaking bones until the people they were working on agreed to comply. Obviously some of their former victims, or perhaps the friends or relatives of people who did not survive their ordeal, have gained influence with members of Castro's secret police. We're convinced that the murder of your brothers was only the first step in a much larger campaign to get even."

Charles Black picked up the narrative.

"They apparently have accused your parents and your older siblings of belonging to an underground organization that is conspiring to overthrow Castro's government. In today's Cuba, proof isn't required. Mere suspicion, or accusations from highly placed insiders, have replaced justice," Black concluded.

"I don't believe any of this. I don't believe these things you're saying about my father and my uncles. I don't even believe that my brothers are dead!"

Brown reluctantly removed two 8X10 photographs from his briefcase, and slid them across the coffee table toward Dolores.

"I don't know of any other way to convince you. I'm sorry, but you're forcing me to show you these."

A man's bloody upper torso and head were visible in each of the photos. Dolores examined them with mounting horror. There could be no doubt that the young men were dead or that they had been shot. Worst of all, there was no doubt that they were photographs of Manolo and Miguel.

Dolores shuddered and slumped in her chair. Her heart felt like a lump of ice being squeezed in a vise-like grip. She felt terribly hot bile rising up at the back of her throat and fought to regain the breath that the photographs had driven out of her body as surely as a sudden and vicious blow to the solar plexus.

Charles Black rose and went to the liquor cabinet that stood against the wall. He poured a large measure of brandy into a goblet and handed it to Dolores.

Silence pervaded the room for the next two or three minutes as Dolores sipped the fiery liquid and fought to maintain her composure. She would be damned if she would let these two agents see how much their news had affected her, or betray the terrible sorrow that now consumed her. Grief was a very private thing; it was never shared with strangers. She would weep alone and recover alone. The world would never be allowed to intrude. She did not speak until the brandy was gone and she was sure that she had regained control.

"If these influential people are so intent on seeking revenge against my father and my uncles, why didn't they simply have *them* executed? If what you say is true they have enough clout to do whatever they like. Why would they kill the kids?"

"In order to inflict maximum pain and suffering. Nothing hurts a parent or close relative more than a child's death, particularly when he feels responsible for that death."

"Won't murdering my brothers satisfy their blood lust? Is it possible they'll settle for the revenge they've already extracted?"

"No! That was only the first step. We're convinced that they plan to systematically eliminate your whole family."

Dolores rose, walked slowly to the liquor cabinet, and poured a healthy knock of apricot brandy into a heavy cut-glass snifter.

"I presume you two aren't allowed to drink while you're on duty. If I'm wrong, speak up."

Both agents declined her offer, so she returned to her chair.

"Okay, it's six in the morning. My brothers are dead and my family's in grave danger. I'm sitting here with a pair of G-men who are about to give me a chance to rescue them in return for some type of quid pro quo. Am I reading you correctly, so far?"

"Like an open book!" Brown admitted, impressed by her fluent English as well as her quick perception.

"Okay. Let me hear your pitch."

"We've made several attempts to eliminate Castro; but all of them have failed for some reason."

"I've heard about them. They were really stupid."

"The United States government cannot afford to look stupid, Miss del Negro."

"With all due respect, Mr. Brown, your government's stupidity factor is not my problem."

"With equal respect, Miss del Negro, it's about to become your problem."

"Run that one past me again."

"We need to eliminate Castro, and you need to get your family out of danger. If you'll agree to help us with our problem, we'll help you with yours."

"I'm all ears."

"We're willing to send a team of agents into Cuba, to extract your family from Havana, and bring them back here to Miami. Quickly and quietly, with very little danger or exposure. The entire rescue operation would be over in a few hours."

"Go on."

"We know you've been working as a Cuban agent for the past year and a half. We have identified your conduit. We also know that you were one of Castro's very first recruits. Fidel has a special regard for his early converts, particularly his guerilla fighters."

Now it was time for Dolores to be impressed.

"Each attempt on Castro's life has been made by a stranger," Brown continued, "so they all failed. This has to be done by a person he knows, a confederate he trusts, someone who can get close to him. In short, Miss Del Negro, someone like you. He trusts you, because until this morning, Fidel Castro was your icon. He has no reason not to trust you."

"Now you want me to assassinate him! How?"

The agents could not suppress smiles.

"We have hundreds of ways of doing that," Brown assured her. "We've developed a veritable arsenal of plain, everyday objects that appear to be harmless, yet can kill the user in seconds, minutes, hours, days, weeks, or even over a span of several months, if that is our objective. To us, method is not the problem; means of delivery is the problem. We need someone who can get close to Castro without arousing undue suspicion. We're convinced that you are that person! We'll train you to eliminate him, quickly and quietly, with a minimum of peril to yourself or anyone else."

"Just like that!"

"No, Miss del Negro! Nothing ever happens 'just like that.' If you agree, our strategists will develop an operational plan. Perfect timing and the systematic completion of every single detail are always vital to the success of any covert operation."

"Could you amplify that a bit for me?"

"Sure! For example, it seems logical for the Castro assassination and your family's extraction to be done concurrently. If we fail to coordinate each aspect of those simultaneous operations perfectly, the whole thing might blow up, and a lot of people could wind up getting greased."

"What about my family and me when it's all over? When we come back here? We might still be targets! We might 'wind up getting greased!'"

"We are authorized to offer you and your family international asylum in addition to a $2,000,000 fee. You will receive completely foolproof new identities and relocation to any place in the world."

"You really want Fidel dead, don't you?"

"Yes, Miss del Negro! We really want him dead!" Then Brown added softly, gesturing at the photos, "Don't you?"

"It's hard to believe that I could suddenly feel such terrible loathing for a man I've idolized for so long. When misery and murder strike close to home, you get a real wakeup call. You're right, he deserves to die—for my brothers and other innocent victims!"

"So, you'll do it!"

"I didn't say that! I only said Fidel deserves to die. I'm going to talk all of this over with Rod before I make a decision. He'll be here for breakfast in a little while. You'll have my answer by lunch time."

"That'll be fine," Brown told her, picking up the photographs and returning them to his briefcase.

"Here's a card with our secure telephone number. Please call us, or have Captain Reynolds call, if you have questions. Otherwise, we'll expect to hear from you around noon."

The agents rose and started toward the door, but Dolores stopped them.

"I guess you think I'm pretty hardboiled. You tell me my kid brothers have been murdered, and I don't bat an eye. I guess I am pretty tough, but I've had a damned tough life. I feel terrible about the kids, and I'll shed my share of tears; but right now I have no time to waste on grief. My brothers are already dead and can't be brought back. Now I must do whatever it takes to save the rest of my family."

She opened the door and watched them walk down the long, dimly lit hallway.

Dolores thought about the government's proposal for the next couple of hours, as she showered, tidied up her tiny apartment, and cooked Rodney's favorite breakfast—Eggs Benedict and mimosas, made with freshly squeezed oranges and California champagne.

Brown had sized up her admiration for Fidel quite well. He had been an icon since the first day she and Tranquilena reported to his mountain encampment.

She ran the tragic event over and over in her mind. Was there any way she could exonerate Fidel? Any way she could convince herself that he had played no part in the murders of her brothers? If he had known about the kids, would he have intervened? Perhaps . . . but, perhaps not! What about the thousand people he had executed—many of them without a trial? If Castro had not participated directly, he had certainly created an atmosphere that was conducive to murder.

Brown had made her face some hard facts. In the two and a half years since Castro had seized power, Cuba had become a terrorist state. Her brothers were only two of the victims. It was too late to help them; but now the rest of her family was in mortal danger of being eliminated by the same band of cutthroats that had killed the kids. She would die trying, before she would permit another family member to perish.

She realized that her choices were clear. She could go to Fidel—swear to him that every single member of the del Negro family was a rabid supporter—then plead for his help and hope he believed her. Or she could accept the State Department's alternative and become the family deliverer. But to succeed, she would have to assassinate her former idol.

As she thought and worked she sipped champagne. Just before Rodney was due, she drained the dregs from the bottle and brought a new one to the table from her wine cooler.

One very large knock of Jack Daniels, followed by two snifters of brandy, topped off by a magnum of mellow champagne would have thrown most people for a loop; but not Dolores. Alcohol had the opposite effect. Each drink seemed to crystallize her thinking, and harden her resolve.

By the time she heard Rodney knock on the door, all of her soul searching was over, and her decision all but made. She would weigh his input because of his experience and good common sense; and most of all because, unlike most other men she had known,

Rodney really cared about her. But unless he came up with a better plan, she knew she had to go ahead.

As she walked toward the door, Dolores smiled, realizing that for the first time in many years her own comfort, welfare, and safety had not been key elements in her decision. Hell, she thought, if I'm not careful, I might turn into a decent person.

Randall Brown and his associate, Charles Black, began their telephone vigil at 11 A.M. They had no intention of missing the expected call from Dolores del Negro. She might decide to call before noon.

For the next two hours they paced and fretted, but the phone failed to ring. At one o'clock they ordered hot Italian sausage subs, with double side orders of spaghetti from a local pizzeria. When the mountain of spicy food arrived, they devoured it like a pair of starving timber wolves. Between bites they glared at the telephone and sipped tepid iced tea. Then they sat in stony silence for two additional hours while their irritation, indignation, and indigestion all grew at alarming rates.

The hot line rang at 3:17. Brown answered it.

"Miss del Negro?"

"No. This is Rodney Reynolds."

Brown's anxiety took a giant leap upward.

"Thanks for calling, Captain Reynolds. I invited Miss del Negro to have you call us if either of you had questions. I assume quite a few have come up."

"It's much too soon for questions; however, I do have some specific demands. Unless you're willing to accede to those demands, we won't even consider your offer. I assume we're talking on a secure line. I also assume that you two don't have the power to negotiate terms and conditions."

He waited for a denial, heard none, and continued.

"I'm going to outline items we need to talk about, and name the location where all our meetings will be held. I'm going to dictate specific terms. Write them down and pass them up the chain of command until they finally reach a level where the reviewing agent is empowered to make a deal. I want to speak to someone who does not need to consult his superior every other minute to find out what his next step should be. Have that person call me. I'll either be at home, at my office, or at Dolores'. Now here are the basic ground rules we'll consider playing under.

"First. Your people will act only as consultants. This will be a CIA operation. The man in charge will be Tracy Barnes. All meetings will be held in his office at Quarters Eye.

"Second. The incursion team that takes Dolores in, and brings her and her family out, will be composed of Green Berets. No State Department personnel will be permitted to go along.

"Third. I'll recruit, train, and command that team.

"Fourth. We won't go to Cuba until I'm confident that the team and Dolores have at least a 75% chance of getting in, accomplishing both missions, and getting out without casualties.

"Fifth. Tracy Barnes will run the entire show. He's the number one man. If he sees fit to call off the raid at any time, even at the last minute, it's all over!

"Sixth. We will not deviate from this ultimatum.

"Those are the terms. There are two choices open to your people. They accept them or forget the whole thing. When you've lined up someone with enough clout to make that decision, have him call me, and I'll arrange a meeting with Tracy Barnes at the CIA.

"Okay! That's it! Any questions?"

"No, Captain. You've made everything very clear. You'll get a call as soon as possible."

"Before I hang up, I want to make sure you two understand something. I think this whole idea stinks. Unfortunately, Dolores is caught in a vice between you and Castro. Since her family is in peril, she feels compelled to do everything possible to bring them out to safety. So we'll go in, and we'll do the job. But before this goes any further, I want to make one thing very clear. If you've lied to Dolores about any of this or if you or any of your agency's people are ever less than completely honest with us, you two are dead men."

After Rodney Reynolds hung up, Brown and Black wondered what had impelled his vehement outburst and the crystal clear warning he had delivered. If they had been more familiar with Rodney's background, they would have known.

He had loved two women in his life. His wife, Amanda, had been the first. She and her unborn child had been killed by a foolish drunken driver who had walked away from the accident without a scratch. Local authorities had done nothing to punish him, and little to penalize him. He received a warning and a year's probation. Like the cautious young man that he was, Rodney never did anything to punish him either. Since then, he had often regretted his lack of resolve.

Now, Dolores had come into his life. If someone's stupidity cost him her love, he would not display any of his former timidity and restraint. He was going to hold Black and Brown personally responsible for their conduct and competence. His promise of death was designed to make them aware of the personal risks they were running. He hoped they would not misconstrue his words as a mere threat. He hadn't meant them as a threat. He had been predicting the future, raising a red flag within the agency, and giving them a reason to back out if they had any doubts about their ability to succeed. If this telephone call turned out to be his final contact with Black and Brown, he would certainly understand why.

# *WASHINGTON, D.C*

# *JULY 21, 1963*

Nearly six weeks had passed since Dolores' early morning meeting with Brown and Black. Since then, nothing had been heard from them or anyone else at the State Department.

Rodney had spent the past two weeks enjoying an overdue vacation. Arriving at Washington National Airport on a 6 A.M. "red-eye" special from Miami, he took a cab directly to his townhouse apartment in Arlington, Virginia.

He was scheduled to attend a strategy meeting with Richard Bissell and Tracy Barnes at 0900. Prior to that he needed to shower, shave, climb into a fresh uniform, and spend at least half an hour in his office at Quarters Eye, reviewing the material they would be covering.

Rod rotated under the shower's stinging spray for several minutes, letting new energy flow back into his tired body. A short time later, a brightly-lit shaving mirror offered mute testimony to the early morning flight's sobriquet of "red eye." He looked like he desperately needed another vacation.

He and Dolores had lolled away the dozen sunny days swimming and sailing, and most of the starry nights dining and dancing at various South Florida hot spots. Avispa, Tranquilena, and their three small children joined them at the beach on two occasions.

They had discussed the State Department plan with Avispa and sought his opinion and advice. He and Dolores agreed that since over a month had passed, State probably had taken both the assassination and extraction plan off the table. Rodney wasn't so sure. He had more experience with federal agencies' exasperatingly slow, snail-like pace in matters of procedure and implementation. He cautioned his friends that a call might still come at any moment saying, "It's on! Let's go! Right now!"

At 0750 Rodney slid his sleek, triple black 1957 Thunderbird convertible into a staff parking spot behind Quarters Eye and headed for the meeting with Bissell and Barnes. When he reached his office, he was surprised to find Barnes waiting for him.

"How is America's finest warrior this morning?" Tracy greeted him. "I see you picked up a deeper suntan while you were deep-sea fishing on Friday?"

"Is there anything you don't know, Boss?" Rodney chuckled.

"A few things. I don't know what they served on the redeye this morning."

"Powdered eggs, soggy hash browns, and bitter, tepid coffee. It brought back the old days in Korea. The bad old days!"

"All kidding aside, I do know something much more important," Barnes said, in a voice devoid of mirth. "The Castro sanction is on. The formation meeting is set for Wednesday morning. Dolores needs to be here for that. Dr. Paul Alexander is the operational coordinator for the State Department.

"Paul has a Ph.D. in international relations and a barrel of smarts to go with the degree. Anyone who ever sold him short has been burned. He told me to tell you he'd heard your ultimatum. If you ever have to enforce it, he said he'll pitch in and help you."

"Did he tell you what it was?"

"No. But I gather the people over at State believed it to be both serious and enforceable. If that were not the case, they wouldn't have spent the past six weeks building a foolproof operation."

"Did your friend say anything else that sounded interesting?"

"Yes, a couple of things. He said Maria Moscardo is the operation's chief strategist and mentioned that State has a jet shuttle flight from Homestead AFB to Andrews on Tuesday afternoon. He reserved a space for Dolores. She's due in at 1600. That should work out well for us."

"I'll call her right away and let her know. Do you know anything about Maria Moscardo?"

"She has a reputation for being as smart as Bissell. So she really must be something. Call Dolores, and I'll see you in Dick's office in thirty minutes."

Ramrod Reynolds spent those minutes brushing up on his notes.

On Tuesday afternoon, Rodney picked up Dolores, got her settled at a Holiday Inn near Quarters Eye, then took her to the *Chart House Restaurant* for a scheduled dinner meeting with Tracy Barnes.

The Beef Wellington and the '59 Chateau LaFitte Bordeaux were an excellent combination. Although it was Tracy and Dolores' first meeting, they quickly established a bond of friendship. Tracy's gentle and unassuming manner impressed Dolores. For his part, Tracy was amazed by Dolores' scope of knowledge and insightfulness—abilities he simply had not expected to encounter. He had seen her State Department file and found it hard to believe that Dolores had only one year of formal high school education. She had taught herself and mastered the English language on her own, as well. Although her vocabulary, grammar, and phraseology were all very impressive, it was her bubbling sense of humor and the delightful lilt she gave to many of her words that captivated Barnes.

"Your language skills and many areas of expertise are amazing, Dolores."

"Thanks!" She laughed. "I acquired my knowledge by reading a ton of books and sitting through some of the most boring lectures in recorded history.

"As Rod knows, I grew up in a nearly destitute family. By the time I was nine or ten, I realized that I would wind up a dumb bunny unless I taught myself. It was pretty discouraging at times because I wanted to know about so many different things. Each nugget of knowledge I acquired was like a particle of sand on an endless seashore. I used to visualize the sand stretching for as far as my eye could see, and there I was dragging a huge empty pail, vainly trying to fill it up, one tiny grain at a time. My pail is still very far from being full, but over the years I've become a knowledge junkie. Now I'm hooked on weird things, like Oriental art, astronomy, and polar exploration. Pretty crazy for a poor Havana barrio kid, isn't it."

"I think it's terrific!"

A waiter brought three Cappuccinos to their table and set a steaming cup before each of them. Tracy sipped, beamed his approval, and then asked an all-important question.

"Are you still committed to the Castro sanction?"

"Yes. Please understand that I'm not happy about the circumstances that have forced me into this; but I'm prepared to do whatever I can to help my family. The State Department people are right. My brothers' murders weren't isolated acts. They were just the beginning."

"You could make a pretty fair circumstantial case that since Fidel Castro had no direct involvement, he doesn't deserve to be directly punished. Have you considered that?" Tracy asked.

"Two of America's famous leaders commented on that exact subject. President Truman said, 'The buck stops here.' He meant that a national leader shares the responsibility for his country's acts—the glory, of course, but also the guilt. Neither one can ever be completely laid at the door of underlings. And in his autobiography, General Douglas MacArthur wrote, 'Every commander is responsible for his entire chain of command. Any leader who does not willingly and eagerly accept responsibility is unfit for command.' I now realize that Fidel Castro is just as guilty as the men who actually pull the triggers. He has allowed and even encouraged the awful tyranny that exists in Cuba. Over a thousand people have already been murdered. Castro may not have directly participated in any of those crimes, but neither has he made any attempt to stop them."

Her face was flushed by a crimson wave of anger.

"I don't know about the rest of his victims, but my brothers were just a pair of innocent kids—they were no threat to anyone. I'm going to make Fidel Castro pay for their deaths."

"Despite the growing violence and misery, there seems to be very little actual unrest on the island," Tracy commented.

"Maybe Cuba's people are still living in a dream," Dolores began. "When Fidel Castro overthrew Batista, he represented a happy new start for most Cubans. The heavy yoke of oppression was being lifted from their shoulders, and they could live happily ever after in a wonderful modern country—where freedom and opportunity abounded. If they admit to themselves that Castro is a tyrant, they will be forced to give up that dream—and that is not an easy thing to do."

"Sooner or later they will *have* to stop dreaming," Tracy Barnes interjected. "How long can an entire nation of people continue to delude themselves?"

"Cubans are just like most other people that were forced to live under tyrannical regimes. Look at Rome's silent citizens who stood idly by while thousands of innocent Christians were slaughtered in the Circus Maximus to amuse Nero. Or the Germans who chose to ignore the obvious fact that Hitler and his Gestapo goons were murdering millions of Jews, Catholics, and Gypsies. In troubled times, ignorance is the most readily available and widespread means of self-preservation. Fear becomes the overriding emotion, and people blatantly deny truth, even to themselves, in their effort to survive. The Cubans are no different than history's other human ostriches, Mr. Barnes. If you plant your head firmly in the sand, you may not find any trouble. And more importantly, the trouble may not find you."

"Castro overthrew Batista," Rodney said. "Maybe another patriot will step forward and depose him."

"That's always a possibility, Querido. Revolution is the Caribbean's favorite sport, and you never know when you'll find a patriot lurking in the shadows." She smiled and gave Rodney's hand an affectionate squeeze as she continued.

"It's ironic. While we were hiding in the mountains and sneaking out to raid the Batistas, Fidel told us that patriots had to be tough on their enemies—that a true patriot did his duty without letting his emotions interfere. Now it seems that the best Cuban patriot of all will be the one who kills Fidel. Only then can honor and justice return to my homeland. I want to be that patriot, Mr. Barnes. But Fidel was wrong; emotions play an important role. They've galvanized my decision and my resolve."

Barnes looked into the beautiful young woman's tear-filled eyes and found himself deeply troubled.

People say the eyes are windows to the soul. If so, he could see that Dolores was either that one person in a thousand who is capable of killing another human being—or she was the finest actress he had ever seen, on or off the motion picture screen.

Tracy excused himself and left the *Chart House* a few minutes later. He had a great deal to do before the next morning's meeting.

Dolores and Rod didn't linger after Tracy left. Since it was still quite early they decided to visit the *Shoreham.* The famous hotel still featured swing music from the big band era that they both loved.

They danced and enjoyed their favorite tunes from the 30's and 40's, until nearly 1 A.M.

When they reached the *Holiday Inn*, Rodney found it more difficult than ever to ignore the tantalizing Dolores' exotic perfume, to kiss her good night, and to leave her standing at the door of her motel room.

He drove home, wondering how long it would be before his moral resolve finally collapsed.

# *WASHINGTON, D.C.*

## *JULY 23, 1963*

The Castro Sanction Committee meeting began at 0900. Present were Richard Bissell, Tracy Barnes, Rod, Avispa, Dolores, Paul Alexander, and Jubal Tyree, Maria Moscardo's chief assistant.

Barnes questioned the absence of Maria Moscardo, the State Department's foremost strategist.

"This is a vital meeting, Mr. Tyree. Why isn't she here?"

"Maria is currently in England, working on a new project. She developed an airtight plan, Mr. Barnes, and briefed me on everything before she left. Don't worry, I'm completely up to speed. Maria would be here if she could, but she's the best qualified person to represent us in London."

"Okay! Let's get started!" suggested the impatient Richard Bissell.

"Sure thing, Dr. Bissell," replied the unabashed and confident Jubal Tyree. He rose and withdrew a folding stand and a large-scale map of the Caribbean from his briefcase. He set the two items up on the end of the conference table, facing the others, then pointed to a dot on Puerto Rico's southeastern coast.

"This is Vieques Island. You and Captain Orizaba will love it, Captain Reynolds. It's a small island with lots of soft sand—great place to run yourselves into tiptop shape."

Rod smiled wryly.

"I'll bet the sand isn't the only reason that we're interested in Vieques Island."

"Right you are, Captain. Vieques Island is one of the three keys to Maria's plan. The second key is the fact that August 13th is Fidel Castro's thirty-seventh birthday. The third key takes a bit longer to explain.

"It all began 450 years ago, when Vasco Nunez Balboa, a debt-ridden planter, fled from the island of Hispaniola. He had himself nailed inside a barrel and stowed away with the ship's provisions in order to escape his creditors. A few weeks after he arrived in Panama, Balboa met an Indian who told him that on the far side of the mountain was an enormous ocean, on whose beaches lay immense quantities of gold."

Tyree glanced around the table and was pleased to see that he had captured the imaginations of his listeners.

"The word *gold* had a predicable effect on Balboa. He quickly organized an expedition and set out to find those great riches, together with 190 equally greedy Spaniards and several hundred Indians. They trekked across the mosquito-ridden Isthmus of Panama, and on September 25, 1513, Balboa became the very first European to see 'The Great South Sea.' He never found any gold; but he did sow the seeds for further expeditions and firmly established Spain's lust for gold.

"Since 1963 is the 450th Anniversary of Balboa's discovery and the beginning of Spanish explorations, it will be commemorated by a flotilla of caravels—ships built to resemble Spanish vessels of the 15th and 16th Centuries, but which have modern safety equipment, navigational aids, and creature comforts.

"The Commemorative Fleet sailed from Cadiz, Spain, last month. They anchored in the Canary Islands for a time and are now crossing the Atlantic. They'll spend four months touring the Caribbean before heading south along the coasts of Central and South America. Eventually they hope to traverse the Strait of Magellan and sail into the Pacific. En route to the Philippines they will anchor at several mid-ocean and South Seas islands. After visiting dozens of ports in the Pacific, they'll sail west, along the northern rim of the Indian Ocean. Eventually, they'll round the Cape of Good Hope, and return to Cadiz. All told, they plan to visit more than one hundred former Spanish colonies and points of interest during their two-year circumnavigation of the Earth."

He paused and sipped from his water glass before he continued.

"One of the caravels is owned by a very wealthy Spanish grandam who is also a staunch human rights advocate. Maria has secured her aid. Her caravel, the *Nina*, will anchor at Vieques Island on August 12th. She'll remain at anchor until her bilge pumps are repaired, then sail in time to arrive in Havana on the afternoon of August 16th. When she leaves Vieques, Miss del Negro and the Green Berets will replace three of the original crewmembers, who will rejoin their ship at Key West, her port of call after Havana.

"Castro has invited the caravel fleet's officers and crews to be honored guests at his big birthday bash."

Tyree stopped and smiled.

"Perhaps believing in the old adage that 'All work and no play makes Jack a dull boy,' Castro has declared a four-day, national celebration. It begins on August 13th and ends with a Grand Fiesta Ball, Saturday evening, the 16th, at the Brazilian Embassy.

"Attendance is by invitation only, and each guest is expected to bring Fidel an appropriate gift.

"Miss del Negro, on the evening of the 16th, you will be escorted to the Fiesta Ball by *Nina's* captain, your patron, Tomas Garcia. At the Ball, you and 'Uncle' Tomas will leave a very special gift for Fidel. A gift the world will never forget.

"I'm sorry; but you Green Berets will have to miss all the fun. You'll have other work to do. One of our Cuban agents will meet you at a downtown location in his dilapidated minibus, and transport you to the del Negro barrio. Miss del Negro will write a note to her father explaining the need for secrecy and speed. Our agent will deliver her message four hours before you arrive. Time to round up all of the family members, but not enough time to arouse suspicions. You and the del Negro family will return directly to *Nina*. When you arrive, they'll conceal themselves in a special section of the bilge, which will be built during your stay at Vieques Island. They will hide there until you reach international waters. Between now and then we'll rehearse each step, eliminate any problems, and debug the entire operation.

"'Operation Baseball' concludes three weeks from today. That permits ample opportunity to prepare for your parts in the drama. If you play those parts well, I assure you that the plan will work to perfection. Maria Moscardo never makes mistakes!"

"Did you say one of your Cuban agents would pick us up in downtown Havana?" Reynolds queried.

"That's correct, Captain."

"At last report, Mr. Tyree, Havana was not a city that foreigners scampered around in. How do you propose we get to that location without being stopped en route?"

"For openers," chuckled Tyree, "don't scamper! Even at a national fiesta, if you and Captain Orizaba decide to do any skippin' around, all bets are off. Seriously, Maria guarantees that on the evening of Castro's birthday fiesta, Havana will be a wide open, happy city. You'll have no trouble whatsoever."

He stopped speaking, frowned, and then continued.

"Let me make one thing real clear to each of you. Getting into Cuba and traveling around once you're there is pretty simple. The hard part is trying to leave without proper authorization."

"How can Maria Moscardo be so damned sure about everything?" Reynolds demanded.

Tyree reddened. Clearly, he regarded the question as impertinent.

"Captain Reynolds, Maria Moscardo is our most successful covert operations designer. Her research, mission controls, and extraction plans are nothing short of legendary. She is certain that the majority of the caravels' crewmembers will disdain the formal dance. They'll join the fiesta in the streets or simply go bar hopping on their own. When they leave their ships, you two tag along. Fiesta excitement will provide your cover."

"What if Maria Moscardo is wrong, Mr. Tyree? What if we're watched or followed? What do we do then?"

"She won't be wrong! You have her guarantee!"

"She'd better be right! The success of the mission, as well as our lives, will be in her hands."

"They could never be in better hands!"

"I have an even more important question."

"Fire at will, Captain Reynolds!"

"How can Dolores assassinate Fidel without being caught red-handed?"

"Before I explain that, I want each of you to examine the fine birthday gift she'll be taking to the party. Please feel free to handle both of these items. They can't harm you—until they've been loaded."

Castro's gift was a solid gold pen and pencil set. At the end of each writing instrument was a small, intricately etched baseball. Tiny, raised, white gold seams were plainly visible on the golden balls.

Although the committee members examined the pen and pencil very carefully, and were impressed by the set's beauty and craftsmanship, they were at a complete loss to explain how objects that appeared to be so delicate could be deadly. When the set had completed its circuit of the table, and was once again in Tyree's hands, he began his explanation.

"As most of you know, Fidel Castro was an excellent baseball player in his younger days. I even heard he had a tryout with the Washington Senators. Although Fidel never played in the Major Leagues, he has retained his great love for the game. This pen and pencil set bespeaks that love. It also bespeaks the knowledge and love of the person who gives him the gift. We're confident that he'll treasure them.

"As you can plainly see, and as several of you discovered when you examined the pen and pencil, they're operated by pushing down on the tiny baseball in order to extend the pen point or pencil lead. When you finish writing, you extract them the same way. The procedure appears simple and harmless. 90% of the time it is—but here's the rub.

"Two special features have been built into the pen's barrel. The first is a hollow, 29-gauge needle. It will be filled with Australian eastern brown snake venom, the deadliest and most undetectable poison known to man. The second is a small, but extremely powerful coil spring, held in place by a rotating disc with ten notches. Each time the ball is depressed to activate the pen, the disc rotates one notch. When the disc reaches the tenth notch, the spring fires the poison needle up through the gold baseball into the thumb of the user. The pen is made from 24 carat gold, which is very soft, and the needle is stainless steel. It goes through the gold like a hot knife goes through butter. The needle is so tiny and sharp, and is fired with such force, that it completely disappears under the skin. The only evidence of the needle's passage is a microscopic hole in the top of the ball. A similar puncture, as well as a slight temporary swelling, appears at the entrance point in the thumb. But the swelling dissipates very quickly, and the tiny holes are invisible to the naked eye.

"Since Castro will be receiving hundreds of gifts at the fiesta, the odds are against him opening this particular one right away; but even if he does—even if he tries the pen a couple of times—you'll be gone before he clicks it ten times. Maria is convinced that the uniqueness of the baseball motif will make the set special to Castro. She believes it will replace the set he always carries in his jacket pocket."

"I'm curious about the poison you're going to use. I haven't heard of it before," Bissell interjected.

"Australian eastern brown snake venom is a presynaptic neurotoxin. It shuts down the nervous system instantaneously. The venom is so deadly that less than a single drop is required to kill the average man. The lethal dose is one tenth of a microgram for each kilogram of body weight. Half of the snakebite deaths in Australia are caused by the eastern browns. They are nature's perfect killing machines."

"What are the chances of the venom leaking out, or eating through the gold?" asked Dolores.

"Absolutely none! Not even eastern brown snake venom can do that. Aquaregia, a volatile mixture of hydrochloric and sulfuric acid, is the only substance capable of dissolving gold. Don't worry, you'll be fine."

Ramrod, Dick Bissell, and Tracy Barnes asked a few questions and voiced several minor concerns; but Tyree answered each question, and allayed every concern in a confident and professional manner. "Operation Baseball" gained unanimous approval in less than an hour. They all agreed that Maria's plan was superb. Everything should go like clockwork.

# *HAVANA, CUBA*
# *AUGUST 16, 1963*

It was less than an hour until sunset. "Operation Baseball" would soon enter its final stage.

It had been an interesting three weeks. Dolores, Avispa, and Ramrod had spent ten days at Useppa Island, learning enough about sailing ships to pass for *Nina's* deck hands on their westward voyage through the West Indies, as well as when they entered Havana's harbor and dropped anchor.

During the layover, the carpenters who worked on *Nina's* bilge had done a superb job. The covert area was almost impossible to detect even when one knew it was there.

*Nina* had arrived at noon, nearly four days after most of the other caravels. As they anchored, three customs officials came aboard to inspect the vessel and validate crewmembers' passports. Documents presented by Ramrod, Avispa, and Dolores were, of course, CIA forgeries.

One member of the trio looked familiar to Dolores. She searched her memory and finally recalled that the man had served briefly in her guerrilla unit.

Dolores was not a woman that men forgot. If she knew the customs inspector, he would recognize her as well. Ramrod anticipated the first glitch in the operation until the quick-witted Dolores took charge.

Clad in a chic white and gold sunsuit, an outfit designed to captivate male attention and hold it, she pranced up to her old acquaintance, patted his bristly cheek, and exclaimed,

"Ramon, how wonderful it is to see you again! You look dashing enough in that uniform to sweep every pretty muchacha you meet off her feet."

Ramon gave the bogus credentials a cursory exam, then laid them aside—to hell with a stack of stupid papers when he could ogle Dolores. The two Special Forces officers nearly burst out laughing. Ramrod turned his back to hide his mirth. If the passport photographs had been Disney characters rather than snapshots of themselves, Ramon would have gleefully approved and stamped them anyway.

They spent the afternoon hours polishing *Nina's* brightwork and holystoning her decks. They were anchored in La Bahia de la Habana, directly below El Castillo de la Fuerza, and hundreds of Havana residents strolled down to the pier for a closer look.

Although every sailor in the caravel fleet had been invited to attend Fidel's Fiesta, most of the off-duty mariners had gone ashore to enjoy the entertainment to be found in the brassier bars along the waterfront as well as in downtown Havana. In her operations plan, Maria had anticipated the crews' preference for such independent entertainment. It was a major key that allowed her covert operations team to move freely about the city and bring Dolores' family out to safety. As usual, she had been correct in her analysis.

A few minutes after sunset, Dolores came on deck wearing a black strapless evening gown and golden tiara. Her appearance catapulted Rodney's memory back to their first date—the evening they had spent dancing in Miami. He grinned at her, expecting her most radiant smile in return, but he was surprised. She looked rather wistful as she took his hand and led him toward the bow of the ship.

When they reached a secluded spot, she turned and came into his arms. As she spoke he felt her shudder.

"I feel like a brazen hussy in this dress. I can't believe the incredible effect you've had on me. I have a conscience now. I've never had a conscience. For the first time since I was a small child, I think about what's right, instead of what's best for me."

She shuddered again and hugged him tightly.

"I've been a pretty rotten person most of my life. I know you're much too good for me; but I'm so crazy about you that being near you makes me tremble. From this day on I have only three goals—to put this night behind me, to see my family living in freedom, and to become your wife."

Rodney started to answer, but she kissed his lips into silence.

"No, Querido, don't speak. I must go now, or I won't be able to go at all. Only the thought of my dreams coming true will sustain me through this ordeal. We have never spoken of it, but my mission is extremely perilous. If I don't return on schedule— and I have no premonition that anything will go wrong," she added quickly, "promise that you'll sail without me. Don't let my family linger in danger! Take them to safety! But if something should go wrong, find a lady who will love you as dearly as I do, and have a wonderful life with her."

He saw tears glistening in her eyes as she kissed him once more, then walked forward toward the gangplank and the limousine that waited on the pier to take her to Fidel Castro's deadly fiesta.

Throughout the afternoon and early evening they all had been somewhat surprised by the hundreds of local people who streamed down to the dock for a closer look at the old fashioned caravels.

Finally, at nine o'clock, anchor watches were set on the ships, to protect them from the eager souvenir hunters; then the rest of the sailors drifted off to the nearby Plaza de la Catedral.

On the far side of the plaza Ramrod and Avispa entered a crowded café that reeked with the odor of stale beer. They found a small table in the rear and ordered a couple of Carta Blancas. Since the meeting place with the Cuban agent was only a short distance away, it was a simple matter to melt into the crowd until it was time to leave for the rendezvous.

At half past ten they left the café, and walked for several blocks along the Desamparado San Pedro to the address they had been given. Less than a minute later, an old black panel truck stopped next to them.

Faded white letters on the side of the vehicle were barely visible — *Frutas y Legumbres.*

"Do either of you hombres have a match?" the driver asked in Spanish.

"We have two!" Avispa told him, completing the recognition signal.

"Bueno! Get in."

Avispa and Ramrod got into the front seat, and the driver swung away from the curb.

"We were told you'd be driving a minibus."

"This is a minibus, hombre. It looks like a produce truck, but there are many seats back there."

Ramrod looked back, then grinned. The floor of the truck was covered with a layer of thin straw mats. If seats had ever existed, they were gone now.

"Lots of space," he commented.

"We only require space tonight, not comfort."

"You saw Dolores' folks?"

"Nearly four hours ago. Don't worry, they'll all be ready when we get there."

The old truck suddenly hit a chuckhole with such force that they were nearly bucked off their seats. Since he was taller than his companions, Avispa actually whacked his head on the dented ceiling.

"We'll be getting to the rough part of the road pretty soon," the driver chuckled. "Better enjoy this smooth ride while you can."

Fortunately, they arrived at the del Negro home while the dim quarter moon was hidden behind a thick bank of clouds. In less than a minute, the ten remaining family members filed out of the small building and found places inside the dark truck. By midnight they were all concealed in the hiding place aboard the ship.

So far the risky operation had gone like clockwork. Crewmembers who had gone ashore had returned at 11:30, and all preparations for getting underway had been completed. Dolores and Tomas Garcia were due to return at any moment. As soon as they did, *Nina* would quietly weigh anchor and slip out of the busy harbor.

Rod had always been skeptical about Maria Moscardo's ability, but tonight he was almost ready to admit that she deserved every accolade she had ever received.

# *THE BRAZILIAN EMBASSY*

# *AUGUST 16, 1963*

Dolores and Tomas did not arrive at the Embassy until 8:45. Fortunately, the long Caribbean summer day still provided ample light to see the magnificent building. On the patio alone were thirty incredible columns—each one had been built with a different colored marble. Along the tops of the high walls in the grand dining room and the great ballroom were paintings depicting the history of the Spanish Main from the first voyage of Columbus to the Battle of San Juan Hill. Every room offered another delightful surprise to savor and enjoy. Dolores decided that the Embassy must be one of the most beautiful buildings in the entire world.

The vast gardens that lay just beyond the back wall of the ballroom were in bloom. Here a plethora of fragrances from thousands of tropical plants blended with Cuba's traditional aroma of sugar, coffee, rum, and tobacco. The aromatic atmosphere and exposure to the garden's tranquility might very well induce an overpowering euphoria if one were unwary. Dolores smiled. If she could bottle the perfumed air from this patio, she could sell it as the world's most reliable aphrodisiac.

Although more than three hundred people were present, most of the eyes turned toward Dolores as she swept into the room on Tomas' arm. One set of those eyes peered out of a bearded face. Fidel Castro looked at Dolores, turned away, then looked again—much more closely this time.

He left the group of dignitaries that he had been entertaining and strolled toward her.

"At the risk of sounding like a Hollywood gigolo, I know you, don't I?" Castro asked.

"I made a dozen raids against the Batistas. I was in Felix Duque's guerrilla force. My sister, Tranquilena del Negro, was your favorite cook while we were camped in the mountains."

"Of course! You are Dolores. Pardon me for my loss of memory, or perhaps I was merely blinded by your radiance. I remember how pretty you were in your fatigues, but tonight you look like every man's dream."

She gave him her most radiant smile and thought 'he's an absolutely ruthless man; but he can certainly be charming when he wishes.'

"Thank you, Comandante. You are very kind."

"Not at all. How do you come to be here tonight?"

"My uncle was invited to the fiesta. He escorted me here this evening."

Castro spied the gaily-wrapped box in her hand.

"Ah! You brought a gift for me! May I open it?"

This was the last thing Dolores had expected. She had planned to place the gift on a long table already piled high with a mound of presents. She desperately searched for a logical reason to refuse but could find none.

She handed over the gift.

He tore off the wrapping and opened the box, then removed the pen and examined it carefully.

"Dolores, this is a wonderful gift. I love baseball, and I love beautiful things. You've given me both."

He held the pen up toward the light, turned it over and over and finally pressed down on the ball. The nib appeared. He retracted it. **ONE.** Then he tried it again. **TWO.**

"What a thoughtful gift, Dolores. I'll cherish it!" His face suddenly lit up. "Speaking of baseball, I want you to meet a very special man. He's the best baseball player in Cuba. You'll like him."

Castro took Dolores' arm and guided her toward the group he had left to join her. When they reached the circle, Fidel placed his hand on the shoulder of a tall, husky man and swung him around.

"Pedro, this beautiful lady is Dolores del Negro. Dolores, this is our best and most famous baseball player, Pedro Gonzales. It's time you two met."

Dolores was a movie buff, not a baseball fan. She knew nothing about Pedro's diamond career; but he certainly was a handsome rogue. His thin mustache made him look like Errol Flynn's twin brother. He could have played Captain Blood or Robin Hood at the drop of a hat or the slash of a sword.

"Introducing me to Dolores is the nicest thing you have ever done for me, Presidente. Senorita, would you do me the honor of dancing with me?"

"Con mucho gusto!"

As they started toward the dance floor, a young boy clutching an autograph book walked timidly up to Pedro.

"Will you sign my book, Senor Gonzales?"

"With the greatest pleasure! Do you have a pen?"

"No! I forgot!" said the dejected lad, hanging his head.

"So did I," his baseball hero admitted.

"You must not disappoint the muchacho, Pedro. Other fans will also want your autograph, and I have here the perfect pen for you to use. It's a gift from Dolores." Castro withdrew the deadly gold pen from his pocket, held it up, and exclaimed triumphantly,

"Look Pedro, it's a baseball pen. Isn't that marvelous? Keep it for now; but don't forget to return it before you leave."

As Castro handed over the pen, Dolores' spirits plummeted. If Pedro used the pen eight more times he would die—and in all probability, so would she.

She laid her hand lightly on Pedro's arm.

"While you give the muchacho your autograph, I have to visit the ladies room, then speak to my uncle for a moment. He hasn't been feeling well. I'll be back shortly."

Instead of heading directly across the dance floor toward the ladies room, Dolores walked around the perimeter of the ballroom until she reached an area at the far end. Here hundreds of the Latin American elite sat at dozens of tables, drinking beverages that were being offered by gaily-liveried waiters.

She spied "Uncle Tomas" sitting beside one of the patio doors, which overlooked the garden. She made eye contact and motioned toward the patio with a slight head movement. Tomas rose, opened the door for her, and followed Dolores into the garden.

"We have big trouble, Tomas. Fidel recognized me the minute we walked in. He came over to chat, saw the gift box, and made me hand it over. Maria was right about one thing; he sure loves that damned pen. The first thing he did was click it a couple of times before he put it in his pocket."

"So we might still be okay."

"We would have been; but now the pen is in the possession of Pedro Gonzales, Cuba's most amorous baseball player. He borrowed it to sign autographs. He's used it once, so we're down to seven clicks."

Uncle Tomas turned a sickly shade of green.

"Carumba!"

"Carumba is right. Look, it's nearly 9:30. If I can keep Pedro busy dancing, drinking, and talking about baseball for the next couple of hours he won't have time to think about signing autographs. At 11:30, I'll maneuver him out here, get him to sit in one of the lounge chairs in that dark corner, put him to sleep, and return the pen to Fidel. I'll tell him you're feeling ill and that we must go back aboard *Nina.* I'll explain that Pedro has fallen asleep and thank Fidel for a wonderful party. Then we can get out of here and out of the harbor."

"How can you be sure Pedro will fall asleep?"

"I didn't say he would fall asleep. I said I would *put* him to sleep. It's very simple if you know how."

"And you know how?"

"You bet I do! You must be prepared for anything. If you sense that something's gone wrong or if you see me raise my arms over my head, like this, come out here at once. Run to the gate at the far end of the garden, and head straight back to the ship. Don't wait for me here or aboard *Nina* because I won't be coming back."

"Wait a minute. I can't leave you here alone. Let's simply abort the mission. We can both leave now."

"I won't do that and you know it. We can't be sure Rod and Avispa will get my family back aboard before midnight. I have to buy enough time to insure their success and safety."

Tomas nodded in understanding and submission.

"Besides, more than a dozen attempts have already been made on Castro's life. None of them have come close. He's like a street-wise tomcat with nine lives. But tonight, we have a chance to get him! If we fail, it may be years before another opportunity this good comes along. I couldn't live with myself if I ran away while success was still possible. I don't want to wake up every day and remember the millions of Cubans who still live in terror because I was afraid for my own skin and fled in panic. No, I'm in this until the end, whatever that end may be."

Tomas realized there was nothing he could say that would dissuade this determined young woman.

"If the plan does blow up, we won't have much of a warning," she cautioned him. "When you leave the fiesta, it will take more than an hour for you to get back aboard the ship and clear the harbor. Even then you won't be safe from Cuban gunboats until you reach international waters. Please! Don't dally! Fly like the wind!"

He nodded. "I will."

"Our original plan still might work, Tomas. If it does, Pedro takes an early nap, we all take an ocean cruise, and Fidel Castro goes down for the count—tonight, tomorrow, next week, next month, *but he goes down!* When he does, the world will be a better place.

Only then will Cubans have an opportunity to live in peace and freedom.

"My alternate plan only deals with the worst case scenario. It means that Pedro Gonzales is dead, that you and the others are fugitives, and that I'm doing whatever I can to delay the secret police pursuit. If I can keep Pedro occupied and recover that damned pen, we'll be fine; but if you see anything ominous, or if I give you the signal, slip away at once."

"You know that if they even suspect you're part of an assassination plot against Fidel, they won't delay or bother with a trial; you'll simply disappear."

"I know! I accepted the inevitability of death when I became a guerrilla raider. So I accept it again now. What I will not accept are the needless deaths of the people I love! So, if you need to run, run like hell! Remember that Castro's secret police play for keeps. One single minute of delay might be the little bit of extra time they need to catch you, and kill everyone aboard *Nina* before she reaches safety."

She gave Garcia's arm a squeeze and smiled.

"Okay, 'Uncle,' I'm ready to go back into the lion's den. Keep your eyes peeled and fingers crossed."

She freshened up in the ladies room, then rejoined Pedro Gonzales.

"I'm sorry for taking so long, Pedro. Did the muchacho get his autograph?"

"Oh, sure. And while I was waiting for you I signed three more. The fans won't leave me alone."

"They'll have to leave you alone for a couple of hours because I plan to monopolize your time until then. I think no one will dare to interrupt us, but if they do, say you'll sign autographs at the end of the fiesta. They can line up, and you can treat them all to your signature at the same time."

"That's a great idea! You're one smart lady, Dolores."

Dolores smiled. She was one hell of a lot smarter than the dandy she was dancing with. She added up the number of times the pen had been clicked. Castro had done it twice. Pedro had used it once for the muchacho, and three more times while she was gone —a total of six times—so far so good. She began to feel more confident. All she needed to do was isolate Pedro from his fans until 11:15, then guide him to an empty table, and have the emcee announce a Pedro Gonzales autograph session.

She would shepherd his fans into line, keep them pacified, and make damned sure Pedro only clicked the pen one more time. That would leave a safety margin of three clicks. When his autograph session ended, she would walk him into the garden, put him to sleep, and return the pen to Fidel. She began to believe she really could pull it off.

Dolores and Pedro spent most of the next hour and a half dancing. On two occasions they left the floor and sipped champagne at the far end of the ballroom.

On their first break they spoke with the emcee, explained that Pedro would be signing autographs, and requested that he make an announcement at the appropriate time. As they sat chatting during their next break, a middle-aged couple approached them.

"Senor Gonzales, my son and I are two of your biggest fans. It would mean the world to the boy if you gave him your autograph."

"It would be my pleasure." Pedro reached into his pocket for the pen; but Dolores, laying a hand on his arm, stopped him.

"To be fair to all of his fans, Pedro will be signing autographs for everyone in a little while," Dolores crooned in her sweetest voice, while wearing her most alluring smile. "We appreciate your patience. An announcement will be made shortly. Thank you for being such loyal Pedro Gonzales fans."

The grateful couple turned away, thrilled that they had been able to accommodate such a great man.

"Dolores, you should have been a press agent. You would have been great."

"With a talented client like you, it would be a very easy job," smiled the clever Dolores.

They finished their drinks ten minutes before the emcee's scheduled announcement, then returned to the ballroom for more dancing. Dolores kept an eye on the microphone at the center of the elevated stage and stopped dancing as soon as she saw the emcee begin walking toward it.

"Let's go, Pedro. It's time to thrill your fans."

As they reached the edge of the dance floor, the public address system began to blare. At the same moment, Fidel Castro intercepted them.

"Pedro has kept you to himself for long enough. It's time you danced with me."

"I was going to help Pedro with his autographs."

"Pedro's a big boy. I think he can sign his name a few times without your help. Right, Pedro?"

"Sure, Presidente. I'm reluctant to share a treasure like Dolores; but I'll try to survive without her for a few minutes."

"That settles it," Fidel said, turning away from Cuba's most popular baseball player and guiding Dolores onto the floor. "You're not only the belle of the ball, you've become the belle of the ball *players*."

Dolores forced a smile at Castro's witticism.

Having Fidel show up like this had been incredibly unlucky. She prayed he would tire of dancing before Pedro opened and closed the pen four more times. Castro said something to her, and laughed, but she didn't hear him—she was praying too hard.

Pedro Gonzales signed no autographs that night because he never reached the table where dozens of loyal fans awaited him. On his way to meet them, he ran into his friend and teammate, Gilberto Fabiano, who noticed the unusual pen Pedro was holding.

"Where did you get the neat pen, Mio?"

"El President loaned it to me. He got it as a gift from the most fascinating woman I have ever met."

"If the woman's as fascinating as her gift, I want to meet her. Let me see it."

Before handing the pen to Gilbert, Pedro retracted the point. The magic number was now three.

Gilberto took the pen and examined the intricate engraving, then he pushed down the ball. The point emerged. He pushed again. The point disappeared. He repeated the two-step sequence a second time.

"It's as slick as a greased pig!"

He started to return the pen to Pedro, but could not resist an impulse to depress the golden baseball one last time. As soon as he did, five things happened.

Gilberto Fabiano crashed to the floor like a stone.

A woman standing near Fabiano screamed.

Before the echo of her scream died away, Fidel Castro stopped dancing and ran toward her.

Dolores stretched her arms high over her head.

Tomas glided out the patio door, fled quickly through the garden, and disappeared into the night.

Although very few people in the huge, noisy room heard the scream, or saw Gilberto Fabiano fall, one of those who did was a doctor. He quickly examined the stricken man and confirmed that he was dead.

"What happened to him?" Dr. Jorge Mendez asked Pedro Gonzales.

"I don't know. One minute we were standing here talking, and the next minute he just fell down."

"Did he clutch at his chest?"

"No! He just fell down."

"What do you think, Doctor?" Castro queried.

"I think it's strange! A heart attack victim usually claws at his chest. A stroke victim tries to touch his head; but this man, a professional athlete in excellent physical condition, died so quickly he had no time to react—yet there is no apparent cause. That simply cannot happen. Someone, or something, killed him."

At that moment, Ricardo Rios, the Director of the Cuban Secret Police, joined them. Rios had been one of New York City's most brilliant and successful homicide detectives for more than twenty-five years.

Although he often used unorthodox means to solve cases and obtain confessions, his tactics had been overlooked until two prisoners died on the same night—the victims of savage beatings. Rios tried to bluff his way through the incident, but he was found guilty of police brutality, dismissed from the force, and deprived of a retirement pension he vehemently believed he deserved. Rios was unquestionably still an outstanding detective, but his bitterness and the carte blanche he received from Fidel Castro were turning him into an ever more dangerous man.

"All of the exits have been sealed," he told Castro. No one will be permitted to leave until I get to the bottom of this business."

"Doctor, tell Director Rios what you just told me," Castro ordered

The Doctor quickly repeated his evaluation.

"Are you saying Fabiano was murdered?" Rios asked.

"I'm saying that healthy young men simply don't topple over without a reason or some warning sign."

"You found no wounds when you examined him?"

"None!"

"Senor Gonzales, if anyone had done something to Fabiano, would you have seen them?" asked Rios.

"Sure! But no one did anything to him."

"How can you be so certain of that?"

"Gil was standing in a corner between the wall and a large plant. I was standing in front of him, against the wall, and that rather large woman (pointing) was standing with her back to him, near the potted plant. Gil was a small man. He was surrounded by people and objects much larger than himself. I don't think he could have been seen by anyone else in the room, let alone touched."

"You say he did not cry out or show any signs of dismay or discomfort?"

"None."

"What were you talking about?"

"I was showing him the baseball pen I borrowed from El Presidente."

"Were you holding the pen?"

"No. Gil was holding it. He was handing it back to me when he fell."

"Where is it now?"

"I don't know. I forgot all about the pen when Gil fell down."

A cursory search of the corner quickly revealed a gleaming object stuck in the branches of the potted plant.

"Perhaps," said Rios dramatically, holding the gold pen aloft, "this is the object we seek. It's a very unusual pen; where did it come from?"

"It was a gift to El Presidente, from Dolores del Negro."

Rios reached into his jacket pocket and withdrew a high-powered, folding magnifying glass. Aided by a small flashlight supplied by one of his assistants, he carefully examined the pen.

"Doctor Mendez, take my magnifier and flashlight. Examine the victim's thumbs and fingers. Look for either minor swellings or discolorations."

Dr. Mendez examined the dead man's hands.

"There is a slight edema in the ball of the right thumb; but I find no discolorations."

"Thank you! I think I've solved the crime."

Rios walked toward a nearby coffee table with the others at his heels. He gingerly dismantled the pen, then laid the various parts on the table, one by one.

"First of all, we have the barrel of the pen; next we have a spring so strong that I am unable to compress it. We also have a notched disc with ten separate notches, and finally we have a hollow cylinder. If you will all watch closely, I will align these parts in their original order. This small hollow cylinder is actually a miniature silo that, until a few minutes ago, contained a tiny deadly missile. The spring is the launching pad and the notched disc is the trigger. Now, this is what happened."

He held up the disc.

"The disc has ten notches. It rotates one notch each time the baseball and a connected holding shaft are depressed. The tenth notch releases a spring, which is driven upward into the firing chamber, very much like the hammer of a pistol striking the primer cap of a cartridge. A missile, which I judge to have been a tiny hollow needle, was fired along the barrel of the pen as accurately as a bullet guided by the barrel of a gun. But this bullet wasn't lead; it was filled with a substance that shut down Fabiano's nervous system and caused his death. Only a few presynaptic toxins can induce instant death. Obviously he was killed by one of those. Now, if you closely examine the top of the golden baseball under a strong magnifying glass, you'll be able to detect a microscopic exit hole made by the poison needle."

He turned and looked smugly at Fidel Castro.

"You're fortunate that you loaned this lethal object to Pedro Gonzales. If you hadn't, a few days from now you might have been assassinated by your own pen and no one would ever have suspected a crime."

Castro was livid with rage.

"Bring that del Negro woman to me."

The Secret Police did not have to look for Dolores. She walked defiantly out of the crowd and stopped a few feet from the tyrant with her head held high.

"I trusted you, and you betrayed my trust!" Castro stormed.

"The people trusted you, and you betrayed them!"

"You deserve to die for your treachery!"

"Far less than you deserve to die for yours!"

"You aren't even ashamed!"

"You're wrong. I am ashamed—ashamed that my plan failed and ashamed you're still alive. I'm ashamed that I once believed in you and fought for you. Most of all, I'm ashamed of what you've done to my people. I only hope another patriot will soon come forth to defeat your wicked regime and end your despicable reign of terror and slavery."

Castro was so abashed by Dolores' fiery courage, and so shaken by his close brush with death, that he was stunned into silence. He stood shaking with fury for more than a minute.

Finally he shrieked, "Get rid of that woman!"

It was nearly 3 A. M. as Dolores stood on the sand at the base of the Morro Castle's front wall. She was pleased. Although her mission had failed, she had protected Rod, her family, and all the others.

Despite several hours of brutal interrogation, she had staunchly refused to divulge anything to Rios. Pursuit by his secret police was extremely doubtful. If it did come, it would be too late. *Nina* had reached international waters by now. Everyone was safe!

Dolores reflected that in the last hours of her life she had finally reached a goal that had never quite seemed possible. She finally felt worthy of Rod.

Her head rolled back, and she squinted up through bruised and swollen eyes at the glittering stars, lying like tiny diamonds in the blue-black velvet softness of the tropical sky. She had always loved the night.

Dolores was smiling when the executioner tied a blindfold in place. She knew Rod would grieve for her, but she hoped his sadness would be washed away by tears of pride. Her last earthly act was a penitent prayer that God would be merciful to a sinner such as she.

# *HAVANA, CUBA*
# *AUGUST 18, 1963*

Fidel Castro sat at the head of a long conference table, listening to more than a dozen of his advisors. His brother, Raul, was the most vehement of them.

"Last October, I warned Robert Kennedy that if another attempt was made on Fidel's life, we would retaliate against the American president. We cannot let them keep trying until they finally succeed."

"As everyone knows, I deplore violence," said the scholarly Dr. Jorge Ramirez, "but in this case I agree with Raul. The Kennedys won't be satisfied until El Presidente is dead. For me, Saturday night was the last straw. I shudder when I think of how close to success that evil del Negro woman came."

"We already waited too long," grumbled Duque. "We must end these attempts and restore our honor. The Kennedys are bullies. We must stop them!"

The discussion continued until late in the evening when the last reluctant one finally joined the zealots. The assassination of John F. Kennedy was approved. They would hire the best assassin, regardless of the cost—a topnotch professional killer who would use covert methods, designed to deceive and mislead the CIA's investigators.

"If the assassination goes well," Raul predicted, "the Americans may never discover we had anything to do with it. They are incredibly naïve!"

"They're gullible, all right," Fidel agreed. "All we need to do is provide a whole lot of red herrings. You're in charge, Raul! Do whatever is necessary!"

***Assassination plot number one was underway.***

# *TAMPA, FLORIDA*

# *AUGUST 25, 1963*

Twenty-four of America's highest ranking crime bosses were seated around an immense cobblestone patio overlooking Tampa Bay. The sprawling estate was the home of the former Havana Mafia chief, Santos Trafficante, who seemed to have adjusted quite well to a new mode of living—an even more luxurious style of life than he had enjoyed in Cuba. The twenty-four Mafia Dons represented the major families in the nation.

The chairman of the meeting was Joseph Bonanno, known in Mafia circles as the "Angel of Peace." He was the organization's most "reasonable man." In addition to heading up one of New York City's five Cosa Nostra families, he mediated disputes in the United States and in Sicily. Other principal leaders included Carlo Gambino, another New York City capo; Chicago's Momo "Sam" Giancana; Giuseppe Molinari, the Californian; and Detroit's Joe Zerilli. Tommy Lucchese, Joe Magliocco, Joe Colombo, Sonny Franzese, and Carmine Persico were other major players.

"The Kennedys used you like a cheap hooker to win the presidential election. The 'graveyard' and union votes you engineered in Chicago swung the whole thing to Kennedy," Molinari, the gathering's most colorful speaker, told Giancana. "We had a free ride coming in exchange for that; but instead of giving us a little elbow room, the Kennedy brothers are squeezing and freezing us out. We can't let Bobby Kennedy pave a road to the White House by building a reputation as a crime fighter. Sam, the man has no gratitude. He treats us like we're a bunch of lousy Communists. We're businessmen. We don't steal from people; we give them what they want! We only facilitate their pleasures. If Bobby Kennedy wants to end America's illegal activities, he should begin with the federal government."

Despite the seriousness of the situation, Molinari smiled, and many of the others laughed.

"Whether we're willing to admit it or not, we are all arguably responsible to every Don, Capo, and button man. As the Cosa Nostra leaders, we must not shirk our duty. We must see it, and then do it."

Joe Bonanno did not fully trust any of the young, well-educated newcomers to the Mafia inner circle, except his son, Bill. Bonanno especially distrusted the glib Giuseppe Molinari, despite his degrees in business and finance from Stanford and Wharton. However, the warmth in his voice masked his distrust.

"The fault was mine more than Sam's. I've known Joe Kennedy for a long time—he's always been a reasonable and trustworthy man. At our meeting in Arizona he offered to make any concession we asked for to put his son in the White House. I consulted with each of you before I sent Tommy to meet with Kennedy. Please tell us about the agreements that were reached at that meeting, Tommy."

"In return for our help, and a very large donation, Joseph Kennedy agreed to Lyndon Johnson as vice-president, and he also agreed to get Bobby out of the country. He mentioned something about making him ambassador to Ireland—instead the little ******* became attorney general. Joe Kennedy doublecrossed all of us," Lucchese concluded.

"I don't believe he intended to," Bonanno said. "I talked to him shortly after Bobby was appointed. He told me not to worry—that his debt to us would be paid. He said Jack and Bobby were coming up to spend Christmas at Hyannis Port and that he would lay down the law about leaving us alone. The last thing he said to me was, 'don't worry—just wait until Christmas.' Of course, a short time before Christmas, he had a massive stroke. Now he can't even control his bowels, much less his sons."

"A hundred thousand thanks for strengthening my position, Don Pepino. The Kennedys have reached a point where accommodation is impossible. I believe we have to eliminate one or both of them before we are eliminated," Molinari said. "The Feds can crush anyone. Look at Al Capone. One day he's a king, pulling in millions of dollars a year from loan sharking, numbers, booze, and broads. The Feds put Big Al in Alcatraz for eleven years. By the time he gets off the Rock, he's a vegetable!"

Every Commission member was listening closely.

"At the turn of the century, Henry Ford spoke about his dream of putting each American family on wheels; but he had a second dream—to get rich! The twenty-four men in this room have given America far better and more popular products than Ford's Tin

Lizzies. The man on the street has embraced them and in the process made us richer than Henry Ford ever dreamt of being. We can't let a bunch of rich do-gooders smash our enterprises. Before they can put us out of business, we have to put them out of business!"

"You're talking about a hit on the President of the United States," exclaimed Guido Luciano, the New Jersey crime boss. "That's impossible!"

"With all due respect to my dear friend and neighbor from New Jersey, I agree with Molinari," Joe Bonanno interjected. "If history has taught us anything, if there is one undeniable lesson, it is that everyone is vulnerable. Assassinating the President would be difficult, but certainly not impossible. Now I suggest that we limit our discussion to the question of necessity. Let us reason together and decide if a hit against the Kennedys would be prudent. Would it be good for business? If we decide, as reasonable men, that it would, one or both of them will die."

"Kennedy has more protection than Fort Knox," persisted Luciano. "He's invulnerable!"

"For many years, people believed Albert Anastasia was invulnerable," Carlo Gambino reminded him. "But on October 25, 1957, Crazy Joey and Larry Gallo walked into a barber shop at the Park Sheraton Hotel, in broad daylight, and riddled Albert with bullets. Nobody is safe if the price is high enough, or the need is great enough."

"If we only hit one of the Kennedys, it should be the President," recommended Sam Giancana.

"Why?" inquired Joe Zerilli.

"Because he's made a lot of enemies in America and around the world. I'll bet a lot of people would be glad to see him dead. But his brother is a different matter. Bobby is a real bleeding heart liberal—a do-gooder who believes the average American is much too stupid to take care of himself. Americans are a big bunch of fools who need a nursemaid to get them from the womb to the tomb. Bobby sees himself as that nursemaid. It may be foolishness to us, but millions of weak sisters will worship at Bobby's crypt when he's gone."

"Molinari's urge to give lectures has become contagious," commented Carlo Gambino.

"Let him finish, Carlo," admonished New Orleans Don, Carlos Marcello. "This is interesting."

"Why go after the Attorney General if a hit points to us?" asked Giancana. "Let's kill the President— the guy with all the enemies. Lyndon Johnson hates all the Kennedys. He'll throw Bobby out on his ear before Jack can be planted in the ground. We avoid suspicion, and Johnson does our work for us."

"If a 'campaign contribution' is colossal enough, Lyndon Johnson will do anybody's work," laughed Carmine Persico.

"Sam makes an excellent case," Molinari said. "If Johnson doesn't ax Bobby, we still have a fall back plan."

"What fall back plan?" Marcello inquired.

"We can still hit Bobby if we need to."

"You've both made good points," Joe Bonanno conceded, "but we still must decide if the hit is our best course of action. I suggest we all relax in the pool for the rest of the afternoon, have an early dinner, and continue our deliberations this evening. Does everyone agree?" Each man nodded in assent.

They met at eight o'clock. Discussions, interrupted by several shouting matches, lasted until midnight, but no conclusions were reached.

They began again after lunch the next day, sifting grains of information, determining whether or not a human life should be snuffed out with as much care as the directors of a major corporation discussing a policy change. To these men, an assassination, or as they preferred to call it, a hit, was nothing personal. It was strictly business. Personal feelings were never permitted to interfere with business.

Despite Joseph Bonanno's reluctance, a majority of the commission members finally decided that an assassination would be in their best interests. Carlos Marcello, Santos Trafficante, and Sam Giancana were given the task of setting up the hit, and ten million dollars was allocated to fund the vital new project.

***Assassination plot number two was underway.***

# *EAGLE PASS, TEXAS*
# *SEPTEMBER 1, 1963*

The ten men sitting around the barbecue pit at this remote Rio Bravo ranch had clout—no doubt about that. Five of them represented giant corporations that were heavily engaged in defense industries where all-time profits were currently being recorded. But that windfall would only last as long as they continued to manufacture and supply vast amounts of armament and material to the American troops and their allies who were serving in Southeast Asia.

The sixth and seventh men perennially appeared in every list identifying the nation's richest individuals.

The eighth man was most often described as an international power broker.

The seedy-looking ninth man was Jerod Athelstan. He had been a federal agent for many years before he was discharged at the beginning of the Kennedy administration. He harbored an abiding resentment toward the Kennedys for their alleged mistreatment of himself and dozens of other old timers who had also been unceremoniously sacked. The pack of new-breed bozos that replaced them were all too dumb to pour water out of a boot without printed instructions. The old U. S. of A. would go to hell in a hand basket if he and the other old timers weren't hired back in a hell of a hurry.

Leaders of this Texas group had hired him because of his familiarity with the shadowy world of covert operations. His assignment had been to find a man with the savvy to coordinate a very risky venture—the assassination of President John F. Kennedy.

The tenth man, Henry Jenkins, was Athelstan's choice for that job. He had come to the Rio Bravo Ranch this afternoon to sell his services.

"I can vouch for Hank Jenkins. He's the very best at what he does," Jerod Athelstan assured them. "To put all of your minds at ease, and to safeguard your anonymity, I frisked him for a wire—he's clean. We can't be seen or heard. There will be no record of this meeting because it never happened."

"Mr. Jenkins, what makes you think you're sharp enough to assassinate the American President?"

This first question came from J. D. Huddlestone. His corporation manufactured combat helicopters.

"Mr. Huddlestone, I believe your tone of voice and curt manner were designed to raise my hackles. You will learn that I don't rattle or rile. But I will provide a simple, straightforward answer to your question. Since it would be impractical to offer a resume of all my achievements, I'll do even better. I'll guarantee to hit the President for a fee of ten million dollars. You'll owe nothing until my mission is successfully completed. Not a cent changes hands until then."

"Assuming that we decide to empower you. What are your conditions?" Huddlestone queried.

"I front all of the start-up expenses—that includes selecting and training the strike force. I also handle transportation, housing, vehicles, weapons, payoffs, legal fees, and any follow-up hits that might become necessary. Covert operational plans and escapes are included as part of my end. Most important, I'll set up the assassination, shooters' locations, the back-up shooters, the target ranges, and the dress rehearsals.

"You'll place ten million dollars, in bearer bonds, in an offshore account, thirty days before the hit. I'll supply the names of five attorneys. You can pick any one of them. When the mission is over, the attorney will furnish me with the account number and code. As I said before, you risk nothing. For ten million, I'll plan the hit, hire the shooters, and front all of the expenses—and most important of all, I buy the local and federal officials that we need to guarantee total success. I lay out all the initial cash because I can't expect clients to display any more faith in me than I display in myself."

"Has anyone ever tried to renege on a deal?"

William White, an assault weapons manufacturer whose weapons seemed to show up on both sides of every war, posed the question.

"Mr. White, if you decided to cheat me out of my fee, would any of you expect to continue living? If I have the ability and skill to assassinate an American president, do you really think I would hesitate to assassinate all of you? Let's be serious, shall we?"

"My colleague was making a joke. Ten million is a pittance. It would cost us a thousand times that much if we did nothing. Mr. Jenkins, if you and Jerod will help yourselves to some of the savory barbecue, and take it down to those seats you see along the river, we'll consider your proposal. You'll have an answer in a few minutes."

"With pleasure, gentlemen. That smoking meat has been making my mouth water since I arrived."

With dripping beef ribs piled high on paper plates, the two highly-paid hired hands made their way to a terrace that overlooked the river, and spent the next few minutes eating and sipping mellow bourbon.

Twenty minutes later they were summoned back to the conspirators' circle.

"How far in advance will we know about the hit?" Huddlestone asked. "We must all have solid alibis—just in case!"

"The answer is, you'll never know. You people are good, law-abiding citizens, with nothing to fear and even less to hide. This is the only time we'll ever meet. The less you know about all of this the better. I have no connection with any of you. Neither does Mr. Athelstan. We can't afford to know you any more than you can afford to know us. By the way, I'll pay Athelstan for his services. You'll owe him nothing. Investigators can't follow a paper trail that doesn't exist. All I need from you is a simple yes or no. Either way, there'll be no hard feelings because we never really met today."

Of course, the answer was yes.

***The third assassination plot was underway.***

# *DALLAS, TEXAS*
# *SUNDAY MORNING*
# *NOVEMBER 17, 1963*

He had been christened Ilich Ramirez Sanchez, but the world would soon know him by a very different name—Carlos the Jackal. He and the other assassins were taking a walking tour of Dallas's Dealey Plaza. It was here, in five days, that they planned to kill the President. The four men walked along the sidewalk on one side of the plaza until they reached a special spot, then the Jackal led the others into the street, and pointed to a steel grill in the curb, which allowed rainwater to flow into a storm sewer below.

"Johnny, this is your stand. As you can see, you'll have plenty of room to aim, track the target, and fire. You'll have a right side head shot from about ten feet away. The speed of the motorcade, and your angle of fire, will precisely duplicate all the dry runs we've made out at the ranch. From here, going through the underground tunnels, the Trinity River is a twenty-three-minute walk—much too far and much too long. That's why you'll exit through the first accessible manhole, which is a five-minute walk. Exactly three hundred seconds after you fire, you'll be able to lift the exit manhole cover, because our ambulance will be parked directly over the hole with the sliding floor open. Just climb back in. Remember, Johnny, everybody else is strictly for backup and confusion. You're the primary shooter. You'll have a pointblank shot!"

"Just like shooting a fish in a bowl!" Johnny assured him.

The assassins continued their walk until they reached a long picket fence that extended to the top of a grassy knoll.

"Dennis, you'll take your stand ten minutes before the motorcade is due. The upper end of these two pickets will be removed, so your field of fire will be wide open. Since you'll be in a police uniform, and a pair of our phony cops will keep the nosey tourists out of your way, it should be like shooting fish in a barrel. Johnny's shot will have already gone home, so your bullet will simply be an insurance policy."

"Just call me the insurance man! I'll see the front of his head and throat long enough to hit him with a rock, much less a rifle bullet."

"After the hit, you and the two phony cops will move up to that railroad trestle (pointing), then walk slowly toward the corner of Oak Street. The phony police car will pick you up there."

The quartet continued walking until they reached the front of the Texas Book Depository, where they stopped again.

"Cheyenne, your job is to draw attention to this building! You can fire from any place on the roof. The kid's periscope is the key. It's so tiny that there's almost no chance of anyone seeing it. Use the periscope until the moment you're ready to fire. As we discovered in practice, your head is only visible for two seconds. Don't worry about hitting the primary target. Select any target of opportunity in the limo. Dismantle your weapon on your way across the roof, then repel down the back wall into the trash truck that will be waiting below."

"We've been over this so often I think I could do it in my sleep. Don't worry!"

"You get paid handsomely to follow orders, not to think or offer advice. The Boss and I will handle that end of things. That's it for today. Johnny, drive the boys back to the ranch. I want five more practice runs before I return at suppertime!"

"No problem. I presume that you and the Boss are going to see Ruby, Oswald, and those cops this afternoon?"

"What we do is none of your concern. Don't forget, five more dry runs!"

Fifteen minutes later the three hitmen were driving down Route 45.

"You know more about this whole thing than Cheyenne and me. We haven't seen the Boss since he hired us. What do you know about him?" Dennis asked Johnny.

"I know a few things. He used to be a high-ranking federal agency guy. He's the best assassination planner in the world. And he's deadly. Screw up once, and you're history," Johnny assured him

"What's Oswald role in this?" Cheyenne queried.

"Oswald is the pigeon—the fall guy—the patsy. The Boss is going to make people believe Oswald was the only shooter. The Lone Assassin."

"How's he going to do that?" chuckled Cheyenne. "Have him wear a mask and carry silver bullets?"

"I don't have a clue, but you can bet your last buck that if the Boss says the scheme will work, it will. Oswald works in the Texas Book Depository. When your shot from the roof draws attention to the building, Cheyenne, the cops will rush in there. That's when Oswald's part begins. He becomes the only suspect, and our 'get out of jail free' card. He's already well known for pulling stupid stunts. Oswald's a natural born loser. A couple of hours after the hit, he'll be a dead loser."

"What's Jack Ruby's part in the Boss's plan? Ruby's a hell of a lot smarter than Oswald."

"Ruby's an ace-in-the-hole. The Boss has hired a couple of cops to kill Oswald. If they don't get him, Ruby's the backup. He's been around for so long that nobody sees him anymore. He blends into the background. He's dying of cancer and he needs big bucks before he checks out. Whether or not he kills Oswald, he's going to put some serious dinero in his jeans."

"I'm curious about something else," Dennis said. "Won't anybody notice some of the windows in the book depository are open and all the roofs around the Plaza are accessible? Last night on the news, they said that every sewer and storm grating along the entire path of the motorcade would be sealed—but the one at your stand will be left open."

"That's why an operation like this costs millions of bucks. If you're willing to spend a bundle, you can always buy the people you need. Cash makes most people act like the three monkeys!"

"What three monkeys?" queried Cheyenne.

"The deaf, dumb, and blind ones. Our monkeys all have something else in common," Johnny told him.

"What?" asked the puzzled Cheyenne.

"They're all gonna be rich," John chuckled.

"In five more days," Dennis observed, "we'll all make a big killing."

The three assassins roared with laughter.

# *EPILOGUE*

## *WASHINGTON D.C.*

## *NOVEMBER 22, 1963*

Rodney Reynolds was seated at a small table in the *Chart House Restaurant* that overlooked the rippling waters of the Potomac River. He was waiting for a luncheon companion; but he had no inkling about that individual's identity. Tracy Barnes had been cryptic and mysterious. He merely told Rodney that an agency bigwig wanted to recruit him for a long-term special assignment, which would utilize many of his unique and specialized talents. Rodney had not visited the *Chart House* since the evening that he and Dolores had dined with Tracy. Reluctant to reopen emotional wounds that scarcely had begun to heal, he had suggested the luncheon be held at a different place. But Tracy was adamant. All the arrangements had been finalized and couldn't be undone.

As he waited, Rodney's mind strayed back to Fort Knox. It was hard to believe he had left there less than four years ago. So much had happened, and so many things had gone wrong. He thought about the invasion fiasco and about Dolores and wondered, for the thousandth time, if there was anything more he, or anyone, could have done to save her.

It wasn't until she was gone that he awakened to his own foolish blindness. He had so zealously idealized Amanda's memory that he hadn't realized how much he cared for Dolores. He wished that he could hug her one more time, and tell her how he felt—how proud he was of her, and how much he loved her. Perhaps she had known in the moments before her death. Somehow he thought she had.

He thought about Maria Moscardo and wondered if she also harbored lingering doubts about Dolores. He hoped not. Maria bore none of the blame. Even if a rebuke needed to be meted out, it could not be laid at her door. Maria's entire plan had been brilliant. Dolores had been victimized, according to Tomas Garcia, by an incredible series of events no one, not even Maria Moscardo, could have foreseen.

He had almost expected Maria to call him during the three long months since Dolores' death, but she had not. Maria Moscardo was known to be a very private person—a bit more phantom than real. Rodney pictured her as a gray-haired, elderly lady, wearing an old flowered smock, so intent on covert operations that she often fell asleep sitting at her overloaded desk—plugging tiny details into the big picture. Sixty-five years old and never been kissed—a lonely legend who tackled impossible assignments and, somehow, found a way through every intricate maze of international intrigue.

His eyes drifted toward a sleek, silver Jaguar sedan that slid past his window and whipped neatly into an angled parking spot. The young lady who emerged was just as sleek as her Jag. Wearing a bright red pants suit that accentuated her lithe grace, she gave every indication of quiet self-assurance and ability. Her chic appearance reminded him of Dolores, but he saw Amanda in her confident manner. He wondered who she was and what she did, and was genuinely surprised by the immediate impact she had made on him.

When the lady in red disappeared into the restaurant, his attention was drawn back to the river, where a few sailboats were scooting about, enjoying the last few days of the late Indian summer, despite the overcast day and intermittent light showers.

"Captain Reynolds?"

He turned and saw the lady in red standing beside his table wearing an irrepressible smile.

"I'm Maria Moscardo. Thanks for coming on such short notice. I've wanted to meet you for a very long time."

She seated herself in a chair he held for her, then continued.

"I've just finished orchestrating a very tough, perilous, and vital covert operation. I designed the entire plan around the talent and ability of one intrepid and resourceful individual. Would it surprise you to know that you're that individual?"

Maria paused and smiled as her eyes locked with his. She plainly saw his eagerness to accept her challenge. A moment later she saw and felt something else, a magnetism that made her tingle. There was no question about it! Ramrod Reynolds was a very special guy.

# *DALLAS, TEXAS*
# *NOVEMBER 22, 1963*

The assassin waited patiently at the opening of the Dealey Plaza storm sewer until the presidential limo turned a corner and came into view, then he leveled his sniper rifle with its telescopic sight, and tracked the various occupants of the black Lincoln as they appeared in his scope. He paused for an extra second as he reached Jacqueline Kennedy, and reflected that she looked pretty in her pink wool outfit. Then he moved the crosshairs past her and centered them on the forehead of John F. Kennedy.

He waited until there was no possible chance of missing, then squeezed the trigger. The silenced rifle emitted a soft *chug* as the heavy bullet left the barrel and sped toward America's thirty-fifth President. As the assassin turned away he paused for a final glance at Jacqueline Kennedy. She didn't look pretty anymore.

# *CHARACTER REFERENCE GUIDE*

## *AMERICAN EXECUTIVES*

Franklin D. Roosevelt, 32nd US President
Harry S. Truman, 33rd President
Dwight D. Eisenhower, 34th President
John F. Kennedy, 35th President
Richard M. Nixon, Eisenhower's Vice-President

## *INTERNATIONAL LEADERS*

Prime Minister Winston S. Churchill - Great Britain
General Secretary Joseph Stalin - Russia
President Charles de Gaulle - France
Generalissimo Chiang Kai-shek - China
Premier Nikita Khrushchev - Russia
Prime Minister Harold Macmillan - Replaced Churchill
Presidente Fidel Castro - Cuba
Ambassador Anastas Mikoyan - Russia
Foreign Minister Andrei Gromyko - Russia
UN Ambassador, Dr. Raul Roa - Cuba
Chancellor Konrad Adenauer - Germany
Prime Minister John Diefenbaker - Canada
President Syngman Rhee - South Korea
Deposed Presidente Fulgencio Batista - Cuba

## *PRESIDENTIAL ADVISORS*

Former Ambassador Joseph P. Kennedy
Attorney General Robert F. Kennedy
Secretary of State Dean Rusk
Robert S. McNamara - Secretary of Defense
John Foster Dulles - Former Secretary of State
Dean Acheson - Former Secretary of State
Senator William Fulbright - Chrm. Senate Foreign Relations
Georgia Senior Senator Richard Russell
Ambassador to Russia, Llewellyn Thompson
Adlai Stevenson - UN Ambassador
Allen W. Dulles - CIA Director
John McCone - Replaced Dulles
J. Edgar Hoover - FBI Director
Arthur Schlesinger, Jr. - International Advisor
Edward R. Murrow - News Media Giant
Theodore Sorensen - Policy & Speech Advisor
McGeorge Bundy - Policy Advisor
Stephen Smith - JFK Brother-in-law

## *THE MILITARY*

General of the Army Douglas MacArthur
Gen. Matthew B. Ridgway - UN Comm. in Korea
Gen. Mark Clark - Replaced Ridgway
Gen. Lyman Lemnitzer - Chairman, Joint Chiefs
Gen. Maxwell Taylor - Army Chief of Staff
Gen. David Shoup - Marine Corps Commandant
Admiral Arleigh Burke - Chief of Naval Operations
Adm. "Denny" Dennison – Ops/Chief/Caribbean

Adm. John Clark - Hunter/Killer Taskforce Comm.
Commodore Robert Crutchfield – Bay of Pigs, Navy CO
Captain "Pete" Searcy - *Essex* Commanding Officer
Commander Mike Griffin, Air Group *(Essex)*
Lt./Commander James Forgy - Assistant Squadron Leader *(Essex)*
Maj. Rudolf Anderson – U-2 Pilot, Killed in Action
Francis Gary Powers - U-2 Pilot, Captured

## *CIA STAFFERS*

Gen. Charles P. Cabell - Executive Project Director
Richard Bissell - Project Coordinator for Bay of Pigs
Tracy Barnes - Bissell's Assistant
Colonel Stanley W. Beerli - Air Force Commander
Col. Jack Hawkins - Ranking Officer, Bay of Pigs
Arthur Lundahl - Inventor of Hi-Level Recon/Photo

## *PRO-CASTRO CUBANS*

Raul Castro - Fidel's Brother and Assistant
Ernesto "Che" Guevara - Avowed Communist
Ramon Fernandez - Castro's Military Coordinator
Maj. Pedro Augustino - CO Cuban Air Forces
Felix Duque - CO Cuban Ground Forces
Enrique Carreras - Cuban Air Commander
Rafael del Pino - " Pilot

## *ANTI-CASTRO CUBANS*

Pepe San Roman - Commander of the 2506 Brigade
Alejandro del Valle - Key Member of """

Hugo Sueiro -"
Ernesto Oliva -"
Roberto San Roman -"
Eduardo Garcia -"
Manuel Artime -"
Sergio del Valle -"
Carlos S. Rodriguez - 2506's First Causality
Captain "Gus" Tirado - Ship Captain
Captain Swen Ryberg"
Captain Luis Morse"
Captain Gilven Slonim"
Andy Pruna - Frogman
Dr. Juan Sordo - Medical Doctor
Dr. Rene de la Mar -"

## *THE MAFIA CAPOS*

Joseph Bonanno – New York City Capo
Joe Zerilli – Detroit
Momo Salvatore "Sam" Giancana - Chicago
Santos Trafficante – Cuba/Florida
Carlo Gambino - New York
Carlos Marcello - New Orleans
Tommy Lucchese - Capo
Joe Magliocco -"
Joe Colombo -"
Sonny Franzese -"
Carmine Persico -"
Johnny Rosselli - Conduit to the CIA

## *SHOW BIZ PERSONALITIES*

Judith Exner Campbell – girlfriend of and messenger between Sam Giancana and Jack Kennedy
Phyllis McGuire – McGuire Sisters' lead singer, and another Giancana girlfriend
Dan Rowan & Dick Martin – Well-known comics

## *ASSASSINATION PARTICIPANTS*

Lee Harvey Oswald - Accused Assassin of JFK
Jack Ruby - Shot and Killed Oswald on National TV
Ilich Ramirez Sanchez - Carlos the Jackal, Terrorist

## *FICTIONAL CHARACTERS IN ODER OF APPEARANCE*

Captain Rod "Ramrod" Reynolds - The Story's Hero
Captain Felipe "Avispa" Orizaba - RR's Aide.
Amanda Mitchell - RR's Wife
Tomiko Ishii - A Wise Japanese Professor
Captain Quentin Moultrie - An Old Friend of RR
Mikhail Potopovich - Russian Ambassador to Cuba
Dolores del Negro - A Street-Smart Cuban Agent
Tranquilena Orizaba -Dolores' Sister, Avispa's Wife
Narciso Mejias - A Bay of Pigs Invasion Victim
Alejandrina Mejias -"
Victor Cabellero -"
Florentina Cabellero -"
Maria Carena -"
Manolo del Negro - Dolores' Brother
Miguel del Negro -"

Charles Black - A CIA Agent
Randall Brown - Black's Partner
Maria Moscardo – A Covert Operations Strategist
Jubal Tyree - Her Assistant
Tomas Garcia - Ship Captain & CIA Mole
Pedro Gonzales - Cuba's Most Famous Baseball Star
Gilberto Fabiano - Pedro's Friend & Teammate
Dr. Jorge Mendez - The Cuban Medical Examiner
Ricardo Rios - Cuba's Chief of Secret Police
Guiseppi Molinari – Mafia Capo from Los Angeles
Jerod Athelstan - A Covert Recruiter
Hank Jenkins - A Soldier of Fortune
**J.D. Huddlestone - A Business Tycoon**
William White - Another Business Tycoon

## About the Author

Bruce T. Clark a Who's Who Historian, has had a sixty year love affair with America's past. He has been a teacher, lecturer, and radio talk show host since his return from military service in 1962. Prior to leg amputation in 1994, he was a six-handicap golfer. "I always found time for golf," he muses, "but never seemed to have enough time to share any of the historical mystery stories that have crowded into my imagination for so long. I hope people think I'm a good storyteller, because I've become a lousy golfer." A growing legion of avid fans are hopeful that the Custer Legacy is only the first of many exciting mystery/history novels.

Mr. Clark and his wife of forty-two years, Dr. Mary Kay Clark, the founder and director of Seton Home Study School, are the proud parents of seven sons, and grandparents of seventeen. They all reside in the historically rich Shenandoah Valley of Virginia.

Printed in the United States
1005200003B